CROSSING OVER JORDAN

ALSO BY LINDA BEATRICE BROWN

Rainbow Roun' Mah Shoulder

A Love Song to Black Men

CROSSING OVER JORDAN

A   N O V E L   B Y

LINDA BEATRICE BROWN

A ONE WORLD BOOK

BALLANTINE BOOKS • NEW YORK

A One World Book
Published by Ballantine Books

Copyright © 1995 by Linda Beatrice Brown

All rights reserved under International and Pan-American Copyright Conventions.
Published in the United States by Ballantine Books, a division of
Random House, Inc., New York, and simultaneously in Canada by
Random House of Canada Limited, Toronto.

Library of Congress Catalog Card Number: 94-94558
ISBN: 0-345-37857-1

Manufactured in the United States of America

First Edition: February 1995

10 9 8 7 6 5 4 3 2 1

I'm just a-goin' 'way over Jordan
I'm just a-goin' over there,
I'm goin' home to see my mother,
I'm just a-goin' over there.
　　　—African-American spiritual

Sometimes I feel like a motherless child,
Sometimes I feel like a motherless child,
Sometimes I feel like a motherless child,
A long way from home;
A long way from home.
　　　　—African-American spiritual

We as a people will get to the promised land.
　　　　—Martin Luther King

CONTENTS

PROLOGUE   3

CHAPTER I: THE FOREMOTHERS   6
March 2012   6
Georgia's Story, 1873   7
Sadie's Story, 1897   11

CHAPTER II: INSIDE THE BOX   24
April 2012   24
1920   25

CHAPTER III: TO PATCH A PLACE   70
June 2012   70
1943   75

CHAPTER IV: HANDYMAN'S BLUES   92
July 2012   92
1933   94
1944   97
1946   114
1952   117
1954   120

CHAPTER V: BIRDS OF A FEATHER   124
August 2012   124
1955   126
1955   137

CHAPTER VI: FREE AT LAST   180
September 2012   180
1957   185
1961   188
1961   191

CHAPTER VII: CALIFORNIA DREAMIN'   207
October 2012   207
1965   211
1967   215
1968   227

CHAPTER VIII: IF YOU KNEW ME   246
November 2012   246
1974   249

CHAPTER IX: ICE STORM   261
December 2012   261

EPILOGUE   287

ACKNOWLEDGMENTS

Thanks to my incredible family, who sat through trial readings, agonies, and bad nerves with patience and much love, and especially to my parents, who made me believe I could do it in the first place.

Thanks to my family in spirit, who are always active and present in the creation of the work, especially my sister, who wanted so much to know how it turned out, to my grandmother, who still whispers in my ear, and to my grandfather, who taught me how to tell stories.

Thanks to all my wonderful friends, who never fail to cheer me on, no matter how improbable my ideas.

Thanks to my school, Bennett College, which gave me the inspiration I needed to become a writer as a student, and the space and support I needed as a faculty member to finish the book.

Thanks to Marie Dutton Brown, my agent, who continues to support me, and to push me to keep doing what I love to do.

Thanks to Cheryl D. Woodruff, my editor, whose skill and sensitivity is beyond price.

And finally, to the Mother-Father of us all. Deo Gratias.

CROSSING OVER JORDAN

PROLOGUE

She is my Longmother, Maasai, and she sits under the tree where we were born, under the baobab tree, the oldest tree in the world, the oldest tree we have ever known. She sits under the tree that gives of itself after its death, under the spirit that is death and the spirit that is life.

She teaches us, the Longmother Spirit, old beyond time, wise before trees. I knew her then and now. I know her before and to come. Her earlobes are wise, pierced with gold rings that reach to her shoulders. Tail tufts of lions hang from these rings. The fierce power of herself is lion. The shining power of herself is gold, and she hears all that we need to know.

Her breasts once gave us child milk, but we are no longer children, and they are flat, dry beauty. She says that now she must give us story, for we have need of it. She has skin black as the night; her head is a noble monument, and she has no use for hair. Her voice is deep as she speaks to me; her voice is blood; the lion is in her voice. The mountain where God lives is in her voice.

The Longmother tells us the story that has always been, under the tree where we were born. . . . She says there is a cave where women made fires. And she says the women must speak because the women have the words to put to the belly of it, to the wraparound pain that comes with the first cry and the last wind sighing out of the body, through the trees and out into the hills.

We remember; we remember that she was there before the ships brought the flesh sellers, before the sorrow chains, before we crossed over the big water, before we were strangers in a strange land. We remember that she was First Mother, and we take her words for we, her daughters, have need of the story that has always been, the story of leaving home and finding the story, of crossing over the waters and coming home. So we look for the cave and we take the Mother's words, and we keep the words simmering in our own pots, speaking them at the quilting frame and carrying them in our apron pockets. And so we have words to give words, in our cupboards and cubbyholes, words in our bundles and corners and closets, and words in the broken places of our bodies. And when we forget our Mother's stories, it is only that the pain shouts louder, for words we've stored up for years, stories to take into the promised land.

We all know each other's songs by heart, songs as old as the baobab tree, and we have been singing the same songs over and over to each other and to our daughters and our daughters' daughters, songs old beyond time. And the words form a crucible and a cradle, and a net of survival and a mystery, and if we listen to these words, they whisper and become the wind. We can hear the breath sighing through the first wind and the last wind, and we can hear the footsteps of the men walking weary, searching, running desperately toward hope; shuffling toward despair; marching, stumbling, dancing toward hope. "And we have found it," they shout to each other, "we have found the covenant again."

And the name of the covenant is "rebellion," and the name of the covenant is "yessuh," and the name of the covenant is "education," and the name of the covenant is "death," and the name of the covenant is "revolution," and the name of the holy, holy covenant is "survival."

We listen and hear the wind sighing through our net of words, our hammock, our resting place. We hear the men shouting "Victory, victory," and we go back to our pots and stir. And maybe they will and maybe they won't, but they'll be home to eat. That much is certain. And women will follow, some of us will go, for perhaps this time the covenant is holy, holy, and the heart wants too much to believe, and after all, they are the beloved.

But we remember the Longmother's poems, and her words in the wind. We remember to give them to our daughters, and to our daughters' daughters—the poems that came with the first cry, and with the last wind sighing out of the body. We must remember, for we languish on the banks of the Jordan, and the journey is not yet done and the sorrow chains not all broken. We must remember, for the stories are hidden in our bones, and in the wise blood that seeps into the ground under the trees in the strange land, the wise blood of the Longmother's voice.

CHAPTER I

THE FOREMOTHERS

MARCH 2012

She watched the old lady out of the corner of her eye. Story was rocking and waiting. Waiting for her to say something, waiting for one
more day to go by, waiting for all of it to be over, Hermine guessed.
After all, when you were that old, what else was there to do? She was
waiting, too. For the old lady to be gone. Gone out of her life. A little freedom, that's all she wanted, a little freedom. Hermine felt a
twinge of shame and wondered why she still felt any guilt at all. She
hadn't abandoned the old woman to a rest home. She had given up
some of the best years of her life to her only living relative. Hadn't
she done her duty? Only the cars on Woodbark Avenue answered

her. She couldn't even read the paper without thinking about her aunt, hearing the annoying scrapes of Story's rocking chair on the porch floor. She couldn't get free of the feeling that her own life was rocking away with every movement of that chair.

How long would it take? It was late March. Unseasonably warm enough for them to be out here on the porch. "I want to get a little fresh air," the old one had said. Hermine had agreed, because she felt as if she would suffocate if she stayed one more minute in that house with all its old-lady nicknacks around her—plastic plants, throw rugs, and photographs covered with dust from the past, of people who were long dead. Grandma McCloud, Aunt Bertie, Grandpapa Temple, people about whom she knew little and cared less. How long would she have for herself? She was already sixty-seven and missing what life she had left, sitting out the premature spring weather with this old lady. And how many more springs would there be anyway? Ten? Twenty if she was very lucky.

So when Story asked her "Is the cold weather comin' back, you reckon?" Hermine rattled her newspaper from the straight chair she was sitting in and didn't answer, hearing, but not wanting to hear, not wanting to be reminded that the old lady was still there, still waiting and rocking herself, rubbing the softness of her thick white sweater. "Maybe," Hermine finally said, in answer to the question. She didn't want her thoughts disturbed; she didn't want to use what energy she had left to answer, to do her duty, to give up one more minute to the dead past. And when her old aunt asked her another question about the weather, Hermine kept her silence, turned to the last page of the paper and kept her silence, even though she had just read that a cold front was on the way.

GEORGIA'S STORY, 1873

Georgia McCloud was my mama. Her name was Georgia McCloud 'cause she come here from Georgia where they done sold her to Massa McCloud when she just a baby. Massa McCloud, he match her up with Tom. He name Tom McCloud 'cause he one a Massa McCloud's niggers. Altogether she had six chirrun. One belong to

Tom, three chirrun belong to Massa McCloud, and two belong to Prince William Rountree, who she married 'cause he so good to her.

Mama tole me one night Massa McCloud done sent for her. She tole me that's how come her first husband Tom run off. Massa say to Toby, "See if Georgia still bleedin' from dat baby she had by Tom." Toby be Massa's body warmer. She tell Toby no, she ain't bleedin' no mo', 'cause she know if she lie, Massa McCloud he come down there an' pull up her dresses, check see if she still bleedin', so she can't lie nohow. So, long 'bout two o'clock, she get ready to meet Massa McCloud. He say to Toby to tell her to come to the kitchen door about two in the mornin'. So she get up out the bed. Tom, he say, "Where you goin', woman?" She say, "You knows where I goin'." Tom, he reach over and pull on her arm so it feel like it gon' break. He got her pinned to the bed. He say, "You ain't goin' no white man tonight."

She say, "Tom, let go, I gots to go!"

He say, "Proclamation say, slavery done be ovah."

"I know," she tell Tom, "slavery done be ovah, but we's still here in this here cabin workin' for Massa McCloud, ain't we?"

Tom let go her hand. He just keep sayin' he swear he gon' kill Massa McCloud one day. He say that ovah and ovah. He cuss and sit up on the side of the bed. He just starin' into the dark.

She say, "Please go on back to sleep, Tom. You kill him, you gets burned alive."

When Mama get to this part, I'se so afraid I gets cold all over. Effin he kill McCloud, de Klu Klux be after him. So Mama say, all she know is she got to go, or both them in trouble. So she go on up to the kitchen slow like, 'cause she don' wanna go, and she get to the kitchen an' stand there by the door wishin', prayin' she don' have to open it, and Massa maybe forgot to leave off the lock. An' wishin' she had run away like she say she was gonna do. So she try the kitchen door and it be open, just like she knew it would be, and it no help for it now. Look like God, He don't answer nothin'.

When she get back 'long 'bout first light, Tom done run off. Fire in the chimney done gone out. His shoes gone, his coat. Baby Alexander hollerin'. She know he might try to come back and kill Massa McCloud, she say.

I say, "Lordy, what you do 'bout it?"

"Lord's will," she say. And sometime after that she say, "I has me a youngun, little tow-headed youngun, 'long Massa McCloud. He don't claim my youngun, 'ceptin' he come down to the cabin see how is his youngun once de while." Tom and her, they done already had them a baby, so now she got two, and every time she stop bleedin', Massa McCloud he send for her, till she got big again. She be cookin' in the house and cleaning and then be takin' care of younguns all the time. Then Mama stop, like she don' wanna go on, only she want to tell me.

"One day Massa McCloud, he come down to the cabin," she say. " 'I want me that boy, the towheaded one,' he say. 'That my son, Hezakiah. I want my son. Gon' send him to school. He a white boy.' "

"Guess Missus was mad about that one," Mama say. "She couldn't give him no son, and he was tired a waitin'. Thought it might never happen." Mama winked at me like we had a joke. "I had to smile a little bit," she say, "knowin' it was my son who was goin' to school and not hers, even though I was cryin' through my smile. I knew I might not never see my boy again, but then I thought about all he was gonna have and what I couldn't give him. My Lord, what kinda choice was that for a mama? I coulda run away with him, but where would I go with three younguns, and how would I feed ya'll anyway? So I cried all night and I kissed him in the mornin' and made him promise to come see his old mama sometime, but I ain't never seen that little one again. Massa McCloud say he gon' raise him white. Reckon he did."

Mama say she have three younguns 'fore Massa McCloud leave her alone. *I was one of those, my name Sadie.* So I got a white brother somewhere I ain't ever gonna know, I reckon, and a white sister so-called I ain't never gonna see again. Hezakiah and Leona June. Long 'bout when Leona June was born, Mama hook up with my daddy, only man I ever called Daddy, that is, Prince William Rountree. Alexander and me, we knew him as my daddy.

Leona June, she done run away when she 'bout twelve. No way I wouldn't know Leona June. Look white but don't look white. Got that slinky brown hair and white skin, but we sisters for twelve years.

'Sides, we look like sisters. Somebody give her some money. Talked
her right away from home. Told her she could be white, and she
took it, took the meanin' of it. Took it like takin' food off a plate. Left
me and my mama and little Alexander like we wasn't family. She
had better look good if I ever see her. It better be worth it. She better
be no down-and-out straggly white trash.

Prince William and Mama done married late in life, after Mc-
Cloud die, and that was good for Mama. Somethin' good need to
happen to everybody sometime. Mama done seen a heap of trouble
in her time. My mama used to say, "Sadie, if you has a man you done
chose yourself, you lucky. Ain't got no business to be lookin' down
the road to somewhere's else." She ought to know, she told me how
they used to do us. How they used to make us bed with who they
wanted. I know I wanted Jacob at first and he my man, but he the
devil to live with now.

Anyway, Mama had her a friend named Penny once, long time
ago. She said Penny love John, they had picked each other out. She
say, "Don' know for sho how old us was." One afternoon, Penny say
she gon' marry John. Penny got a head of thick hair. She says she
gon' wash her hair 'cause she gettin' married. She got this big bar of
soap. Octagon soap, she done took from the storeroom. It just that
soap they be usin' to do the clothes, but that's all she got. Say she
gon' bathe in the creek, 'cause she don' wanna be stinkin' when she
marry John, and she ain't gonna have no nasty head. They be
laughin', take off all their clothes down at the creek, where can't nobody see, they think, in the bushes. Penny say she wish she have a big
old bathtub like Missus got, where she could sit down. Mama say, "I
tell her, you sit down here, your bottom gon' be full of mud for your
weddin'." They laugh. Creek water feel good. Breezes blowin' by,
sky blue. Sunday they gets afternoons off. Penny say she gon' pick
some wildflowers for her bosom. Mama says, "Naw, Penny, these
just weeds." She don' care, she love John and they gon' get married.

They gets all soaped up, and then Penny got trouble. Just when
she dip her head in the creek, Massa McCloud step out the bushes
where he been watchin'. They naked. He grab her by all that wet
hair and say, "Who give you permission to use that soap?" Penny lie,
say she got it from Missy Caline. He jerk her head back, and she starts

to hollerin' and cryin'. Then he say ain't gonna be no marryin'. Penny start to cry good then. He say John been sold off, and anyhow, he got some buck he want to bed her with, and he drag her off by her hair, tell her to shut up that caterwaulin'.

Mama say, "My head wet, soap drippin' in my eyes. I'm standin' in the creek, my heart 'bout to bust for my frien'."

So I tell my friend Louvenia, maybe I should stay with Jacob. What else can I do? 'Least ain't nobody makin' me be with somebody I ain't chose.

SADIE'S STORY, 1897

My name Sadie Evelyn Rountree, now Temple. I used to live with my mama over on the McCloud place, and it got to be too hard over there, be who I is. So one day, I'se about fourteen, I heard from some folks down at the company store, they has work at the Cook plantation. So I says, "Mama, I goin'."

She say, "Where you goin', gal? You ain't nothin' but a little striplet. You ain't goin' nowhere."

I say, "I goin' work on the Cook place. They got work. I got to be my own person."

Mama, she say, "I reckon it time. We can't get you no schoolin', and your hips be getting too wide be settin' in the dirt with the pickaninnies. Next thing I know, you be makin' pickaninnies." So the last thing my mama see of me, I'se goin' down the road. Had my hair in two long plaits, and they be switchin' back and forth. I'se totin' a ole cloth bag Mama give me, all my clothes in it.

Anyhow, I went to the Cook plantation, and they say they has work for nigger gals in the kitchen. It be a big place, not like where Mama was. And they has lots of hands to feed, and so they hired me and I stayed on there for a long time. One day I showed up at Mama's with my man. It was on toward evening, and I said, "Mama, this my man Jacob."

She say, "Well, he black as tar, I see dat. Bring it on in here, den."

So I had Jacob by the hand and I brought him in. I say, "Set down."

She say, "What you in the mind to do, gal?"

I say, "Mama, we gettin' married. You know. It's time."

My mama look at me real hard. She say, "Gal, you big?"

I say, "Yeah, Mama."

She say, "How long you been knowin' you big?"

I say, "Two, three month."

She say, "Well, I reckon you best be havin' the preacher say the words; don't be jumpin' over no broom."

I say, "Mama, folks don't be jumpin' over no broom no more." We laugh. "We gon' have the preacher say the words. Can you come?"

"I reckon I can come," she say, "'pendin' on what Missy Mc-Cloud got for me to do. Go 'long home now." So me and Jacob we left, and then we gets married Sunday afternoon. Mama be there.

'Bout two months later I lost that first baby, but life be okay after a while, and we go 'long, till Jacob, he turn mean.

—

Miz Cook and Massa Cook, they done gone off 'cross the waters. Left Massa Dylan there by himself; he not but 'bout fifteen, but he a big boy, and he gon' be big boy always. He ain't never gon' be a man, I think. He stay by hisself while they gone, 'cept he have the servants with him. He come in the kitchen one night, say, "Com'ere, gal."

I say, "Massa Dylan, what you want?"

He say, "Sadie, you know what I want. You a pretty little nigger gal. Always have been a pretty little nigger gal."

I think Massa Dylan, he done got in Massa Cook's drink while he had the chance. Anyway, I knew that he wasn't in no kitchen to get no food. I said, "Massa Dylan, what you want? Want me to fix you somethin' to eat?"

He say, "Gal, you know I don't want you to fix me nothing to eat. Now you come on over here and let's have us a party."

I say, "Massa Dylan, you don't wanna do that." It's 'long 'bout time for me to go home. "I got a husband now. I'm near about nineteen years old now; you ain't but fifteen, you sho don't want me to do that."

He say, "You a pretty nigger woman. I been watchin' you for a year. You know what I want. You don't give me what I want, you gon'" be sorry." He come over to the side of the kitchen where I was standin', grab me roun' my neck, say, "Scream, nigger, and I'll cut your throat," and he pull out a pocketknife as long as my hand. I'se so scared, I didn't know what to do. Only I knew I want to see my family again.

So, Massa Dylan, he got what he wanted, and he was 'bout 'sleep on the floor, still feelin' good; I gathered up my skirts and I seen that pocketknife on the kitchen table. Then I say, now what I want to be strung up for some ugly cracker like that? And I ran on 'cross the road.

Come to find out Massa Dylan got me in a family way, and I didn't know what I'se s'pose to tell Jacob. I thought, what if this baby come here lookin' white? 'Course, I 'bout bright and light enough. But Jacob, he pretend like he thought it be his baby. I didn't know what I'se gon' do, and then the baby came here stillborn, a little gal.

Jacob actin' like it was his, but knowin' something else. He ain't never been the same since. He say he love me, but he don't really trust me, and sometime he look at me real funny, like I got a scent he don't wanna smell, or a secret he don't wanna know. I never did know how he knew what Massa Dylan done. Maybe he didn't know for sho, but he know enough. I wasn't 'bout to take that doubt away. I lost that pretty little gal, but then I felt kinda like it was God's way of takin' care of me. 'Cause I could tell when I saw the baby, even though she was dead and all, that baby was gonna be almost white, and she looked too much like Massa Dylan for comfort.

Jacob say, "Why that baby so bright?"

I say, "Jacob, that baby is dead. Why you say such a thing? Jacob, my daddy white. You know how baby's be gettin' their color from way back in the family."

He mumbled something 'bout "this baby'd done got her color from 'cross the road." Like Mama said, Jacob black as tar.

Anyway, we buried the baby, an' he didn't hardly speak to me decent till the twins come. And then he turn mean. Not mean so other folks could see it, you know, just mean when the door shut in the house with me.

It was a long time before I got in a family way again, and the granny say we gon' have twins, and Jacob was all the time prayin' they'd be all right. Askin' God not to "visit us with his wrath," and on his knees everytime I turned around, even after they got here. He said I didn't pray enough. And later he say he was sho I didn't pray enough and that was why God punished me. He said God had put a curse on him for somethin' he'd done in the past, and maybe somethin' I done, though I searched my heart and I couldn't find nothin' that I'd done that I thought was that bad. It wasn't my fault, what that Dylan boy done. It wasn't nothin' I could do to fix that but die.

My twins was my heart. I thought Jacob was goin' back to his old self after they come. He say his sons was his hope. It was God's gift to him. They was his hope for justice. Somebody got to pay for his mammy and daddy. Twins was my hope too. I thought they give Jacob a little sweetenin'. Jacob, he have his own cross to bear, though, and sometimes he get so he don't talk for days. His wife had been messed with by a white man, and other bad things. Things make me sick to think about.

I remember 'fore the twins gone, Jacob tell me about a long time ago, why he so quiet sometimes. Why he sometimes walk off and don't come back till way over in the mornin'. I got so I could bear his goin', and then I got so I liked it 'cause I rather be alone. But once when he was young, I say to Jacob, "Why don't you speak to me some days? Why you go off and don't come home all night?"

Mostly he say it's not my business.

This time he find me cryin' my eyes out when he come back at four o'clock in the mornin'. He say, "I been alone since I was ten years old. It ain't nothin' to be alone. My mammy was alone when she died." And his big eyes the color of tree bark liked to filled with tears. "I believe in God," he say, " 'cause-a my mammy. She done tole me God's day would come. This white man is got to pay somehow for his sins. Last white boy I spoke to good got my head beat. My mammy couldn't save me. It wasn't nothin' she could do.

"This white chile called himself my friend. His mammy say I lookin' under her dress. I'se ten years old. Five years after the war done stopped. I'se in the house with my mammy, who be cleanin' this white man's house before freedom and after freedom too, cannin' his peaches, weedin' his garden. And I was totin' the firewood like always, and took it upstairs for her fireplace. She was in the room, and opened the door for me 'cause I got the wood, and I know she done had on her corset, but I don't know what else. I ain't seen nothin'. I just try not to look and put the wood down, and then she say I'se lookin' at her. So when his daddy come home, David, he done tole. We was playin' in the barn all evenin', and then his daddy come, and Missus say I done looked at her. David get scared and he say yes I was in his mammy's room, and I was, but that's all I was doin'.

"Marse David's daddy, he said did I want him or the Klu Klux beatin' on me, 'cause he wasn't a member but they would find out what I done and come after me and kill me. So I chose him. And he done took me out to the shed. I remember he say the corn was high and I should pluck it after the beatin', cool as he wanna be. I see that corn glimmer like fire in the sun, and he strip me and whip my behind till it raw meat, and then he beat me upside my head till my mouth so swollen I couldn't talk. And then I had to pluck that corn hurtin' like I was. David, he was always around me all my natural childhood. We hunted crawdads together. But he done lied on me without blinkin' an eye.

"There ain't nothin' they won't do for white blood and nothin' they won't do to us. That's why we got to be strong and teach our younguns to be strong. Be strong in the Lord. Take your punishment. After that I had to go away, had to leave the house. Marse David Senior, he send me to work in the furniture factory, carryin' water, sweepin' up, choppin' wood, cleanin' the outhouse, sleepin' on the floor. I learned how to do some things there, how to make a little money, what white folks need and want from us, but I ain't never seen my mammy but twice more, and my daddy, he was already dead. That was after the bad thing happened."

Jacob stopped talkin' then. It got real quiet in the house. Me sittin' there with my eyes red from cryin' all night, him sittin' there with his eyes I reckon red from bein' up all night. "Ain't nobody got no business knowin' all this," he said. "We should let the dead rest." And I started to get up to wash my face at the washstand, and he said, "Set down! I'm gon' finish this, since you made me start it. I'm gon' finish it once and for all." And I set down, and he say, "Was right after freedom and the war over. And my daddy was dead then." He took a real big breath, like air comin' out when somebody die, and let it all out, so I wasn't sure he was gonna tell me, and I knew I didn't want to hear it now anyway. But he wasn't gonna stop now. Was like he was bein' sucked through a hole by somethin' big and evil, and he couldn't stop till he got to the bottom of that hole.

"My daddy dead 'cause he thought them white folks meant what they say, that we could vote for real, so he went to sign up to vote, and I remember he got all dressed up in his Sunday clothes 'cause he said we was citizens now, and we had business to look like it, and he went to the courthouse to sign up, and I ain't never seen him again with his hands."

I looked at Jacob to see if he said what I thought he said. There was tears lappin' over his chin, and he was starin' through the walls of the room and not at me, and he said it again, *"I ain't never seen him again with his hands.* They done brought him home to Mammy in them white sheets, come knockin' on the door. Mammy afraid to open it up, and they say, 'We got you a votin' nigger here! Let him go vote now!' Mammy, she opened up the door, and they done threw my daddy in on the floor, and all I remember was blood. Blood and white, blood and white sheets, Sunday suit gone. Mammy was screaming and movin' all at the same time, wrappin' up his stumps like she could put them hands back if she just wrapped enough old rags around where the hands used to be, but the life was drainin' out so fast you could see him dyin' by the inch, and 'fore Mammy stopped hollerin', he was cold."

Jacob was quiet a long time afterward, and I was shiverin' in the bed just thinkin' about it, and not knowin' what to do to help him. He said, "I ain't never seen Mammy smile again after that, but she say, 'They got to pay, they got to pay,' every night before her prayers. One time I come home from the factory and she look real old, like she sick, and the next time I go back, she dead and nobody done tole me. I ask Marse David, and he say she been sick. Coughin' and got the fever. I know how it was. They done worked her to death. Didn't stop workin' and sick like a dog.

"I didn't never want to see that house no more. I knew how to work now, I knew how to work for myself, thank Jesus. I got strong, or else I be dead today. I'se eleven years old, fightin' off big boys. I see things I wouldn't tell nobody, and I done some too. That David wasn't nothin' but a white bastard, and his mammy a naked whore. That's what I think. I go sometime to the place where they laid her down when I was ten years old. And I think about how she say, 'we got to be strong. God's justice is gonna be done,' and that's how come I decided to be a minister, 'cause God's justice is the most important thing. Till then, we all alone. It ain't nothin' but the way life is."

Then Jacob, he look at me like he could kill me for makin' him tell that story. "Don't you never ask me where I been again," he say, his face all wet. "I'll kill you. You got more of me than any woman should have of a man."

—

After that, look like it was even harder to think he just bein' mean for meanness sake. I mean, when did he ever have a lovin' hand? His mama was a mule for Marse David's daddy, and what they done to his daddy was a sin to pay for in Hell. I sat a long time after Jacob tole me that. Sat there real quiet, starin' down into my two hands, into my bones that I still had on my arms. Thinkin' 'bout us and life and how I'se meanin' to tell Jacob he didn't treat me right, but then I couldn't. Thinkin' 'bout Jery and Lucas, Mama tole me about. How Mama's voice always come to me like Jacob's mama's voice. "Bible say you gon' reap what you sow," she always said. How could I tell Jacob I wasn't happy?

"Happy? What's happy?" he'd say. "Ain't no colored folks happy I know about. It ain't about happy, gal! Hand me my supper."

"Bible say you gon' reap what you sow!" Mama said, and then she tole me that story 'bout Jery and Lucas. "I sho do hope the Bible is true," she say, "but I don't see no such thing in this life. Folks just does they devilment and gets away with it, far as I can see. Once I went to the barn where I'se s'pose to feed the chickens. Them hens clucking 'cause they hungry. Old Jery come out the barn. All wild-eyed he was. I could sho see somethin' wasn't right, and then Massa McCloud he come riding by and say, 'Jeremiah, where Lucas?' Lucas ole Jery's youngun. Not really his, but he been like a grandbaby to Jery while he growin' up. Jery been sold away from his own younguns when he sold to Massa McCloud. Lucas 'bout twelve then I reckon, don't know fo' sho. He gettin' to the age where things be dangerous for him. Might be sold away, might do somethin' bad 'cause he comin' on a man now.

"Ole Jery say he don't know where Lucas go to. Massa McCloud say he gon' find him and he gon' get the rawhide when he do, and he ride off; dust be flyin' everywhere."

She just a little girl, but she remember this part real good. Jery take off runnin', tryin' to find his youngun; tryin' to get to him 'fore Massa McCloud do. Don't nobody notice her; she just standin' there with the chicks. Then she watch Jery get littler and littler out in the cotton field, and he fall down, and get up and run around like a dog when he chasin' his tail, and he fall down again. She run out to the place where she see him fall, and he be grabbin' at his heart like it 'bout to come out' his chest. She run fast, try to get help, but don't nobody listen to a little gal when they being watched by the overseer, and by and by they gets there, and ole Jery gone. They say his heart just give out 'cause he ole. Mama say, "I know better. I know he be trying to save Lucas."

They tole her Lucas been caught out all night more than once and he done took more than his share of rations from the storehouse. But she know that was 'cause old Jery was needin' meat to keep his strength up. That was the onliest pappy Lucas ever knew. They done foun' Lucas, and he just run wild when they say his pappy dead. Ole overseer man beat him till the blood run down. That's what got me to wonderin' about reapin' an sowin'. I wondered what did ole Jeremiah ever do, 'sides raise him a son? And why did he have to die in the corn like a ole dog, runnin' till his heart bust? And what did Lucas ever do, but be a good son, and why his blood have to run and mingle with the barnyard dust?

And I didn't ever ask no more when Jacob leave me at night, where he been, and I didn't never say I wasn't happy, 'cause I figger he ain't had no chance to know what happy was, less even than Jery and Lucas, who maybe had a little while to feel like they was pappy and son, 'least a little while longer than Jacob ever had.

So I was the most surprised one when the twins come and Jacob look like he was gonna let the past rest a little while. For two years look like he was a man who could smile at least once a day or any-time he looked at them babies. They was just beginnin' to walk good so they could go where they wanted to go, just beginnin' to like the world a little, and they went out behind the privy. They was only two years old. They didn't know no better. I was hangin' up some clothes on the line and I didn't see 'em go behind there. Pretty soon I started callin', but the chirrun didn't come.

I was only washin' the clothes. That big ole black pot that I boiled the rags in was away near the pump, and I just had so many clothes, I reckon that's all I could think of. I went lookin', and found 'em be-hind the privy, drinking something outta some old dirty bottles. Come to find out later it was poison. My babies was lying on the ground sick as dogs. My heart was jumpin' in my chest so, I couldn't hardly scream for help. I tried to pick both my babies up at the same time, but I just couldn't. They was throwin' up and jerkin' so bad, I left them on the ground and run to hitch up the mule and get Jacob. I tried to fly in that old wagon we had, and when I found Jacob, he threw down his tools and took off with the mule. I run all the way home, my hair flyin', heart poundin'. When I try to reach for my chirrun, Jacob knock me clean down. He say, "Get away, bitch. You done kill my sons. They dead! Don't you touch my boys!" And I pass out.

———

When my younguns died, I like to died. Jacob said it was the work of the Lord. I say, "What kind of Lord take my babies away?" He said I blasphemin', to shut up.

They was layin' out in the parlor, them two little bodies that I loved. I was standin' in the kitchen, so low I couldn't do nothin' but cry. That's all I remember about most of that funeral time. They was other folks around, church folks and neighbors, I guess. I recollect Jacob was in the parlor with the boys. He told them folks to keep me away from there, but I say, "Now! I goin' to see my babies now!" and I bust in the door. Jacob start beatin' on me then. He holler, "You the cause, you supposed to watch 'em. What was you doin', bitch? Havin' you a party? Havin' you a party with some other white man? You done already had one white baby!" And every time he take a breath, he hit me some more. Everybody tryin' to grab onto him and stop the beatin'. I don't even care if he kill me. My younguns dead. My husband hate me. Don't nothin' matter to me no more. He beat me till preacher could hold him still and calm him. Look like my inside pain so bad, the outside pain somethin' I can't even feel.

It was a long time after that before I could pray again. Jacob didn't know I was pretendin', only sayin' the words. Only on some days, for a minute when I forget my heart's gone. It was the awfulest thing that ever happened to me. The angel of death just rolled out that black carpet and rode down on me and took my heart right out in his two hands. I ain't never prayed the same since.

—

Good thing I knew how to shoot. Learned that on the Cook plantation when we was still in Alabama. I took my coat and put it on. Put the bullet in the shotgun, walked out on the porch. They were standin' there yellin' dirty words, "Nigger, black coon." I had lost my twins. Story was my fourth chile. I had lost my first baby and my twins. No cracker children was gonna take this child away from me. I pointed the gun. They were no more'n nine, ten years old. Ugly faces in the afternoon sun. Don't know what Story did to make them mad, but it didn't matter then. Ain't nothin' she coulda done so bad they hadda act like a bunch of hoodlums. She got a strong will, though. I'd find out what she did, teach her she had to learn to be careful. Runnin' her home from school with rocks like a common houn' dog.

I pointed my gun. "Ya'll go 'long home," I said. "Get outta my yard or I'll shoot ever' last one of your hides off. Go 'long away from here." They scattered like chickens in a barnyard. I watched them all the way down the street. Story had to learn if she was gonna grow up. She had to learn just like I did. A colored woman's job is to keep her mouth shut and mind her own business. Otherwise she'll get herself and her family in trouble, and her menfolks killed. That's just how it is. I knew I had to teach her a lesson quick. We got to be strong and not be askin' for trouble. They's enough trouble you don't ask for. That night the Klan was on the march, and I ain't tole Jacob about Story smart-mouthin' them white chirrun. Couldn't bring myself to.

She too little for him to be beatin' on her. But Lord have mercy, I'se scared to death.

It got nearly dark, Jacob come in the house quick, started blowin' out the lights. "Lock the door," he said, so quiet my blood stopped. Then he got his gun from under the bed and we sit, all us quiet as mice in the front room. Jacob sit in front of the door, gun pointed out. "They come in here," he said, "take them girls out the back door." And then they come, 'bout ten, fifteen men in white I guessed. I ain't seen 'em 'cept in my mind, but I know what they look like. Jacob prayin' under his breath. We had the curtains drawn tight. Lights out. I could hear my heart up in my arms. And I can't get his daddy's hands out' my mind. I reckon he can't neither. I could hear every little thing. My heart and blood, my breath, a leaf fallin' outside, a cat whinin' next door, a dog barkin'. Baby is started to tune up to cry. I put my hand over her mouth and rocked back and forth. They walked right down our dirt street big as brass. We seen the glow of the fire from the cross they was carryin'. I kept thinkin' maybe I should have tole Jacob what Story done, I shoulda tole. But they wasn't after us, thank you, Jesus. The marchin' was so loud, so loud I wanted to scream. And then they kept goin' right past our house, and we sat in the dark what seemed like all night till Jacob say, "Go to bed, they gone."

Next day, we find out nigger song and dance man was caught with a white woman. Jacob say don't say "nigger," and besides, just the devil claimin' his own. I just can't stand thinkin' 'bout that Klan. Can't get his daddy's hands outta my mind. Reckon he can't neither. Adelia next door say the man was caught in a white folks' hotel room downtown. I holler, "Lord have mercy!" And she say the woman scream, "Don't take my Johnnie, I love him, I love him!" and they dragged the nigger out of there and all the way down the steps and to the jail. Then we found out later his mama was called to the jail to claim his body. Dead. The next day. And then the Klan marched. We never knew what really happened, thought maybe the woman meant him to be caught. Somebody told, I reckon. I keep my girls safe as I can. They say another man was lynched down in Chillum County that same week. White folks put a hot iron in his throat and set him on fire. Terrible. Make your blood run cold. Jacob says we

livin' in the last days. I don't know, but it's a terrible world, first and
last. My girls get outta line, they get a beatin'. That way, Jacob and
me know they behave, and maybe they be safe. Mama was right. She
always said, "Don't nobody care 'bout us in this world but us."

——

Me and Jacob, we has bad blood between us, I reckon that's what
you call it. I ain't goin' nowhere with these chirrun, though. Bible
say you got to stay with your man. I can't make no money cleanin'
and doin' laundry, 'least not enough for a decent house for my girls.
Anyhow, how I'm gonna raise my girls with no man?

It wasn't never the same since I lost my twins. Guess it was my
fault. I did love Jacob when we was young, but can't nobody love a
man who got a rock where his heart should be. I try, though. Jacob,
he think I'm no good. Sometimes he say he forgive and forget, but he
never forgive nothin'. Story born in 1916, three years after I lost my
twins. It was a hard birthin', and I thought I was gon' die, but the
Lord spared me to see her raised, I reckon, her and her little sister
Bertricia. Last Saturday, Louvenia come over, we was havin' some
coffee in the kitchen and talkin' 'bout birthin' babies and raisin'
chirrun. She tole me her husband have two chirrun by some other
woman. I don't know about Jacob. I think maybe Jacob be 'fraid he
gettin' old now. His hair be gettin' thin. I'm thirty-five and he forty-
seven. You know, he still look nice when he dress up for church with
his black suit and his gold stickpin, but I think he scared. I think he
just be believin' the womenfolk be evil too. No help for it, he just
think we got a weakness that make us sinful. "Louvenia," I say, "I
does my best. I ain't never messed around with nobody, but I sho be
tempted. Jacob is a trial and a temptation. It ain't easy to be a Christian woman married to that man. I done thought 'bout runnin' away.
But where I gon' run to?"

Then I say I hope to God I don't have no more chirrun, and Baby
Sister be it. You know he won't use nothin'. Claim it's a sin to keep
babies from bein' born. More I have, more I got to do. I just gets so
tired; so much to do, I can't see straight. Put me in the mind a my
mama. Then I told her about bringin' Story here and how I almost
died and how I named her Story 'cause it was such a story to tell 'bout

her birthin'. She come out crooked you know, backward. My heart almost give out. Soon's I say I name her Story 'cause it was a story to tell 'bout her birthin', Jacob come in the door and he hear me.

"That ain't true," he say, standin' at the kitchen door. "I named her 'cause I wanted one of these babies to remind you of your lyin' mouth." Well, I just didn't know what to say to Louvenia. I ain't never touched another man since we moved away from Cook's. And that one ain't my fault. What was I gon' do? Jacob woulda killed him if he find out for sure about the baby. I knew that. And then he blame me for the twins. So I just sat there lookin' at my coffee, and he walk on into the bedroom. Louvenia, she say, "I see you later, Sadie, girl," and pat me on the shoulder, leavin' real fast. She know about Massa Cook and everything else. I don't know what I'd do without her, 'cause I don't have nobody else but my girls. You sure do need a friend sometime. I hope to God my girls don't be marryin' nobody like they daddy. I just hope to God.

CHAPTER II

INSIDE THE BOX

APRIL 2012

Story looked out of her kitchen window, and poured the water from
a glass into the sink, noticing that the leaves were very green. It was
hot. It was always hot now, she thought. Even in winter it didn't
seem to get cold much. She leaned on her walker, running another
glass of water from the water filter. She had always liked the sound of
running water, even as a little thing. Hermine was different that way.
She had never liked water, never even liked to take a bath when she
was a child. She'd holler and scream whenever her water was being
run. Hated to be undressed.

She could understand that. Somebody somewhere all through

your life is forever trying to undress you, trying to make you take off your clothes and reveal yourself. Somebody is always trying to strip you, to take away what they can, especially men. She had always been curious about Hermine's intimate habits, though. The girl's sexual life was a peculiar mystery to her. To her, Hermine seemed to be a creature without control. For Story sex was always a nuisance, even though it offered an occasional thrill. Taking off your clothes was okay as long as you knew when to stop, 'cause they'll ask you to show your soul for a dollar if you aren't careful.

Story chuckled to herself. It had been so long, she'd almost forgot what it was like. Nothing wrong with a little heat as long as you knew where to draw the line, and didn't give yourself away. A lot of people would give far too much, and a lot of people would take far too much. Best to remember that it was just a little heat—that's all it was.

Story bumped her way into the living room. Hermine was getting groceries somewhere. She hoped the girl would get something fresh. She always came back with those cheap frozen things, telling that lie about no fresh vegetables because of the lack of rain, or the early freeze somewhere, or a strike somewhere. Story thought she deserved better. She'd given up a lot for that girl; a lot. No tellin' what she could have done without Hermine. Her legs hurt today. The old lady flicked on the television even though she couldn't see it very well. She wanted the noise. Something on about a river somewhere. Time running out for the river. Time running out. It was polluted. Time's running out for lots of us, she thought. Me too. Fish dying; river running out. She remembered a creek somewhere. She had always liked water. That Sam person, she thought, had taken her to the beach once. A creek somewhere . . . a little thing. She was just a little thing.

1920

Story was running along the creek bank. The water was running with her, running over the rocks and calling to her. It talked about some other place and time. It talked about warm moss, and dancin' birds, and a tree that sang to her. She wondered where this place was, if it had ever been real, and then she knew it was real because she remembered it. It was her place—like a home. In that place there was a blue star under every leaf, and behind that was a door that opened like the doors opened in her head when people said things that made her go away . . . go away to someplace else. Papa said things that made her go away sometimes. This was not the only place where there were people. She knew that. You could dance there with no shoes on. And folks had long, wild hair, and she could play with no clothes on, not nasty. She always wore only flowers around her neck in that place. Story took some steps toward the water. The water was laughing. She swayed from side to side to its music and hummed with it, waving her dark brown arms in the sun. Three steps in and three steps out and side to side to side. Then she remembered. She remembered the last time she danced, and she made her feet stop.

When it happened, she was out here by the creek. Rosanelle was in the yard with Junior Lee. Junior Lee had a mouth organ. He was six. She knew that 'cause Rosanelle said it. It was a hot day and they was drinkin' water out' the creek down on their knees. Then they leaned back on the scratchy grass. Grass tickled her legs, and Junior Lee played on his mouth organ. Rosanelle had on a dress with flowers all over it, red dress with yellow flowers. She picked up her skirts and said, "This is how grown folks do the 'cake walk,' " and she started tryin' to look "grownie." So Story wanted to try too, so she picked up her skirts and showed the tops of her high-button shoes, and they danced to Junior Lee's music. Till Papa came. He came around the house to see what was all the noise.

Junior Lee stopped playin' soon's he saw Papa. He said, "How do, Reverend Temple." She remembered Papa didn't say nothin'. He had hold of her arm and it hurt, and all she remembered was his belt and the black buckle on it and he was takin' her in the house fast. When they got inside, her mama was in the kitchen, but she didn't say nothin' only kept on makin' biscuits and lookin' out the window. Papa took her to his and Mama's room. She remembered the sun on the curtains. She was so scared. Papa's face was mean and ugly.

"That's enough. I done tole you about dancin'. Ain't I tole you enough? Dancin' is a sin. Dancin' will take you to Hell. Don't you know no better yet?" And then he hit her on her sittin' down place with his hand and it hurt, and she started to cry real loud. "Shut up!" he said, but he was real quiet sayin' it. "Shut up!" And he covered her mouth with his hand, and she couldn't breathe good 'cause she was cryin' and her nose was runnin'. He was standin' up. All she could see was the top of a table with a big oil lamp on it and the buckle on Papa's belt. "Shut up!" he whispered, and he started to take off his belt. She wondered why he would be takin' off his belt, and then he hit her real hard, and she screamed again and he said it again, "Shut up!" only he was whisperin'. He said, "I got to or you'll go to Hell. You got to be clean. I got to make you worthy."

Then she didn't remember no more, but she tried to remember about dancin'. She should remember it would take you to Hell. She got down on her knees and looked into the water. Under the water she saw rocks and stones and sand. The rocks looked shiny under the water. She stuck her finger into the water and rubbed one of the red-brown rocks. The water was very cold. Story put her wet finger in her mouth. The stones were no bigger than a pea, and the sand ran between them and swirled around, running with the water. She leaned over and put her mouth in, tasting it; she liked the way it moved across her face. She loved when things moved. Maybe that made her a bad girl. She wondered what Hell was like anyway. There was supposed to be fire there. Big fires that burned you up. Maybe everything danced there and that's why dancin' was a sin. All she knew was you went there if you were bad. She didn't want to burn forever. Sometimes she dreamed about that. One time there were ugly things there and it rained all the time. There was no fire, just gray rain. One of her braids trailed in the water and her ribbon came off and was lost in the moving stream. She had lost her ribbon. A blue ribbon, playing, and dancing, and maybe it went to the blue star place and maybe it was free.

———

"Old rags, old rags for sale." She heard the junk man's wagon way down the street. "Old rags," he sang, "old rags for sale." He got farther and farther away and she couldn't hear his old horse's hooves anymore. Last night was like a dream. They came and got her and took her to Miz Robinson's house. And she had to stay there and go to bed right after supper. She was a lady who lived down the street. She didn't look like Mama. She was old and fat. Miz Robinson gave her milk and cookies and said to go to sleep 'cause she couldn't have it unless she went to sleep.

Miz Robinson's bedroom was smelly. Story didn't like sleepin' in her bed with that old lady, but she took her rag doll to bed with her. Baby Lizabeth was her doll. She had always been her doll. It smelled funny, and it was too hot. There were pictures of cats all on the walls. Miz Robinson had three kittens. Two slept downstairs. One of them slept upstairs with Miz Robinson and Story. Her name was Lavender. She was gray. Miz Robinson's milk was too warm. She didn't want it. The cookies were good. She didn't want Mama's surprise either, not as much as she wanted to go home. Miz Robinson's house smelled like pee to Story.

She was awake now. It was mornin'. She had to wash her face and put on her clothes. She felt the sun comin' through the open window. Miz Robinson pulled Story's dress over her head. She said, "Your papa'll be here directly." Then they had grits and another glass of warm milk and someone knocked on Miz Robinson's door.

"God has sent us a baby sister," he said as he came in. He didn't look at Story. "But praise God they both all right."

"Yes, praise God for that," said Miz Robinson, pushin' up her dress sleeves.

"I think God is tryin' me by not givin' me another son," he said, "but praise God for His gifts." He told Story to stand up straight, and then they walked home. The road was dry and dusty. The sun was very bright. She saw a small rock in the road, and then she stumbled over it and dropped her doll. Papa said, "You can't hold onto that doll better, you oughten to take it away from home." She wanted to know what was a baby sister. She wanted to ask Papa. But she waited too long, and then they were walkin' up the porch steps and a lady from the church opened their screen door.

"Where's my mama?" said Story because she couldn't wait any longer. "What's a baby sister?"

"Hush," said the lady, and started tellin' Papa where to find his breakfast in the kitchen. Then the church lady turned her head away, and she ran to the back of the house to look for her mama, call-ing her. She was goin' to her mama's room and she was carryin' Baby Lizabeth. The lady she didn't know grabbed her hand and said, "Wait here like a good girl," and she went in Mama's room and shut the door and said somethin', and then she opened the door. "Story, come and see your mama and your baby sister now," she said. Then she saw the dirty rag doll. "Let's leave your baby doll here, darlin'," she said. "It's too dirty for the new baby."

Mama was there in the bed. Why was Mama in the bed in the day-time? She said, "Hey Story, how's my big girl?" It was asleep, a little baby doll with its eyes all closed. It had almost no hair, and then it moved. She wanted to touch this baby sister. Mama put up her hand to warn her not to touch. "Her name is Bertricia," she said, "Baby Bertie." Then the lady from church said it was time to go, and she took her hand and pulled her out' the room and shut the door.

"Time to go out and play?" she said, like it was a question. "Ain't that exciting?" Story saw Baby Lizabeth on the floor, and she picked her up and held her tight. She felt that feelin' like she was in a dream again. It was not right to see Mama in bed, and she didn't know why a baby sister was exciting. The lady said, "Time to go out and play?" and, "Didn't you like your surprise?"

Story didn't answer the questions, and then she said, "Where's my surprise package?"

The strange lady who only spoke in questions said, "Now ain't that a sweet baby sister? Now, you don't want to be a ugly little girl do you?"

It was a long time before those ladies from church went home and her mama got up. Sometimes Story could see the baby sister and sometimes she couldn't. She heard her cry a lot, though. And she knew Baby Sister messed in her diapers and had to be changed, but she couldn't watch. She wanted to watch every time, but nobody would let her watch. When she was all wrapped up in blankets, she got to hold her once, and she didn't like that much 'cause Baby Sis-ter wiggled under her blankets and she was scared she'd drop her or somethin', like she'd dropped Lavender at Miz Robinson's, but she didn't drop her. She wanted to see her all over, see if Baby Sister looked like she did when she took her clothes off, only littler. She could see Baby Lizabeth all over. She was different 'cause she was a doll baby, and she was rags all over. Her back and legs and wee-wee place was rags, and she was not like Story at all. All she wanted to do was see Baby Sister. See if her skin was the same as hers and if she felt like her and to touch her.

———

It was a box with a lid on it, and it was always in Mama's room. Those little people on the sides of the box were whittled out of wood and they were always dancing. Dancing around trees. They were all brown people, but they were never angry or sad. On really awful days like today she could imagine she could get inside. Pull the lid down and hide.

"It was awful, terrible," they said, "and maybe she was Satan's chile." Maybe she wasn't clean, 'cause you weren't supposed to look at her. Her sittin' down place hurt terrible. Her stomach hurt and it hurt terrible where Papa strapped her. She would like to get inside the box somehow. If she could make herself small. It was about as big as a hairbrush, and it always stayed in Mama's room. Her stomach hurt; she had been bad, Papa said, so Mama said she'd have to learn to behave or nobody'd like her, and God wouldn't like her 'cause she'd be unclean. If she could get inside the box she could hide, and then when she was bad they wouldn't know. Inside the box there was a little hole just big enough to see out of it. She could look at every-body, but they couldn't see her. She only wanted to look at the baby. She was like a doll. See her all over. See if she was like her all over. Just once, but she'd never look again. Never.

They took Baby Lizabeth and gave her to the junk man. She didn't have a rag doll now. The junk man took her Baby Lizabeth and went away. Baby Lizabeth wouldn't be there when she went to sleep now. Nobody would be there. She wasn't a good girl. They said it wasn't enough to strap her, so they took Baby Lizabeth.

Baby Bertie was like a doll, but it was a sin to look at her all over, especially her sittin' down place. Then she got strapped at her sittin' down place 'cause he said she had been real bad. So they took Baby Lizabeth away, and she watched them put her on the junk man's wagon. "Old rags, old rags," he sang, all the way down the street, and she heard his horse and she heard his song while she was cryin' in bed. She closed her eyes and she remembered Baby Lizabeth's rag doll arms, and she could see her on the rag heap, her big button eyes lookin' up at the sky. "Old rags," the old man sang. "Old rags . . . old rags . . . old rags."

Inside the box, they could never see if she was doin' anything bad. Never see. She could touch the little brown dancing people. She was standin' in front of the box on Mama's dresser. She reached out and touched the little people. She didn't feel good. She was sup-posed to be in her own room, she wasn't supposed to be in Mama's room. Mama would find her, and she wasn't supposed to be in here. She was getting sleepy. Her stomach hurt and her bottom hurt. She had looked at Bertie to see her all over. Bertie was crying in the kitchen. Mama was busy. Mama was busy a lot. Maybe she forgot about Story being a bad girl today. She probably forgot about Baby Lizabeth too. Mama's bed was soft and her eyes burned from crying. She had to be a good girl. God wouldn't love her if she wasn't . . . a . . . good . . . girl.

The button man had come to get her. He was completely covered with buttons sewn into his clothes, and his pants were held up with three belts. He carried a long heavy stick and a little brown box. She was afraid to go with him, but she would, she had to. He never said anything that was mean, or threatened her. "I came to get you for your own good; we got to make you clean," he said. That was all he said. Then he buttoned her to him and they set off.

They walked a long time and there were lots of tall buildings, like she had only seen pictures of. They were on a long road under a hot sun. She was still afraid, and he still didn't say where they were going. The buildings looked like they were under water, and they began to sway back and forth like they were trees in a storm with pieces of rags dripping off them. She was very dizzy. Maybe she should ask where they were goin'. She was afraid of the tall buildings that moved like trees. She was goin' to ask him, but then his mouth was buttoned closed.

Then her Sunday school teacher rode by on a horse and waved to her. The horse was moving very fast. Story tried to call her. She was afraid of this button man, but her teacher wouldn't stop, and she looked funny. She had on Baby Lizabeth's rag dress, and she called to Story in a high voice and said, "You got to be worthy." Her teacher's face was white, like it had been painted white. So she tried to ask the button man where they going, but this time his face had disappeared! There was nothin' there where his face should have been! There was nothin' but buttons covering that space. Her stomach twisted like a snake. She thought she was going to be sick. She looked at all the belts. There was no way to get away from him. She was buttoned to his coat sleeve, all the way up to her neck on one side. There was no way she could undo all those buttons without being caught.

The trees turned into buildings again. They began to sway more and more, and looked as if they would come down any minute. Her heart was beating fast, too fast, and she felt seasick. The button man was laughing at her confusion. His mouth was wide. The buttons had come undone to let out his laugh, and when she tried to open her mouth to scream, she felt buttons on her face. It was buttoned shut, closed all the way across, and no sound would come out. She struggled to breathe, but there was no way she could open her mouth, and no way she could get away; she was buttoned to the button man, all the way up to the neck. The buildings were about to fall, and she knew they would be killed. One of the buildings seemed to be leaning over her. She was being shaken, the building was falling. Her mother was shaking her. Her mother. She had a dress buttoned up to the neck on both sides, and her wide mouth said, "Come to supper, Story. Wake up and come to supper."

———

"It's time," the Reverend Jacob Temple preached. "It's time for you to come to the Lord. Yes, it's time now before you run out of time. The clock is tickin' and the hands move across the face of the clock like God moves across the face of the waters. Give up that drink before your time is up. Time and death wait for no man. And no man is above the march of time, my brothers and sisters. I say to you this maunin', no man stands above the march of time."

Jacob's voice got louder. "The hands of the Lord will bring you down to perdition before you blink twice. For a thousand years in His sight are but as yesterday when it is past and as a watch in the night, and so we know not when God will come. Sanctify yourselves against tomorrow! Lord teach us to number our days, for we know neither the day nor the hour when the bridegroom cometh.

"No man knoweth when he will be called upon to pay the price. No man knoweth when the Lord will call upon him like Father Abraham in the wilderness to sacrifice all he has for the Lord God. Do you think God give Abraham a warnin'? It won't no warnin'. No! No! It was early in the maunin' and God appeared to Abraham and said, 'Take thy knife,' he said, 'and offer your son as a burnt offering. Take up thy knife,' he said, 'and give me your son as an offering.' For the Lord is a jealous God, yes He is, and we must pay the price, whatever it is when God calls, whatever it is, even if it means the sacrifice of the one you hold dearest. Yes Lord, you never know when you will be called upon to pay the terrible price, to prove you love the Lord. And not one of us know when the bridegroom will appear and say to us, you must make a reckoning of your sins. For there ain't no warnin'. You must count the sins and the seconds you have squandered. You must answer to the terrible voice of the Lord."

Story knew his voice would get louder and louder as he neared the end of the sermon. "No man knoweth!" he shouted. She concentrated on her shoes. Her Sunday shoes hurt, but she was pleased with them anyway. Very pleased, as a matter of fact. They were shiny black button-up shoes, and she had on new white stockings. Between Papa's "Yes Lords" she counted the buttons on each shoe. There were eight on each and that made sixteen in all. "Count them," Papa said, "count the days, the hours, the seconds that you have squandered in liquor, and multiply them by eternity. That's how long you will pay for your sins! That's how long you will burn in Hell!" Story jumped. She hated when Papa talked about Hell. His loud voice was scary. He was louder and louder now. "For the children of Israel were brought out of bondage, Yes Lord, they crossed over the mighty river Jordan, Yes Lord, but there was a sinner in their midst who transgressed the covenant of the Lord. And the Lord said, neither will I be with you anymore except to destroy the accused from among you. Sanctify yourselves against tomorrow! Yes Lord! Sanctify yourselves, Yes Lord! Or else it were better you had not crossed over into the promised land! For he that is accused, he shall be *burnt* with fire; he and all his family, Yes Lord, shall be burned also. Amen."

"Amen!" echoed Brother Wheeler in the corner seat. She counted more buttons so she wouldn't have to listen. Maybe he'd say something about things she'd done wrong. Maybe she'd end up in Hell like the babies God took. She stared hard at the buttons. Sixteen. That made sixteen in all, Story thought, shutting out her papa's voice, and then she had at least ten down the front of her dress, and that made twenty-six, and then there was one or maybe two on her bloomers, and that made twenty-eight . . . and Mama was glaring at her to bow her head 'cause Papa had said, "Let us pray," and the choir was singing "You Must Be Pure and Holy." She was thinking how glad she was it was time to go home and dinner would be fried chicken like it always was and that maybe they'd have apple pie 'cause there were dried apples in the sink Mama had got out from the pantry that mornin'.

—

Their house was small and southern. Her address was 333 Mill Street. There were two bedrooms which they'd added after the girls grew up some. Papa had added on to the house every time he got a little money. They started with two rooms, but by the time Story was seven they had a dining room and a parlor. The parlor picked at her, like a bird peckin' after a bug in a tree, because she wanted to go there too much. She'd sit and think about it after school. And when Mama wasn't listening, she'd open the door just so she could see part of a chair or a corner of the fringed lamp, because she was afraid one day it would go away and become heavy like the rest of the house, and she wouldn't have anyplace that was hers, that was a separate place where things weren't too much for her to bear.

The parlor was a treasure box with a forbidden but visible key. A surprise package, an escape from out there, from something, something she didn't want to know and didn't want to name and too much for her to bear. Too much quiet. That was it. It was quiet.

One day, though, the quiet was there and it was good. Papa was out in the yard. She went out there with him 'cause there was nothin' to do inside. Bertie was sick. She had a cold and couldn't go out.

Mama was sewing. Papa was choppin' wood. He said she could stay and watch him. She sat on the fence and watched him chop a long time. Once, he got tired and came over and leaned on the fence. His face was dark and the sky was light blue. Papa said, "Man can't get nowhere in this country." He sounded like he was talking to himself. "Ain't no justice. Only God's justice, I reckon." Story was quiet. He looked at her. "You do good, gal. You my last hope. You be a good gal. I be tryin' to raise you like a son since I ain't got no boys. You got to be strong. You my las' hope. You promise me now. I think you can do it. Bertie, she weak. More like woman. You the oldest one. I pinnin' all my hopes on you."

Her heart was pounding. It scared her a little bit. He had never talked to her like this, always seemed to be talkin' to the air, or to God or somebody else, but not to her. But he was really talkin' to her this time. It made her scared and happy. "Okay, Papa," she whispered, "I promise," and she felt as if something had opened between them and she had her own secret that nobody else knew. Her own special secret with Papa.

When Papa got home after work, the quiet that bothered her got to be as big as the dark through their window at night. Sometimes Mama would be smilin' behind her teeth and she'd say, "Evenin', Jacob," and sometimes they'd even talk a little about things Story'd try to puzzle out and didn't understand. But most of the time Story knew there was something that felt like a secret she'd never know about, something under the house she was afraid of.

She remembered a long time ago, one day when it wasn't quiet. It was at first and then it wasn't. Jimmie had to go home. Jimmie was a girl, but she had a boy's name. It was gettin' cold. She had to go home. It was against the rules to stay outside alone, especially for Baby Sister. So she took Baby Sister by the hand and they came in. Baby Sister wanted to play with her dolls. She went into the bedroom. Story wanted a drink. She went to the kitchen, and the basement door was standin' open. There were voices comin' up the stairs. Mama and Papa. But they were mad voices, and Story knew it was bad to say she wanted a drink. And she was afraid to track dirt on Mama's floor. Mama's mop and bucket were still in the kitchen. The floor was wet over by the window. Story went to the sink and tried to get a cup. She heard something downstairs that sounded bad. Papa's voice was loud. He said, "Shut up!" and she heard a crash like something fell down and crashed, and then she knew Mama was cryin', and Mama said, "Jacob stop! Jacob stop! The children will hear us." Story walked over to the basement door.

"Whose baby is she?" Papa kept sayin', and everytime there would be a noise and Mama would cry and things would fall down. She remembered it good. She was scared of Papa's voice. He said somethin' like "sin" and "shorn." He said, "Let her be shorn," and then she ran out of the kitchen and back outside on the porch, and she sat in one of the rockers and rocked back and forth so it would make noise 'cause she couldn't hear it out there and she didn't want to be scared.

And then Papa opened the door and she looked down at his shoes, and he had on his coat. He didn't say nothin' to her. Just walked down the street. And then Mama came to the door and she said, "Story, come in the house," and Story remembered her eyes were real red and she had a bad place on her face, but what she remembered most was Mama's hair. Mama's long hair was gone. It was just short around her ears and stickin' up all over her head. All Mama's beautiful long hair. And Story knew she better not say nothin', and so she didn't. And Mama went and put a blue head rag around her head, but you could see her hair was short under her head rag. Nobody said nothin' else to her that day. It was quiet again then. Her mama was sick that night. They had to go to bed after supper.

Irene and her brothers and sisters could make noise, and they were "dirty and foul-mouthed," Mama said. It wasn't quiet in Irene's house. It wasn't that quiet, heavy thing; it wasn't in the air, on the shelves, in the food and in the washtub. She had her secret, though, and it always made her feel better to know she had made a promise to Papa. Maybe Mama had this kind of secret too; maybe. The parlor was quiet too, but not the same quiet. It spoke to her, and told her about other places and times. Other people's lives. She liked her secret about the parlor, about the way she felt it was her secret place, but it didn't always make her feel good; sometimes it was too heavy. She had promised to be good, and sometimes she didn't want to. Sometimes she wanted to be like Irene and be bad.

She had to dust the parlor every Saturday. The first time Mama went in there with her and showed her how to pick up everything correctly so it wouldn't get broken, and how not to dust around things, but to move them and dust under them. Story barely listened to her mama. The room was wonderful to her because it was all new. She had never seen these things. She didn't really know what was behind that door. It had always been locked, and Mama said it was not for children, so she couldn't go in. A secret room where she couldn't go in, and a door she couldn't open.

Papa had said it was time she learned more about what a woman was supposed to do with her life, and that Mama should give her more jobs to do around the house so she wouldn't be a foolish woman. She looked around slowly. There was the dark green lamp with fringe around the shade, but it didn't work because Papa didn't ever get around to wiring the room. And there was the wine-colored fuzzy chair, and it had feet like bear claws. And a sofa with wood behind your head, so if you leaned back, your head would hit the wood. A little table with a big Bible on it in front of the big window, and a little table with another big book on it that said Family something on the front. She didn't know the word.

Mama left with instructions about where to start dusting, and told her to work her way around the room and come and tell her when she was finished. Story breathed in deeply, standing on tiptoe at the door. She could hear her mama in the kitchen, stoking up the fire to start supper. Bertie was asleep or maybe outside. The house was silent except for the kitchen sounds. She took her dust cloth over to the table with the big book on it, an oversized velvet-covered book with the words Family something lettered on the cover in gold, or what looked like gold to her. Very carefully moving across the letters FAMILY ALBUM, she mouthed the words silently; she just had to know what was inside. She knew the word "Alboom, Albioom," trying to sound it out. Family something. Family—people who live together, people related to you. Mothers and fathers. Sisters and brothers. Was there something in there about her? About Bertie?

The dust cloth lay forgotten on the table. She dared to crack the cover. The big buckle was not locked. It seemed to be calling her. She finally opened it all the way. There were pictures in there. Pictures of people. All kinds of people! She stared at the first page. It was Mama and Papa. He looked like that every Sunday and on Wednesday evening at the prayer meeting. He always wore that black string tie and that black suit with his stiff collar and that belt with the big buckle. But mostly he looked mad at somebody, like he did when they were slow getting dressed, or if supper wasn't ready when he was hungry. She had never seen Mama in that dress, and she looked very young, but Story knew it was her mama. Sadie Evelyn had on a high-necked striped dress that looked silk. There was a ruffle around her neck and buttons along the shoulder. Her feet were very, very close together and she was sitting down holding a baby. Story thought it must be her, because Bertie wasn't in the picture anywhere, and she was the oldest.

She was glad she was the only one in the picture, 'cause she had Mama and Papa all to herself. Now she had Papa to herself. She was the one. His last hope, he said. She had to be strong. She couldn't tell what color dress she had on. Probably pink or white, she thought. She had tiny shoes that looked black or brown, high-tops. Her mama had on black shiny high-top shoes too, and a straw hat that Story remembered, only when she remembered her mama wearin' it, it was old, and in the picture it looked new.

Mama's hair was pulled back from her face, and she looked like she did on Sunday mornings too, all straight and snappy like you had just done something wrong. The baby looked too hot, and stuffed into all those ruffles. Maybe she wasn't the baby. Maybe it was one of Mama's babies who died. Maybe God was mad at those babies. Maybe God was mad at Mama and Mama was payin' for something she did. Mama said God took those babies. Nobody at home ever talked about those babies. She thought maybe God looked like Papa. She was scared of God. She wondered if it hurt when you died, especially if you were a baby. Babies didn't know nothin'. They wouldn't know about dyin'. They hurt a lot, though. She remembered when Bertie was a baby and she cried all the time because she had colic, Mama said, and her stomach hurt.

She looked at the baby really hard to see if she could tell if it was her or not, but she couldn't. If it was a baby that died, she hoped it didn't hurt to die. You was supposed to go to Heaven if you died repentant of your sins, Papa said. If you didn't, you'd be sure to go to Hell and burn in the everlastin' fires. She looked at the baby again. Did she repent of her sins? she wondered. How did a baby tell the reverend she was sorry? How did a baby pray? Babies didn't know nothin'. She looked at the little baby feet and thought of the ever-lasting fires burning up the little feet. Mama was callin' her. She had to close the book and finish dusting.

After that, every Saturday, Story would tiptoe over to the biggest book she'd ever seen and very carefully open the heavy cover to the front page. She was only allowed in that room if Mama sent her there to get something or to dust it, or when there was company and she and Bertie had to sit on the sofa and be quiet, dressed and wrapped up like two birthday packages with two bows on their heads. Looking at the album always meant her heart would be knocking so loud that she was afraid she wouldn't hear if her mother was coming to catch her. She'd feel this noise in her chest and stare at the old tin-types, looking, looking, trying to see through them.

She knew she was doing something bad. She wasn't supposed to play with things, only clean them. Things had to be clean. She wasn't supposed to be "messin' " with Mama's stuff. It was wonderful just to touch these grown-up mysterious objects, to look at those pic-tures. Like touching Mama and Papa might be, touching their skin and knowing what it felt like. One time, she felt Papa's face when he was sorry he had to beat her. But this was like putting out a finger and touching the back of Mama's neck, which she would never dare to do. Papa would pat her head now and then and say she should be a good girl. Mama would touch her forehead to see if she was sick or take her by the hand to cross the street, and she was always pecked on the cheek by Mama for good night. Papa would hold her by the shoulders if he was strappin' her, and then he would hold her close and say, "You got to be strong." But this was like what she could only imagine it would be to rub her finger across the eyelid of her father, to trace the lines of the inside of Mama's hands.

These pictures were magic to her. She would creep up to the table very slowly; it made her shake a little bit to think that she was doing something besides what she had been told to do. She fingered other things, things that made her dream. The crocheted tablecloth that

covered the small round table was made with a circular pattern—
pieces made and then sewn together to make one cloth. Story's fingers would lightly caress the crocheted work; she wondered how her
mother's hands could actually know how to do a thing like that.
Then her eyes would move to the candlestick that always had a white
candle in it, and finally to the book itself in its velvet and gold glory.
It was hinged with two large brass pieces, and though it was never
locked, there was a leather strap that wrapped from back to front, and
a keyhole. She wondered where the key was, and one day she even
looked in the drawer of the table to see if it was there. The drawer
was empty of everything but dust. Sometimes by the time she got to
the keyhole she'd hear Mama calling her. Sometimes she could actually look at a few photographs before that happened. She could
rub the mysterious dark red velvet slowly. And touching the FAMILY
ALBUM letters with her finger, she'd get more and more excited as she
neared the M of the ALBUM and knew that she could open it as soon
as she finished the M. And then she'd carefully lift back the heavy
cover and choose the page she wanted for that visit.

Once, she got to see the album three times in one week. When
that happened, it was like having three quarts of ice cream. On Tuesday she had dusted the parlor for company. And then it was Wednesday and the ladies came. Mama had left her and Bertie there alone
for a few minutes and taken the company outdoors to see her rose-
bushes. They were supposed to sit still, "not move a muscle," Mama
said, and "not touch anything." She was not supposed to be looking
at the album. She knew that. She might make it dirty. She might
make a mess. Mama said to sit still till she came back, and she always
meant what she said. But Story couldn't stand it. Her second chance
that week! She didn't dare do it. She was sure she'd get caught. The
devil punished people who had too much fun; she was sure of that.
She shouldn't upset things. Saturdays were her days, but maybe if
she took too much, she'd have to pay for being bad. So she sat on the
couch where they had left her in her pink starched dress and stared
across the room at the album. Secrets, she wanted to know their secrets. Did they hit people? Did they get scared? She wondered about
Mama. Was Mama worthy? Did she have to be beat to be good?

Papa said females were the devil's temptation. They had to pay. What about Grandma McCloud? Was she in the book?

Bertie was just sitting like a doll, afraid to move. "I'm going to open it," Story said. Bertie just stared at her and shook her head no.

"I'm going to," Story said again. Bertie was too young to dust the parlor, and so she had never seen Story's daring disobedience. She opened her mouth but nothing came out. Neither one of them dared to look at the Bible, and Story was not interested in it anyhow, though she never told Bertie. It was full of long boring words, she knew that from church, and there were no pictures of real people, only fake people, and none of them were black. But she knew that the ALBUM was full of real people, that some of them were related to her, and some were even still alive.

Story was thinking about last Saturday, and she wanted to find those pictures again. She liked the picture of a place that said "Stein's General Store" on the building. There were three people in that one, three men dressed in suits and hats. They looked dressed-up to her. They had cigars. She liked the one that was a chair and an old lady and flowers in the back of her. She had a cane and a long dress on. The one that scared her the most was the one of a dead man in a coffin. There were lots and lots of flowers and people lined up behind the coffin, and they looked very sad, and they had black things around their arms. One lady had something black over her face.

Story stared at the man's body a long time. She thought the lady behind the veil had a secret too. She had one hand up near her face. Maybe she wasn't ready when they took the picture. She was sure the lady had a secret. Mama had a secret too, and Story knew what it was, she thought, but she wasn't supposed to tell. It was a bad secret about her hair bein' cut off. The secret lived in the basement, but Mama never would tell. She knew because she heard the secret a long time ago. Mama was like the lady behind the veil. Maybe the lady's hair was off behind the veil.

One time she turned the big page and there was a picture missing, and that was a mystery too; you could see where it used to be, and it was outlined and no picture. That picture was a secret. It wasn't there. There were lots more pages with no pictures on them for the rest of the book, but the pages talked to her anyway. The pages talked about a world outside their house. The people in this book told her they might not be like her. They were secret people. They might be different. She didn't know them, but she wanted to ask them questions. What was it like? Was everybody like Mama, Papa, Bertie, and her? What did you do when you knew a secret that you didn't tell?

She edged forward on her seat, straining to look out of the parlor window. Bertie clapped her hands over her eyes. Mama and her friends were just past her view on the side of the house where the roses were planted in front of the screened-in side porch. They were laughing about something and talking about somebody. As she got to her feet, she plotted her course. Edge around the maroon mohair chair, which was not facing the window, squat down just a little, and she'd reach the ALBUM with no trouble. That is, as long as they didn't come back inside before she got there and got back to her seat. She was light on her feet, sliding around the back of the chair before Bertie had taken her hands down from her eyes. When Bertie could bear to look, Story was slowly opening the first page. She had one eye on the photographs and one eye on the window. Then they heard the ladies' shoes on the front porch, and Story was composing her hands as if she had been straightening her dress when her mother opened the door to the parlor.

The ladies left at three o'clock. Mama didn't speak to her for an hour. Story was sure Mama didn't know she had left her seat. Sneaking looks at the album was getting to be very easy. She changed her dress and took off her hair ribbon. Mama said to wash up for dinner, and then Story had to clear the table after they were excused by Papa. Bertie was playing with one green bean. "Finish your food, Baby Sister," Papa said.

Bertie looked up and blinked her eyes. "I'm full, Papa," she said in her high voice.

"Finish your food, I said. So I can excuse you from the table." He was rubbing his chin and looking out of the window. Bertie put the bean in her mouth, chewing as if she was trying not to taste it, and swallowed it almost at once. There was no way she could have chewed it up that fast, Story thought.

Papa pushed back his chair. "You're excused," he mumbled, and went into the dark hall to get his coat and hat. Story and Sadie cleared the table in silence until the door slammed. Then Mama looked at Story. "You enjoy the pictures, Missy?" she said.

"What pictures, Mama?" Story said, blinking three times.

"I hate a liar and a sneak," Mama said, slamming the plate she was carrying on the kitchen sink. She held Story's eyes with her own. "You know what I'm talkin' about."

"I didn't do nothin'," Story said, her voice low, her eyes to the side. Bertie was rubbing her finger around in the butter dish, making swirls in leftover butter.

"Oh, Lord have mercy," Mama said. She jerked Bertie's hand out of the greasy mess and wiped it furiously with a dish rag. "Go 'long away from here," she said, "go sit down. And you, Missy, you been lyin' about messin' with them pictures. I tole you to sit still, don't be messin' with nothin' 'less I say so, don't *move* if I don't say so, and you done disobeyed me again and again. I'm gon' have to tell your papa for sho, and you be in a mess a trouble. Does you want another strappin'? 'Cause you sho askin' for it. You got to learn how to be in this world. You got to *learn*! Girl, don't you know I'm tryin' to save you from your papa?"

"I didn't do nothin'," Story said. "You don't never do nothin' to Bertie. Why doesn't Papa ever beat his baby girl?"

"Shut your mouth, girl, shut up that lyin'!" Sadie turned around from where she was washing dishes and slapped Story on the mouth with her wet soapy hand, and they heard Jacob's step in the hall. He had come back.

"Now you done it," Sadie said, "ain't nothin' I can do for you," and she turned back toward the sink. Story's face was streaked and shiny with soap and water. She was hot with fear, but she didn't care anymore. It wasn't wrong. All she did was look at pictures. Why was it wrong? She didn't do nothin'. It wasn't a lie, it wasn't nothing to do. It wasn't a sin in the Bible to do that. It wasn't nothin' but some pictures. Her papa was standin' in the kitchen door, his black coat and brown hat still on. Story's face still smarted from her mother's slap. "What's she done?" he said, his voice low and quiet.

Sadie mumbled, "It wasn't nothin'."

"You slappin' her for nothing'? I said, what she done!"

"She told a story," Sadie said, "but it wasn't nothin'. Jacob, let it be." He didn't ask about the story. He didn't ask why. He didn't even care why.

"Woman, you mean she lied. I ain't out here preachin' God's word to let my flesh and blood go to Hell." He unbuckled his belt. Story tried to tell him about the album. About the pictures and the secrets they had, like their secret. "Shut up your mouth," he kept saying. "Shut it up! You done let me down. You done lied more'n once. You ain't worthy to take my son's place. Shut up!"

She looked at her mama, but Sadie didn't say anything. She never said anything to stop it. There was no place to run. She wanted to hide behind the veil like the one on the lady's face in the dead man's picture.

"You think I don't know," he spit out, dragging her to his room. "You think I don't know you and that riffraff you play with got a dirty book? And you think I ain't heard you up at night? Just what are you doin'? Are you readin' that book?" He made her lie across the bed. "It ain't seemly for you to know nothin' 'bout that. Nothin'!" She was afraid to cry. Her throat hurt terrible; it was closin' up so tight she felt like she couldn't breathe.

Then he got real quiet and looked at her and took off his belt. He said, "You know what we got to do so you be pure." She began to tremble, and he said, "Pull up your skirts, pull them up!" And she was shakin' so, she couldn't do it, and her eyes began to run and her nose was runnin', and because she was afraid of what he'd do if she didn't, she did it. She thought she was gonna die, and every blow he made with the heavy brown belt made a welt on her thin brown legs, and every time he hit her, something in her said it was wrong, it wasn't fair. And she whispered into the mattress, "I didn't do nothin'," and the tears streamed down her face into the bedspread. She could hear him saying things between those awful pains. Things like, "We've got to beat out the curse," and, "You got to pay for your sins." Finally, on the last one, she cried out, and he stopped because she had given in to the pain, and he pulled down her dress real soft like always and pulled her off the bed and held her from behind, and she knew he had been crying 'cause she could feel his tears on her neck. But she wouldn't turn around. She didn't care. They had had a secret, and he had let her down. It was Papa who was wrong, and she had decided. He whispered in her ear, "You got to pay for your sins. We got to beat out the curse of the evil one."

Her legs and calves and hips burned like fire. She had made Papa cry, but she didn't care. He touched her shoulders lightly, and then when she didn't move, he backed off the bed slowly and left the room. She didn't care how much it hurt. She had decided. She would hide inside herself forever like the lady frozen behind the veil in the picture of the dead man. Forever. And there would never be another time that she would share a secret or a promise with anybody. She would go back to the picture book whenever she wanted; he couldn't make her stop. She wasn't afraid of his beatings anymore. She had made him cry. And she wasn't sorry. She thought because they had a promise together, that she was special to him, that he would listen, that he wouldn't beat her. They had a secret together. But not now. He wouldn't listen to her. She wouldn't be his last hope, and she had a secret now. She could make him cry. And she hadn't let him down, she hadn't. It wasn't a lie, and he had beat her anyway. She didn't care if she had to pay, she would hide like the lady in the picture and she would never come out, not for anybody's secret.

—

One Saturday she saw a picture of her grandmama. At least she thought that's who it must be. All she knew for sure was it was a picture of a very old lady whose head was wrapped in a white bandanna. She was standing in front of a big white house with white columns. She looked very clean to Story. Her long, long skirt was covered with a white apron, and she carried a baby so little you could only see the white blanket it was wrapped in. Story knew it was a baby 'cause she'd seen babies carried like that at the general store when she'd gone there with Papa. But the old woman's face was the second thing she noticed because it was one of the oldest faces she'd seen in the book. Mama had told her Grandmama, her grandmother Mc-

Cloud, died at the age of sixty, way before she was born, but to Story she was older than time, older even than old white Mr. Hattenfield, who was so old the town was named after him. She had only seen him once, passing in the only motor car in town, and sitting in the back because a black man was driving him.

More than anything, more than how old she was, it was her eyes that fascinated Story. They stared right at you, but they didn't seem to be looking at anything. They looked almost dead, like the fishes' eyes she saw when her mama cleaned fish and cut off their heads. Those big dead eyes, staring at her from the black face that was surrounded by white. They reminded her of someone else's eyes. She wanted to know why her grandmama's eyes were dead, if she was her grandmama, but she was afraid to say that. That was just the kind of question Mama hated. There were some questions she was glad to answer, questions like the teacher would ask, like, "How many states are there in the United States?" or, "What is the capital of North Carolina?" Story knew Mama wouldn't talk to her if she asked a question like that, she'd just keep doing what she was doing or she'd say, "Don't have a foolish mouth." So she held her peace, and looked at her grandmama whenever she had a chance to open the ALBUM.

Every Friday they had fish for dinner, and every Friday her father would bring the fish home and fling them in the sink for her mother to clean. He'd call out to her, "Sadie Evelyn, Sadie Evelyn, fish is heah!" And her mother would stop whatever she was doing and come running to clean the fish, because she knew that he wasn't going to put them on the ice, and if they spoiled, she would be blamed. And so she'd grab her big knife, cut off the heads, scale the fish, and pump up some water to wash them good. Story would watch her mother's hands, and sometimes she'd feel a fish scale hit her face as the scales went flying in every direction. Her mother's hands could move fast, and they always did it right, they never made a mistake.

The first Friday after she noticed her grandmama's eyes, she had forgotten that it was Friday and that her father would be coming in soon with the fish. When he threw them in the dry sink, the fear rose up in her and dangled like one of those fish on a hook. She'd have to look at her grandmama's eyes as her mother cut the heads off the fish. Something kept her from running outside, even though she couldn't stand not to look. The eyes were there waiting for her; even if she didn't look, they would be there waiting for her, and even after her mother threw the heads to the cats, the eyes would be there waiting for her. Maybe she would dream about them. Maybe her grandmama would be in the dream with a fish's head.

Her mother was coming. She had heard Papa's call from where she was, out in the vegetable garden getting greens. Story walked slowly over to the dry sink. She stared at the fish, slightly hunched over, afraid to get too close.

Her mama came in the back door. She said, "Girl, you sick?" and didn't wait for an answer. Instead she said to Story, "Get my knife," and the back door slammed behind her, fish swinging into her dress.

Story picked up the knife and walked outside to the stump of the old tree where her mother killed chickens and scaled fish. She waited through all of the beheading, splitting, and scaling. She realized that she wanted somehow to save the fish, that she felt related to them, the creatures with dead eyes, with her grandmama's eyes, 'cause they couldn't talk. They couldn't say anything about anything. She was quiet as her mama fed the heads to the cats who had been hanging around like buzzards, rubbing up against her mother's skirts and her own dress. Story stood and watched the cats devour the entrails and heads of the fish and then cry for more as if they were starving. Flies had settled on the stump, and more and more flies were coming. Their dog, Spider, came up, sniffing around the blood. Her mother had finished and was hurrying back to her garden. She was always hurrying.

"Get the bucket, girl, and rinse off that blood," she threw back over her shoulder. "Don't just stand there like you dead or somethin'!"

That's how it was, Story thought. Maybe somebody had said that to her grandmama, and they had scared her so much she felt dead, dead like the fish in the sink. Maybe she had felt her body go all heavy like it wasn't here. Maybe she had pulled all of herself in the back of her head, so she could hide into a tight little ball that left her eyes flat, just like those eyes in the sink. She was sick feelin'. How would she be able to eat her supper? Her papa would strap her for wastin' good food if she didn't eat. She swallowed her sickness like she did when she was punished and got the bucket.

Flies were everywhere. They rose up in her face as she threw the water over the stump and washed away the fishes' blood. Maybe if she told her she was sorry. She could look at the picture and talk to her and say how sorry she was that she had to eat that fish, and explain that the cats had to live too. Spider made a move as if to chase the cats, but there were four cats and only one of him. He backed off, barking from a distance. One of the cats was dragging off part of a fish head, taking it somewhere to finish it. Both eyes were gone. She kicked the dirt, looking for somewhere to go. She'd go down by the creek, only there were fish in the creek. Live fish with dead eyes.

———

Papa had put a pantry on the side of the house, where they stored dried fruits and kept the canned food that Mama put up every summer. Story used to hide in the pantry whenever she got the chance. One time she saw Papa take a drink of something she was sure was liquor, when she was in there looking through the space between the wide boards that the door was made of. He came in and took a glass from the white kitchen cupboard. All the cupboards had glass in them, so you could see where everything was. Then he hitched up his pants like men were always doing, and looked out the back door. She figured he was looking for Mama. This was a wash day. Mama must have been washing clothes around the side of the house in the big washtub. Papa looked way back in the bottom cupboard and pulled out a bottle. He poured a little bit, stopped it up with the cork, and pushed it back in there behind some things Mama didn't use much. Then he swallowed the whole thing fast, throwing his head back, and wiped off his mouth with his hand, sighing loud, like he was letting a big wind out of him. He looked out the door again, and left the kitchen. He didn't rinse it out with the sink pump like Mama always did.

Story remembered his last preaching on the evils of strong drink, and wondered if her papa was lying to folks on purpose. It was strange and confusing to her. She felt sad. Maybe this drink was something different; maybe it wasn't really what she thought. She checked the kitchen through the crack in the door and tiptoed out of the pantry. She didn't like seeing things like that, but there was no other way to see what was going on. There was no other way to keep from being punished for things she didn't do. Would God get Papa? she wondered. Couldn't God see everything? Papa was a minister. Lots of people came to their church to listen to him. He knew about Hell and damnation and all that stuff. Would God get her for spying on His pastor?

She was afraid suddenly. Maybe she had committed a terrible sin by spying on Papa. What if it wasn't strong drink, but just something like medicine he had to take? She was glad Bertie didn't see her coming out of the pantry. Bertie might tell Papa. Then she'd be in trouble with Papa and God. She could try praying and ask God to forgive her. Then as long as Papa didn't know she spied on him, she'd be all right. Maybe she could give God something He wanted so He wouldn't be mad. She'd have to think about that.

Bertie could never understand the point of spying. But then Bertie was never in trouble. They thought she was some kind of angel. Their baby. The point was to get something on them, so you'd know what they did first, and then you would always know what was coming. And of course, the only way to do that was to spy on them from a safe distance. She had learned how to be safe from the button man dream. It was to think of the button man for a few minutes before she went to sleep. Spy on him, see what he was doing, and then she would know, she would know he was only an empty suit with no face, and she could ball up the button suit, stuff it in the furnace and watch it burn. After that she could sleep without having that dream. She had tried to tell Bertie that, but Bertie never knew what she was talking about, and it just made Story angry, so she gave up talking to her about her dreams. Story laughed when she remembered she used to think the button man was God. Now she knew better. He was just a bad dream.

But she also knew you had to pay God for what you did wrong. So one day after Papa preached about Abraham and Isaac, she knew how to pay God. She found her mama's sewing basket and her needles and pins, and one day while Mama was dusting, she took a straight pin. It was during their playtime. Bertie was making mud pies. Story went behind the big pecan tree and sat on the ground and then she closed her eyes and said, "I'm sorry I spied on Papa," real fast, and she stuck the pin in her finger. The blood came out in little drops, and she squeezed it so there'd be three drops of blood in the dirt, one each for the Father, Son, and Holy Ghost, and then she heard Bertie coming, so she covered it over real quick with her foot and acted dumb like she hadn't been doing anything. But she knew she'd paid God. She sacrificed some of her blood.

—

They couldn't leave for school without being checked. First there was the underwear, and then the sweaters, and everything had to be fresh. Story and Bertie had to do their own laundry after they reached nine years of age, and so every night found them ironing in the kitchen.

"I'd never let a boy do that to me," Bertie whispered. "That's dirty, Mama said so." Bertie's round sweet face nodded in agreement with herself. She had two long brown braids that bounced.

"And Papa says you'll go to Hell." Story mocked her father's preaching style as she ironed their collars. " 'Change your low-down ways, sisters and brothers.' " She had heard it all her fourteen years. "You'll go to Hell for this, you'll go to Hell for that. You'll go to Hell if you look cross-eyed at a monkey, according to Papa!" She was not quite whispering. Papa was not home. Bertie looked crushed. Story frightened her. She didn't understand how she dared say some of the things she said. Story got strapped for things she did. She worried about her sister's soul. Bertie was ten now and had been recently called to the altar on a Sunday morning and confessed Jesus as her personal savior. Bertie was almost always good. She almost never got a strapping. Story got sick of her sometimes. She thought, If I just had a buddy who could talk to me.

"Let me tell you, Bertie, Hell could be fun after this. I'm leaving this place when I get old enough. You'll see. They'll all see." They heard their mother coming. She wore laced-up oxfords and stepped rather heavily.

Story was not afraid of her mother. She knew her mother was afraid most of the time of a lot of things. She thought her mother was nosy, but not mean. She thought, Fraidy cat. Mama is a fraidy cat. Her mother sang the same little tune all the time. "I've tried, God knows I've tried." She had lived through hard times right after slavery, and she never let them forget it. "Dealin' with white folks," she said, "meant findin' out what they wanted most from you and makin' them think it pleased you to no end to give it to them." Story knew the song by heart. "She'd done her best with their daddy. God knows."

One day Story overheard her mother talking to herself. She was rolling some damp clothes up for ironing. "Meanness sit on his shoulders like a burden," she mumbled. "I do what I have to do, and they'll have to do the same. All I can do is teach them the rules. That's all I can do." Story couldn't help wondering why it had to be that way. She didn't plan to live like her mother did, afraid all the time. Afraid to tell somebody to stop beatin' on her, to stop beatin' on her children.

"Girls, now let me see your collars," she said, coming in the kitchen to check on them. She pursed her lips, weary with the day's work. "You don't want no black marks on them, no dirt. Story, you got to teach your sister how to look respectable and clean. White folks respects cleanliness in colored people. How many times have I told you that?" Story thought of Irene's house. It sure wasn't clean there. It was a mess. She was going over there tomorrow. Irene had asked her to come over after school.

Irene lived in a two-room house. They had an outhouse in the back, a kitchen, and a main room where they all slept on cots and two sofas. There was a water pump off the back porch, and a wood stove in the kitchen. Story was their honored guest whenever she visited. They always called her Reverend Temple's daughter. "It's so nice to have Reverend Temple's daughter to grace our table," Irene's mother would say, looking right at Story like she was talking about somebody else. Story loved to go there, even though she never ate much of their greasy food. They almost always had turnip greens and biscuits that they would slop up a kind of gravy with, and even the gravy looked a lot like grease to her. Still, it was a lot of fun to be treated as if she was special, and Irene's mama made Irene wait on her, which was the best part of all.

Irene's family was light-skinned. This had always been a mystery to Story, because she thought when she was a little girl that all light colored people had better clothes and nicer things than dark colored people. But they were different, and they treated her like she was high yellow or something. They never seemed to notice that her hair wasn't very long or very straight. She decided that it was because she was always clean, since Irene's house always stank of chitlins and wasn't very clean. Irene always went on over her clothes, said she dressed like white folks, and had even asked if she could have one of Story's dresses when Story got tired of it. "You must be rich," she said one day, picking at Story's shirtwaist. "You rich?"

Story knew they weren't rich. As a matter of fact, she knew Papa often fussed around the house about her mama's spending for what he called "foolishness" and "the devil's own trinkets." He was always telling Mama to "lay up treasures in Heaven." She knew they sometimes ran out of cash money and lived only on what was in the garden. She knew Papa did handyman work for white folks to make extra money. But Irene made her feel so good, she said, "Yes, we're rich." She didn't care if it was a lie. It was just a little lie, and besides, to Irene they were rich.

They were in the sixth grade. Sixth grade got out at 2:45. She'd go by after school, and Irene's mother would always ask her to have a piece of pie or something sweet. She couldn't stay long because she had to be home by 3:45 or she'd be in trouble with Mama, and then with Papa, but for a whole school year she went there after school without Mama knowing. And sometimes they looked at the dirty book Irene found in her daddy's drawer, but they couldn't figure anything out. Finally it was all ruined, though, and she wasn't treated special anymore and she lost her friend, Irene.

Irene's parents played cards and drank. When she walked in with Irene, the house was full of men gambling. There was cigar smoke floating in the air, and they had dishes on each table with money in them. There were bottles of some strong drink sitting around. Over in one corner there was a woman sitting in a man's lap, running her hands all over his head and whisperin' in his ear. She had on the tightest dress Story had ever seen, and her face was painted. They were kissin' each other on the mouth. Story looked away. She wanted to look but she knew it would be a sin. Irene said "Hey" to her papa and started on through the room to the kitchen, as if nobody was there. As if she was used to seein' things like that. So Story just followed behind her.

One of the men was staring hard at her. Before she reached the kitchen door, he said, "Ain't you Reverend Temple's girl?" She looked at her feet. She wished he didn't know. If Papa found out, she'd never get to come back. And she would have terrible trouble with Papa.

"Yeah, that's who she is, man," another man said. "Let's play cards."

"Naw, naw, wait a minute," the first one said. He was near drunk. "That's the man said I was goin' to Hell and not to come back to his church. Naw, man, naw." He pushed the hands away that were attempting to restrain him. "He said me and all my kids was goin' to Hell 'cause I was gamblin', and I got a message for him. I got a message for this pretty little gal to take to her papa. She gonna be a purty thang, ain't she? Look at them long lashes and that sweet chocolate-brown skin. She gonna be a fine chocolate mama one day."

Story moved closer to Irene. She didn't like that man. It wasn't right. His voice was dirty somehow. The words were not bad words, but she knew they were wrong, and she was wrong bein' there. She felt like a bad girl, like she was lettin' Papa down. She knew the message wouldn't be a good one, but she didn't know what to do.

"Aw man, look," said the one with the big cigar, "she just a kid. Les' play cards. I come here to play cards."

He had not even heard the objection. He was staring at Story now, at her clean clothes and her nice shoes. "You tell your daddy, little girl, you tell him you was at a gamblin' house today, and that Mr. Bobby Lee Bocard said tell him you folks ain't so high and mighty after all; he guess . . . aw, forget it . . . I'll tell him myself." He settled back in his chair and took a drink.

A fat man with a plaid shirt on and a kind face said, "Man, you drink too much. You ready to play cards?" They ignored her. Irene's eyes were stretched wide open. She pulled Story out of there by the hand.

"I got to go," Story said. "I got to go now." She knew she could never go back now. Somehow the word would get back to Papa. And even if she lied and they believed her, she'd have to come home earlier than ever and Mama would be checking up on her. She ran from Irene's questions, covering her ears with her hands, tears streaming down her face.

She couldn't ever go back there. Papa would beat her if he ever found out. When she got to 333 Mill Street, Story tried to straighten up her shoulders. She wiped her face with her hankie. It wouldn't do to let Mama know she'd been crying. There would be questions, too many questions, and Papa would be sure to find out where she'd been.

She opened the screen door and let herself in. She was earlier than she had been in a long time. Mama expected her at three forty-five. It was only three o'clock.

"Well, what you doin' home so early, Story?" she said. "Didn't have debate club today?" Her mother was sitting down; for a little break, she said. Unusual for her.

Story kissed her mother lightly on the cheek. "No, ma'am," she said quietly, and sat down on the couch. She was glad she was not really lying. Of course, that didn't say where she had really been. Something in her eyes, her voice, something gave her away. She had always thought Mama had a real strange way of knowin' what she was doin'. Sadie looked into her eyes. She fingered the crocheted doily on the arm of the green overstuffed sofa.

"Story, you ain't tellin' me the truth," she whispered. Papa was in the bedroom. Story heard him opening and closing drawers. Sadie never stopped looking at her.

Story's whole body shivered. God, please don't let Mama tell, she prayed. Please don't. She was still holding onto her books. She decided it couldn't hurt to try. If she didn't say anything, she'd get strapped for insolence. If she said, she'd be in trouble for going to

Irene's. "I just went by Irene's house for a few minutes, Mama," she said in a tiny voice. She was looking down at the dark green rug, praying to herself.

Her mama sighed, and at the same time her papa opened the bedroom door and walked down the hall. He said quickly, "I'm goin' out, lock the doors." Story held her breath and listened to her heart. Then he was gone. She let out a long breath, put her books down, and went to lock the door.

Mama looked very tired. Her hair was pulled back in a bun behind her head. She had on her "workin' dress," as she called it. She only looked up when Jacob's step could no longer be heard on the sidewalk in front of their house. Story had always been glad they had sidewalks. Most black people she knew lived on unpaved streets with no sidewalks. Story could smell soup simmering. The clock ticked. She didn't know where her sister was, and she wished Mama would say something to let her know if a beating was waiting for her that night. She sat back down.

"I ain't gon' tell him this time," Mama finally said. She sighed again and shook her head. "You know your papa; he a good man, he just be awful hard sometime. But I know he don't want you runnin' with no trash." Her voice got a little louder. She looked into Story's eyes again. "You a strong, willful filly," she said, "and you bound to make him mad sometime. I reckon he can't help who he is, and you neither. But if you ever go over there again, it be too bad for you, you hear me?"

Story was so relieved, she began to cry, silently, her eyes open and lookin' at Mama. She could feel her face getting wet. Then Mama handed her a hankie and she blew her nose. They just sat in silence for a while. Story thought Mama seemed glad she had not told Papa. "So what you learn today? 'Sides runnin' roun' with that common gal?" she said.

Story talked about arithmetic and history. Mama told her a funny story about Bertie, who was at piano lessons, she said, and then Story thought that maybe she could ask about the secret she had always wanted to know. She had always wanted to know about Mama's hair. Story remembered when Mama had a long braid straight down her back almost to her waist. Now Mama almost always wore it in a bun, and it had not been long like that for a long, long time, it seemed to Story. And they were sitting there side by side on the couch, and Mama didn't seem in a hurry to work for once, and they had been together about Papa this time. So she said, all of a sudden, "Mama, why you cut your hair that time?" It just came out without her really thinkin' it. She remembered a day when she was little, and loud voices in the basement, and Mama's blue bandanna. But she knew as soon as she said it, it was the wrong thing to say.

"Because I did," Mama said, giving Story another sideways look. "That's for me to know. Why you askin' that?" Her voice was tight.

Story wiggled her feet. She was sorry she had asked. "Just did," she said. Then she said, " 'Cause."

" 'Cause what?" Mama said, glarin' at her.

" 'Cause I remember one day when I was little one day, I remember somethin'."

Mama sat up suddenly and looked straight into Story's eyes. "Well then, you know why I cut it, and you ain't got no business askin' me what you done already remembered, 'cause it ain't none a your business. Some things is just better left alone."

Story knew what the secret was then. She knew somehow that Papa had done it, cut her hair off, and that Mama's black eye was 'cause she had done something Papa didn't like. It was like rememberin' through a fog, but she knew, and she knew she was right. Mama had secrets too. Sometimes she heard what sounded like slaps and bumps in the night and somebody cryin'. Sometimes Mama had big blue places on her arms, except mostly she wore long sleeves and you couldn't see her arms. Somedays after school Mama would look like she'd been cryin', her eyes all red and swollen up. Story wanted to tell her to stop him doin' it! Stop him doin' it! Maybe he would listen to her. She could try, couldn't she. Couldn't she try?

Mama got up from her chair. "Got to look after suppah," she said. "Your papa be back soon." Story knew that was it. She would never try again, because she had already said more than she had ever dared. She had already remembered too much and said too much. But at least she knew what the secret was, except she wondered what Mama had done that was bad. She wanted to thank Mama and hug her, for savin' her a beatin', but Mama would say somethin' like, "Don't thank me, just behave," so she didn't do it, she just helped out a little more at dinner, and at night she would listen for sounds, and some mornings she would know what the dark circles under Mama's eyes were all about.

Irene told everybody at school Story thought she was cute and too good to be her friend anymore. There was never another after-school place for Story from then, and until high school she came straight home every day.

———

Luther was a boy in her high school class, and that's all he ever was destined to be to her, just some boy in her high school. It was Miss Courtfield's science class. They all went to her house for the class picnic. School was almost over. Honeysuckle was blooming; it was a semi-nice day. Not too hot, shady-sunny, you didn't know what the day would turn out to be really. Most of the girls had on white, or plaid pink dresses, with big bows tied behind their backs. They had primped and preened all morning in preparation for the picnic. Miss Courtfield had a big house with a big yard on the edge of town; almost in the country, right at the edge of the colored section, and not too far in toward where poor folks lived. It was in the area where most of the colored teachers and the two colored doctors in town lived. All the young people met at the school at eight-thirty A.M., and then Miss Courtfield marched them over to her house. Girls and boys were divided, of course. There were ten girls and thirteen boys, and so Hungerforth Smith and Raymond Williams had to march together. All the boys snickered and whispered about it, and one even laughed until Miss Courtfield said this was inexcusable behavior and they knew they had better home trainin' than that, and so they shut up, and T. P. Sanderworth marched in between the boys' line and the girls' line by himself. He was the smartest boy in class, and so Miss Courtfield gave him that honor. Miss Courtfield herself headed up the girls' line. All the girls had lunches they had fixed, lunches for two. Miss Courtfield would have three extra lunches at her house for the three odd boys.

Story walked with Fannie Holdon. They were friends; not whispering friends, but friends nevertheless. Fannie liked Luther. She talked about him all the way to the house, whispering and giggling. Luther was at the end of the boys' line. "He is just so handsome, you know," she said, squeezing Story's hand, "and he looked at me twice this morning. Not once, but twice; so I know he likes me, he just hasn't said so."

Story was interested in this, but very cautious. Everytime she thought of having a boyfriend, she got kind of scared, scared of Papa, of what he said of such things. She knew Mama and Papa would kill her for even having some of the thoughts she had. She knew what the Bible said about such things, or what Papa said it said anyhow. Fannie was playing with fire. Story listened to her, jealous, repelled, fascinated. Only married people should be thinking about such things.

"So have you?" she was asking Story. "Have you?" Kissing. Kissing, thought Story. Dirty to put your mouth on someone else's, but something awful in her wanted it. She wasn't worthy and she shouldn't have such thoughts. Fannie had even told her of nasty kissing when you did something with your tongue. She shuddered when she thought of it.

"No, of course not," she answered. The sun was getting a little warmer now. They were closer to Miss Courtfield's house. "I'm not that kind."

Fannie was suddenly quiet. She didn't speak any more until they had reached the house.

Miss Courtfield had organized games for the morning and nature walks for the afternoon. Only two boys were to take five girls not too far from the house, past the tree that had been struck by lightning, down by the blackberry bushes that ran behind her house and back again. Each group had fifteen minutes of walking time. They were to pursue the beauties of nature and report on the species they observed when they returned. Luther and Story were in the same group, much to the dismay of Fannie, who ended up in T. P. Sanderworth's group; the boy in the class who wore glasses, and carried a pocket watch just like his father's.

As soon as they were out of sight of Miss Courtfield, the group paired up, two boys with two girls, leaving the three extra girls to work together. Luther walked over to Story. "Walk with me?" he said.

He was tall and had a beautiful smile and deep brown skin. Story thought about Fannie's question. Had he ever done it? she wondered. Luther slid his arm around her waist. She was slender; her white eyelet dress showed her figure to its advantage. Story froze a little, and then she felt proud that he would pick her out, the most handsome boy in the class. That was really something! She smiled. His arm felt good. They strolled behind the barn. The others were up ahead. She knew Miss Courtfield would be watching for them, and she began to get very nervous. The sun came and went. It looked like rain, then it didn't.

"You know I've been watching you," he said. Story felt something tremble inside herself. What would she do if he tried it? "And I think you're the one," he said.

Story looked away from him, nervous. She glanced at the tree that had been struck by lightning. Only one little green bough still hung on to life. There was a long black scar where the tree had been struck and burned. Her eyes came back to him. She didn't know what to do with her hands. "The one, Luther?"

"Yes, the one to give me my first kiss." He was very close. She would have to push him away if she didn't want to do it. There were little bursts of something like lightning going up and down her body. He leaned over her and pressed her lips with his. It felt awkward to Story, but he must have liked it because he kept pressing until she pushed hard on his chest.

"It's time!" she whispered urgently. "Miss Courtfield will be waiting!" The others were on their way back. Story looked from left to right to make sure they were still alone. If they were discovered and Miss Courtfield spoke to her parents, she would be in for it. Mama would never stop talking about it, and there was no telling what punishment Papa would come up with. She started to bolt and run until she had looked at her shirtwaist. It was crooked and one button had come undone. She fixed it quickly. He pulled on his tie.

"Not bad," he said, trying to sound sophisticated. "Not bad at all.

How about meeting me somewhere later?" She was busily straightening her dress and hair.

"Just don't get any ideas," she said. "Just don't get any ideas."

They made it back just in time. Her anxiety faded as soon as they joined the others and she knew she was safe. Story shared her lunch with Luther and enjoyed watching Fannie go from frustrated to angry. Luther watched nobody and nothing but Story. She could tell her first kiss had rendered him helpless and she had just found out how good it felt to be powerful.

———

Late that summer, Luther started coming to her father's church, to Sunday school. And all the next school year they saw each other at church or lingering after school a little. Luther was eighteen, two years older than Story. He knew more than she did about where to go to sneak a kiss or two, and he hung around Story as much as he could, calling her his sweetheart, putting his arm around her waist, trying to touch her when people weren't looking. She liked it enough to think about him at night. She liked getting all hot and soft for a few minutes, but it scared her too. Soon Luther asked her to meet him every Thursday after glee club practice, when they had an excuse to be home late.

Story walked slowly around to the back of Jamison High. The leaves made a pattern of shadow and sun on her brown coat. Luther walked up behind her and leaned into the wall. He was very close to her. Story turned around. He smelled slightly of sweat from the long day at school. And she could see his Adam's apple bobbing up and down as he swallowed.

"So," he said, "what's sweet Story gonna do today? Can I have a little kiss? Little blue ribbons?" he said, touching her hair. She didn't move. She didn't want to move. His lips were nice on her, really nice, and she felt herself move into his arms with so much urgency it scared her. She could feel herself sinking, giving in. "Can we go somewhere?" he whispered into her neck. "Can we go somewhere, please?"

Story was aware of his hardness pressing into her. It was wonderfully dangerous. She had never felt this before, but she knew what it meant. She had to stop it. This was more than she had expected. More than she wanted even. Somehow, she had to stop this.

"Please," he whispered.

"Luther," she hissed, "it's too dangerous! My father! My father will kill both of us."

He kissed her again. "We can go to the woods behind the mill," he whispered heavily. "That's where all the guys take their sweethearts."

She really wanted to go with him. If only . . . "I can't! It's a . . . You know that!" The thought of her father was enough. "No, Luther . . . no . . . No! Stop! Someone's coming!"

It was too much. Her coat was half off, her hair was in disarray, and Mrs. Marley was upon them. The youngest and the prettiest teacher in the school. Her debating and speech teacher. "That's just about enough," she said severely.

All Story could think of was what would happen to her at home. "Please," she pleaded, "please, Mrs. Marley, nothing terrible happened. Please don't tell my parents."

Luther had his hand over his eyes, as if to shield himself from being seen, the way little children do. Mrs Marley was outraged. "I hold you both responsible. This is inappropriate behavior for a gentleman under any circumstances. I am shocked," she said. Her head trembled slightly. "Shocked and dismayed. Two of the brightest and best students at Jamison High. And I am most dismayed at the young lady's behavior. The leader of our debating team, the bright light of promise for our future. You should both be expelled. What kind of street behavior is this?"

Luther spoke up, wringing his hands, standing first on one foot and then the other, like he might need to go to the bathroom. "Ma'am, Mrs. Marley, she was trying to resist my overtures, she was trying."

Mrs. Marley glared at Story. "Is this true, Miss Temple? What do you have to say about this? And you a Christian daughter of a pastor!"

Story took in sharp, short breaths. She had started to cry. Oh, just let her have mercy please, she prayed to herself. "Yes, ma'am, it's true. He was just carrying my books home, and then he started this—this—"

"Never mind," Mrs. Marley said. "Never mind the details. I can see what happened. Story, go inside and clean yourself up and go home. I'll think about what I ought to do. It's a serious thing to ruin your reputation. Once tarnished, you can never be made bright again. Now, you march!"

Story wanted to hear what happened to Luther, but she ran, tears covering her eyes. Also, she wanted to kill Luther. It wasn't fair; it just wasn't fair. It was all his fault. He had made her act like that. Boys always got what they wanted. She just knew Mrs. Marley would be easy on him. They were bigger and stronger and they had it easier. He made her feel all fluttery and weak just 'cause he wanted to, pushing and pushing, and then they got in trouble, just like she knew they would. Leaning on her, pushing her, like that man at Irene's house that time called her a "fine little chocolate thing." Like Papa leaning on Mama, making her do what he wanted, forcing her.

She was really crying now, and as she ran down the hall to the rest room, was afraid the janitor would see her looking like a loose woman. Her blue ribbon fluttered off and was left on the hall floor. She hated herself like this, all messed up and crying like a baby. And it was her fault too. She shouldn't have met him there. She shouldn't have let him kiss her like that. She had almost said yes! She couldn't believe she had almost said yes! If that's what sex made you do, made you lose control and act stupid and silly, it wasn't worth it. She washed her face and fixed her hair as best she could, dismayed that she had lost her ribbon somewhere. She prayed her mama wouldn't notice that. She didn't have time to look for it. It was getting terribly late. They'd be locking the school doors soon. She'd have to walk fast and make up some story to tell Mama on the way. If Mrs. Marley didn't tell, maybe she could save herself a beating. There was no guarantee. In her haste, she dropped her satchel and all her books fell out. "Damn!" Story swore. Something they were strictly forbidden to do in their house or anywhere else. She gathered up her books, stuffing all the papers in helter-skelter, and hurried home, running as much of the way as she could.

It took two weeks for her to feel safe at home, and she held her breath for those two weeks. Mrs. Marley was silent for two weeks, and both Story and Luther worried for twenty-four hours a day, wondering when the blade was going to be lowered on their necks. Finally, Mrs. Marley called Story into her room and announced that she had decided that the damage done to Story's reputation would be too great if anyone else found out. And so out of deference to the outstanding work Story had done as a student, she would give her a second chance.

She and Luther stayed away from each other for several weeks. She didn't know what Mrs. Marley had done to him, but he was doing something every afternoon after school for her. Story didn't know what it was. She thought it might have been yard work and cleaning, but she didn't know, and they had to sneak a minute or two to see each other, for fear Mrs. Marley would catch them together. One day she saw him through the barbershop window sweeping up. He winked at her, and she walked by as if she hadn't seen him. She couldn't risk being caught. Eventually they managed to get notes to each other, and she told him it was no use. She was a Christian girl. She told him not to act crazy. Mrs. Marley had saved his senior year. If he messed up, he wouldn't graduate.

Story would put the notes inside his book satchel, which they had agreed he would leave behind the risers in the choir room, and he would leave his notes in there for her.

"I love you," Luther wrote, in his rather cramped hand.

"I can only see you in class," Story wrote back.

"I'll be graduating soon and we can get married. I love you."

"I'm going to normal school. I can't."

"Can I just walk you home? I love you."

"What if Mrs. Marley catches us?"

"Meet me on the corner at Carnegie Library. She lives in the other direction. I love you."

He wouldn't take no for an answer. He hung around after school, standing far enough away so that he wouldn't be noticed. Finally, he planned it so that he met her at the library. There was nothing she could do except run. She didn't really want to run. She was glad to see him. She knew there was no danger. Mrs. Marley was in a faculty meeting.

He was shy after their close brush with disaster. "Hi" was all he said. And then, "I'm sorry."

"Yeah," was her answer. They walked most of the way in silence. After that he met her there almost every day and they began to relax, but Story felt different. She began to think maybe he wasn't as handsome as she had thought. Maybe she didn't really like the sound of his voice so much or the way his hands were made. He did have one attraction that was still there for her, however. Luther wasn't an outstanding student. He was a little lazy in school, but he was brilliant in one subject, the one that had made his reputation, biology. He had offered to help her when she had trouble, and she had trouble often with biology. She decided she'd take him up on it. Soon he was helping her with all her biology projects. One day after school, she let him walk all the way to the front porch with her. He told a joke. She didn't laugh. She could tell he was afraid to say the wrong thing, and so he said stupid things.

"What happened?" he said after he had tried to hold her hand. "You liked me at first."

"I still like you, Luther," she said, "only as much as I should, not more than I should." She knew that it wouldn't satisfy him, and it didn't. But she had decided. He would not lean on her again. She would not be a little butterfly for him, fluttering around, getting caught, and maybe getting pinned to a board like those bugs in biology lab.

"I'll wait for you, then," he said in despair. "I'll wait for you to love me."

Sometimes she thought about those lightning sparks that were there the first few months they had known each other. Because her parents weren't home, she leaned over and let him kiss her, right on Papa's porch, even though she knew there would be an awful scene if she was caught. Nothing. Boring, she thought. Luther thought he had made some progress. "Can I come calling on Sunday?" he said timidly.

"Maybe so. Papa doesn't like me to have callers. I have to ask." She was thinking of her biology projects, which were due Monday. "I'll ask if you do one thing," she said, ever so slightly pouting. "If you'll write up that biology project for me."

By the time graduation came, Luther's father had died and he had to move to Virginia with his mother and little sister. That year, he had written up at least eight biology projects for Story and given her a cheat sheet for the final. But he had given her a lot more than biology lessons. Luther had taught her that her beautiful, smooth skin, her little white teeth, and her ample breasts could make men come and go for her. Oh, the feelings were fun, all right, but that wasn't the important thing. She had learned that she could use those feelings if she stayed outside them. It was all about how to get what you wanted. Men did it all the time by making women afraid of them. By using women to get what they wanted. Luther taught her that she wanted to be the user and not the used.

After Papa got through with her for kissing Luther good-bye, she was certain. It was after graduation, so she thought Luther deserved a little kiss, only Papa caught them on the porch. It was terrible, but she made up her mind. She was not going to be like that tree that had been struck by lightning in Miss Courtfield's yard. She was not going to be like Mama, letting a man beat on her and use her. She'd enjoy the feelings and that was all. They would be her feelings, and she would belong to herself and no one else. No man would ever use her against herself.

———

It was over very suddenly, and all of them had trouble with the change. When you have always lived with Armageddon, what do you know about the time of still waters? She felt like there was a fall in the forest and she wasn't there, but she heard it; they all heard it, all three of them. Every twig, every crack and sizzle of the hardened, encrusted bark, every soft bounce of fungus that grew along the broken places. She knew she had heard every limb and joint as it crashed into the ground and splintered into a thousand, two thousand, ways. They heard it all, she thought.

"And so freedom come," she remembered some old folks sayin', "and so it come with a proclamation, with a jubilation, with a shout and a juba, and then folks went on back to the quarters and commenced to go back to work, 'cause what else could they do?"

And so this is freedom, she thought, a great big empty place in the sky, and no way of knowin' what to put in there, and nothin' for the eyes to do but shut and open, and the same for Sadie, who now had nothin' to do but be afraid, because that's all she ever knew how to do, and so it was empty she was afraid of now, and then too. And the same for Baby Sister, who wandered about the house with her big eyes full of unshed tears, not knowin' why she should be sad, but she was anyway, maybe just 'cause it was habit.

And Story was sixteen and free at last of it all, but didn't know at first who the great emancipator was, and thought in her young eyes, which had not had a chance to feel, ever, that death or what passed for God in her life had done it. His dying, she thought, was like one of the huge trees in California that had lived out its stubbornness, and in its meanness made time irrelevant. And his fallin' took years and his dyin' took years, all of her sixteen years at least, like a great tree fallin' and scattering everything soft and fine and afraid that was in its way, like Baby Sister, who didn't know which way to turn, but was wanderin' around the house like a deer in the forest who didn't know where the sound came from. His dyin' left her, too, with nowhere to turn and come about, and not knowin' how to do that. And her mama bein' quiet about what she knew again. She knew and had always known, but also had always known how to step out of the way of falling things.

They went to the little white church neat with funeral flowers, stinking of them, the smell creepin' out under the front door and even into the back hall and making her sick, the choir singin', "You must be pure and holy, you must be pure and holy, you must be pure and holy to see God feed His lambs." And all the sisters gathered to weep over the pastor's untimely death. "Yes, death wait for no man," she heard them say, "time and tide wait for no man. And you never know when the bridegroom will come in the night," they said, "never."

Story heard all this, thinking and not thinking. Thinking behind her veil which was not a real veil because she was too young, but her own private one that she remembered even more now because of the dead man in the casket in the picture. The dead man who was not her papa, but now was. The brown inside, white outside, church that was wood. And clean, so that you could eat off the floor if you dropped a piece of fried chicken by accident. And the waxy smell mixed with funeral and weeping and women with perfumes.

Story watched her mother watching the dead man. The dead man who had sealed his death warrant because she had reached her limit. Paid is paid and done is done. Paid for with the blood of the lamb. Paid for with the blood of the lamb. Paid for, this blood between her mother and her father. Sadie would see who made it to the promised land; can I get a witness, Lord? An eye for an eye. Story knew the twins were sacrifice enough. No more, no more. It was twins for that baby her papa always called "that white man's chile," an offering up of innocence, and Sadie for the twins. God's Abraham only had Isaac to give; her papa himself preached on that, and Abraham's God only asked for that one chile. So when they sat in the first pew with their silk dark and heavy, Sadie's veil was coverin' not grief, but surprise, because there was no way of knowin' what to put in the great big empty place, because she had never known enough. Story knew it had not been fate or destiny or God's hand, but just that enough was enough for her mother, and there was no room left inside Sadie for any more fear. So she refused, just like she would have refused another piece of turkey at Christmas dinner, because there was no more room left for any more fear.

It was that boy Luther who insisted on kissin' her good-bye, because he was movin' away. She let him walk her home when she didn't even like him, and Papa caught him tryin' to kiss her. He dragged her in off the porch and back to the bedroom, and slammed the door and took off the belt, and it all started again. Mama was left with nowhere to put her fear but in the future, and when the dark lid of the box came down over Papa's head, she screamed "Enough!" Finally. She sank to her knees and said, "Lord have mercy on me and mah girls!" But her face was like she'd been slapped or somethin'. Story could see that she didn't know what to do with the space Papa left, and there was nowhere for Mama to go but down, so she got herself ready to take over the house and to care for Baby Sister. Mama

was all used up in the great effort contained in her one small cry—
"Enough!"

"Enough!" was what she had said when she opened the bedroom
door, and Papa pullin' her panties down and his hand just ready to
touch where it oughten to be and had never really been before, no
matter what Mama believed. Mama kept askin' how many times,
how many times, like she didn't know how many times he had
preyed upon her, and Story kept on sayin', "He never did nothin' but
beat me, he never did nothin' but beat me," because that much was
true.

They walked along holdin' hands like three widows: Story, Sadie,
and Baby Sister in navy-blue silk, because Mama said she wouldn't
wear no black ever again after her two boys died. They threw in the
dirt and turned around and walked back to the cars. Story never
cried a tear, not then, not ever. She walked straight as a ramrod,
holdin' up Sadie, holdin' onto Baby Sister's hand. She was thinkin',
So this is freedom, this is emancipation, this word "enough."

When the door burst in on Papa, she knew he was finally gonna
give in to his hunger. She was stiff with fear; he was finally gonna put
his hands on her. And then she saw Mama wavin' that fireplace
poker and Papa's hands rose in the air like flutterin' birds who,
though lookin' for a place to land, see crouchin' fur and glittering
green, and she knew they were finally free. She couldn't go to sleep
after that for the tremblin' and thinkin' about "what if"—and she
knew it wasn't God who'd had enough, it was Sadie.

The mornin' came after a longer night than she ever lived, and it
came with a screech and a howl and a just barely blue-gray dawn,
and a tree stretched out on the bedroom floor. A whole tree it looked
like, till she looked again at the dark hands at the end of the shadow
holdin' the sheets. Facedown into the hardwood floor where it had
fallen straight forward, and Mama's white, white sheets clutched between his hands like he had tried to cover himself 'cause he was
naked, and for the first time she saw his naked and black body
stretched out before her in perfect supplication.

"I done killed him," she heard someone sayin' and later she realized it was her mama's strangled tone, so unnatural that she didn't

recognize the voice. "Oh Lordy, I done killed him," she said again, knowin' his heart had quit because she had looked at his flutterin' hands, had looked at his sin and unflinchingly said, "Enough!" She had meant, "If you touch her, I will kill you!" And his heart had had nothin' to say in return, and so had stopped.

CHAPTER III

TO PATCH A PLACE

JUNE 2012

Lately, she had been killing as many as ten a day. They seemed to be drawn to the porch, sticking to the screens as if something sweet had been smeared on the door. If you opened the screen, they would fly off, buzz around a bit, and come back settling on the door, watching, waiting. Story had spent a good part of that summer day swatting with her rolled-up newspaper. She had had her evening meal, which Hermine cooked and served on a tray (though not on time) in the sunroom. Now the sun was rather low, it was almost twilight, and so the light filtered through the plastic and real plants lined up on glass shelves attached to all the windows in the front room. The windows were dusty and the air in the room was hard to breathe. Story had lived in it so many years, she never noticed how heavy and closed it felt, like an old unopened box. Hermine heard the newspaper flop every few minutes.

Bertie would have killed all those flies, Story thought. She had always been a good housekeeper. She'd have taken her time with those shelves and had all the plants dusted and polished. Too bad things had to turn out the way they did, but she had done her best by Bertricia. People make their own beds; have to lie in 'em. Someone had to put some sense into that Bertie's mind. She was a child with a child's sense. She got herself in that fix. Story swatted at a fly. Somebody had to get her out of it.

Nobody had ever looked after her, though, Story thought. Old Story always had to look out for herself. When her heart was broken or she was in pain she had to pick up the pieces and go on. Nobody ever cared that she had loved to dance when she was a tiny thing, and nobody cared that she had to take care of that white man's filth in order to go to normal school. Nobody cared that she had to save the family name either, least of all Bertie.

She was the oldest. She had to teach Bertie. Be an example. Be the strong one. Be Papa's last hope. She'd never forget how they punished her because she didn't want Bertie to wear her new straw hat. The hat reminded her of Mama's hat in the picture she saw in the album. She tried it on and felt pretty and grown-up. Then Papa said something she'd always remember. She was standing in front of the little round mirror that was attached to her chest of drawers. He walked into the room using his big preaching voice. "Where you get that hat?"

Story jumped. The little swinging mirror trembled. "Mama got it for me for Easter, Papa," she said, sure that she was going to get a lecture on the sin of pride, or something he called being "vainglorious."

"Put me in the mind a your mama when she real young," he said, flipping the ribbons that hung down her back. " 'Cept, you gon' be somebody when you grow up. You gon' do somethin' when you grow up. That look real nice, Story," he said. "Make me proud of you."

There was a soft look to his eyes she wasn't used to seeing. That's all he said, but that was a lot for Papa. He never gave compliments. He turned and abruptly left the room.

It was still a mystery to her. She had never quite understood her father anyway. But what he said about the hat was a real surprise, and she was excited about wearing it because he liked it so much. She could tell he liked it because he didn't say a word about vanity and pride going before a fall. And he had said she looked like Mama, and she was going to be somebody. That's why it was a special hat. And then they didn't let her wear it.

It was Easter. The day everybody would be at church. More people than any other day of the year. More people than Homecoming Sunday. And everybody would be "dressed to kill." Everybody who had anything new would wear it, even if they had to borrow something from somebody else, somebody who wasn't going to their church, so nobody would know they were wearing their cousin's hat from last year. Ladies would have yellow and pink flowers with white shoes or navy-blue shoes and straw hats with feathers and roses and veils, or they would have on navy-blue and white dresses with navy-blue and white shoes and navy-blue and white pocketbooks that smelled like the cologne on their handkerchiefs.

These handkerchiefs were never used to do anything like blowing their noses; they were only taken out of the blue and white purses to pat the perspiration away from their upper lips and their foreheads when it got too hot in the church. When the sisters started to get happy, when the deacons started their "amens" in the front pew and Papa's voice got loud and raspy, then they would take out their handkerchiefs and carefully wipe the mustaches that you couldn't see unless you were very close. And if they got happy, they would wave them in the air like flags, a sign of how much the Spirit had entered into them and how much power was coming from Papa's sermon.

Story remembered the first time she saw one of these ladies shout. The lady was sitting behind her and Bertie and Mama in the second pew, and as Papa's voice got more and more exciting, the lady handed her pocketbook to the woman next to her, and took off her wire-rimmed glasses, which were held together with a little safety pin, and she gave them also to the lady next to her, and then she rose like a big boat rocking back and forth and raised her hands in the air with a loud "Jesus" and began to dance, shaking the floor of their church with her black tie-up oxfords. Finally, two lady ushers and a man took her under the arms to keep her from falling, and when it was all over, she sat back down in the pew and wiped her face with her handkerchief and put her glasses back on as if nothing had happened.

Story knew there would be lots of shouting today, Easter Sunday, and lots of people being saved. The pastor's family was invited to dinner after church in the church basement. It was important to look nice. Her hat was cream-colored straw, and it had a navy-blue ribbon that ran around the crown and streamed down the back, and it went with her navy-blue dress, exactly. They were all standing in the hall ready to go, and Bertie started crying because she didn't have a hat for Sunday school and church. Her big eyes filled with tears. Mama said, "What's the matter with Baby Sister? What's she tunin' up about?"

"Just this ole hat," Story said. "She wants a hat too."

And Papa said, "Well, give it to her and let's go. We ain't got no time for foolishness." It was the hat he liked. The hat that had made him proud of her.

Story couldn't believe it. She couldn't believe they'd give her hat to Baby Sister without so much as a by-your-leave. Mama didn't move. Maybe she didn't believe it either.

Papa said, "Didn't you hear me? I *said* come on. The pastor can't afford to be late!" And he started out the door, certain that they would follow his orders.

Mama snatched the hat off Story's head and slammed it on Bertie. "Now you hush," she said, " 'fore you gets in trouble. Story, get me my Bible I left on your bed by the nightstand."

Story was standing there with her mouth open. Mama had taken her hat, her new Easter hat, and given it to Bertie! Before she could move, Bertie said, "I'll get the Bible," and ran for their room.

"I tole you to get it, Missy," Mama said, "and I notice you ain't moved a muscle."

She moved as slowly as she dared, and when she reached the bedroom, Bertie had fallen all over her school books trying to get to the Bible, and Story's beautiful English homework was all crumpled up under Bertie's feet. It would have to be copied all over again. She looked at her sister in her hat, and slapped her across the face.

What with Bertie's hollerin' and their bein' late, and Papa standin' out there on the sidewalk, Story knew Papa would know what she had done, and she didn't care. She had never even worn it. She had never even worn it, and they took it right off her head and gave it to Bertie to wear for Easter! Bertie's head wasn't even big enough for the hat, and Story thought she looked stupid in it, and she didn't care about the strappin' to come for hitting her little sister, she just didn't care. They all marched off to church like nothing had happened. Story lookin' straight ahead, Bertie sniffling and runnin' to keep up with Papa, who knew the choir would already be standin' there in their red robes.

The little wooden church sat up on a hill. It had a white cross on top, and was white outside but was all brown inside. Brown walls and floors. Brown pews. Brown pastor's chair, all oiled and polished for Easter. The only thing not brown was a big picture of a white and blond Jesus behind the pulpit. Only today there would be lots of white Easter lilies that people had given to remember their dead relatives, and the whole place would smell like perfume and Easter lilies. As they marched down the center aisle, Story looked at Bertie in front of her, holdin' Mama's hand and wearin' her hat. She wanted to snatch it off Bertie's head and smash her in the face. Nobody really cared. Papa would beat her, and nobody would know how it hurt that she didn't get to wear her hat, and nobody would ask. Well, Baby Bertie could keep the hat, Story thought as she slid into her seat. They could beat her till doomsday and she'd never wear that hat again, and she'd never forgive any of them.

Well, Bertie was gone now, and she'd looked after her right to the end. Big Sis was always goin' to look after her baby sister, they said. And she'd done it too, right to the end. The strong one. She wouldn't take any guilt to her grave. She'd looked after it all, right to the end.

1943

Bertricia pulled on her stockings one leg at a time and fastened them to her girdle, careful not to run them. She saw a snag she had fixed with nail polish. She inspected her body carefully, sure that the signs of pregnancy were everywhere, though she had only known for a week that it was true. She would have to get several new dresses, and enough yard goods to make at least three outfits. Maybe Story wouldn't mind her sewing on the Singer.

There was a bottle of In His Arms on the dresser. Bertricia sprinkled some on her temples and sighed. For a minute after she had told her sister, she thought Story was going to hit her. She would certainly never be forgiven. There only remained the task of telling Herman the news. She was sure he would want to marry her right away and avoid any disgrace. He was respectable and decent. She pulled her dress over her head and put one foot in each black pump. He was due any minute now. She'd go downstairs to read the paper and wait for him.

—

Story put the coin in the phone.

"Maybe you could give me some advice. I mean, you know Bertie so well, and, well . . . this is a personal matter, and I just need your help so much. Could we meet? Perhaps after school?" She had called him from the corner near school, sweetness in her voice, a little nervous in spite of herself, but that only helped her to convince him. They made arrangements for four o'clock. He would meet her at the colored side of the bus station. She could walk there from school.

Yes, she was nervous, and that made her furious at herself. She couldn't believe she was doing this, and yet she could. She had always known how to get things done. Just make up your mind and that was that. She hadn't stood all that mess with Papa for nothing. It sure made you strong, pain did. Such a dumbbell to be nervous. It was necessary, that was all there was to it. She went to the colored rest room. What would she have to do to keep him from marrying Bertie? she thought. Men were never quite clean, and she was sure they didn't wash their hands after using the bathroom. A chill ran over her body. She watched the water run out of the cold faucet and down the drain.

She dropped her hankie and wrapped her arms across her breasts, holding her shoulders with her hands. She sat there in the colored waiting room and wondered if there was something wrong with men that they were always late. She guessed it might hurt. So, it would hurt. Bloodletting was a condition of life. Story crossed her legs. A young couple kissed good-bye. She wondered what *they* did at night? Public display was vulgar and common. Then she saw him come into the waiting room, and she was aware her hands were cold. As they drove to his house in his small pickup truck, she kept her head turned carefully to the side, hoping no one she knew would see her.

They drove up to a small-frame, two-bedroom house, close to the ground, with dirt spots where there should have been grass. He had never been too much on yard keeping. Too busy tryin' to make a decent living. There was a small dog tied to a stake, who began to bark, but it was a friendly hello, not a threatening one. Story saw a pot of geraniums on the porch and a ladder-back chair where she imagined Herman sat after work taking a smoke.

"Would you like a little something to drink, Miss Story? A little sherry maybe?" He was ill at ease and looked quickly into the corners of the small living space, suddenly aware of how disheveled and dirty the place was.

She stood looking carefully about her for an empty chair. There was a gold-upholstered one to the left, with shiny armrests, that was free of papers and other debris. He asked her to sit. "Well, Herman," she began, "to tell you the truth, I'm worried about my sister. She seems to have become a little unbalanced over you, a little distracted, you understand." Herman cleared a chair for himself, sweeping some mess onto the floor.

"Could you be a little clearer, Miss Story?" he said, adjusting the tie he had put on for this occasion.

"I mean she seems very nervous and upset these days, almost hysterical, and yesterday she wouldn't eat all day and insisted on sleeping through the dinner hour, which is strange when we've always had dinner together." She rose, paused, and walked up to his chair, fingering his coat sleeve.

"I think maybe you're too much man for her. You know what I mean." There was a long pause. "I think," she said knowingly, "with a good man like you taking an interest in her, courting her and all, she should be happy and full of life all the time."

Herman's eyes widened slightly. For the first time, he noticed that he liked her mouth. "After she sees you, she gets distraught and a little hysterical. . . ." She faded away, looking very intently at him and opening her mouth just a little.

He took her hand very carefully. "Miss Story?"

"Well, I mean, I think you give her kind of . . . women's trouble, you know." She blushed and looked at the floor.

She'd been kissed a few times by Luther when she was almost seventeen, in a few foolish moments, and she'd played with Mr. J. But she suddenly remembered that this was much more than kisses she was going for. She would have to do it all this time. She would have to turn his head, and then she'd drop him. And it would be finished between him and Bertie. She was sure she could fix it. Bertricia had made a pure fool of herself, and there was no other way. She just couldn't let her marry this man. He was too crude, too ordinary, and he would draw them down to the place they had worked so hard to rise from. Bertie would have to live in this filth. He'd never make anything of himself; she was sure. Story thought she might end up having to support them both. Bertie would never be able to make him do any better. She didn't have it in her to push him forward like he ought to be pushed. He was a "common nigger," the kind who was loud and uneducated, and besides, he was too dark; they'd have a house full of black babies. She closed her eyes.

"Miss Story?" Herman had reached up and put his arm around her.

Her eyes invited him to touch; the mouth, the tilt of her head. Any woman would have seen through it. For Herman it was irresistible. She was talking slowly, watching him react to what her eyes were saying. She looked at him intently. "Surely you don't intend to marry *her?*" She rubbed his moist hand with just one finger and sighed.

Herman had never been thought to be a stupid man. He was a hard worker, a man not used to fine things, but certainly not stupid. He liked a good woman. Kind of took the starch out of things. This one was interesting. She wanted something; he wasn't sure what. But as he thought about it, he'd kind of like to be out of the other one's clutches. She was a little too sad sometimes and she grabbed at him. Maybe he could get something he wanted here too. And it might be fun. She was undoing his shirt. He put his hands on her.

She was forced to unbutton her own things; the buttonholes and zippers were smaller than he'd ever seen. There was little or no preliminary touching. He gave her what he thought she wanted, moving in and out of her rather gently. She gritted her teeth with pain and thought how simple it was, and how many fools were out there in the world. Somewhere in the back of her mind Papa's face flashed. Is this all he wanted? she thought. Is this what the talk was all about? The sentimental trash about first love, the thrill of losing your virginity? It was hard to believe how much energy people put into it. She closed her eyes on his face as he grimaced in this strange enjoyment.

She'd drop him, she was sure of that. This had to be kept secret, and she hoped he'd never ask to see her again. But then, of course, she knew he would. He cooed and moaned and said it was wonderful, and she acted just enough pleased so that he wouldn't think she didn't want it. Her mind moved with anger, to school, to marriage, to Bertie, to marriage. She wondered if she'd ever marry. And then she thought of her mother, stuffed with fear, of her years of suffocation, afraid to move or to be still; to speak or to be silent. She would never belong to a man. She would never give up her freedom. She dreaded doing this for the rest of her life; experiencing the pain, of exposing herself like this, like a piece of meat. She had no intentions of being any man's slave. Herman spent himself eagerly and turned over, asleep in a few minutes.

—

Bertricia settled into the mud-brown mohair sofa and switched on the reading light, beginning to read a book called *The Correct Way to Be*. Maybe this would help her to be a good mother and wife. Story was late today. Perhaps the children had been difficult and she'd had to keep them after school. Finally she heard the key in the lock, and her sister stepped quickly across the threshold, out of the gathering evening.

"Hello, dear, how are you?" Story's voice was lilting and fresh, not the usual thing after teaching all day. "Let's get some dinner, shall we?" That was Bertricia's signal to go to the kitchen, but she was expecting Herman, and she hesitated briefly. He was very late. Story tilted her head, slightly annoyed. She went upstairs.

Bertricia didn't wish to argue. She just wanted Herman to come on. She had to tell him. Today. She walked through the hall to the kitchen and put on the potatoes. Their pendulum clock on the mantel struck. It was five-thirty. Herman was an hour and a half late.

The green beans were simmering when Story came through the swinging door singing "It's All Right with Me" to herself. She looked at her sister's shoes and stockings. "Bertie, why *ever* are you so dressed up?" She reached out for the candy dish and then changed her mind. She had to think of her figure after all.

"I have an appointment, Story."

"An appointment? What do you mean, dear? How could you have an appointment? I mean, you don't work! You couldn't possibly have an appointment." She chuckled.

"Well then, a date." Bertricia grimaced and busied herself with the dinner. She hated her sister's questioning.

"A date? Really? Is that what they call it now—you mean someone's coming to call, don't you? Who's coming?"

"You know who's coming, Story. You know I wouldn't see anybody but Herman. Especially not now."

"And what time is your 'date,' Bertie?" Story was leaning on the sink, looking a little too pleased for Bertie's taste.

"Four o'clock," Bertie whispered. You could barely hear her.

"Four o'clock?" Story said out loud. "It's almost six! What kind of man is that? Two hours late. Really." Story laughed a short laugh.

"Well," she said, "I hope you're not disappointed this time. I mean, in your condition I wouldn't count on it!"

"What do you mean 'this time'?" Bertie held the salt shaker poised in midair.

"Really, Bertie, this is tiresome. Let's eat, please."

"You eat, Story; I'm not hungry." Bertie left the salt shaker on the white counter and rapidly climbed the stairs to her room. She would do the dishes in the morning.

———

He never apologized for not coming that night, and he just kept giving excuses for not keeping regular dates. He was too busy. His uncle had needed him. He was out with his men friends playing cards. Bertricia kept herself busy. She had dusted the house every day for a week. She thought maybe she could get a job, but Story had said there was nothing she could do that anybody would pay for, and she was probably right. She thought of scrubbing in some white family's kitchen, and she thought of finishing teacher's college, but now she couldn't, of course, not with a baby coming. The days stretched out in front of her, and she cried most of the time, praying, hoping silently that she would see Herman soon. Maybe he was just going through a phase. Men did those things, she supposed.

She remembered hearing rumors about a woman's husband who ran off with Rita Stevenson, her high school classmate. He stayed for two weeks and came back, and his wife took him back. She didn't understand that then, but now she knew why his wife took him back. She'd take Herman back if he did something like that. She knew she would. It was late February. Gray days stretched out like winding sheets. The clock ticked so that it hurt her ears, and she began to throw up every time she tried to eat. She was watching the rain form puddles in the street. Tired, so tired, when she finally decided she had to call him.

They had had a phone put in a few years back, after Mama's death. She sat down and stretched out her hand to dial his number. It fell limply to her lap when she heard her sister's step on the stairs. "No sense you callin' him," she said. "Men do what they want. He wanted you, and he got you, and now you're in a mess. You should never give men what they want. Mama learned that." Story laughed her little short snort and went outside for the paper.

It was dark, nine o'clock. They were sitting at the dining room table. Bertie was reading, trying to think of something else. Out of the silence Story said, "Well, you can get it fixed, you know." She didn't look up from the dim light. There was a stack of papers filled with sixth grade handwriting on one side of her, and three or four sharpened pencils on the other side. The furnace was rumbling in the background. It was chilly in the house. They both had on heavy sweaters. "There is a way you can make things right," she said, squinching her eyes to be sure she saw whatever she thought she saw on the child's paper.

"Story, what do you mean?" Suddenly she could taste sickness in her throat. Could her sister really be suggesting that she have one of those awful operations? Bertie clenched her fists in a sudden rush of fear. She couldn't do that. She couldn't. It was dangerous. It wasn't legal. What if someone found out? And what if the whole town discovered she was pregnant and unmarried? another voice said in her head. What then? How will you survive *that* disgrace, and who will help you take care of this baby? "God punishes us for things like that," she said aloud.

"God is about doing your duty in life, that's all," Story said in a flat voice. "You don't do your duty, you get punished, pure and simple. You don't play by the rules, you pay for it, that's all.

"Of course, you probably wouldn't have the courage to redeem yourself," her sister said. "You never did have much backbone, Bertricia. You could never even stand up to Mama and Papa." She put a very neat red D on the paper, and picked up the next one on the stack.

Story had never answered her question. Bertricia closed her book slowly. She pushed back her chair and made her way to the bathroom as if moving under water. It was the only way to get to the toilet without making a mess. She clenched and unclenched her hands, and as she vomited, her nails made bright red bruises in the palms of her hands.

———

By the end of two weeks, she was sending him notes by the milkman. She finally called Herman, once when Story was out, begging him to tell her if he was angry, if she had done something wrong. She'd soon be two months gone. People would know. Her eyes were puffy with tears. People would know soon. They had to get married. He'd promised!

Thursday of the third week. She was at the meat market buying liver and onions for dinner. She had been too sick to eat anything all day, so she walked slowly, her head aching, just a dull pain. She went in quietly and was standing, concentrating intently on the meats in the glass case. "I thought he was courting the younger one," a female voice said.

"Well, girl, all I know is I saw him kissing her over in the park near the A & P grocery."

"Herman?"

"Yeah, Herman. You know. Yeah! Herman Greene."

There was a giggle. "He need to get his sisters straight."

"Sho do!"

She looked for a way out. Just leave. Not be seen. Not have to be the butt of another joke. Never another one. Just find a door out. A door out.

The liver was left lying in a white paper on the counter. "Hey girlie," the clerk said. "Hey! Hey! You paid for it!"

She walked as fast as she could, going wherever her legs wanted her to go. She must do something. She'd heard about drinking some salt stuff. There were coat hangers and hot baths.

When Bertie got home, Story had come and gone out again. But there was a note on her dresser in Story's handwriting. It read, "Bertie, call Selena Davis 62–30042. She can fix it." Story had said there were things people could do to make things right. There were ways you could fix it. Bertricia was sure this was that girl who'd been in trouble in the seventh grade. She dialed the number.

By Saturday she was sitting on a bench at a downtown bus stop with Gloria. Gloria was a little overweight, but she had a kind of too-ripe beauty. Her cheeks glowed with rouge and sweat and her lips were very red. She had on bright blue pumps, red-fox stockings, and a black dress. The dress was short enough to allow her thighs to show in the late March wind.

"Honey, I know some folks. But you sho you ready for this? You sho you can't get that man to do right by you?"

Bertricia's hands trembled. She wet her lips and whispered, "There is no way. No other way."

"Honey, you got money?" Gloria lit up, and put the Lucky Strike pack back in her handbag, waving the smoke away from Bertie.

"Enough," was the answer she barely heard.

"Well, now, I could get in trouble, you understand, but you do look serious, and I could use the cash myself." She crossed her legs. The short dress revealed a hint of hot pink underpants. Bertie slipped the bills to Gloria and promised to keep her mouth shut. Gloria put the bills in her bosom and gave Bertie an address and a time. The last she saw of Gloria was a flash of blue shoes climbing up the steps of a crowded bus.

———

There were soldiers in that neighborhood. White soldiers and black soldiers who hooted and howled at her as she went by. "Hey, nigger gal, how bout a li'l taste?" Their hands reached out to grab. "Hey, hot twat!" She swerved to miss them and stepped up the narrow, dirty staircase.

Her left eye was jumping. On the last step her right leg gave way and she had to catch herself to keep from falling. The name on the door read "F. E. Wyeth. Palm Readings."

When they woke her up, she could barely stand. They gave her a drink of something hot and pushed her out the door. Somebody, she never knew who, helped her down the stairs, and she was on her own. She just barely made it home before the blood came. The key, she had to find the key to open the door. It hurt so much she couldn't see anything. Feeling around in her purse, she found the right key as if by braille, and opened the door. The large dark stain was seeping into the carpet when she fell.

It was late afternoon. Story had been out with Herman, and was returning home feeling rather pleasant about the whole idea of sex.

It did have its nicer moments, she had to admit. She let herself into the house, wondering why Bertie had left the door unlocked, and saw her sister sprawled in a puddle of blood. Bertie's eyes were locked open as if in pain. Story sat down abruptly on the umbrella stand seat in the hallway. The gray day slid into darkness as she calmed her nerves and decided what to do.

How could this happen? she whispered to herself. How could she die, how could she die! Her legs trembled slightly. What to do? How to keep the world from knowing what the girl had done? She had always been silly and childish. She told Herman how unstable Bertie was, and now look! What to do? Why didn't she use any self-control, ever? They had given her everything she wanted. An occasional light spanking, and she was forgiven. She had had no discipline in her life, a fool with no discipline. If Bertie had just waited; if she had just waited and let her handle it. If Bertie had just told her she was really going to call that Selena girl. But now look at this mess. And all left on her shoulders, always on her shoulders.

Her stupid legs wouldn't stop trembling. What doctor could be bought off to keep quiet? She racked her brain for a name. She had to move quickly so it wouldn't look unnatural, like she had waited too long. Dr. James. He would probably do it. Neither his practice nor his reputation had ever amounted to much. They were black women. She guessed he wouldn't care; one less black woman and one less black baby.

He came in shaking his head. "So you say you found her there on the floor a few minutes ago? We'll have to call the police, Story, if it turns out to be a suspicious death. You got somebody you can call to help you, gal?" Story looked frightened, nervous, and was on the verge of tears. She fought to keep her control.

"I can call my friend, Aleatha, sir," she said, aware that she needed this white doctor's indulgence.

"Good, you do that. Now, can you help me move her to a bed or somewheres?"

He pronounced Bertie dead while Story called Herman and Aleatha. She told them to come in two and three hours respectively. And then she hid in the bathroom and let the bitter and desperate tears come. Dr. James was in the downstairs bedroom with Bertie where their mother had died years before.

" 'Pears we got a problem here, gal," he said; his southern drawl sounded thicker than ever to Story. "Your sister's either lost a baby in a miscarriage or she had herself fixed. You know she was carryin' a pickaninny?"

"No." Story swallowed her words. "No, sir," she whispered. "No, sir, I sure didn't. But sir, I don't think she'd ever had herself fixed like you said. She was just a little country girl, you know what I mean, she wouldn't know nothing 'bout that. But Dr. James, you think she just couldn't carry no baby or somethin'?"

He cleared his throat and looked around him at the room. He thought, it seemed nice enough for a nigger family. "Well now, I don't know," he said, "without an autopsy, but I should report this as an unnatural death of an unborn child. That's illegal in this state. Or I could forget it, Story."

Story said, "How much do you charge, sir?"

"You know, I've always liked you. I'd best be calling the funeral wagon, now. I reckon as twenty-five'll do."

Story noticed his coat collar was soiled. "If you excuse me, sir," she said, "I'll get my pocketbook." What a piece of slime he was, she thought as she went to get her purse. His usual fee was ten dollars.

He folded the bills. "Okay, Story, have the undertaker call me if he's a mind to." He slammed the door, glad to be out of there.

Story sank into the sofa and called the undertaker. The death certificate read, "Miscarriage."

———

It was so quiet, she thought. So quiet. They took her away quickly. It always seems to be so fast when they take them away, it's like they leave a big hole in the wall. When a body's there, it takes up all the space; there's nowhere to breathe. And then they come with their uniforms and their wagon and they wrap it up and take it out like a vegetable from a grocery story, and it's gone, and you wonder how something so heavy could be so gone in a blink of time's eye.

They had been together a long time, Bertie and Story; since Story was four years old there had been Bertie. She looked down at her hands and saw their lines, crisscrossing, connecting to each other. She and Bertie had been connected like that. In a strange interlocking of life. Not love ever. There had never been love, but there had been a linking together. They had had the same parents, but then, maybe not. Maybe they had not even felt the same strange *creature* their parents were together. But it was the same juggernaut they'd both had to deal with, and living something that was not over even after death.

She had been staring at the rug but not seeing it, but when her eyes shifted, she saw it and the blood seemed to move and shimmer. What was she to do? She realized then that people would be coming over. She wasn't just anybody, she was a schoolteacher. She was Reverend Temple's daughter. Her children's parents would be paying "their respects." They'd all be trooping over, peering in corners, nosing around "to see if they could help out," could "do anything for her," bringing food. She had to be ready. She had to do something about that blood on the rug. And she had to do it fast. After she looked at her hands, she knew there was something she had to do if she was to continue living in that house.

Herman was stunned. He just kept saying, "Didn't know; I didn't know," and shaking his head. "But I didn't know. Why didn't she tell me?" Story threw herself on his chest and sobbed, from fatigue, from desperation.

"Now, honey," he said, "it ain't your fault. It's my fault if it's anybody's. Poor girl was just desperate, I guess. And it was no way you could have known if she didn't tell nobody. I know you didn't know nothing 'bout this." His voice was slow and sad. He rubbed Story's hands and wiped her tears. "What about the police? Will they be after some more information, you reckon?"

Story shook her head. "Don't know," she whispered. "Don't know. I don't want anybody knowin' what she did," she said fiercely under her breath.

The doorbell rang. It was Aleatha to sit up with her. Herman went out the back door quickly. She hadn't felt she had time to ask him to help with the carpet. Story didn't want him seen there. There had been rumors he was seeing her. She knew things were being said.

She had to find a way to keep Aleatha from asking too many questions. She went out on the porch to meet Aleatha. Story saw her peeking through the screen curiously, but she quickly closed the storm door behind her. Aleatha hugged her, genuinely upset. "I'm so so sorry. What in the world happened to the chile?" Story was shaking and wondering how she could make up a story that would convince Aleatha that it was a "normal" death.

"You . . . you don't want to go in there," she said. Her nervousness was real. Whether grief or something else, people would be convinced. "There's blood on the floor." Aleatha grimaced and shook her head. "You know, Aleatha, she always did have terrible trouble with her time of the month. I think the poor child must have had—" Then she just broke down and didn't finish her words. Aleatha would have no problem filling in the blanks. And if she told everybody there were tumors, so much the better. "It was a hemorrhage," was all Story could get out. Aleatha just shook her head and hugged Story.

"Lord, Lord, Lord," she said. "What a cross to bear. So young. So young." Aleatha finally left, promising to spend the night after taking care of her family.

While Aleatha was gone, Story took Bertie's largest sewing shears. She went down into the basement where she and Bertie used to wash. There was a piece of carpet down here somewhere. Mama had always said you could never tell if you'd need to patch a place. Over behind the mason jars and old screens she found it, rolled up in a piece of canvas. Her arms got scratched by the screens, but she dragged it out, determined to put upstairs back together before people started ringing her doorbell. The blood had covered a good five square feet or so. Story began to cut the damp carpet her sister's life had spilled on, cutting through the roses their mother had prized so much. As she cut around the red edges of the stain, her hands also began to get soiled. She stopped and wiped them on her skirt, careless of her outfit and driven to make the place clean again.

She had almost stopped thinking. She was doing it, just doing it, so that things would look as normal as possible, so there wouldn't be the embarrassment of questions, the pitiful looks, the sorrowful sighs and the raised eyebrows. "Just do it," her arms said. "Just get it done."

She just pulled herself into a tight ball and did it. There was nothing for her but the carpet and the scissors and the smell of blood. She cut until she could no longer tell the difference between the bruises that came from cutting and the dark red stains on her hands.

Finally, she pulled the heavy thing out, lifting it on one end, dragging it to the door and out on the front porch. The wind was up just a little. It blew the smell of placenta into her face. She suddenly panicked, realizing that it was too big to fit in a trash can the way it was. The shears were sticky and hard to work. It took another hour and a half to cut the mushy carpet piece in half, stuff it in the garbage can, fit the old remnant into the space, wash herself, and change her clothes. She had barely finished when Aleatha rang the bell, bringing friends. Not one person missed the contrast between the old carpet and the new inserted piece, and not one person mentioned it.

—

Two days went by. She'd made funeral arrangements at her father's old church; Aleatha was enjoying being in charge of the house and phone, and calling friends. The third night when Aleatha went home to look after her family, Story used the time she had been waiting for. She went into Bertie's room and gathered up what things were left. Bertie hadn't had much, and in the two days, Story had given lots of things away to the poor fund at church.

What was left she gathered under her arms, along with the few letters in her sister's drawers, an old rag doll named Cecelia left over from Bertie's childhood, and a few pairs of stockings. She'd come back and get the books later that evening. In the kitchen there was an old Franklin stove Papa had never removed. When the new stove was bought, he'd just never removed it, though he always meant to. It still worked, but usually it had a box of something or other on it, or a sack of potatoes. Story threw everything in her arms onto the floor and began to build a fire in the stove with fireplace wood and paper. As they burned she thought, There was no way. There was just no way for her to keep that baby anyway. Who would have taken care of it? Who would have supported it? Herman didn't care about Bertricia enough to take care of her child.

Herman had lodged himself in her life like dirt in the corners un-

der the stairway. He said he thought she was the most wonderful
woman he'd ever known. She had sucked him in, and he was too
willing to follow her wherever she wanted to go. He was totally cap-
tivated. He told her if she left him he'd never be the same. She
didn't know what her plan was yet, but she knew she had to find a
way. She threw some of Bertie's underwear into the fire. The flames
gave off a strange odor. It was Bertie's cologne she smelled. Story
stood there for hours, burning piece by piece. She wouldn't be tor-
mented the rest of her life with remembering every time she saw
those things; she'd do the room over. She'd paint the walls and
change the furniture and Bertie would be gone. Forever. The smoke
rose over the house and little bits of charred cloth blew out into
space—a bit of lace, a bit of sweater. At last she put in the doll and
put the lid on the stove. An old song came back to her, and an old
memory. "Old rags for sale." Baby Lizabeth. The day Bertie was born,
all mixed in there together in one awful week. Story turned off the
lights and left the kitchen. Long after she slept, Cecelia's rag hands
glowed red beneath the iron lid.

—

As soon as the funeral was over, it started. It was Aleatha who first
mentioned it. She prided herself on being "a good friend," and so
when Vanetta said it, that she'd seen Story behind the schoolyard,
Aleatha called Story the very next day. "I sure hate to add to your burden of sorrow, honey," she said quietly, "but it's somethin' you ought
to know."

"Oh, yes?" Story said. What was it now? she wondered, and Herman's face outlined itself in her mind. Aleatha was talking very
slowly. She didn't want to say it, whatever it was.

"Now, honey, you know I don't believe this," she said, mumbling,
"Folks do need to mind their own business," between her first state-
ment and the next.

"Believe what, Aleatha?" Story said rather too brightly.

"Well, well . . . some busybody done said you took Herman away
from Bertricia and that, well, and that she caused it to happen."

"Caused what to happen, Aleatha?" Control came natural to
Story. She knew how to pull it all in. All the nervousness, all the

panic. She brought it all into a little place behind her neck. Her voice was perfectly normal now.

"That she, well, that she killed *herself somehow*. Folks say you been messin' roun' with Herman. Ain't that awful. Just made me too mad! And I told 'em you ain't done no such thing, that your sister had cancer and you has more principles than to be sleepin' roun' unmarried."

Story's mind was moving fast. How much did Herman really know? Did Bertie ever have a chance to tell him? What would he do if she left him? Something crazy, something mean? Would he expose her? The school superintendent required strict morality from his teachers. They were cautioned to be exemplary models. She'd even heard of people being fired for less than this. For rumor alone. Then there was her father's church, and Lord what would those people think? Aleatha was waiting for a response. "Don't worry, Aleatha," Story said, "they are lying. It'll all be cleared up soon. And thanks so much for calling. It does help to know what's going on."

She hung up quickly and leaned her chin into her fist. It was a matter of making the best of a bad thing. They had her forcing Bertie to kill herself. God, people were such dirt daubers. She had done no such thing! And she had thought the park was safe! Someone must have seen them. It was nearly dark. Who could have seen them meeting there? She was sweating. Still, they had little proof that Herman had promised to marry Bertie, little or no proof at all. She wondered if Bertie had told anyone else that she was pregnant, a girlfriend perhaps? Probably too scared, she thought. Poor Bertie had probably thought she was going to Hell for sure and was too mortified to tell anyone at all.

She would have to lay all this to rest as fast as possible. Before it got any worse. She would just have to take it one step past where she thought she could stop.

The next day, Herman told her he had knocked somebody down at the brickyard who asked him about that "hot schoolteacher lady." And Story knew what she had to do then. Getting Herman to agree was the easiest thing she'd ever done.

Story suggested to several people at school that she had been upset about her sister's mental health. "She had these fantasies," she said, "that Herman Greene was in love with her. But of course Herman and I are very close, you know, why would he even be thinking of her?" She looked wistful and said, "She was so sick, poor little thing. Maybe the cancer had affected her mind." Story also let her teacher friend of a gregarious nature into a "little secret"—that she and Herman had been keeping company discreetly for two years and that there might be "interesting developments" ahead for her. He thought they should make the engagement public after a decent time had gone by for her to grieve over her sister, and it was a consolation to her that he was such a gentleman.

Herman was ecstatic. He had felt sorry for poor Bertie, he really had, but he just never intended to marry her, not from the beginning. She was just a sweet little "piece" to him, but he sure didn't want her for a wife. Story, on the other hand, was his weakness, and he knew it. There was no way to deny it even to himself. He knew he'd always be running after her like a river running downstream. There was no getting her out of his blood, so he might as well get married. He thought she was beautiful. The smoothest sweet skin he had ever seen, almond-shaped eyes that were heavy-lidded, and a low-pitched voice. Not only that, she had a figure a man would kill for. During their waiting period he decided not to tell Story he knew Bertie had been carrying his child, and he never volunteered the information. He didn't know what she might think of him if she knew he wasn't entirely innocent, and she was doing such a good job making up stories, there was no need for him to look bad.

CHAPTER IV

HANDYMAN'S BLUES

JULY 2012

Her head dropped just a little and she seemed to snore. Her skin, which had always been perfect ebony, was now blotched and uneven in color, and the skin folds hung around her beautifully placed eyes, covering her lashes when they were closed.

The only sound on the porch was the fifty-year-old rocking chair. Her mind almost always traveled backward now. She remembered all right. Clear as day; her mind was twice as good as Hermine's, who called herself taking care of somebody. It would have been much better if she had ever become a lawyer, like I told her to do, she thought. Story had never understood it. The girl had a good mind too, in spite of who her daddy was. She was always a reader. She was always smart. Just didn't have any gumption. Just didn't care about making something of herself. Lost in those silly fairy tales—like *Heidi*, all that stuff that didn't mean a thing.

Story had thrown one of those books away. That *Heidi*, she thought it was. Hermine got to asking questions that weren't safe. About grandfathers and fathers. Digging into the past, which needed to stay where it was. Still, she had to ask, Story thought; had to force me to lie. She just wouldn't leave it alone. Questions about a father who would have only dragged a daughter down to his level. So she threw the book in the trash, while Hermine was asleep. She never asked again about her daddy. And she never did anything with all that education.

Story swatted a fly without opening her eyes. Hermine told her all the time that they were living in a new century, like she thought Story should keep up with the times. She didn't know about all that, but she did know that what was ahead for her ought to be better than life was now. "Humph," she said aloud. In 1962, when she had moved into this house, things had been different. It was brand new then, the envy of all the niggers, or "African-Americans" you had to say now, and some of the white folks. White folks sure didn't want you to get ahead in those days, and they made it damn hard to get anything worth having. You had to ransom your soul to get a mortgage loan. All the same, teachers' salaries bought a lot then in a place like Hattenfield. Also, folks with class were easy to spot, and it was clear who people were.

Hermine was on the plastic lounger. She appeared to be taking a nap, but Story never knew for sure. She might have been doing that "meditation" she talked about. Bunch of foolishness. She should be up fixin' that sofa. It looked like they had come from nothin', patches everywhere.

"I must say," Story said in a low voice, "you could be doing that sofa over that needs recovering. Just because I'm old don't mean I should live in filth." Occasionally she made grammatical errors, but not often. Story's eyes closed slowly. She was silent again. Hermine didn't answer. Sometimes she really missed the old days when she was a young working woman. There was always something going on, someone interesting to talk to. Hermine was just too . . . she didn't know what. Dull maybe.

Story cleared her throat, but she didn't open her eyes. She moved one hand slightly. Thinking. Thinking about the past. She had spent six long weeks on that job. Cleaning up someone else's house and body was disgusting work. The thought of doing that kind of work all her life had pushed her into school.

1933

The husband's slop jar had made her sick at the stomach every one of those forty-two days. With Mama and Papa gone, she had to work, to support herself and Bertie, to try to go to school. He had been wounded at some French place during the war. She didn't remember the name of the battle, but she remembered the scar and the smell, and that woman's arrogance, and she remembered Mr. J. She bet he never forgot her either.

The day she was hired, the wife had said, "Now Story, Story—I just love that name, it's so-o-o quaint—now Story, I want you to be one of the family. You just take Mr. J.'s bedpan to him three times a day and make sure he gets to sleep on time, ya heah?"

Story smiled, thinking how she had left him on the right day, when Mrs. J. had gone to visit her mama for the weekend in Charleston. One day she found some pictures of his mother and a piece of an old letter in the drawer. It was a love letter, torn in the wrong place, so she couldn't see who it was addressed to, but she thought it was probably to Mrs. J.; that made sense, though she didn't know how he could have felt that way for her. The bitch was too pale. What her mother would have called "po' lookin'." Thin as a rail.

She enjoyed the letters. There were more of them in a packet tied with blue lace ribbon, and a picture of Mr. J. in his doughboy outfit. "My Darling, I long to run my hands through your hair, and over your beautiful breasts," he wrote. And there were other things that Story thought were dirty and common.

She was deep into the letters one day when she heard him calling her. "Story," he called from downstairs. His voice came through the ceiling to where she was reading his love letters. She closed the drawer rapidly and went down with a dust cloth in her hand. "Listen, gal," he said, "you want to bring me that book on the table? I guess I'll read me some of this day away."

She looked at him carefully. He was still a young man. "Well now, Mr. J., you want anything else?" She plumped up the pillows behind his head, and let her hand stroke his neck lightly, as if by accident. "You know, I understand, Mr. J. My people have always been, well, close to the earth. And you just tell me if you'd like someone to talk to." He looked at her as if he'd never seen her before. She was seventeen and just blooming. Story smiled. "Ain't nobody ever said the races ain't supposed to touch. They just not supposed to marry, ain't that so, Mr. J.?"

He was turning pink, but very slowly becoming curious, being taken in. He had never had a nigger woman before . . . before the war. They were supposed to be really something, like animals. Still, she must have known there was nothing he could do now.

Some days she rubbed his back. Other days they had tea, and sat on the porch while he told her war stories. He finally got around to telling her about the day he was paralyzed. He had never told anybody the details. He couldn't stand it. The curiosity of people, their fascination with pain and violence. The fear that froze in his blood when he discovered he couldn't escape, and the smell of his own blood on his pants. The day he told her, that was the day she held him close and let him cry, something he had never let his wife do. That was the day she stroked him and felt his poor shriveled-up thing, and she undressed for him so he could touch her breasts the way he had wanted to touch his wife's breasts like he said in the letter.

Then he gave her his old army tags because she was so interested in the war, and she said she'd keep them to remember him. One day he gave her five dollars and told her to buy herself a new dress, and after that she seemed to change some. He had never understood it. She came in and fixed his lunch, and then she said she had to study for normal school, and she left him sitting all day, quietly puzzled. She'd met a nice young man, she said. Mr. J. told Story he bet her boyfriend was a "big fine buck, because he'd have to be a real man to satisfy her." And he could see her mouth pucker a little bit. She said, "I don't know, sir, I don't know what you mean." And he had slapped her behind and laughed out loud, talking about how she'd soon find out if she didn't know already. Big bucks with big peckers to make their gals happy. She'd know all right.

The next day she came to him as sweet as she ever was, gave him a bath, wore that gardenia perfume that he liked. She'd probably bought it with the money he gave her. While he was lying there helpless, she leaned over and gently lifted one breast for him to suck. "Mr. J., you like your wife?" she said, putting on her uniform slowly.

"Well, Story, you know how it goes, gal. You do what you can to survive. Mrs. J., she's got family, you know, and she makes all this possible, the house and all the rest of it."

Story nodded. She went to the kitchen to fix his lunch. When the tray was ready, she heard him calling for his bedpan. She poured the milk, left the green peas and salad on the tray, and wrote a note to Mrs. J. "Dear Mrs. J.," it said, "you can clean up your husband's shit from now on. Also you might want to know, it's not completely dead. He does feel something. Maybe you ought to find you another nigger gal to take lessons from. P.S. Ask him how I know." It was signed, "One of the Family." As she quietly shut the front door, she heard Mr. J. calling for his bedpan and getting desperate.

———

It was almost dark. It never got really cool till it was dark. They were still on the porch. Well I certainly haven't lived a dull life, Story thought. Poor Bertie wanted to add a little spice in her life, then she bungled it. Didn't know what she was doing. Picked that man with no class. That was why Herman had been so fascinated by her and why things had turned out the way they did. People with no class had no business mixing with people with class.

There was never any question for Story that she would leave Herman, it was just a matter of when. He was more than a little crude. Still, he had served his purpose. We all end up being used in one way or another, she thought. He had served his purpose, but she sure got more than she bargained for.

1944

The wedding was quick and small. Story wanted to keep her house. She believed in a woman having property of her own; you never knew what life had in store for you. So they rented it out and moved a couple of hundred miles north, where Herman's mother lived, and where he could find better work.

During that first year, she put him off as many times as she could. There was no use trying the excuse of illness. Story was never sick, and playing sick would have meant she'd have to stay home from school, something she would not do unless forced. With a new school, a new job, she was determined to be there every day. After four or five nights without sex, Herman would begin to try everything he knew to ply her. He just made things worse, sticking his tongue in her ear, pawing at her body's private parts. She could tell when she was going to have to do it so that he'd leave her alone for a while; so she could have some peace.

Their room was painted a deep pink. There were three windows that fronted the house, and so Story kept them heavily draped for privacy. During the day she used electric lights and kept the deep rose curtains shut. The bedroom furniture was an ordinary oaken color, vaguely Early American, and their spread was flowered roses with a dust ruffle around the bottom. Under the ruffled lamp on the dresser, Herman had hung up a picture of his mother in a round frame, and so she looked down upon their marriage all day and all night. The room smelled faintly of mothballs that were kept in a small closet. There was a short walk to the bathroom, which was also pink, down a dim hall with one incandescent bulb overhead.

The bulb flickered slightly. It was lightning and raining heavily. Story sat at her dresser thinking of tomorrow's faculty meeting. Over the storm she didn't hear Herman come into the room. "Nice night to be a little close," he said.

She sighed and said nothing. There was no way out of it tonight. She'd have to play along until she could find a way to end this marriage. His mouth made a kind of apologetic half smile. "Just a minute," she said, "I'll just finish my hair."

There were no lights on. They made two black figures in the close

room. Herman fumbled for her breasts. Her nipples got hard, a bio-
logical reaction to the friction. He rubbed them slowly, sensitively.
Every brush of his fingers gave her a shudder, which he took for passion. He began to suck. Gently, gently. She felt it in her tongue and
held onto the sheets and blanket, counting until he tired of the ancient symbolic act. Now, she thought, now he'll touch me and I will
have to open my legs and I will have to bear the pain of knowing he
has me; knowing he has the most private thing I have. She smelled
the mothballs. She could hear the last trickle of rain in the trees.
Concentrate on the mothballs, she thought, on the rain, on anything
but his ugly hands opening me. He worked and worked at it. There
was no softening her. There was no flowering and no yielding. Finally he gave up and took her, desperate for relief. Story could bear
the pain of being dry. It was knowing that after the pain she would
have another week of being alone that got her through it.

Herman finished and almost fell on her with a deep groan. He was
sweaty. It was too warm in the little room. She smelled the semen
and the male sweat and longed to open the windows. She pushed at
his body heavily, and he rolled over off of her. They didn't speak. In
a very few minutes he was asleep. The rain rushed down the side of
the house where the gutter was broken. The gutter she had asked
him to fix at least six times. There was bile in her throat. She had almost thrown up. She eased out of bed, went to the pink bathroom to
take a bath, and made a bed on the couch. In their separate passions,
she had forgotten that Herman had not used any protection.

—

It was hard not to drink too much. A man has to do something to
keep himself together. That's why he kept going to church. It
seemed to help him face Monday anyway. Something to do. Story
went to her own church. He wouldn't change, and she wouldn't
change, so he dropped her off and kept on over to the other side of
town unless she got a ride from some of the ladies at Deliverance
Baptist. After church he'd go by to see Mama. He thought of her
arthritic hands lifting those heavy black pots she always cooked in.

She had been happy for him to marry, but she never understood
"that Story," and she never really got over Story's snubbing her.

"Well," she would say, "I reckon she done forgot how she got to be a schoolteacher." And she'd go on doing the best she could with her housecleaning and singing "Blessed Assurance Jesus Is Mine."

Then later, Story and Herman would have another fight about Story never going out there to see Mama and never having Mama over for a meal. "We still live on the nigger side of life," Story said. "Doesn't mean I got to parade down there in Shantytown for all to see. We all got to better ourselves, Herman, you included."

She had not been to "Shantytown" to see his mama since their first meeting, and Reesie Greene had never been to her son's house either. The introductions had taken place a full week after the wedding, his mama declining to come to a church where she didn't feel welcome and to a wedding that was "too hasty to be sanctified."

Herman kept putting it off and acted for all the world like he was scared of introducing them. Story insisted, saying it wasn't respectable not to have met her mother-in-law before the wedding. So a week after the wedding, Herman reluctantly drove her to his mother's neighborhood in his truck. She would have to do something about that truck, she thought. She didn't think she could stand being driven around in it much longer. As soon as they could, she'd see that they got another car.

Reesie Greene lived on Center Street across from Sister Ever-Virgin. Of course, Story didn't know where Sister Ever-Virgin lived, but she had heard rumors. Rumors that gave her enough information to know that the woman so-called had a highly questionable reputation. The story was that she ran a gambling house or something like it, and that men and cheap women went there to drink. The truth was that Sister Ever-Virgin sold drinks for a quarter a shot and that she tolerated only mild drunks. Any rowdies were thrown out by her two "nephews," who were large enough to keep most folks behaving. The truth also was that Sister was a churchgoing woman who, far as anybody knew, had never had a man in her life, and whose daddy left her with one jug of white lightning during Prohibition and no mama. She had a handmade house strung with permanent Christmas tree lights, and she was Reesie Greene's best friend, only even Herman didn't know that.

When they passed Sister's house, Herman looked the other way, hoping Story wouldn't ask any questions he didn't want to answer. They pulled up in his mama's front yard, which was part grass and part driveway, but very neat on the grass side. There were day lilies blooming in the ground, and pots of every conceivable kind of flower everywhere else. Flowers were planted in anything that would hold dirt, including pots and pans. Seven or eight birdhouses made of cigar boxes were attached to posts stuck in the ground. Story had never seen as many containers for anything and everything as she saw on that little porch.

Reesie was sitting there in her rocking chair, moving gently, silently, back and forth. "Mama, this is my lady, Story," Herman said. Herman had Story by the hand. They climbed the steps slowly. "Mama?" he said, so quietly he could barely be heard.

"Don't tell a body hey, don't say 'How you, dog, cat, kiss my ass even.' Can't you speak?" Reesie looked straight past him out into the yard.

Herman drew in his breath and started again. He kissed his mother on the cheek. "Hey Mama, how you?"

"That's better. Now we can talk." She pointed to a chair, and still looking at Herman, she said, "Sit down, daughter. Now Herman, what you got to say for yourself?"

"Mama, this is my wife, Story, and . . . well, we was married last Thursday."

She nodded and rocked and then she looked at Story. This was the way too many of their people were, Story thought, backward, country. And this old woman was looking her over like she was on display or something.

"Well, daughter," she said, "look like you done landed you a man. But don't you forget, 'There's many a slip between the cup and the lip.' "

Oh, God, she is from the dark ages, Story thought.

Herman grinned shyly and cocked his head at Story. "Story teach school, Mama," he said.

Teaches, Story thought. She sighed, again biting her lip.

"Mama, you needin' anything?" Herman said, rather urgently, as if he was already about to leave.

"Well, now as you ask, 'pears you could take time outta your busy schedule to check out my back steps," she said. "I heard something creak other day when I went down the steps. Don't want to fall and break these old bones." She got up slowly and straightened out her skirts. As Reesie went into the little house, Herman looked back at Story, still sitting in her original position. He started to tell her to come along, then hesitated, and then he followed his mama without saying anything.

It took a whole hour to fix the steps. She heard them all that time talking and laughing, but she never moved and she was never invited to the back steps. At one point she hard Reesie say, "Fetch me that bottle, son," and she knew they were drinking together. Story just sat there staring at the birdhouses and pots and pans and sighing every ten minutes. She thought about going in the house, but there was nothing in there she wanted to see, she thought. Only more of the same junk that was out here.

When the truck pulled away from the yard, Story had already decided she'd never set foot in that house, and though she didn't think it through then, it would never occur to her that Reesie would ever set foot in her house. The idea just never came to her mind.

In a few months, he told his mama, he wanted to build up his business slowly. Maybe he could get on with Bob Barlow; they sometimes hired colored who were skilled bricklayers. He had these plans. Plans to build a brick house for her one day. Story, she'd change her mind about babies soon, though sometimes (and he didn't say this to Mama) he thought she wasn't natural. He thought women were supposed to have kids. Maybe it was that thing with Bertie dyin' like she did. Maybe it scared her. It was Story who scared him sometimes. She could be so sweet, and then she'd turn, she'd turn into someone or something he'd never known before, a stranger looking through her brown eyes, speaking words that sounded ordinary but somehow weren't.

"She a strange woman," Mama said. "You don't want no chirrun by her. They be cursed, or something just as bad. Women like that can turn a man's head all the way roun' twice and open his nose clean up. That Story done put a spell on you," she said, "and only death can break it."

He laughed at Mama. "Let that old stuff go, Mama. Folks don't believe in that nonsense these days. It's the twentieth century, Mama, time for colored folks to give up all that old stuff. Story's just different. She educated and all."

"Humph." She pulled on her undergarments under her dress and smoothed herself down in the back. "Best to listen; don't, you'll give up your soul to devilment and go straight to Hell."

Herman enjoyed these visits. Maybe Mama was old-fashioned and she didn't smell sweet most times. Maybe she was mostly too tired these days to keep herself clean, with no runnin' water and nobody to haul it for her. But Mama cleared out a space inside him like sweepin' in him with a broom, a wide light circle, like she had opened a window in there. And he couldn't get that anywhere else he knew about. She still took in laundry when she could. He always stopped off at her latest customer before goin' out there so he could save her the long trip and carrying that heavy basket. And he always took her a pint, because she said it kept her warm between visits.

Herman let the old chair rock him slowly. His mama just kept on scrubbin' her pots. Herman was quiet, thinking. He thought about the comfortable house they were living in; it wasn't nothing fancy, but it was warm in the winter and cool in the summer and there was a bathroom. And he thought about his mother's rounded shoulders, and finally he said, "Mama, you should just come on and move in with us."

His mama stopped scrubbing and looked him full in the face. "I'll lie down and go home to God first," she said. He knew there was no more discussing it. When he left her, she said she'd pray for him 'cause he'd need it with that woman he'd married. He left her rubbing her knuckles and muttering about "people who couldn't give you a decent hello if they life depended on it."

———

There was a plan in her mind. A plan she'd been thinking up since she first went to normal school. There was a way out of this black-bottom, end-of-the-line life she was living, and she was going to find it or die trying. She didn't care how much it took, she was going to be the best teacher in the black public schools. She'd made herself known and respected and desired, and then she'd be able to get some money to go for a degree. Other black women had done it. She might even be Dr. Greene some day. There was one thing she knew. She wasn't going to be stuck here all her life, here with this life of barbecues and beer and court jester monkeys with the whites of their eyes showing just like they did in the movies. Here with these plantation mammies like Sister Ever-Virgin and her *mother-in-law*. She'd die first.

Story wrote off for catalogues to Howard University and Atlanta University and Fisk. She went to the colored library frustrated that she couldn't take the information from the Canfield County Library because she wasn't white, and she tried to find out what scholarship help was available to blacks. She called her old normal school teachers at Hattenfield Institute. She wanted to become a school principal, and she was determined to do it. Then her period didn't come, and she was caught, like a rabbit in a snare.

She just didn't want to believe it. Not now. Not ever. Children were not a part of her plan. Why was he so stubborn about using some protection? He couldn't have forgotten. She was sure he had done it to her on purpose, to ruin her life, to keep her tied down at home. Like her father. He was just like her father. A bully, using her for his own needs. He only sounded nicer. She didn't know whether he had had the damn thing on or not. She always tried not to look at his body, and the lights were out anyway. Besides, she was trying not to feel anything she didn't have to feel. Bertie was probably somewhere laughing at her, but she wasn't going to be stupid like Bertie, running to some sleazy butcher who'd kill her. She wasn't about to do anything like that. The child's father would just have to raise it. It was his fault, and he would just have to raise it. She was going to go on teaching, and she was going to become the first black woman principal in North Carolina, child or no child.

———

They had been invited out to a party. They were both tense because they almost never went anywhere together. Story was always embarrassed, and Herman was always confused at her reaction. Why she never liked for him to have a good time was beyond him. Everytime he felt good, she was sour. Everytime he and his friends started "telling lies," she left him alone with some remark about common niggers. The last party they had been to was a barbecue down at the Burrises'. They had a yard full of friends, a tub of beer, and all the trimmings. Herman, who made great barbecue, was standing over the fire in his apron with a dauber in his hand. It was something he liked to do, preside over the fire and play the dozens with those guys who weren't cooking, with a beer in one hand and a fork and a saucer dauber in the other. It was his playtime, and all his buddies and their wives always got him to take charge of the ribs. Leon cracked a joke about his secret ingredient. "Ain't nothin' but ketchup and a little Dr. Brown's tonic mixed in," he said, "and it's more Dr. Brown's than ketchup 'cause everybody knows you can get drunk on Dr. Brown's!"

Herman had laughed so that the whole backyard could hear it, and he tilted his head back all the way for the last swallow of Pabst Blue Ribbon when he caught Story's eye. She was not amused. She was thinking how crude he was and she turned her back to him. He said, "Shit! The ribs are burnin'!" and threw his beer bottle to one side, ignoring her scorn. It was always that way. He'd have a great time and she'd be pissed off, as if he had no right. What did she want from him anyway? He wasn't no holy-rollin' stuff-shirted minister like her daddy, and he wasn't no schoolteacher tied up in knots. Everytime they went out, she found some way to spit on his good time. He had started going to the "260's Colored Club" to have a drink or two on Saturday afternoons and then on Sunday afternoons. Most of the time she didn't know where he was, and she didn't care. They were going out to the Fosters' for a card party and supper. He wasn't sure why she was so eager to go to this affair. Seemed to be all geared up to go and determined to have him there. He really couldn't say why he had given in, but now that he had, he wouldn't go back on his word.

Time to go home and get into his suit. He put in the last brick, smoothed over the edges with his trowel, and collected his tools. It was just early enough for him to stop at the 260's for a drink first. He jumped into the driver's seat of his old truck. It sure could use some attention, he thought, but there was never enough extra money for anything.

It was six-thirty. He had had four beers. One more than he could have without being on the edge. He got home at seven. She was pacing silently. He changed his shirt, got out his tie, and tied it with the knot that she didn't like. Story had arranged her hair with slick waves on the side and a pompadour up front. She had on a little rouge, and there were two tortoiseshell combs placed just so in the careful arrangement of her straightened hair. She had on silk stockings, black peau de soie pumps, and a mauve silk dress. She did look nice. There were three worry lines in her forehead and one pearl in each ear.

"Did you clean out the truck, Herman?" she said, straightening her seams. "You know how I hate to ride in that thing, and it just adds insult to injury if it's dirty."

"I'll get it, Story, I'll get it," Herman said, not moving. He put his cigarette out slowly, taking his time.

"Well? I'm ready to go, Herman." He looked at her, locked the front door, and they walked over to the truck. He swept off the front seat with his hands and moved a few tools on the floor so she could get in. Story took a rag from the floor behind the seat and wiped the leather she would be sitting on before she climbed into the truck.

As he slammed the truck door, she gritted her teeth one more time. How many more days and nights would she have to ride in this truck? Peau de soie and silk in a truck! She could smell beer on Herman's breath and the faint odor of underarm sweat. He had not bathed. She waited for him to say, "Well, let's go," and he did. "Well, let's go." He always said the same thing everytime he got in a vehicle. God, he was so predictable, she thought. She knew they would be the only ones driving up in a truck. She knew Herman's tie looked stupid, she knew he smelled of beer, and she knew he'd be too loud and say something crude tonight. Not only that, but she just knew they'd be the last to arrive. She was right. They were the last arrivals. The cards had started. "I told you I don't play no cards, Story." Herman looked patient but tired, and he knew he had had too much beer. He could feel a buzz, and the evening had just started.

"All sophisticated people play cards; just watch me," she said, and knocked on the door. "You can do it."

There were four tables of card players and a Louis Armstrong blues piece being played on the record player. Only one or two women were playing cards—mostly men. The women were watching, and on the edge of the room, fussing with food. Herman found a soft chair and sank into it with a sigh, listening to Story's voice go higher and higher with the excitement she found in being social. That was always the way it was. She'd be silent and cold at home, and then as soon as she began to talk to someone else, she sounded like a real peach of a woman. He sat there most of the night. He sat there all through supper, filling his plate with fried fish and corn bread and returning to his seat to eat it. He sat there while the tables were cleared and when the dancing began, and he sat there through her obvious attentions to James Framington, the colored doctor who was visiting the Fosters; while she did the hoochy-koochy with him and strolled around introducing him to people who might not know he was from Chicago and just here visiting relatives for a week; while Bessie Smith sang the "Handy Man Blues." Herman sat there and chewed on his bottom lip and decided he'd go see his mama and tell her she was right about the devil. He even sat there when Elijah Williams asked him, "What the hell is eatin' you? Where is mah old life-of-the-party buddy?" He was still sitting there when Story announced out loud that men who worked at physical labor all day had no energy left for parties, and when the woman in the blue print dress began to twitter and encourage Story, suggesting that "a party there wasn't the real test, but the real test would be the party after the party, the party at home. The party after the party," the woman slurred through her drink, "was a workingman any good at that? That was the real question, wasn't it, Herman? That was the real question!" She nudged Story and laughed loudly, almost spilling her drink on Story's silk dress. Other people laughed, and some looked at Herman sitting in his chair. There was a loud grating scratch, and a "damn." Somebody had just ruined the "Handy Man Blues" by carelessly pulling back the needle as they turned the record over.

Story was leaning on James Framington's arm, her eyes wide, and looking right at Herman. She smiled sweetly and said something under her breath that sounded like, "Even a man with no class can get a baby." They heard her say it, and he heard her say it. A baby. His baby. She stared at him with no expression on her face, as if she were staring at a bus driver or a postman. Waldo clapped him on the back. "You old son of a gun! Damn, man, we coulda been drinking to your son all night!" Everybody roared. People began to dance again. That was it. She had told a whole room full of people before she told him. He sat there wondering why, staring through the smoke, and wondering why he sat there.

Things were never the same for Herman after that. There wasn't any point in askin' why, there wasn't any point even in hitting her. And besides, he didn't believe in that. If he could just understand it. He hadn't planned it this way. Life. He couldn't figure out what was wrong with this wife of his. Not wanting this, not wanting that. Being as cold as fish in bed, or not sleeping in the bed at all. Poor Bertie had never been cold, at least. And everytime he mentioned her name, Story said that name was never to be mentioned again, and he should let the dead stay dead, like she didn't know it was his baby that had died with Bertie. His baby that he had just as much as flushed down the toilet, because of lustin' after *her*. She'd look at him like she was made of stone and say, "I don't know why you insist on talking about that woman. She's dead and buried and probably burning in Hell." Made his blood run cold to hear her say that. Sweet little Bertie never did mean nobody no harm, and as far as he could see, she wasn't the one who ought to be burnin' in Hell, it was him. And probably Story.

He thought about leaving; he thought about telling her to get out of his house. But now there was the baby. And he thought maybe things would get better with a kid. Maybe. And so the days went by slowly, and just as slowly, little by little, he got so he could forget the look on her face, hangin' onto that doctor's arm and saying, "Even a man with no class can get a baby." And Story began to swell, and he felt his old tenderness come back, just around the edges of his hurt.

The months dragged by for Story. She went to work faithfully, and as elegantly as possible in her maternity clothes. She had hired the best black dressmaker in town to make her wardrobe. She wore linen and other fine fabrics. Herman fussed about the cost, but he could have saved his breath. She reminded him that none of this would have been necessary if he had just taken responsibility for his actions. She wasn't going to look dowdy because of some stupid mistake of his, and he'd just have to pay for the clothes.

———

I used to stick a pin in my finger and let the blood drip down into the dust to pay for spying and all the ugly thoughts I had about church and Papa, she thought. I thought I was paying, I thought that was blood. But that wasn't enough, three or four drops of blood from my finger. And another pain washed in over her mind around her waist and down into her belly, and waves of memories were obscured and ran together like watery colors. Memories of Bertie and blood and Papa yelling about Hell. And the blows from his belt and the day he fell down dead. Mr. J. calling her name, and Herman's face over her, his weight on her body, and then Bertie and her blood again. I used to let my blood drip down. . . . I'll do anything, she prayed, anything to make it up. . . . I'll do anything, if You, You just make it stop.

Nurses came and went. Stupid nurses who didn't know enough to come out of the rain, who looked at her and poked their fingers in her and left. She had no sense of how much time had gone by. Someone came into the room and rolled her away somewhere. Mama and all those babies, she thought. And after all this, some of them had died on her. After all this, and Papa yellin' about Hell. What did men know about Hell? Not much. I thought I was paying for my sins, and Papa yellin' about Hell, and for what? So I could suffer like this? And what did God know about it anyway? What kind of God would put women through this mess just to bring unwanted children into the world? Mama and all those children. Three dead and two living, now only one. Her lips tasted like blood. The bed-clothes were wet. There was no air-conditioning, just fans going over her head, whining and whining; it made her sick to look up at them. Then came another pain and the thought, If only God could be bargained with; if only Herman had worn some protection!

When she checked in, there was a dirty broom and a dustpan leaning against the wall, and then the long form to fill out and the sickly brown and green walls, sick colors for sick people. "Relax," the doctor had said; she bit her lips again even though it hurt. She didn't notice the pain then, but noticed the sound of the fan that didn't bring any breeze. She was aware of the other women in the ward with complete clarity for a minute, and realized most of them were moaning and crying. She was hoping she hadn't cried out loud, then another pain came around the back and into the pelvis with a force that took her breath. Then she remembered only a dimness and a bright, bright light, and someone saying, "Push, bear down harder," and her last thought was that she used to think God was the button man, and that He might as well be for all the good He was to her. Then she heard it crying.

———

She was floating back through the twilight when somebody started punching her in the stomach. She struck her without thinking, without a word to herself, a motion that came from a need, a choice never to be struck again without striking back. The nurse cried out, startled, on guard. She moved back quickly. "Mrs. Greene, I'm just the nurse. Just the nurse." She was backing off, fearing more blows. Story lay tense, like a wild thing ready to strike. She blinked at the nurse. "We've got to get it all out," she said. "We've got to get the afterbirth out or you'll be sick."

I'll be sick! Story thought. She began to laugh. "I'll be sick!" she shouted. "I *am* sick, and the afterbirth is wrapped up in that sweet little pink blanket out there in the viewing room. That's the afterbirth, twenty-one years worth of after. All that time ahead of me, all those years of being burdened with someone else's mistake!"

Story said nothing more to the nurse, who finished her work timidly, as if afraid to touch the woman. She had never had such an experience with a patient. She didn't know how to talk to this woman. All her nursing training had not prepared her to treat a patient who acted like she didn't want her baby. In school they had never mentioned the possibility that there were women who wouldn't automatically love their children. This was unnatural to her, and strange. She didn't like it at all, and she didn't like this woman Story Greene, but she'd try to do her job. She bathed Story's body quickly with the pan of water she had brought. It sloshed upon the bed sheets once or twice. The young nurse couldn't finish fast enough.

Finally, she said quietly, "Are you ready to see your baby?" Story didn't answer. The woman stopped her work and left, looking confused and rubbing her face. Her plastic name tag said MYRA SIMMONS. She walked quickly, blinking back her tears. Someone else brought the child to Story with a bottle and left them alone for a feeding. Story looked at her daughter's face through a pool of her own tears. She didn't bother to wipe them away. What did it matter anymore? The world was a muddle, and her path was full of stumbling blocks. She didn't know now how she'd get the money to pay for another degree, much less the time and freedom to study. How could she go off to school now? Days and days of being trapped with a baby in this nowhere town with these backward country black people stretched out before her. She reached for a tissue to wipe her nose. Years of being stuck with Herman and diapers and dishes and washing greens. "A mess of greens," country people always said. A "mess" of turnip greens or mustard greens, canning peaches, picking beans, common work. She hated it. Mama would have known what to do. She would have taken the baby, Story was sure. Story had always hated housework. It was her life that was the mess now, and she couldn't see how it would ever get straightened out. The baby was beginning to fuss. Story stuck the rubber nipple in the small mouth and stared straight ahead. The baby stopped crying, but the mother's tears were still falling. She felt entirely alone. It was the only time she ever missed her sister.

—

They named her Hermine. When he was sober, he loved her more than he had ever loved anyone.

The night before her first birthday they had their worst argument. Herman was late, as usual, he had alcohol on his breath as usual. Story had been waiting for an hour so that he could stay with the baby while she shopped for the birthday party. By the time he got home, supper was cold, the baby had to be changed twice, and Story was furious.

"You wanted to have this party," she said lightly, "and invite all your friends and their children. You wanted it, but I'm the one who has to do the cleaning, the cooking, and the shopping." Herman sat slumped on a chair, waiting for it to be over. He had Hermine propped on his knee, half listening to his wife. He looked at Hermine, chucked her under the chin and held her up to throw her in the air.

"I told you not to do that, Herman! She just gets sick and throws up and it makes more mess to clean. Plus it stinks." Herman continued to play with the baby, and Story was talking even louder now. "All I asked you to do was to come home and watch her for one hour! Now the stores are about to close and I'll have to get half the things tomorrow and there'll be everything to do in one day! The least you could do is listen to me!" Hermine threw up on the carpet, and Herman carried her into the bedroom and put her in the crib. The baby's milk vomit began to smell. He walked back into the living room and looked at Story. His voice was low and tense. This was all he was going to take tonight.

"Listen to you? Listen? Bitch, I have listened to you for the last fuckin' time. If you don't want to do this party, then don't do it, okay? I'll do the fuckin' party, I'll do it myself and you can go to hell for all I care." They were standing on either side of the little pool of milk. "You never wanted to do anything a normal woman would want to do. You don't even love your own baby daughter. You aren't a *real* woman!"

She stood there with her fists clenched, still in her navy-blue coat which she had put on to go out to the store. "Oh, so you think I'm not a real woman, then," she said. Her mouth tightened and her nostrils flared with each word. "Only a real woman would have put herself on the line to keep a stupid, silly girl from disgracing herself in front of the whole town. Only a real woman would have hidden the disgraceful ugly thing she did so well that not even her boyfriend knew the real truth. I only married you to keep the world from knowing what a fool my sister was. And you're right, I never wanted a baby, I never even wanted a *husband*. I only married you because it was the only way to save my family's name and my own reputation. You clown! You stupid Sambo clown!" Tears of rage began to run down her face. Somewhere in the background the baby was yelling. Neither one of them heard her.

He started to hit her and almost stepped in the pool of milk that was slowly sinking into the rug. His foot slipped a little and it threw him off guard.

"Goddammit, don't you call Bertie a fool. Call me what you want, but don't you call Bertie a fool," he snarled. "She ain't done nothin' you didn't put her up to. You forced it on her. I know you now, goddamn you, you forced it on her sure as I'm born. I ain't never gon' forgive myself for that. I hate I left her. I hate it. They said you made her kill herself, and they were right. I should have listened to the gossip. I was the fool. I knew she didn't have no cancer. You made her get rid of my baby, didn't you?" Herman grabbed Story by the arms and shook her. When she lost her balance, he almost threw her on the floor. "You ain't worth hittin'," he said. He grabbed his coat and stomped out of the house.

Slowly, Story began to come out of her fury. She wiped her face with a napkin and took her blue coat off. When she heard the truck start up, she realized the baby was screaming, and she went to see about her almost with a sense of relief and concern, because it gave her something to do. At least it was out, she thought. The truth of their feelings was out. Her body was sore from the trauma and the anger. She picked Hermine up, changed her, fed her, and put her to bed. Nobody ever cleaned up the milk spot.

The next day, on Hermine's first birthday, Herman had been gone for twenty-four hours. That evening he went out and got high with some friends. He boasted and bragged about her at the Club 260's, where he had spent so many hours brooding about Story. His baby was a whole year old; he had a right to brag! He probably spent more time with her than any of these dudes with their kids. Some of them didn't even know their kids; hell, they just got 'em and kept rollin'. Well, he knew his child, and she was goin' to make one hell of a woman someday!

After the last friend left him at the table, he had a few more, just to get his courage up. He never knew what he would have to meet once he got home. In the smoky blue light of the place, nobody saw him weave his way to the door. He had driven his old pickup truck. Story's favorite vehicle, he thought with a smirk on his face. He couldn't remember where he'd parked that motherfuckin' truck. "Story's favorite vehicle," he mumbled while he looked for his truck. "Story's favorite vehicle." Shit! This old truck helped him pay for all those clothes she claimed she had to have. He fell into the front seat, looking for his keys. When a man couldn't get no pussy on a regular basis, he had to have somethin' else. "Where those god-damn keys get to?" One thing he didn't ever do, he didn't ever drink in front of the baby. That was against his rules. Poor Bertie. At least she had been a woman, warm and sweet. He began to cry, driving nowhere, thinking of her and how she went through that thing all by herself. He was a fool, that's what he was.

He was thinking of her and his own little baby girl, linking the two of them together as if they were one and the same person when the old Ford truck finally stopped. It had knocked over a lamppost and run into a tree. Herman's blood was spread out over the front seat. They found Hermine's birthday doll all wrapped up in fancy paper under the seat next to her grandmother's pint.

While he lay in a coma for two weeks, Story had the time she needed to pack. Before the yellow mums had shriveled on his grave, she had decided to go to graduate school on the insurance money, and rented the house, and she and the baby were on their way home to Hattenfield, home to the house that Jacob built.

———

Reesie Greene had had only one child. After Herman, there just weren't any more. That was good and that was bad. It was good not to have to worry about how she was going to feed a houseful of chil-dren. On the other hand, it was lonesome. The man she married had been there today and gone tomorrow for thirty years, and he never would have been much help with children. He'd appear and reap-pear with a regular rhythm, but Reesie never minded too much about it. He was good to her when he was there, and that was what mattered to her. Still, it would have been nice to have company. She was a company-lovin' woman, and children were at least underfoot all the time.

Reesie knew that woman Story wasn't angry. She knew people

cried angry tears at funerals. Those weren't sad tears; those were angry tears. She knew if people could kill God, they'd kill God when someone they loved was taken. But that woman Story wasn't angry. Her man was gone. Who'd given her a baby girl. Who'd been a good and faithful husband. She was supposed to be laid low with anger, cursing God and calling on his angels for mercy at the same time. Instead Story stood there at the grave lookin' too good in her black silk. Story didn't even see her; Reesie, who wasn't going to give her a chance to ignore the mother of her dead son, and who stood in the shadow of the big swamp oak on the edge of the colored graveyard. Reesie didn't curse God. She cursed Story. She knew why Herman was dead. He died of thirst. He was runnin' from a pain that had him hot and thirsty, muscles achin', crying out for joy lost, body full of alcohol, dyin' of thirst. She knew he was runnin' when he started comin' to see her every Sunday. A grown man who's happy don't come home to his mama every Sunday, 'cause he be living with his hand on the cup of joy and that cup ain't never gonna be far away from him. He be too busy drinkin' in the joy, and that joy ain't at home with his mama. That joy be living with some other woman. Her boy died runnin', all right, runnin', thirsty, full of alcohol, and drunk on sorry. There were two women who didn't cry at that funeral. One of them was thankful to God. And one of them knew that God was just, and that she had work to do before Old Death came knockin' at her door.

1946

It was all hers now. Jacob Temple's home. The front parlor where the Bible was always kept, and the other forbidden things, like the red-velvet-covered Family Album that had gotten her in so much trouble. The front window where the green-fringed lamp always sat on a table. The kitchen with the wood stove and the gas stove. The wood stove where she had burned Bertie's rag doll and all the other pieces of her life. She walked from one room to the other in the still, empty place. The basement where her mother's hair had been sacrificed to some idea of judgment and divine retribution, falling like rain on the dirt floor in the desperate attempt to claim restitution for a lost life. The bedrooms, where so much concentrated pain was finally prostrate in a still, dark tree of a fallen man. The living room rug with its still newer patch made it impossible to pretend that she didn't think of Bertie, that she didn't think of all of them caught in a photograph in her mind. But Story didn't want to see the soaked form of Bertie by the front door, so she didn't.

Mother, she thought. What is Mother? A cook, a maid, a servant to a tyrant? She was in the house and a mother now. It was all here, but she would gather herself in and refuse to let it touch her. She would be a caretaker, yes, but never a mother. So she told them that her in-laws had been killed in a fire and there was no one to take the baby. She told them, the old and distant friends, that the child was homeless. That with Herman gone, she needed company. She told them, and they thought the baby was a blessing in such a tragic time for her. God does provide when all else fails, they said. The old and distant friends who had never known about the child anyway were happy for her. Even though the baby was from an obscure in-law, they said, she could still call herself Aunt Story, and so Hermine, the daughter, became a niece to them and to her. And once the idea took hold, it seemed a perfect solution to the frozen feeling in her stomach when she said "Mother."

She walked into the parlor just as baby Hermine reached for the dust dancing in the sunlight right where that sofa used to be that she and poor Bertie had to sit on, to sit on and hold themselves in tight like their shoes, laced all the way up their ankles. Hermine sat in a beam of sunlight streaming through the window, and a halo rose above her head like one of those Renaissance paintings. Hermine did look like a little angel. Soft curly hair all around her face. Those big liquid eyes and golden skin. Maybe she had been wrong to deny her, maybe she'd be sorry. Not the dust, baby, she thought, catch the sunlight, if you can. For a minute or two she watched in silence as Hermine played. There'll be plenty of dust in your life, she thought. No need to reach for it.

She cared for this child more than she wanted to admit. Wanted things for her. Good things like money, security, and education. But she couldn't bear the burden of it. And nobody to help. People would always leave you in the end. You couldn't count on other people's love. She was afraid. Afraid of somebody needing her so much. Everybody wanting a piece of her. Papa and Mama and Bertie wanting her to be something, do something for them. Hermine wanting her to be somebody she couldn't be. This was why she had to claim herself.

She didn't want to be anybody's last hope, and she didn't want anybody to be her last hope. No dependency. The baby's chubby arms reached out for her, and she picked her up and rubbed her head and stood in the sunlight where she had once been so defiant. She thought about how Papa had beaten her because of it. At that moment she knew she'd never beat her child and that she couldn't be a mother. All that love mothers were supposed to have. She didn't have it in her. Not that much love. She didn't know where it was supposed to come from.

She wished they'd all leave her alone. Mama, Bertie, and Papa. She wished all the memories would go away. It was too much. People putting burdens on other people. It was all too much. She'd care her way, the only way she could. She'd make the memories leave her alone.

Story walked through the house, Hermine toddling around in the empty rooms far ahead of her.

—

Sometimes, by herself at night, Story would remember she was a mother. She would remember the pain and blood of childbirth, and sometimes when she shut her eyes she would see Bertie lying in a pool of her baby's blood. Especially when Hermine cried—and it seemed to her that Hermine was always crying—she would remember when Bertie was born. She was born in Mama's bedroom, and Story remembered being kept all day by some strange woman; and then somebody showed her the smallest baby she had ever seen and the baby was screaming.

Baby Bertie screamed all day and half the night with colic and teething, and so did Hermine. Once during a long night of being up and down with Hermine, Story dreamed that she could hear people crying all over the world, and she found herself going through room after room of children crying, but there was really only one baby crying over and over in all those rooms, and it was Bertie. And all the rooms were in Jacob's house, now her house, she corrected her thoughts. Now her house. Some nights, Story would put her fingers in her ears to shut out the baby's cries, and pull the covers over her head, anything to shut out the baby's cries. It made less of a lump in her stomach.

There was something low and unrefined about being a mother, cleaning up messes day after day, Story thought. She pictured Mama on her knees scrubbing floors, making bread, killing chickens, scaling fish, unmaking beds, on her knees, the hands never still in the house Jacob built. That was not at all the Story she wanted people to see. She would show them only what she wanted them to see. A Story who spoke well, dressed well, and worked at a desk was the Story she liked. She remembered herself on her knees, cutting that bloody carpet, and shuddered. The picture of Bertie lying in a pool of her own blood flashed through her mind again. "Well," she lectured herself, "at least things never got messy." Story was expert at keeping things in order. Things had to be in order or else life got completely out of hand and then *nothing made sense*.

1952

"That's the one," she said. Hermine pointed to a doll in the department store window. The display window had everything in it a little girl could dream of. Wedding dolls in frilly lace dresses, and Swiss mechanical dolls, and old-fashioned dolls dressed in silk nineteenth-century dresses. Miniature dolls, and two-foot life-sized dolls, and baby dolls of all shapes. There was even one doll with brown skin. Story had Hermine by the hand because the crowd was thick with holiday shoppers. She had a horror of losing the child in crowds. Suppose she wandered off in all this confusion? The Salvation Army bell sounded out its regular beat, dee dum, dee dum, dee dum. It reminded Story to get Uncle Dee and Uncle Dum a present. Just as she thought about their awful names, Hermine piped up again. "That's the one, Aunt Story." She looked more carefully at the doll.

It was Bertie's doll! It was exactly like Cecelia, the rag doll she had burnt up in the old stove. How could they still be making Cecelias?

Story recovered quickly. "Oh no, honey, see all those beautiful dolls. Look. Wouldn't you like something really pretty?" She pointed to the wedding doll, a large blond, surrounded by white tulle. "Wouldn't you like that one on your bed? Wouldn't she be pretty?"

Hermine shook her head firmly. "Uh-uh. *That's* the one I like. I like *her*." Cecelia's button eyes stared at Story. She could have sworn there was no difference in the two dolls. The same calico dress with a white ruffle around the neck. The same pink cloth moon face, and the same yarn hair. The only thing they added was two perfect little black shoes.

"Let's go in, Hermine. We'll go and look really close at them. Then maybe you'll change your mind." Story wasn't sure Hermine still believed in Santa. A smart seven-year-old, she often understood more than Story realized and said things that she wouldn't expect.

They went into Hattenfield's biggest department store and made their way through the crowds, jostled by women, children, and even fathers doing Christmas-week shopping. "Jingle Bells" was coming from some loudspeaker somewhere. The toys were on the third floor. Story liked Christmas. She liked celebrating it in her own way. She no longer had to worry about anybody telling her what to do. What was right, what was wrong. She only went to church the Sunday before, that was it. No all-day prayer meetings. No dreary Christmas afternoons sitting in church. A Christmas tree decked with elegant trimmings bought from a lot, not left over from some empty field. "You can ask Santa for two other things," she said to Hermine.

"Can I take off my coat?" Hermine said. "It's too hot." She was hypnotized by the glitter and the music and all the people. She struggled out of her coat, her fat braids askew.

"Wait until we get off the escalator. Wait," Story ordered. "We mustn't drop these packages."

At the third floor they stepped off the escalator, and straight ahead about fifty feet was Santa Claus on his throne. His forced ho-ho-ho rang out above the noise. There was an unending line of children waiting to see him, all with mothers in various stages of exhaustion. Story hated the thought of waiting in that line with all those squirmy kids, but she felt obligated to ask. Mothering, she reflected, is one long wait. Waiting for Santa, waiting to see the doctor, waiting to see the principal at the school, waiting for kids to grow up. Story looked at the colored water fountain, where there was a long line of people waiting for a drink. There was only one colored fountain in the store. How long would they have to wait for fair treatment, she wondered?

"Aunt Story, my coat," Hermine said, bringing Story back to the present, the blue coat half off already and hanging partly on the floor.

"Well, you'll have to carry it yourself. I have too many things." Hermine grimaced, but let the coat slide off the rest of her body and picked it up off the floor.

"Hermine, for goodness sake! That's a clean coat!" Story shook her head and bit her tongue. It was Christmas after all. "Shall we see Santa?"

"I want to look at the dolls. I don't believe in Santa anyway," Hermine answered, adjusting her coat. "I want to see that doll."

"Well, all right, Madame Grown-Up." The dolls were in the toy department to the left. Rows and rows of dolls, smiling and dressed to kill. Of all dolls! Story thought. Why would she want that doll? I hate that doll. And there it was, staring back at her from behind the counter on a shelf. Along with all the other baby dolls.

"We'd like to look at several," she said to the clerk. "She's trying to decide what to ask Santa for, you know."

"I *told* you," Hermine sang out, "I don't believe in Santa anymore."

Story pretended not to hear the child's noise. "We'll see; let's see the wedding doll, and that one in the red and white satin, and oh yes, the Raggedy Ann."

"No," Hermine insisted. "*that* one over there."

"Oh yes, that one," Story said to the clerk, nodding a little. "Just to see it, you know. The little rag doll over there."

She brought them all, and in spite of herself, Hermine looked at them all, fingering their dresses, looking for details like socks and underwear.

Story looked at the prices. The wedding doll was very expensive, twenty-five dollars. "Cecelia," on the other hand, was only two dollars. "Oh, aren't they beautiful, honey?" She cooed to Hermine. "Especially this wedding one." She really couldn't afford that, but anything to avoid having Cecelia around forever. Hermine's small determined finger pointing at Cecelia, and her big brown eyes, suddenly struck Story's memory and startled her. Hermine looked a lot like Baby Bertie. Story had never realized that before. She looked more like Bertie than like her. She was sure it didn't mean anything. The doll, the resemblance. But something in her ached for a minute, for Bertie, for her parents, for Bertie's lost baby, for her own lost motherhood.

"*That* one," Hermine said, pointing, after she had satisfied her curiosity and looked over all the dolls.

Cecelia would go home with them. There was no help for it. The lady put them all back. "Well," Story said, "I was hoping to surprise you, but since you insist on this one, I'll wrap it for you and put it under the tree with your other gifts."

Story resigned herself to Hermine's Cecelia.

1954

"Who you be?" she said. Her skin looked like the bark of a cypress, so old was she. Myra Simmons looked at her with great kindness. She had been a visiting nurse now for ten years. This old woman had no living children. No family at all, as far as she knew. "I'm Myra Simmons, Mrs. Greene," she said, loud enough to be heard next door. She had been visiting Reesie now for three years, but Reesie often forgot who she was.

"Myra Simmons, used to be you work at the colored hospital. That right?"

Myra was stunned. How would this old, destitute woman know that? Reesie cackled from her place on the bed. Her favorite position was to have her feet on the very edge of the bed and turned almost diagonally so that her head was near the other edge of the bed. That way if she needed to get up, she could swing her feet with less trouble.

"Ah knows who you be. See, Ah knows. Ah knows a lot more'n

folks give me credit for. You worked in that hospital when mah granddaughter was born. Ah found out who worked up there, years ago, years ago. An' Ah ain't never forgot."

Myra was paying very good attention now. She had found no record of any living relatives for the old lady. A granddaughter? Maybe she was just imagining something she wanted. She knew old people often had delusions about things, fantasies. But to know that she worked there at the hospital?

"And what's your granddaughter's name, Mrs. Greene?" she said gently.

"Hermine. Hermine, after her father Herman Greene. Mah only chile. After he died, did me some checkin'." Suddenly she grabbed Myra by the arm, looking up at her from that curious diagonal position on the bed. Myra wished she'd straighten up. Kind of gave her vertigo to look down on her that way. Reesie held on tight. "Remember," she said, "remember good. A dark pretty woman with expensive nightgowns. Marcelled, I thinks that's what they called her hairdo. Remember? Remember her? Story Temple she was before she was married mah only son. Ah had to know, was that my chile she was havin'."

How could she forget? The one who hit her. The only patient she had ever had who hit her! That was at least ten years ago! "Yes. Yes! I do remember her," Myra said, not believing that she was playing into the old woman's fantasy and taking it seriously. She tried to free her arm.

"She run away to Hattenfield after she killed him. I want you to go to Hattenfield and find that woman after Ah die. Find that woman and finish it. Finish it."

"Mrs. Greene, Reesie, you're not going to die soon. You're not sick, you're just tired today. Calm down now. Come on, let's get you ready for dinner." Myra had other clients to visit. She was anxious to get Reesie Greene settled down.

"She killed her sister. Mah son done said it; said she helped her git rid of her baby. Said he thought she knew about the baby. Didn't do nothin' about it. Tried to drink his guilt away. We got to finish it." Reesie's eyes were burning. She knew. She knew there wasn't too much more time. She had heard death knockin' at the door last night. She had Myra's arm in a fearful grip. A grip that comes only with the strength of dying. Myra tried to draw on her professional manner, but she knew there was something strange going on and that she was somehow involved in it now, like it or not. It gave her the creeps. She shivered and tried to pull her arm away.

"Find her, find her and save mah grandchile. The woman Story is goin' to Hell. She'll take Hermine with her if you don't help. Does you want that on your soul?"

Myra was beside herself. She knew that Reesie was too excited for her own good. If she said no, there would be a struggle. "All right. All right. I'll find her," she said, not knowing what in the world she was promising to do. Reesie relaxed her grip and her body. It was as if a great burden had fallen from her. She slept. Her face was wet with sweat. Myra wiped it, put away the uneaten dinner and left.

The next day, making her rounds, she found Reesie's door unlocked. She pushed it open, calling for Reesie. It was very clean in the one room that served as a living room and kitchen. Everything was put away somewhere, though it was hard to know where it all was in that tiny space. She wondered if Reesie had been up during the night. When she reached the bedroom, she found her, slippers neatly placed beside the bed, robe folded, Reesie's head and feet still turned diagonally across the bed. There was a little package resting on her stomach, wrapped in an ancient, withered Woolworth's bag spotted with grease. Someone had penciled in a very wavering handwriting, *For Sister Ever-Virgin 1313 Center St. and to be for her only to know.* What would she do with that package, and who was Sister Ever-Virgin? Myra tucked the legacy into her coat pocket. A remembrance of some kind, she imagined. She supposed some of the neighbors would know, and remembered that she had assumed Reesie could not read or write. Reesie's hands were on her chest as if she'd been waiting for it to happen. All Myra could think of was how in the world could she "save" Hermine Greene from her own mother?

The child would be about ten now. She couldn't just walk into a perfect stranger's life and say she'd come to save her daughter. But she could at least call and see how they were in memory of Reesie. The operator in Hattenfield had a Story Temple Greene. She put her through. Story answered her phone. Myra said, "Mrs. Greene, I'm calling for your mother-in-law." Story said nothing yet. "Well, she died yesterday. And she was especially concerned about her granddaughter." There was only silence on the other end of the phone. Myra talked faster and faster, feeling the weight of the silence and getting more and more uneasy. "She wanted me to ask about how little Hermine is." Silence.

Finally Story said, icily, "I'm sorry. I don't know any Resa Greene. You must have the wrong person." Myra felt absolutely foolish. Like she had been had. Whatever it was all about, she didn't want any part of it. Reesie Greene was dead, and she'd never know whether Myra went to Hattenfield or not. That was that. She was going to close the door on this whole thing. And she did; until she had a granddaughter of her own, she did.

CHAPTER V

BIRDS OF A FEATHER

AUGUST 2012

The sun was coming through the living room windows now, just before it set. There was a purple haze on the old sofa. Story pushed the remote button and turned off her television. She reached for her chocolate candy. That had been a stupid movie. It reminded her too much of the past. "Nobody needs to see all of that stuff now," she said, fussing aloud to herself. The movie had been about a seventies drug bust. Just when drugs had begun to be a major problem in the northern cities and for white people in the suburbs. The villain of the story had been a black man—handsome, mean, and ruthless.

Story settled back in her favorite chair. Her wrinkled hands rested on the armrests. Drugs and sex, she thought, the ruination of more people than you could count. Now Papa, what would he have said about drugs? 'Course, he drank, on the q.t., but he sure drank. Maybe it was the drink that kept him so mean. I sure wanted him to love me, she thought, and I tried to teach the children in my classroom how families are supposed to work. And I even tried some with Hermine. I remember how smart she was even as a little thing. She learned to talk early, and I tried to talk to her so she'd learn things right. I paid for those dance lessons for a whole year, so she could do what I didn't get to do. Why, I would have given my right arm for dance lessons as a child. But somehow she just let it fizzle out. She let most things fizzle out.

I wanted her to have the best. But she didn't have what it takes. She just couldn't do it. Looked like one of those Disney elephants. Couldn't pass the bar either. Couldn't get her body off of the floor. I bought her costumes for the recital, and then she just quit on me. Said I didn't think she was any good or somethin'. Takes offense at everything anybody says. All I said was, "You look like a teddy bear in tulle, can't you do any better than that?" and she wouldn't go back to the studio. I never could please that girl, no matter what I did or how much I spent on her. Tried to talk to her, tried to lead her in the right way, tried to talk her through law school, tried to make up for her daddy, the way I never had anybody to do. Me and Bertie, we had to make it the best way we could. Papa never gave nothin' to us except orders; brought us nothin' but pain. . . .

Story chewed her candy slowly. Her mind flashed back to her papa's condemning face. "Women ain't good for nothin' but wipin' up the mess that a man leaves behind," he said. Story looked out of her living room window; there was one small maple tree, leaves twisting in the breeze. All she saw was a green blur, but she could smell a rain coming. Pieces of memories floated through her head like an underwater sequence in a movie. Hermine trying to do a ballet dance in the living room. Hermine in an Afro. Hermine screaming and stomping her feet. Something about running away. Somehow it had to do with Sam. Yes, now she remembered, Hermine was hysterical, and that was the only time in her whole life she had hit Hermine. It was the only thing she could do to calm the girl down. Crying and screaming about her friends; her friends indeed. My life was in a shambles, and she's hysterical about some childhood friends. They were trash anyway. The whole lot of them.

Her memory drifted with the breeze. At least Hermine never got on drugs, that she knew of. God knows what she did out there with those women. She should thank God she didn't come down with that AIDS thing. Story fumbled around with a tissue to wipe her eye with. It ran tears once in a while.

Hermine was such a strange little girl too, sour-faced and unhappy, for no reason. She always had everything she needed. If she'd known what was good for her, she would have been less rebellious and more determined, and she would have spent less time with certain kinds of people. I always told her not to take up with trash, Story thought. They won't do anything but drag you down. She picked up the remote again. The worst part about being old was having to depend on that girl. She should come and shut the front door. It was beginning to rain and there was a draft. The white light of the screen lit up the now dark living room.

An old "Cosby Show" rerun had come on.

1955

The witches always got it in the end. She was glad of that. "The princess was in mortal danger; the ancient hag leaned over her, her gray and white hair swinging across her glittering eyes. She laughed diabolically, but just as she reached out to grab her, the witch fell headlong to her death." The witches never ended the story. Hermine looked up from her book. The princess always won, and sometimes she was rescued by a handsome prince, and sometimes the poor girl was transformed into a royal princess or queen in the end, but the witches never won.

She hoped Aunt Story would be here soon, and then they would go. They would go to see Mrs. Henredon, whoever that was. And she had on her best brown oxfords and navy-blue skirt and white blouse. Aunt Story said she had to uphold a certain standard. What did that mean? Aunt Story said she had to go get the kinks straightened out of her hair today. Hermine wished she was old enough to have her hair straightened. She would have to sit and wait for Aunt Story while the lady did her hair. She could smell all the smells in there just thinking about it. Cigarettes and pomade, and shampoo, and hot hair being straightened and curled. It was always boring, and it took too long, even though she could watch the ladies who looked really funny with their hair standing up all over the place.

She wished she had long hair like the fairy princess. Then she wouldn't have to worry about it ever. She didn't like her outfit. The princess never wore oxfords or plaid dresses, only homespun before she was rescued and silk afterward. Her oxfords were new, kind of hard. Her long socks itched. She was tired of waiting. Mrs. Henredon was probably white. That wasn't a name she remembered from church or even from school. Mrs. Henredon probably had lots of money. She was going to give some money to something, maybe their church. Aunt Story had called it a charity.

The radio announcer was talking about President Eisenhower; that was boring, but then some music came on, and then she decided to read another story from *The Complete Fairy Tales of the Brothers Grimm* that she got for Christmas when she was eight, or maybe she'd start *The Lion, The Witch and The Wardrobe* again, and she thought how wonderful it would be to have a secret place where Aunt Story wouldn't be able to find her when she wanted to hide. She could go through the wardrobe and disappear into Narnia. She would take her paper dolls there, and stay all day under a tree, and she'd never have to draw anything Aunt Story liked, because mostly she hated what her aunt liked. Plaid dresses and brown oxfords for school and red velvet skirts for church. She hated them. Once, they went shopping and Aunt Story bought them both navy-blue pleated skirts and said they could be look-alikes. Hermine tried never to wear the skirt but couldn't because Aunt Story would ask, "Where's the skirt I bought you that looks like mine? You look like such a lady in that, especially with your white blouse. Oh, you look prettier in that." Hermine noticed Aunt Story had the same kind of blouse, which she wore to work every Monday.

Playing paper dolls was one of her favorite things to do because she could draw herself in all kinds of costumes that were different from the clothes she had to wear in real life. She could draw herself in a ballerina costume or a little Dutch girl outfit or a cowboy outfit. She could even put herself in "dungarees," as Aunt Story called them. Blue jeans were what the kids called them, but Aunt Story wouldn't buy her a pair. She drew herself in a bathing suit that she thought was very sexy. "Sexy," she would say under her breath, knowing that she had spoken a forbidden word. "Sexy," she would whisper, and she would feel the sound of it and think about something else quickly because it scared her a little bit, even to say it. She thought "sexy" must not be so bad because she heard kids say it, and people on the radio said it about ladies, and it sounded good. Anyway, she liked the bathing suit costume because she was something different then. In her favorite fairy tale, the princess had to wear a costume that made her look old and ugly, but then she turned into a beautiful young girl with long blond hair in the end. She liked that story, she liked that story the best.

"But how the maiden was transformed! You've never seen anything like it in your life! After the gray wig had been taken off, her golden hair flared like sunbeams and spread like a cloak over her entire body. Her eyes sparkled like glistening stars in the sky and her cheeks gleamed with the soft red glow of apple blossoms." Hermine closed her book of fairy tales and sighed deeply. She wiggled her feet, looking at the shoes she hated. Stood up and sat down. Stood up and sat down.

The furnace made gurgling noises in the basement. Maybe Mrs. Henredon would serve ice cream and cookies, if they ever got there. She heard Aunt Story's car now in the driveway and straightened her back, so she wouldn't have to hear about her posture as her aunt opened the front door with her key.

———

It was too good to be true. Her uncles were coming soon to visit, and when her uncles came to visit them, Hermine felt just like the princess in her story. She was "in bliss," like it said in the story, for as long as they stayed; but they never stayed long enough for her. The wonderful magic was always over too soon. Uncle Dee and Uncle Dum were Grandma Georgia's twin boys, so that made them Aunt

Story's uncles. Hermine didn't know what they were to her, but she called them uncles anyway. Their real names were Dandridge and Dannell McCloud, but she always called them Uncle Dee and Uncle Dum. Aunt Story said they got "those ridiculous names" when they were born a long time ago in Alabama, but Aunt Story always called them by their "real" names.

Her uncles were cowboys. They said that during the great migration of the twenties they had gone out to Oklahoma to start a new life. Hermine didn't believe there were any colored cowboys until one day when she saw them actually walking up to their front door in jeans and cowboy boots. They had on those hats, too, like she had seen pictures of. The kids at school who had television sets talked about Hopalong Cassidy, and she heard the Lone Ranger on the radio, but she knew that he was white. She hadn't really believed until she saw their hats and boots, and then she was convinced.

Aunt Story was always nice to them. They came to visit their niece about every two years, so the first thing they had to say was how "Little Niece" had grown like a desert weed. Wachomis, Oklahoma, seemed so far away that Hermine couldn't imagine what it would be like there. Uncles Dee and Dum had a ranch where they lived with their wives and children and grandchildren, and they kept horses and cattle. They could tell all kinds of stories about real Indians who were alive today, and about horses and cowboys, and she thought the life out there must have been about the coolest thing she could think of. She could tell Aunt Story enjoyed all their tales of the West too.

Uncle Dee was tall and thin and had brown skin, and Uncle Dum was just like him, except he had a potbellied stomach because he liked beer. They were both gray and they wore wire-rimmed glasses. Sometimes they took her to King Sam's barbecue place. They said King Sam's barbecue beat anything they could get in Oklahoma, and they always looked forward to their visit to King Sam's. Aunt Story wouldn't go with them. She said that place was too much for her, so they always took Hermine.

The year she was ten they said she could have absolutely anything she wanted, anything at all. Uncle Dee said even a taste of beer, but just a taste, and Hermine thought she'd just die with excitement when he said that. He said everybody needed a little strong drink to grow up right, said it made you courageous, brave enough to face life. Uncle Dum said he thought that was "bullshit." Said beer was just good stuff and ought to be enjoyed for itself. They didn't mind tossing in a few cuss words now and then, which they only did in Aunt Story's absence. Hermine thought it was thrilling.

She felt so free with them, like a real person, not like a paper doll, a cutout, made in Aunt Story's design. Hermine ordered ribs, beans, slaw, french fries, and a Coke, and they let her taste the beer in their glasses.

"So," said Uncle Dee, "what important stuff is Little Niece doing these days?"

Hermine thought she wasn't doing anything important, so she just said, "No important stuff."

"Look, little prairie dog," he said, "never say you're not doing nothing important. Ain't you breathin'?"

"Yessir," she said.

"And ain't you sittin' there shovelin' in those fried potatoes?" She nodded, her mouth full.

"And ain't you bein' my niece?"

He didn't wait for an answer. " 'Course you are! You are important as long as you breathin' and bein' my niece, which you will be forever, even after I'm gone on to glory, praise God. What you doin' important is *bein'*. That's enough, and don't you let nobody tell you no different. I tell my grandkids that every day." Uncle Dee had four grandkids and Uncle Dum had one, but he said that was enough because he was married to the most beautiful woman in the world, present company excepted. Aunt Story said he always said that to any female who was present, no matter who they were, if his wife wasn't with him. She said her uncles were full of themselves, but Hermine could tell her aunt liked them a lot. Aunt Story talked a lot about their big ranch and how successful they were, and she put up with a lot from them that she wouldn't have tolerated in anybody else.

Hermine reached for the ketchup. Uncle Dum said, "What are you plannin' to do with yourself in this life, little lady?"

"I took dance lessons last year," she said, pounding on the bottle. "But I stopped."

"Stopped?" Uncle Dum said. "Stopped?"

"Yeah," said Hermine, chewing her french fries.

"Why?" both uncles said together.

Hermine only shrugged her shoulders.

"We have to see about that. We just have to see about that." They looked at each other and shook their heads at the same time.

"So. What are you plannin' to do when you grow up?" Uncle Dum asked.

Hermine had no idea what she was planning. She was only ten years old. She knew Aunt Story had talked a lot about college, so she said, "Guess I'll go to college."

"Well, that's a fine idea, a fine idea," Uncle Dum said, "but what you gonna do with all that education?"

She had no idea what to say.

"What," he said between bites of barbecue and gulps of beer, "you mean you don't know?"

She shook her head.

"You got to have a plan to bring your power down," he said. "Not power *over* people, but Hermine's own private power. You must find your power place and use it to shape your life." He took off his glasses and looked at her with piercing brown eyes. He had bushy gray eyebrows. "I don't care what anybody tells you, Hermine, sugar. And I do mean anybody. If you don't want life to push you around, you have to find your place—your power place. Don't ever forget what I'm saying to you. Me and Uncle Dee done seen a whole lotta life go down. And some of it good and some of it ain't so good. But these two old uncles a yours, we *knows* a thing or two about survivin', and we do know life will do you in if you don't know where your own power place is hidin'."

She ate as slowly as she possibly could. Every bite was a minute away from home, a minute away from feeling trapped again. Her uncles had a pocket full of quarters to put in the jukebox. Each table at King Sam's place had its own little machine where you could look at the list of songs with a number for each one. And then you put the quarter in the big jukebox and punched in the number. They let her play whatever she wanted over and over, not like at home where she had to be so quiet all the time. She played "Lawdy Miss Claudie" and then "Rock with Me, Annie." Aunt Story said that was a disgraceful, ugly song. Hermine loved it and she played it at least three times. Then she played "Caldonia, Caldonia, What Make Your Big Head So Hard?" and then "Lawdy Miss Claudie" again and again until even Uncle Dee said he had run out of his music quarters and she needed to finish her barbecue before it got completely cold. But it was wonderful, and the food was wonderful too. She was just like a princess in one of her stories. She could have whatever she wanted. When she finally finished and it was time to go home, she felt awfully sad. She wished somehow someday she would not feel this thing that made her want to cry. It was always there in the corners, in her dreams. It was always there waiting for things to get over so it could come out again and take over her thoughts.

On the way home in her uncles' car Hermine was quiet, but she tried hard to be cheerful so they wouldn't ask her what was the matter. Still, she saw them looking at each other over her head. She was sitting between them on the front seat. They were talking to each other without words, the way grown-ups did a lot around kids, talking with their eyes and squinching their lips to the side.

She wanted them to ask her something, and then she didn't. What would she tell them anyway? Would she tell them her friends were afraid of Aunt Story? All except for the Joyce kids. They just said she was peculiar. Would she tell them that she dreamed a lot about having light skin and long brown hair because she thought Aunt Story would love her more if she looked like that? Would she tell them about that Friday? She thought about it hard. She thought about it hard because maybe it would go away if she thought about it enough. All she wanted to do was to have a slumber party for her birthday, and she got in trouble just because of that. Friday, Aunt Story asked, "What do you want for your birthday?"

So Hermine said, "A slumber party. I want to have five girls over to spend the night."

"That's not suitable," Aunt Story said. She was tucking in her white blouse that had come out of her skirt. And she had on those brown shoes that Hermine hated. She could hear them all over the house, click, click, click. And she said, "No, I meant a present, a suitable present. What do you want?"

Hermine paused. "That's what I want, Aunt Story, a slumber party."

"Well," said her aunt, clicking around in the kitchen, "when you can give me a real answer, I'll give you a present. You know I don't approve of people lolling around on the floor and messing up the living room with food. Besides, none of you girls needs to be talking about what you're likely to talk about if you spend the night together. Might give you ideas. And who would you ask anyway? Those Joyce girls, who don't have good personal hygiene, and who else? No, no, it's not a good idea."

The uncles' car rounded a corner. Hermine thought about the milk bottle again. She went over the details in her mind again and again. It happened before she knew it was going to happen, before she could stop it.

She was holding onto it with both hands, standing there looking at the brown shoes, and her hands just let go of the bottle, and there it was, milk all over the floor, and someone was yellin', "You never ever let me do anything! I hate you! I hate you! I hate your white blouses and your brown shoes, and your pleated skirts and everything!"

But she was yelling at the shoes, the voice was the shoes, which were just sitting there on the maroon linoleum, brown and maroon, brown and maroon, and then she felt someone grab her arm and shake her, and she looked up and it was Aunt Story saying, "That's enough, young lady, enough! You will clean up this mess. Do you hear me? You will clean up this mess and you will spend the whole day in silence at home. You will not go out of the house until church on Sunday; and you will clean up this mess and polish my shoes; do you hear me? And there will be no birthday presents of any kind. The mop and the bucket are out there," and she pointed to the back porch.

Story was speaking very slowly, as if the words were stuck somewhere. At first Hermine didn't know why her aunt was so mad. What had she done? There was milk all over the floor, and a pair of brown shoes standing in it, splattered with white milk.

"And you will never, never speak to me like that again as long as you live. Do you hear me? Or I swear I will move you to the Children's Home where they put difficult children who don't respect their elders."

The mop was heavy and stinking with whatever it had mopped up before. There was a big long handle, and Hermine wasn't very tall for her age. The handle kept bumping into the cabinets, and she had a headache before long. The milk was beginning to smell. She hated this. She hated the milk and the smell and the heavy mop. When she got it all up, she started to put the mop away, but then she knew what would happen. The mop would turn sour, and she would be blamed for a filthy mop head. So she had to rinse it out somehow. By the time she had rinsed out the mop with Spic and Span and put it back, and wiped up the water she spilled, the afternoon was almost over and it was getting dark. And she still had to clean and polish those shoes. But it didn't matter. She was going to be in the house all weekend anyway. Nothing mattered now that she couldn't have her slumber party.

The car slowed down, pulled into the driveway, and brought Hermine back to the present. Uncle Dee got out first and rang the doorbell. Already the sad thing inside her was gripping her tight. Hermine thought about the witch costume that the princess had. She had to put it back on. She wasn't a princess anymore.

Hermine heard Aunt Story coming to the door. The grown-ups said things to each other like, "How did you enjoy your afternoon?" Then Aunt Story asked if she had behaved like a lady, and Hermine went upstairs because she could tell they wanted to talk grown-up talk. But she heard some of it. She sat by her bedroom door and she heard Uncle Dum say, "That child needs to have some fun." Then he said something and "too tight, Story, too tight." Then they moved into the living room somewhere and she couldn't hear anymore except when she decided if she'd go to the bathroom and she could hear more on the way down the hall.

She heard Aunt Story raise her voice and say, "Dandridge . . . my responsibility, I know what's best for her, Dannell," and she sounded very angry. Hermine couldn't believe it. They were really talking about her, and the uncles had made Aunt Story raise her voice, something she always said a lady never did. Then someone closed a door and she couldn't hear anymore. Maybe things would be better now because of her uncles' visit. Maybe Aunt Story would let her play the radio and sing and have more clothes that were like some of her friends had, and maybe they could even convince her to let some girls come over for a slumber party. If she could have a slumber party, she'd just die of happiness. She wanted that more than anything; to have girls spend the night and pop popcorn and talk until morning.

Aunt Story is always saying no, she thought. No to everything I want to do. Hermine wrapped her arms around herself tight, and held onto her rag doll, Cecelia Too. But if her uncles could . . . But she knew it would never happen. She had dropped a whole bottle of milk and said terrible things to Aunt Story. She'd never get to have that party now. She knew that for sure.

She was still sitting at her door fifteen minutes later when she heard Aunt Story calling her. "Hermine, Hermine, would you come down, please? Your uncles want to ask you something."

Her heart fluttered just a little. Maybe, just maybe, they were going to let her have the party. When she got to the living room, Aunt Story was putting on a record, "The Blue Danube" waltz, it was. As it started, she said, "Your uncles want to see you dance. I told them you had taken dance lessons for over a year, and they want to see what you learned. Of course I told them you were not the best student of dance, but they are insisting."

All of a sudden Hermine felt too warm. Her stomach turned over. She couldn't tell her uncles no. They loved her. They were expecting her to do something they could be proud of. If she did well, Aunt Story would be proud of her too, and maybe she could have her party.

"Come on, Little Niece," Uncle Dum coaxed. "Let's see it. Let's see you dance. So I can go back to Wachomis and tell them about my niece who could dance like a ballerina."

Her power place. She could try to show him she had a power place. She knew she wasn't the best, but she could try. They all sat there looking at her. She had to do something.

Aunt Story started the music over at the beginning, and the melody of "The Blue Danube" filled the living room. Hermine thought she remembered it. Maybe she could make up what she didn't remember. Arabesque, arabesque, turn, levez. In the middle of the levez she noticed Aunt Story's arms were folded, and her head, cocked to one side, was not smiling. The three-four time of the waltz kept going, but she couldn't remember any more. The whole second half of the dance was still to come, and she didn't know what to do. She began to stumble. It was so hot in there. She could feel the sweat on her face. She couldn't keep turning around and doing the arabesque over and over. After a long minute Aunt Story pulled the needle off the record and the music stopped abruptly. Her uncles clapped politely.

"That's enough," her aunt said evenly. "Go start your homework now."

Uncle Dee grabbed her before she could run out of the room. "Whoa! Just a minute," he said. "Give me a big hug, little one. I was mighty pleased to see you dance, mighty pleased. You take good care now, ya hear?" And Uncle Dum insisted on giving her a big kiss, and he said, "Now you go on back to those lessons, you can do it. I'll never forget that you danced for me, sugar, I sure won't."

"Go along now, Hermine," Aunt Story interrupted. "She obviously needs lots more practice," she said, turning to the uncles.

Hermine ran all the way upstairs and slammed her bedroom door. It was all ruined for her. She had forgotten the steps. How could you forget the steps to a dance you knew by heart? Now they'd never think she was special anymore. She could tell she had embarrassed Aunt Story too. If it was inside her head once, how could she have forgotten it like that? How had she made such a mess? "Don't fail me," Aunt Story said all the time. "Don't fail me, and embarrass us." And that's exactly what she had done. Aunt Story was right. A teddy bear in tulle. That's all she was.

When they pulled out of the driveway to head back to Oklahoma, Hermine's eyes were full of tears, and Uncle Dum whispered in her ear, "Don't you ever forget what I told you last night, about your power place." Hermine nodded, promising to remember always.

She thought about hiding in a wardrobe or maybe even in an ordinary closet and wondered if that's what they meant by a power place. It was a place to hide, a place where she could do what she wanted. But Uncle Dum said her power place was hiding somewhere inside her. It puzzled her. She wanted somehow to know. But there was no time to ask in private, and when they drove off, she felt very small and very alone, like the princess who had to put her ugly costume back on, and there was no one to ask about how to find the power place if it was inside you. She thought maybe it was a fairy-tale thing like her stories, and that power places only existed in books. They had promised her one day she could come and see them on their ranch. She would ask them then, how to find this power place.

1955

She brushed it out and it floated down to her shoulders. The room was lined with mirrors. Everywhere she looked she saw her face, smiling happy, as she had never been happy before. Relieved, mostly, that now she was better. She'd finally done it, wished something true. Bobby McCollum said you could do that, so did Alice. They were both in her class, but she was scared to play with them. They always knew everything. She looked and smiled again. It was still there—the lovely dark brown hair that floated when she brushed it. The lovely cream-colored skin that was as light as Aunt Story's mama in that big photo book that her Aunt Story had.

She couldn't wait to tell Aunt Story. It was a beautiful day. There was sun everywhere. It began to get in her eyes. She rubbed them a couple of times. The mirrors began to give back a very bright reflection, so she was losing sight of her face in the blinding sunlight. She covered her eyes, rubbing them, but she had to look one more time. She had to make sure she looked the same. She had to make sure she didn't go back to the way she was, and so she dared another look . . . and "No" . . . someone crying . . . crying . . . "No" . . . and suddenly she was screaming, "I have no head. My head is gone." And she woke up rigid with fear, holding the covers over her head, and then without thinking rushed to her mirror to look. Afraid, hoping, hoping, Hermine looked at herself. Afraid, hoping, hoping, but it was just herself. Her little plain brown face, her curled-up pigtails, her half-open sleepy eyes. It was all gone. All the light. All the beautiful hair. She was not prettier. She was not like the princess in the story.

She turned her head, remembering the dream, and then she remembered to be angry. The dream was a lie. It wasn't fair. It wasn't fair that she should be lied to by a dream. When she woke up she thought it had really happened, and to find out she had dreamed a lie just wasn't fair. Her eyes burned with tears. Our teachers are always telling us to better ourselves, she thought. Aunt Story tells me to better myself by marrying well. I think she really means I should marry someone lighter than me with "good" hair. Things will work out, grown people always said. But they lied. All of them lied, she thought. She didn't have any power place. That was just another lie. Life was a lie—just like her dreams. She stood in front of her narrow mirror, her small brown body rigid with anger, her mouth grimacing, as ugly as she could make it, the tears coming faster now. She shouted without sound into the mirror, too afraid she'd be heard. "Life is a lie, life is a lie, life is a lie!"

———

Hermine called it the House of Children, and she loved it.

She called Mrs. Joyce "Aunt Aleatha." Aunt Aleatha had four children who were always tumbling over everything and all over their mother. They were so close in age, Aunt Story said, "because the Joyces didn't have any self-control, just like white people always said about Negro people. We have too many children, one right after another." They were messy and "unkempt" and Hermine loved it at their house. She would have gladly moved in with them. Hermine always had to be neat and clean. She hated that she had to wash up after school for supper and stay clean until bedtime. The Joyce children played in her yard after school, but Aunt Story didn't like having them in the house. They tracked in dirt and were "spillers and breakers," her aunt said. At their house Hermine never had to mind her manners. Her shoulders could come down. When she was at Aunt Aleatha's, she could move better and she could breathe. She had to be very careful not to get dirty, though, because Aunt Story really got upset when she was dirty.

Once when she was over to Aunt Aleatha's, she got dirt all over the front of her dress. They were outside playing and she fell and scraped her knees and messed up her dress. There were streaks of red dirt all over it. Aunt Aleatha put something soothing on her knees and she stayed as long as she could, afraid to go home. Aunt Story was very quiet when she saw the dress. She only said, "Take it off and wash it out," but Hermine knew how angry she was. There was a big icy feeling in the room when she said that. Hermine felt the coldness follow her all the way up the stairs. She put on her play clothes, washed out her dress, and she began to cry. She wished she lived with Aunt Aleatha and her children; she wondered if she wished hard enough, would her wish come true.

One spring Saturday, Aleatha decided it wasn't too early in the year to have a picnic. She packed up all her children, ages five, six, seven, and nine, and Hermine, who was ten, and they all went out to Paul Lawrence Dunbar Park, which was in the colored section of town. There were nice roses there that had been planted by a group called the Colored Neighborhood Improvement Association. There were red and pink roses, and there were honeysuckle vines and wildflowers. Hermine loved that place, and she only got to go there when she was with Aunt Aleatha. Story always said no, she didn't have time for parks, and besides, Hermine ought to be improving her mind, and reading. "Besides," she said, "it wasn't in a good part of town. There were too many rough people there."

Later in the summer there would be lots of children there, because it had the only swimming pool where black children could swim. Sometimes the pool would get very crowded with kids. Still, Hermine thought it was wonderful. One day she had been there with Aunt Aleatha, and some older boys who were maybe ten or twelve saw her sitting on a bench with Jamesina, the oldest Joyce child. They started teasing them, especially Hermine, who was wearing glasses. She hated that she wore glasses, because it made her even more different than she already was. Living with Aunt Story was already weird enough. Then she had to wear those dumb glasses. (When she got old enough to buy them herself, she was going to buy some of those glasses she'd heard about that fit right on your eyeballs. She didn't care if they did hurt. It would be better than being called "Four Eyes" by stupid boys.) But anyhow, nothing, not even stupid boys, could keep her from loving the park. She just moved away from the bench, toward Aunt Aleatha. The boys were practicing for a yo-yo contest, and wanted to show off how good they were, so they followed them for a little while. One of them said, "Betcha can't do Rock the Baby in the Cradle." Hermine was holding the Royal Crown Cola that Aunt Aleatha had bought her and Jamesina. She just kept on drinking and walking toward the adults, and most of the boys wandered away, but two of them stayed behind with a couple of rough and tumble girls. "Hey, Four Eyes," one of the boys said, "where you stay? We never seen you before."

"Leave them ole girls alone, JoJo," one said. "Come on, let's play ball. You said we could play with you. Come on."

"Aw girl, wait a minute," said the first boy. "I think I know this one. Her auntie work at the school."

"No wonder she look so stuck-up," said a girl dressed in overalls. Hermine and Jamesina tried to walk away, but they were surrounded by the group, who could see they had found captives.

"Ole Four Eyes got a friend too. What's your name?" said one of the girls. She snatched Hermine's glasses off before she knew what happened and waved them in the air, moving toward Jamesina slowly.

Everything in Hermine's world had suddenly blurred at the edges. "Her name is Jamesina," Hermine answered. She tried to sound like Aunt Story's voice did sometime, cold and unfriendly. "And give me back my glasses."

"Jamesina, Jamesina," they sang out. "Bet your mama don't know you playin' with this ole girl," they said, turning to Hermine.

"You got a problem with that?" Jamesina yelled. "You give her back her glasses!"

"You give me back my glasses!" Hermine squeaked. Her voice didn't sound familiar to her. It was like someone else had said it.

"You want to start a fight?" someone yelled. "You talkin' 'bout they mamas, callin' them outta they names."

Somebody kicked a stone in the dust. "Aw, let's go. We got things to do. Why you wanna mess with these ole girls anyway?" said one of the girls.

They still had Hermine's glasses. Jamesina had no notion of backing off. She handed her cola to Hermine. "Hold this," she said.

"Give me back the glasses," she ordered, her jaw set. She walked out into the middle of the circle. Her sturdy legs never wavered.

"So what chu gon' do about it?" the girl in overalls said. There was only one thing that could happen now. "Aw, you can't fight, you can't fight, you sissy girl." The strange girl was moving around in the dust, rolling her eyes at Jamesina. She was in her element.

Hermine didn't know how to fight, and had never dreamed of doing it. The very idea of getting hit scared the pants off her. In the meantime, Jamesina was squaring off. She had done this before, Hermine could tell. Everybody was yelling "Fight! Fight! Girls in a fight!" and making a circle around them. Hermine was beside herself. Where was Aunt Aleatha? And where did these kids come from so fast? Before she knew anything, the girls were at it, rolling in the dust. She should get help! There was no sign of Aunt Aleatha or the little boys. The last thing she saw was Jamesina's shirt being torn. Hermine threw the cola down and ran for the park rest room. It was some ways away, but maybe that's where she was. There was only one colored rest room in the park. Oh God, it was so far away, and she couldn't half see. They'd kill Jamesina! Hermine tore through small bushes and trees and stumbled over a log that was in the way. Her arms and legs were full of scratches. The park outhouse finally came into view, but she couldn't see the colored men and colored women sign very well. She didn't know where they'd be. She just couldn't go in the men's side! At that moment Aunt Aleatha emerged from the women's side with her two boys in tow.

"Come . . ." Hermine said. Her breath was frantic. Her side was killing her. "Come quick! She's gonna get killed! She's gonna get killed! Those kids started a fight! They took my glasses!"

Aleatha started off at full tilt, but her unborn baby held her back. She was breathing heavily before she had run too many feet and she had to slow down. As they got closer they could hear the kids yelling through the trees.

By the time they reached the circle, it was all over. Jamesina, nose bloody, blouse torn, and face bruised, was sucking in the dust, grinning. And she had her trophy. A pair of broken horn-rimmed glasses that belonged to her friend. The girl in overalls was being helped away, and the boys had been distracted away to a ball game without a backward glance.

Hermine was awestruck by her friend's crazy courage. She grabbed her arms. "Oh, Jamesina, are you all right? Are you all right?" Aunt Aleatha picked her daughter up out of the dirt. She was holding her big stomach.

"You okay?" she said, trying to get her breath. "Oh, Lordy, I got to sit down."

Jamesina seemed much too casual for Hermine, who couldn't understand how she could be so calm.

"Yeah, Mama," Jamesina answered. "That girl, she stupid, and she don't know how to fight either. Here your glasses, girl; sorry they got broke."

They looked at each other and smiled. Hermine was overcome. She couldn't believe any of what had happened. A girl fighting and not being afraid! A friend who'd do that for her! She put her arm around Jamesina and thought, I'll be her friend forever and ever. She still hated her glasses, but she put them on and laughed. Things looked so funny through the shattered glass.

"Well, let's eat!" Aunt Aleatha said. "No sense lettin' a bunch of hoodlum kids, ain't got no home trainin', spoil a good picnic!"

They set out their food. Fried chicken and potato chips, and Royal Crown Cola and cookies and fruit. Hermine thought it was the most wonderful food she had ever eaten.

Aunt Aleatha's youngest were the two boys, Harold and Thomas. They were rolling on the ground, pretending to be cowboys and Indians. Francis and Jamesina were jumping rope. Jamesina was bruised and her blouse was torn, but other than that she was feeling fine. Aunt Aleatha settled down on her quilt for a rest. She was expecting the baby soon. Hermine plopped down beside her. She thought about a lot of things. About Aunt Aleatha's husband, Uncle James, who worked at the cotton mill at night and slept during the day. About how different Jamesina's life was from hers. "Aunt Aleatha," she said, "Aunt Story says this is a bad neighborhood. Why you think she said that?"

"Not enough . . . well, you know," she said slowly. Aunt Aleatha's voice was smooth like honey. She was overweight and had pretty brown skin and wild hair that she could never keep in place.

"You know what?" Hermine persisted.

Finally Aleatha said, "Your aunt sort of different." She means "stuck-up," Hermine thought. "Your aunt Story, I reckon I'm the only friend she's got that's like I am. You got to understand, some of these folk ain't never had nothing they could call their own. They works and works and they just can't get nowhere, and then the men-folks get to painin' over that and they just walks off or they beats up on their wives. It's a sickness, a sickness brought on by bein' hungry and tired and nothing to nobody all their lives. Now there's other folks who goes to church regular, *every* Sunday, and do they best to fight the pain or the devil, I don't know which. I reckon that pain might *be* the devil. Me, I never had too much to do with the church, too many folks there want to mind my business. Always askin' me if I'm saved. If I'm saved, it's between me and the Lord, not none of their doin'. I just minds my business. I does believe in God, Honey, don't want you think I don't, but I don't want them folks runnin' my life.

"I'm kind of poor and just plain me. I ain't had no schoolin' to speak of. But I guess your aunt Story like me somehow, maybe she think I been a good friend to her. Anyhow, ain't enough educated folks around here for her. We just plain workin' folks; works in white folks' kitchens and white folks' mills, and that's not enough for your auntie. She need more somehow. Guess it her upbringin', home trainin', you know."

Hermine wasn't sure she had understood all of that, but she did know that Aunt Story was lucky to have a friend like Aleatha. She thought Aunt Aleatha was wonderful, and she never really felt as safe at home as she did right now, lying on the quilt, looking up at the white powder-puff clouds and blue sky through the trees. The leaves turned and turned in the breeze like little silver-green kites.

———

One day Story had left Hermine at the Joyces' and picked her up after supper. Aleatha was discussing the behavior of soldiers in town

with Story, and started complaining about their unruly behavior.
"The whites worse than the blacks," she said, as if this were hard to
believe. "They steal too. I saw a bunch of 'em down town at Woolworth's and they were acting up like po' white trash does, you know,
and I was just there fixin' to buy my red-fox stockings for the month.
I happened to see one of them soldiers take three pairs of stockings
and stick 'em up under his coat quick as lightning! I said 'un-uh' to
myself; you can't tell me them folks don't steal. They all the time
talkin' about us. I take little things once in a while myself, Story,
'cause you can't tell me they don't owe us a thing or two, us being
black, them bein' white. They owe us!"

Story looked over Aleatha's head out into space, thinking about
her next move on that Sam person. She wondered if he'd be free this
weekend. She made a mental note that Aleatha was a thief. It might
be useful to know someday. Aleatha was quite generous with her information, and with most other things. Despite her "flexible" sense
of morality, she knew how to be a good friend.

It was Aleatha who told Story that Sam's wife had died some time
ago, way before her time. Just dropped dead one day. And Sam was
that rare thing, a black man of marriageable age who wasn't attached. He was also a black businessman, which meant every black
woman in town who was husband hunting knew who he was, and
who he was currently "talking to." It was said that Daisy Eldridge
even knew he had a suit for every day in the week, and what color
they were, and great conversations were engaged in, based on the
question, How does Daisy know the colors of the suits?

Sam owned a barbecue joint, a small restaurant that sold great
barbecue and fried potatoes. Not incidental to the barbecue business
was the pool that was played there on Sam's pool table. Folks went
there to eat or to watch, or to play pool. You only went to Sam's to do
one thing at a time. People who went to eat barbecue didn't go to
play pool, and men who played pool had too much on their minds
to be "greasin'," and some folks just went to watch the happenin's.
They might have a bottle with them, or they might order a beer. Sam
didn't have no truck with trash either, so it was said. He ran a respectable eating establishment where folks could bring their kids for
a barbecue sandwich, so there was a limit to the cuss words you

could use. "Motherfucker" was reduced to "MF," and the kids had to stay along the back wall and eat their barbecue, especially if they were watchin', and to mind your mouth if you were playing pool.

The teachers' lounge was a great place to pick up on the latest gossip. It was said that Sam had once been in prison for something, nobody knew just what. Anyway, Sam made a right good living and was known as King Sam, the Barbecue Man, to most of the regulars. He was a big man who knew how to make money; he drove a maroon Buick with white-walled tires that were never dirty, and he fascinated Story. She refused to believe that prison stuff. "Niggers," Story said to Aleatha one day, "will pull anyone who's got anything down to their level, just for spite." Any black man who could make money and keep it fascinated her. He was in charge. He had respect from those pool-room types who bought his barbecue. They stuffed their faces and stayed ignorant, while Sam got rich. "I bet he laughs at them," she said, "I bet he calls them 'plantation niggers.' "

Story had never been inside King Sam's, of course. In the first place, it was in the wrong neighborhood. There were too many dirty, loud, and uncouth Negroes on the streets there and in and out of places like that. She had no way of knowing about Sam's rules firsthand, never having been in a "place like that" in her life, and she didn't even drive through "that section" if she could help it. Those were the people she imagined hung out at Sam's place. Her father's church was uncomfortably close to "them," however, and every Sunday morning she carefully parked her car on the far corner so that she could go in by the back door. That way she could avoid looking at the shotgun houses across the street, and at the dirty little children with runny noses who played in the dirt yards facing their church. She had headed up a committee of folks who wanted to raise money to build a new building in a "more appropriate" part of town, closer to the teacher's college. Her papa would turn over in his grave if he knew what "his folks" had to look at every Sunday morning, not to speak of Hermine being exposed to that everytime they went to church. Common, sinful riff-raff, folks who didn't have the gumption to go out and better themselves. Didn't have what it took to make it in the world. One thing you could say about him. He had worked hard every day of his life, and built that church up too.

The building committee didn't get very far because they already owed for the new car they had just bought the pastor, and then there was her daddy's mausoleum, which had cost them a pretty penny, so folks were not in the mood to talk building; but she would bring it up again, and she would keep bringing it up until something was done. They deserved better, they really did. They had all worked hard to get where they were in life, at least most of them. They still had a few shiftless types in the congregation, but for the most part she thought it was a good group of people, good workers even if they were kind of ordinary.

Story finally met Sam at a school function. He had a young daughter who had attended the school where Story worked, and one year she'd been in Story's room. One night he showed up at the school for a program the youngsters were in, and Faith had introduced her teacher to her father. When they were introduced, he said softly, "*Very* pleased to meet you." Story thought he was attracted to her. She carried herself with dignity. She had class, and was certainly above most of the women he'd seen lately; she'd put money on that. She thought there was a good chance he might really be interested. At first it never occurred to her that he might be looking for a wife, but she certainly knew how to wear the clothes he could buy her.

Finally he asked her out for dinner and dancing. They went to the Sideways Club, a kind of dinner club where there was a small dance area and you could get a good meal. There was a cover charge, which was beyond the reach of the types who came to his place.

They arrived at the Sideways about nine-thirty. It was on the outskirts of town, past the last house in the black neighborhood. Story wore a gold taffeta dress with a gently flared skirt and a low-cut, figure-flattering bodice, just low enough, but not so low it was cheap. The gold color set off the dark brown of her velvet skin. She had chosen small rhinestones for earrings and a small decorative hat. Her high cheekbones seemed accentuated, and her eyes were very bright. Sam was all eyes when they crossed the threshold of the small but nicely done club. It was painted blue inside, and there were small tables with blue candles on them and blue and white tablecloths. Sam ordered piña coladas for them, and the live jazz band played something blue and modern.

Late in the evening they were up for their last dance. As usual someone who had had too much to drink tried to make trouble, this time by trying to cut in on Sam and dance with Story. When he first tapped Sam on the shoulder, Sam said, "This one's taken, son." Then he tried it again, a little rougher. "I said, this lady's taken, son," Sam repeated. "Try elsewhere." The third time, Sam didn't waste any words. He simply said "Excuse me" to Story, lifted the drunk up by his lapels, and propelled him toward the front door. When he returned, the whole dance floor was turned in Sam's direction and the music had stopped. Sam motioned to the band, and they seemed properly impressed.

Story was beginning to be quite interested in this man. She fantasized about life as his wife, and remembered life as it had been with Herman. It had been a long time since she had had a man. She wondered if it would be any different after so long. Would it be any better? Once in a while she had flashes of how it could be. She'd dream of doing it with men of all kinds, handsome men, rich men, some white, some black. The dream was always better than the real thing had been. She always woke up hot and ready, but then there was no one there to see her flushes or hear her moans, and she was glad. No one should ever see anyone like that. She didn't even know how it happened. It seemed involuntary, beyond her control. The whole business was disgusting and degrading; she remembered Mr. J. and how weak he was. It was one of life's humiliating necessities, like going to the bathroom or washing under your arms. Sam could give her money and security, though, and that just might be worth a little sex. Security and a maid and a house in that new development for blacks.

She liked his good manners and his careful dressing. Sam had been around enough to romance a woman like Story. He knew how to give just the right present with the right touch of gallantry. He had brought her a box of imported chocolates, not the common drugstore type, but French. Each one was wrapped in its own little gold wrapper. That night he came in with a bunch of cymbidiums, and he even knew what to call them. Story was thrilled, but she wore them as if she were used to such extravagance and deserved it. He said he liked that about her, she was never ordinary, never common, and never seemed naive. When the Sideways Club closed for the night, she sat as close to him as she could without being too forward, and the shiny maroon Buick pulled out of the parking lot.

After that night they were together almost every weekend for practically a year—dancing in the black nightclubs around the state, going to art museums that were open to colored, finding respectable black restaurants in places like Raleigh and Charlotte, traveling in his fancy car.

Aleatha was excited for Story, pushing her to keep after Sam for a possible husband. "You won't never have to worry about a thing, Honey," she said, slicing the air with her left hand, a regular gesture of hers. "You won't never have to worry about no bills, and about educating little Hermine. Girl, you don't marry him, I'll beat you with a stick!"

Story grew to like being squired around and shown off. This was what she had never had with Herman. He wouldn't have known anybody important enough to show her off to. Sam introduced her to a lot of people. He knew lawyers in the area and aspiring black politicians, educators, and others whose professions she couldn't identify; but they all had one thing in common—they all seemed to have more money that she did. She had never known there were that many prosperous blacks in the South. Sam was invited to lots of parties. She was glad to have somewhere to go, places where people could appreciate her good taste, where people knew how to live. Sam Tucker had plenty of money. He talked to her about his business plans, opening a chain of restaurants and investing his money. Maybe someday, he said, he'd even give some money to one of the black colleges.

Soon they were a "couple" in town. People were curious and envious of them. They were thought of as "classy and rich." The day she took him to church, they made an entrance just before the service started. Story wore a smart cream and gray suit with a hat to match, and Sam was clean and lean. She knew heads were turning as they walked down the aisle together, and she liked it. Her papa's church was hers that morning. One of her friends at church had made a joke after meeting Sam on Sunday. "They tell me," Riva had said, "that you might be in a position to help out the building committee soon. They tell me King Sam's more than a little interested in takin' himself a new wife." She and Story were walking to their cars after the building committee meeting.

"Oh now, don't start that, Riva." Story blushed. "Don't start all that."

"Well, they say you looked like a million bucks at the last Teachers' Association dance. That's what they say." Story was a little embarrassed, but she loved outclassing folks, and she knew it. She had to admit that even to herself. It gave her some satisfaction that people had already started associating her with money, even though she was just a public school teacher. Being linked with Sam gave her the aura of the unordinary, and she loved it; she licked it up like a child with a batter bowl.

Once in a while when they were out together Sam would stop "on business" at places she thought looked a little shabby. But she never questioned him. He was a businessman, after all, and she supposed he knew what he was doing. He'd get out of the car, and she would wait one or two minutes for him to reappear. She never questioned much of anything he did. He made it so easy to be comfortable and excited. There was always something to do that was different and fun.

It wasn't long before Sam wanted to marry her, though he didn't tell her right away. After almost a whole year of dating, she still hadn't gone to bed with him. He thought she was just "that kind" of woman. Story had her reasons, which were her own business, of course. She thought holding out was effective as long as it kept him catering to her wishes, giving expensive presents, taking her on trips. When she sensed he was right on the edge, about ready to give up and go looking elsewhere, she gave in. He was everything she had fantasized about. She had never felt this good with any man. Before they had even put their clothes on, he proposed.

He wasn't like any man she'd ever known. There was nothing conventional about Sam, except what he wanted the public to see. He thought most people were fools and said so; and he said he was just playing a game with them, so he could stay on top. He liked Story's class, he said. She was no fool, and underneath her facade of perfection, Sam had tapped into a part of Story that had never been tamed.

"That preacher daddy of yours never knew you could do *that*," he said, roaring with laughter after an hour or two of lovemaking. "I'm exhausted, girl. You 'bout to give me a heart attack!" He had given her some sex magazines; he said they would warm her up. Story reluctantly looked at the photographs, ready to be repulsed. She was shocked, but to her surprise, very excited. She had never seen anything like these pictures. The women were shamelessly voluptuous. They wore skimpy, suggestive underwear or were naked, and they were posed in all kinds of sexual positions with men and with women, "I got them from 'a source,'" he said when she asked him where they came from. "You can't buy these anywhere in stores."

It was a whole world she didn't know existed. The photos made her want to do things she had never thought of. It was almost frightening that something could have this effect on her, but she loved it. She had never felt anything close to these feelings with Herman. She loved letting herself fall loose and almost swimming in these feelings.

"How'd you know I wouldn't throw you out of my house?" Her laughter sounded like low, watery bubbles, very unlike her usual sharp, tight guffaws.

"Oh, I know you, girl, I know you better than you know yourself. I know there were some still waters there that the right man could stir up. Could tell by the way you walk," he said, patting her on her behind.

Somehow with Sam, she felt she was not being used, being leaned on. Story thought she was just as much in control of things as he was. Sam was different. She nearly forgot the decision she had made at sixteen, never to let herself be taken in by a man.

They took to looking at the books together every time they went to bed. She took some home in her large purse one night, so she could enjoy them while Sam was out of town. It was their little secret.

He was building her a magnificent house. Brick. Eleven rooms. Surrounded by a brick wall. There would be two plaster lions, one on each side of the driveway. It was so big that it dwarfed all the other houses in the colored development. Aleatha said it looked like they were building a school or something, but then she wouldn't know any better. Every week they'd go to visit the house and see if his instructions were being followed to the letter. Sam had imported the front door from England, and there were custom-made cornices over all the windows. He wanted the wedding at the Negro Episcopal church instead of at her father's church. Sam said all the best people went there. Story wondered where that left her, but she agreed. She was beginning to think of this as an adventure, after all, and he was paying for all of it.

He wanted her to wear French lace, cream-colored. She was sure she looked better in a color—rose especially. The day she was to pick out her dress in Raleigh, he insisted on going. "But Sam," she said, "it's a woman's thing. You'll be bored to death. I'll take Aleatha." He would *not* have her going without him.

They parked the Buick in front of the expensive shop, called Birmingham's, and walked in. One of the women working there walked quickly toward them. They weren't used to having colored even come into their shop, and routinely asked "negras" to leave, but these two were well-dressed. There was something different about them. "What can I do for ya'll," the woman said loud enough to be heard by the security guard in the back. A second woman had disappeared through a door in the back of the room.

Sam had known how it would be. He had known that he might have to be very insistent in such an exclusive shop. He was used to handling people, even some white people. It was 1955, after all. The Supreme Court had just ruled on school desegregation last year. Things were beginning to change, and he wasn't about to be humiliated. "We'd like to see your finest French lace," he said in a booming but cultivated voice. "Suitable for the lady's wedding." He could see a large muscular man leaning not so discreetly against the back wall. All the clerks looked as if they had just been invaded by aliens. They seemed to be immobilized.

"Just a minute, sir," one of the less timid ones said. She was not about to let this woman try one of their dresses on. "Uh, what size does the, uh, lady wear?"

Story looked her most dignified. "Nine," she said quietly.

"The *lady* wears a nine," Sam said. The word "lady" stood in the air like a living thing. The clerk flinched.

"Well, that is just the size of our model, Miss Jenine. Ya'll just have a seat," she drawled, "and she'll be right out to model for you." The head clerk pushed "Miss Jenine" into the back with one hand, while she was indicating where they were to sit with the other. Then she disappeared into the racks to select something, and brought out the tackiest, most expensive thing in the shop. It was tight-fitting down to below the hip line, and then there were rows and rows of lace around the knees. The neckline was cut very low.

Sam said, "I *said* a wedding, not a honky-tonk." She got the idea and slipped another dress to Jenine without a word. The security guard continued to watch them.

Story whispered something to him about rose or blue. "Now, Honey, you know I want to see my lady in something that'll make her look gorgeous," Sam whispered back. He was fingering a long cigar that looked imported. He patted her on the knee. "Just you wait. You'll like it." It was a nice dress. It made Jenine look better than she probably ever had, and Story thought it really was a pretty dress, but it wasn't her. She would never buy it for herself. "Miss Jenine" pranced up and down for a while, clearly not used to being a model. And then Sam boomed out, "We'll take it," before she had a chance to ask about seeing anything else in the shop. He flashed his cash around, paid the whole three hundred dollars, and lit up his cigar while Jenine got back into her own clothes.

"Give the girls in there something to talk about for weeks," he said to Story on the way out to the car. And they laughed about it all the way to Hattenfield. Through all the laughter, Story was thinking about a beautiful rose dress she had glimpsed in Birmingham's. She was laughing with Sam, but part of her laugh was lost under that cream-colored dress she really didn't like. When they got back that night, she decided not to ask Sam in. She decided she didn't feel like it. Story kissed Sam lightly and ran into the house, saying she was anxious to check on Hermine, who had been left at Aleatha's for the night. She needed to call her and see how she was. Sam looked puzzled, but he seemed happy enough to give in to his bride's inconsistencies.

Story stayed up for a long time that night. It was a hot summer. She could hear the insects buzzing outside. She was thinking of Bertie. Being with Sam today had reminded her that she seemed to be acting like Bertie more and more lately. It didn't do to jump too fast when he called, she thought. She let Sam call the tunes too much. All his money wasn't worth being the kind of woman who let herself be led around by the nose. On the other hand, she sure wouldn't want to make him mad. He was a valuable asset in her life, probably the best thing she'd ever done for herself. Maybe after the wedding she could ease in her own opinions more, be more herself. She certainly didn't want to be anything like Bertie, crying after a man, bowing and scraping to him. She didn't much like the thought of that. She didn't like the thought of that at all.

When she remembered it later, she knew it was his wedding that got planned that summer; his wedding all the way. His dress, and his flowers, and his wedding guests. She had invited about fifty people. All the rest of the 250 people were invited by him. His daughter would be the maid of honor. Hermine was too old to be a flower girl; but he had a niece just the right age.

Story could tell Hermine was really enjoying the whole business. She got to spend a lot of time with Faith Tucker and a lot more time with Aleatha's children. It was convenient for Story; she didn't have to worry about getting home early, and so Hermine stayed away from home almost every weekend, either with Aleatha or with Sam's daughter. Story was excited and lighthearted, and less annoyed with Hermine than she had ever remembered. Hermine was to wear a pink dotted-swiss dress and to help with the gifts. That was what she had asked for, a pink dotted-swiss dress.

The fabric store was on Jones Street near the hardware store. They had the best material in town, Story told Hermine.

"Well, do they have dotted swiss?" Hermine asked.

"Of course, silly." Story laughed at Hermine's straightforward practical way of looking at things; the child was always so sober. She went right to the heart of things, that was for sure.

Story pulled the car up in front of Kraus Hardware. Early Saturday morning it was full of farmers and workingmen getting ready for a day's work. The weather was fine, clear and cool, a beautiful blue sky. One of the white farmers actually tipped his hat at them as they got out of the car. Story smiled at Hermine and winked as if they had a private joke. Hermine smiled back. "White folks are certainly strange," Story said. "One day they are lynching you, the next, they are tipping their hats. Be careful, though, Hermine, don't ever forget. They never forget who you are. Look at what they do, not what they say. We're always niggers to them."

Hermine didn't answer. The saleslady in the fabric shop knew Story. She often had her clothes made, and shopped there to select unusual fabrics. The clerk thought of her as that "colored schoolteacher" who was "different," and had said as much to Story. "You're so classy, different, you know," she said. "It's a pleasure waiting on you always. You know, you have such beautiful manners and all." Story knew that she really wanted to say "different from those other niggers who come in here," but she bit her tongue. The clerk made a big fuss over the wedding.

"The little girl wants dotted swiss in pink?" she said in her southern drawl. "Well, I've got just the thing." They ambled to the part of the store where those bolts were stacked up among the yellow and white cottons.

"I want her to have the best," she said protectively.

"Such a cute little girl," the clerk drooled. "Now she's your daughter, isn't she? Or . . ."

"Niece, she's my niece." This woman was truly trying her patience. Story turned her back on the woman and pretended to be looking at some fabric. She looked at Hermine to see if she had noticed. Hermine appeared to have missed the reference to a daughter.

"Oh, I'm sooorry. She looks enough like you to be a daughter! Now ain't you a lucky little thing to have such a smart aunt?"

"Could we . . . ?"

"Oh, yes," the woman said. "Here we are!"

She pulled out three bolts of different quality material. "Now this is your ordinary kind," she said. "Twenty-five cents a yard, thirty-nine inches wide." Story shook her head no. Hermine was silent but very interested. "And this," she said, "is our good quality. Most of our colored church ladies buy this." Story fingered the second roll and dismissed it.

"Well," the clerk said, "if you want to spend sixty cents a yard, there is the top quality." She pulled out the pink bolt. Hermine grinned. It was thick and lush and the dots were soft and just right.

"We'll take three yards," Story said. "But we must look at the patterns first." The patterns in the big books that looked like paper doll books seemed to fascinate Hermine. "You would love to have one of these, wouldn't you?" Story said. "You could make up some paper dolls with this." She smiled at Hermine again. "Now you just have a good time and see what you want the most." Story was very patient. She felt a kind of satisfaction. She was finally going to have something good that she didn't have to fight for. Finally she would have some money, a way to have the things that made life worthwhile. Someone to help her with everything.

Hermine chose a full-skirted pattern with puffed sleeves. Story liked another pattern. An A-line with capped sleeves. She thought it was elegant. "Are you sure, honey?" she said. It was one of the few times in Hermine's life she had called her by a pet name. Hermine nodded.

"Well . . . fine, it'll be fine. We'll put flowers in your hair. Won't you look pretty?" She squeezed Hermine's hand.

Hermine hugged the package to her chest as they passed Kraus's and got into the car. "How about an ice cream soda now?" Story suggested. "We could go to Chavis's little place. You know we can't go to Woolworth's. White people think we goin' to poison them, I reckon. You sure have lost your tongue today, Hermine," she said, starting up the car. "Smile! It's a beautiful day!"

—

Every morning she felt like she'd had two glasses of champagne—picking out dresses for the girls, anticipating the reception. The last time she was married, things were not right. Aleatha and some friend of Herman's standing up for them in that dismal country Baptist church on First Street. It was dusty and depressing. But she had her second chance now, and nothing was going to stop her happiness. Story bubbled over and smiled more than she ever had. It was wonderful to have enough money to do things right; it was wonderful to imagine being Mrs. Sam Tucker.

She knew Hermine thought that Faith was going to live with them. One day she asked Story if she'd ever have to stay alone in that big house. Story thought she'd tell her later that Faith would be going away to a private school up north. But that would come later. She didn't want to do anything unpleasant now, and she knew that Hermine would be a big baby about Faith's leaving. She'd tell her after it was all arranged. That would be better. She'd tell her they'd have a maid and she'd never be alone.

—

Sam Tucker's daughter was sleek and beautiful. So sleek and beautiful that Hermine didn't know any words to think about her. She just felt warm all over when Faith came to the house, or Aunt Story said she could go over there to spend the night. Faith had a bedroom like Hermine had seen in the movies. It had white dotted swiss curtains, and pink chenille bedspreads, and twin beds. "Faith Tucker," Hermine would say to herself. She didn't know anybody else with a name like that. The bedroom had a white chifforobe and pink throw rugs in front of each bed. On the chifforobe there was a ballerina music box, and Faith called the ballerina Marie. It played "The Blue Danube" waltz. They looked under the bottom and saw that Marie had blue eyes and blond curls, and Faith said she was beautiful. Everytime they wound it up, Hermine thought about her dancing lessons and she felt bad again. She was too embarrassed to tell Faith about forgetting "The Blue Danube" waltz. It was just too terrible. Faith said her boyfriend had given her the music box.

There was a window seat in the room that looked out over some trees. It was spring and the leaves were just tiny buds. Hermine couldn't wait until summer. She would come over every day if she could sit and stare out of that wonderful window seat. Her room looked out into the street, and all she could see was the milkman, Mr. Petree, coming every morning to deliver a quart of milk. Faith had a bookshelf with grown-up books on it, and she told Hermine she would read to her when she had time. But best of all there was a dressing table. A dressing table with a skirt of white dotted swiss, and a mirror glass top that was almost as magic as the ballerina. You could see yourself in the mirror on the table and in the mirror in front of the dressing table. She didn't always want to look in the mirrors, because it would remind her that she wasn't grown-up or even pretty, but she looked anyway.

Faith had lots of powder and stuff on the dressing table. She was sixteen and she could wear that stuff. Hermine thought it would be an eternity before she got to be sixteen and she would be allowed to go to the beauty parlor and get her hair fixed so it would sit on her shoulders like Faith's. An eternity before she could stop wearing those braids and those glasses. Faith said her mother had been real light and had had good hair, but she got some of her father's hair and some of her father's color, and because of that she had to have her hair straightened. Anyway, Hermine still thought she was the most beautiful girl she had ever seen.

She and Faith could be sisters, because she didn't have a mama and neither did Faith. But Faith was lucky because she had a daddy and her daddy was rich. She'd like to have a daddy too. Faith's daddy was real nice to her. He let her do anything she wanted. Faith said so. But Hermine didn't have a daddy she could talk about; she only had Aunt Story, and Aunt Story wasn't enough.

Faith had a book about a girl named Heidi, and Hermine asked her to read from it over and over. Heidi only had a grandfather. She didn't have a mother. But her grandfather was real nice to her. He gave her strawberries and cream, and they lived on a mountain, and Heidi had a friend named Peter. Sometimes she'd close her eyes and dream about being like Heidi and having a grandfather just like Grandfather in *Heidi*. And she would live in a little mountain cabin and eat strawberries and goat cheese that her grandfather made. If you had a grandfather, you had to have a father. She wondered a lot about her father. Maybe she had a grandfather someplace too. She wanted to ask Aunt Story about it, but she was scared. She was scared it would be the wrong thing to ask.

One day Aunt Story took her to Hattenfield State Library with her because she had some work to do, and Hermine brought Faith's book with her, but it wasn't Faith's book anymore, it was her book. Faith had said, "Take it. I don't read it anymore, and you love it. You can have it."

While she waited for Aunt Story, she looked at the pictures of Heidi and her grandfather. After about an hour Aunt Story was ready to go. All of a sudden she asked it before she had a chance to be scared. "Do I have a grandfather, Aunt Story?"

Aunt Story shushed her. They were still in the library. As they walked down the steps, she said, frowning, "Now what did you ask me?"

"Do I have a grandfather?"

"Of all the ridiculous questions. Don't you think if you had a grandfather you would know it? Of course not, child."

The silence settled around Hermine. She screwed her mouth around slightly. They got in the car.

"Why *not*?" she said finally.

"Hermine, you do ask the most annoying questions. If you do, I don't know it. I would assume he's dead by now." She changed gears and stopped for a light.

"What about my father?"

Story sighed. "I told you. He's dead."

"Why?"

"A car accident. I *told* you. They were killed."

"Was he rich?"

Story looked at Hermine briefly and then back at the traffic. She shook her head and sighed again. "Of course not. Whoever gave you that idea? Faith?"

"What did he look like?"

"This is enough of *this*! Stop reading such silly books that put silly questions in your head!"

When they got home, Aunt Story unlocked the front door. Hermine clutched her copy of *Heidi* and ran up to the bathroom. At dinner there was mostly the sound of chewing and the clicking of forks and knives. Hermine thought about strawberries and cream and goat milk while she ate her mashed potatoes and chicken. She knew she'd be alone in her room after dinner and Aunt Story would be busy reading or working. She'd be in her room, Aunt Story would be in her room. And Hermine would feel alone like she did most of the time when she wasn't with Faith.

———

Faith told her stories about what sixteen-year-olds did, about boys and stuff that was important. They sat in her beautiful bedroom and talked. Hermine liked the smell of powder and lipstick and perfume, and she liked looking at the pictures of Faith's boyfriends on the walls. Faith had a yearbook from her high school, and there was a picture of her with a real short majorette skirt on; Hermine always asked if they could look at the yearbook first. Faith was one of the best majorettes in the school and she had a real silver baton that she twirled with rubber balls on the end. Hermine wanted more than anything to learn how to twirl that baton. Faith promised to teach her some afternoon, but mostly they just sat while Faith talked on the phone to one of her boyfriends. Hermine would remember the time she saw Faith throwing her baton up in the air, and her long hair flying out with the wind, and her eyes sparkling. Her legs would move in time to the music, and she wore wonderful white boots and Dunbar High's colors, red and white. The colored high school had ten majorettes, and she was the head majorette. Hermine would sneak looks at Faith when she was on the phone so she wouldn't be staring. Aunt Story said staring was rude and people wouldn't like you, and she wanted Faith to like her. More than having long hair, more than being a majorette, she wanted Faith to like her.

Faith was her "babysitter," but Hermine hated that name; she wasn't a baby. Faith called her her "little friend." One day she said, "You're my 'little friend,' how's that?" Hermine thought about it all day. Faith's face when she said it, the smile on her face, her perfect teeth, her beautiful brown eyes, and her warm hand in hers as they crossed the street.

She couldn't go as much as she wanted to, because she wanted to go every day. She wanted to live there, at King Sam's house with Faith. She felt safe with her; warm and safe like the hot cocoa they sometimes had at night at home. She felt like someone would always be with her and she wouldn't ever be alone like she was at home.

One day maybe she'd come home and there'd be nobody home, and nobody would ever come home again. She had dreams about this sometimes. And one day maybe she'd have to go to the Children's Home. But she thought Faith would always be there, at least she felt like that when they were together. It felt warm, like good times, even when Faith was busy doing her homework.

Aunt Aleatha was like that, but not as much, because she had all those children. She couldn't be hers alone like Faith. Faith said she didn't babysit for any more "little friends." Hermine was the only one. That made her feel real good. She was flying inside when Faith said that. She even practiced walking on her toes like Marie, the ballerina. She felt like flying right up to the moon and never coming back, and she and Faith could live there together. They could live happily ever after somewhere.

Faith was King Sam's daughter and she always had lots of money. She bought Hermine lots of treats—ice cream at Woolworth's and popcorn at the movies. They'd go to the colored door and take their popcorn upstairs to the colored seats. Faith said it was shameful, but what could they do about it? Hermine didn't know, but she believed Faith was right. Maybe it was shameful. Maybe colored folks did something to be treated like that. She didn't know, but she was glad to be with Faith. Sometimes they went to King Sam's and had free dinner if Aunt Story was out for the whole evening, and that was the best of all.

Faith had had lots of slumber parties. She told Hermine about them. How the girls talked girl talk and rolled up their hair and stayed up until five o'clock in the morning. One time when Aunt Story had to go out of town to a meeting, she had to go so far away that she went on a train, and Aunt Aleatha had to take care of her mother, who was sick, so there was nowhere else for Hermine to stay except with the Tuckers. Faith kept her and she taught Hermine something secret. Something secret about things Hermine didn't know.

They had dinner at King Sam's. Great barbecue and french fries. And then they took a walk and listened to some of Faith's records. Sam Cooke or the Dells. She got records for free, she said, because her daddy had a friend who was in the recording business. Faith was very excited. She was going to the senior prom with the most popular boy in Dunbar High School. He had a scholarship to Howard University and he was going to be a doctor. One day she would marry him and they would have lots and lots of money and six babies and a big house. She talked to Hermine just like she was one of her girlfriends at a slumber party, telling her all of her secrets.

They were in Faith's room, and the milk-glass lamp was lit on the dressing table, and it made the pink bedspreads even pinker. Hermine felt sleepy after her bath. She had on her flannel pj's and her hair was rolled up in paper curlers. Faith said, "I'm goin' to show you how we do it," and she tore the strips of paper and twisted them, and then she twisted Hermine's hair around the paper strips. "Tomorrow," Faith said, "you'll have curls just like mine." Hermine felt all warm and squiggly. She scrunched down in her bed opposite Faith, wishing, wishing she lived there in that house.

"Do you know what they do?" Faith said.

Hermine had no idea what she was talking about. "Who?" she asked, pulling up her covers.

"Boys. They make you feel all warm and hot," she said, slipping her feet out of her baby-doll slippers. "Boys are wonderful, but you have to know how to treat them. They shouldn't think that you're easy, or they can have you just because they ask. You have to play hard to get."

Hermine watched Faith take off her robe. It was made of some white soft stuff. Under it was a long nightgown with little blue flowers on it, and she pulled it up over her knees and crossed her legs on her bed. Hermine could see she didn't have any panties on, but Faith didn't seem to notice. Hermine turned her eyes away, embarrassed.

"You have to fool them into thinking you don't want them to do it even if you want them to. That's what nice girls do anyway."

"Even if you want them to do what?" Hermine asked. She felt too hot under the bedspread and threw it off, leaving only the sheet.

"Even if you want them to, you know, kiss you, or touch you *there*. I've known some girls who've done it already."

"Done what?"

"Don't you know *anything*?" Faith said, plumping up her pillows.

She didn't want Faith to think she was dumb and a baby. "Sure I do," Hermine lied. "I know. Aunt Story told me a little bit. Something secret."

"Well then, I know some girls who've done it. And they said . . . oh gosh, they said it was the best thing that ever happened to them." Faith shivered a little and got under the covers. They were very quiet for a few minutes. Hermine was thinking about anything she might have heard that she could say Aunt Story had told her. Anything at all. She remembered some bad words she got in trouble for asking about, and somehow she knew they had something to do with boys and stuff, and babies. She thought it had something to do with how babies got born, she thought.

Faith looked up at the light on the dressing table. "Go turn off the light, Hermine," she said. Hermine slid out of bed. King Sam was out. They were alone in the dark in the house. She was standing there in her yellow flannel pajamas, with her hair rolled up in paper-bag bows.

"Why don't you get in with me?" Faith said. "It'll be more comfy that way. We can keep each other company while Daddy is out. I don't like being in this big old house without him downstairs." She moved over to make room in the narrow bed, and Hermine squeezed into the space. Hermine lay with her legs very straight. Were you supposed to touch or not? She had only slept with Jamesina and Francis in the same bed at Aunt Aleatha's, and there was not enough room to keep from touching them. Besides, it seemed different somehow, more secret, more scary. They weren't playing under the covers to see if they could make each other laugh, or tickling each other. It felt too quiet. They both had the covers pulled up to their chins.

"My girlfriend, Rhonda, she told me what they do." Faith's voice was whispery and thin. "They touch you on your arms, and maybe even on your titties, and then on the legs, and then, you know what? Between the legs." Hermine knew it was true. It had to be true because Faith was saying it, but she didn't want to hear it. It was too exciting, and scary, and she didn't want to hear it, and there were funny feelings going on in her body that she didn't want to feel.

"And then," Faith said, "you get all watery inside, and then they stick it in. You know," she said, without Hermine asking anything, "their *thing*. They actually stick it *in* you." Her voice was tight and she sounded as if she was talking with her mouth closed instead of open. "They stick it in and move it in and out and you go crazy, and you're never the same again in your life!" Hermine could feel their legs touching all the way down to her feet.

"Let me do it on you," Faith said. She turned her head toward Hermine. "Let's just *see*, and then we'll know what it's like. And you can do it on me." Her voice was like tissue paper. Like Christmas wrapping paper. Hermine was sure it was wrong. It was secret. Nobody was home. It had to be wrong. She opened her mouth to say no, but nothing came out. "No," she said finally, barely moving her lips.

"And then," Faith said, as if Hermine had not said anything, "and then we will be blood sisters forever because we touched each other *down there*, and it'll be our secret forever! And we'll belong to each other, always."

It had to be wrong. You weren't supposed to touch anybody down there. Maybe something would happen to her, and Aunt Story would find out. It was only right if people were married, and girls never married girls on the radio or at the movies. You weren't supposed to touch if you weren't married. But maybe if they would really belong to each other, maybe then it wouldn't be so bad. And anyhow they didn't have a *thing* to stick inside. It was only touching like hands touching. And she would belong to someone. She would really have a sister who was hers, and no one could ever take her away. The beautiful majorette, who danced on the football field and threw her silver baton in the air, and caught it every time, every time. She never made a mistake. Faith must be right, and she would have a secret from Aunt Story. You weren't supposed to touch yourself down there, Aunt Story said it was filthy, but she didn't ever tell her why. But Aunt Story would never find this out, never as long as she lived.

"Please, Hermine, just a little bit. I just want to see what it's like,"

Faith whispered. "I'll be sweet to you forever, and you'll never have to be alone again. I won't hurt you. You'll be safe with me."

Hermine could smell Faith's toothpaste and soap, and the baby powder she had put on after her bath. She was so scared, and she was shaking, and maybe if there was a Hell, she would go there, but she didn't care right now. She loved Faith. It would be okay.

Faith moved her hand down Hermine's shoulder slowly. "I saw it in a movie," she said, "it's slow like, and then they kiss." And Hermine felt her lips being touched by something warm and soft. It made her tingle all over. She loved Faith. It would be okay. They would be blood sisters forever. That makes it okay. That makes it okay. She felt Faith's hand move slowly between her legs. She would belong to her forever. Forever. And that would make it okay.

"Now you do me," Faith said, with her voice all breath, like she had been running. "You do me just like I did you."

Touching yourself was filthy, but touching someone else wasn't. And they would be blood sisters forever. It was easy; just put your hand there and pet like you were petting a kitten, just like Faith had done to her. She could see the moon through the open dotted swiss curtains. The moon threw its light on their bed, and she put her hand on Faith. She could see the shadows of the young leaves through the open windows. "You promise," she said, "you promise to let me be your little friend, and your blood sister forever and ever, and never to tell anybody as long as you live?"

"Of course I do," Faith said, and she hugged Hermine, and Hermine could feel Faith's breasts under her white nightgown with the blue flowers on it. "Do you love me?" she whispered in Hermine's ear. "Do you love me enough to do it? Oh, please just do it before I die!" And she took Hermine's hand and put it on the soft hairs between her legs. "You have to put it *in*," she said, "or it doesn't count." She parted the hairs and put Hermine's hand where she wanted it. "Oh, God," Faith said, "if it was only John, oh, God."

Hermine had felt her own body, only her own warm place. She didn't know it would feel good doing it to somebody else too. But it did. It did feel good, and she couldn't help it. "Now are we blood sisters?" she said to Faith. "Is it forever now?"

"Oh, John," Faith said, her voice muffled in the pillow. "Oh, John, oh, John, oh, John." She didn't say anything to Hermine. She just kept calling that boy's name, and curled herself into a little ball.

Hermine shook Faith's arm. "I did it," she said. "I did what you wanted. Are we friends forever now?" There was something on her hand that felt like blood. She didn't know what it was. She couldn't see what it was in the moonlight. But she wanted Faith to answer her, to hug her and tell her it was all right. Faith belonged to her now. She turned Faith's face toward her and looked at her in the moonlight. "Now are we what you said?"

"Go to sleep," Faith said. "We'll do it again sometime. Go get in your bed."

———

They did do it again, every time Hermine spent the night. And Faith would squeeze her hand when Aunt Story said, "Can you keep Hermine tonight?"

And then Aunt Story had told her the big news. She was going to marry King Sam and live in a big new house. They were just going down the aisle in the grocery store like everything was normal, and suddenly Aunt Story had said, "Oh, by the way, Hermine, I have some good news for you. Sam Tucker and I are going to be married this summer." She said it just like that, while she was throwing pork chops into the cart.

Hermine's mouth opened in surprise. What did it mean? What did it mean for her? She couldn't believe it, even though she knew her aunt had been going out at night with King Sam, and Faith had said, "My daddy likes your auntie, did you know that?" Still, she didn't really imagine Aunt Story would ever marry anybody. She was too old. She was, well . . . she was just Aunt Story. How could anybody marry her?

"Oh, come along Hermine. Don't be so silly," Aunt Story said. "Close your mouth and push the cart." What Story wanted to know was, would she get to see Faith? Would they live together now? She couldn't concentrate on peas and greens now. It was just too exciting. Would King Sam be her father? Or stepfather? She was full of questions she was afraid to ask. They finished the groceries with Aunt Story chattering about prices, and though Hermine started to ask her questions two or three times, she was just too scared.

But very soon she had something else to worry about. John was around all the time. And John would go with her and Faith to the park, and John would go with them to the movies, and once in a while Hermine even saw them kissing. Hermine had to go in the rec room to give them some more time for grown-up things, Faith said. Or she had to go in the living room if they wanted to use the rec room to play records.

Summer was coming fast, and Aunt Story would be out of school, and maybe things would be different after the wedding. One day Faith would graduate from high school too. Hermine was worried about that. John was going away to school. Maybe Faith was going too. John loved Faith. Hermine could tell. John sent letters and notes to Faith, and she would tell Hermine about what John would do when they were alone at the drive-in movie. And she thought Faith loved John too. She could tell by the way they kissed, and she was beginning to feel more and more lonesome when she stayed with Faith. They didn't do their secret touching very much at all, and after Faith talked to John on the phone until midnight, she just told Hermine to go to sleep in her own bed. It was too late, Faith would say. Or they had to get up early. John was going away to college soon. Hermine hoped he'd go to summer school this summer, and then maybe she'd have Faith all to herself again. After the wedding they'd be sisters for real. And they would be safe, and she would be Faith's "little friend" forever and ever.

—

The phone call that changed all their lives came two days before the big day. There were boxes everywhere. They had almost finished packing for the move. The phone rang and Aunt Story answered it.

When she hung up Story's face had changed so much, she almost looked like another woman. And then as she turned to go up the stairs, someone rang the front doorbell. Hermine saw Story's face and she saw the policeman standing on the other side of the screen, and she knew something terrible had happened. She ran into the kitchen and shut the door the way she always did when she was afraid of her aunt Story's anger. The white policeman was standing on the other side of the screen with a piece of paper in his hand. She heard him say, "Are you Mrs. Story Temple Greene?"

"Yes," she said.

"Is this your residence?" he said.

"Yes," Story said.

"Ma'am, I have an order here to question you."

Aunt Story opened the door. "Yes?" she said.

"Ma'am," he said, "do you know a Mr. Sam Tucker?"

"Yes," she said. Hermine cracked the kitchen door and peeked out.

"Well, ma'am," he said, "we just picked Sam Tucker up on suspicion of selling drugs. We also have an order here for searching your premises, for concealment of drugs. It may not be necessary for you to come to the station if we're satisfied with our questioning and our search, but we need to talk to you," and he motioned for another policeman, who was standing on the porch, to come inside. Story led them into the living room. Hermine could still see her aunt, but nobody else. "Please sit down, ma'am," he said, inviting her to a seat in her own house. She sat down and he sat down. "Now, Story," he said, "our sources inform us that, uh, you and Sam Tucker were planning to get married, uh, this coming Saturday. Is that correct?"

"Yes, sir," Story said, looking directly into his eyes with her stony gaze.

"Well, uh, now how much do you know about Mr. Tucker's activities, Story?" He had dropped the "ma'am" in favor of the old southern custom of calling all black people by their first names.

"Nothing," she said. "Nothing at all."

"Uh, based on our information, we're inclined to believe you. But you understand, we have to check some things out."

Story said, "Yes, of course I do." Her voice was a monotone.

Back in the kitchen, Hermine was trying to listen and trying not to listen. She closed the door and sat on the floor with her head down in her arms, wondering what awful things would happen next. Uncle

Sam, "King" Sam, was arrested on some kind of charges she didn't understand. She knew that that meant the wedding was off, and that it probably meant they wouldn't be moving into the new big brick house. She didn't care about the house. It meant leaving her friends, after all. What she cared about was what would happen to her now that Aunt Story would be upset and mad, and probably mean again. It was just that Aunt Story never had loved her before this summer, and she seemed to have loved her a little ever since she had known King Sam.

She let her visit the Joyces as much as she wanted. She hugged her and touched her. She even sang songs in the house while she worked in the kitchen. And Hermine had Faith, and they were going to be real sisters forever and ever. She didn't know if she could go back to being without Faith and being afraid all the time. There probably would be no more hugs; there probably would be no more singing in the house. She felt sick to her stomach.

It must have been another hour before she heard things moving in the living room. She couldn't hear much conversation, just snatches here and there. She heard people moving around now, opening drawers, going upstairs. She went into the backyard and sat under the tree that she always sat under when things got bad. They were looking in the kitchen drawers, up under the dishcloths, behind the food, even in the refrigerator. She didn't know what they were looking for, but she knew it was something terrible. She was going to ask Aunt Aleatha what had happened. Aunt Aleatha would know; she knew everything. She knew all kinds of things Hermine was afraid to ask her aunt Story about. She'd ask her aunt Aleatha. She wanted to run over to Aunt Aleatha's house, but she was afraid to move. Maybe they would arrest her for running away. She heard that when people ran away, it seemed like they were guilty, and she wasn't guilty of anything that she knew about.

Maybe Aunt Story would have to go to jail. That would just be too horrible to believe, too horrible to think about. She sat under the tree and dug a little stick into the ground, making a hole deeper and deeper, a hole she thought it would be nice to crawl into if she could get it big enough. She saw a little ant that crawled into the hole and the dirt fell in over it. Poor little ant; buried in the dirt, buried alive.

Finally she heard the police car start up and pull out of the driveway. She could go back in the house now, but she was afraid to see Aunt Story. Maybe they had taken Aunt Story away with them. Maybe she was all alone in the house. She crept back in the house, opening the screen door and shutting it so quietly that no one could have heard her come in. Hermine pushed the kitchen door gently and looked through a tiny slit into the dining room. There was nobody there. There seemed to be nobody in the house at all. She walked through the dining room, through the living room, and then she saw Aunt Story, slowly walking up the steps, holding onto the banisters like an old, old woman. And her face looked like it had aged ten years in the last two hours. She wasn't crying, at least not on the outside, but she was clutching the banister almost as if she had had a heart attack, and walking slower than Hermine had ever seen her walk before. She just looked at Aunt Story, afraid to open her mouth.

Story looked at Hermine, and what she said was a complete shock. "I don't want you going over to that Joyce household unless I tell you you can, and maybe never again. And you're never to see that Faith again either." Then she disappeared around the landing on the way to her bedroom. Hermine could not believe her ears! She couldn't mean it. It couldn't be true! She couldn't go visit the Joyces. She couldn't see Faith! Her special blood sister. The one she belonged to and touched! She couldn't see Aunt Aleatha or Jamesina or Francis or Thomas or Harold or even the new baby. What had happened? What awful thing had happened?

She ran to the telephone. At least she could call up and find out. At least she could call. She dialed the number, TE-23345. She couldn't get her words out. Finally she managed to squeeze out "Hello."

Aunt Aleatha said, "Hermine, baby? Is that you?"

Hermine wiped her wet face with her arm. "Why can't I come over there?" she said through the sobs. "Aunt Story says I can't come over there until she says I can, maybe never. Something awful happened. The police were here and she says I can't come over there anymore."

Aleatha didn't know what to say. She had no idea what had gotten into Story's head, but she knew it had something to do with Sam and this whole mess. "I don't know, baby, 'bout you comin' over here, but I know King Sam done got hisself in a bad mess. Look like he ain't what your auntie thought he was. He's a bad man, and he got bad trouble, sellin' that stuff that makes people crazy, that stuff they call dope. Folks pays a lot of money for that stuff. Anyhow, you should be glad they caught him 'fore your Aunt Story got herself married to the likes a him. Then she sho 'nuff be in bad trouble. And don't you worry. Let a little time go by. She'll give in and let you come back. I gotta go see 'bout the baby now. You can call me any time, okay?"

Hermine let the phone down slowly. She didn't want to let Aunt Story hear her crying. Her head hurt and her shoulders shook. There was nothing to do, nowhere to go. Faith's daddy had been arrested. He was a bad man. There would be police over there, everywhere. She was afraid to call. Maybe they would arrest Faith too. Maybe Faith would be sent away. She thought she knew the way to Faith's house. She would go there, but it was across town, a long, long walk. She would run away, pack a bag and go to Aunt Aleatha's or to their neighbor, Mrs. Stroud down the street.

She started looking for a suitcase, wiping her eyes with her hands and blowing her nose with toilet tissue. They were somewhere in a closet, she thought. She mustn't make any noise going upstairs. She must get away to Faith somehow. Hermine opened all the closets upstairs except for Aunt Story's, afraid to make any noise, afraid to be caught. What had happened to the suitcases? Then she remembered. They had all been packed for the move. They were all in Aunt Story's room.

It had started getting dark outside. She sat down on the stairs and put her head down in her arms. The police were out there now, and she'd forgotten the way. It was too far to walk anyway. Maybe I could just die, she thought. If I never ate again, I would die and it would all go away. She held herself by the elbows and rocked back and forth. The carpet was soft and gray through her tears. She ran her finger through the dust on the baseboard next to the carpet and moved down another step, sitting down. It was too hard to go and too hard to stay. She'd never belong to anybody now, she knew that. Faith wasn't really her sister anyway. Hermine drew another line in the dusty wood. Faith loved John anyway, she thought, as she scooted down another step. It was just like everything else; it was too good to be true. A fairy story, not true. No blood sister, no little special friend, no belonging to anybody. She had moved all the way to the bottom of the stairs. Her hands were filthy.

———

Story sat holding herself in, holding herself still so that she wouldn't fly apart into two thousand pieces. There was no need to question why or how it had happened. It had just happened. The way marriage to Herman had happened, the way Bertie's death had happened, and having a baby had happened. And now the only thing to think about was how to survive this disaster. How to put her life back together so she wouldn't look like a complete fool to people. She could not find the words for her anger. It felt like a fire inside her, or a deep pit of dark swirling water. Even when Bertie did what she did, people didn't know exactly what had happened because she had hidden it. But there was no hiding this. Everybody who knew them would know that she had been led to the slaughter like a stupid sheep. Would know that she had connected herself to a man who was lower than the worst wino on the street corner. A man who tried to be something he wasn't.

How could he have allowed himself to get caught? she thought. How could he have put her in that position? And how could I not see any clearer? How could I have been taken in? It's as if I was high on one of his drugs without taking anything. I should have known that no black man could have that kind of money without doing something illegal. It just didn't happen in this world.

It all stood before her like a great wreck—the house, the wedding. It all looked ridiculous and clownish. The house would become the symbol of her folly. "Story's Folly." The plaster lions would be pointed at. The eleven rooms would be discussed. The oak paneling and the custom-made drapes would be clucked at. And for years to come people would ask why that great house was there in the middle of a development for colored, and someone would answer, "Let me tell you about what happened." She would become the object of laughter and ridicule, a melodramatic story that people told when they wanted something to tell at parties that would make other people laugh. How many people had she told she was going to have a maid? A fairy tale. She had believed in a fairy tale, in dreams coming true! She had seen herself presiding over that damn house, having parties, serving canapés, dinners to important people! Stupid, stupid. She was too angry. Suddenly she found herself shaking all over. She didn't know what to do with anger like this. Her stomach cramped. She ran to the bathroom with diarrhea.

It was too familiar. Too much like being a child again. Maybe if she'd lie down, she'd have some control over her body and she could think better. She hadn't felt so helpless in a long time. Not since Papa's beatings. She thought about moving away, but that seemed impossible now that she had only her income to fall back on, and she had put too many years of service into that school system. She had run up lots of bills, bills that she thought Sam would be paying. She went over it and over it, looking for a way to fix it, but there was no way out of this humiliation, this exposure. She felt naked, like she was standing at the top of a hill and everybody in town was standing in the valley laughing and shouting and pointing. That's the way she felt, naked.

She began to drift off to sleep; it was easier to sleep than it was to face what had happened. It was a restless and terrifying sleep, dreams peopled by strange creatures walking in fearful landscapes. But the most frightening thing of all was a dream about Bertie standing over her bed.

At first she wasn't sure who it was, but then she knew her. Bertie looked exactly as she had looked on the last day of her life, and she was wearing the dress she had been wearing when Story found her on the bloodstained carpet. She was carrying Cecelia, and Story saw something on Bertie's arm. It was her dress, the dress that Sam had bought for her to get married in. In her dream she was more frightened than she had ever been in life. She said to Bertie, "What are you doing with my dress?" It was the dress that Sam had picked out, except it was not the color that Sam had picked out, it was that same dress, colored rose.

Bertie spoke. "You didn't think it could happen to you." She laughed diabolically. "You didn't think so. You thought you had it all under control. You didn't think the same thing could happen to you that happened to me, did you?" She laughed again. "Well, now you know, and I have it; I have your wedding dress, and I'm going to destroy it. You thought you could control me and Herman, and yourself, and anybody who got in your way. You were just like Papa, only you were a sneak. You had it all wrapped up in neat little boxes but you found out different. You found out that life turns on you and there's nothing you can do about it, and there are people in life who are stronger than you. You thought you knew it all. You thought you were smarter than everybody and knew it all, but you're helpless now, aren't you? You're helpless to do anything about it. I knew it would happen to you sooner or later, if I waited long enough, and now I'm going to take your dress downstairs and cut it into tiny little pieces and burn it up. Like you cut me up in tiny little pieces. You tried to burn me up, didn't you?"

She laughed wildly again, waving the old rag doll. Story was hypnotized. She experienced that terrible paralysis that happens in dreams, and she tried to get out of her bed and run, but her body wouldn't move an inch. She didn't know where this strange apparition had come from, but she had to have that dress back; she was obsessed with having that dress back.

"Leave me alone, and give me my dress," she shrieked at Bertie. Her arms felt as if they were pinned to her side. The more she struggled, the more she was powerless to seize the dress.

Bertie backed out of the bedroom door to the stairs, turned and ran wildly down the stairs, laughing, holding the dress up over her head. "I've got it," she sang back in a singsong. "Ha, ha, I've got your dress, big sister." She ran into the living room. "You never let me have anything. You thought you were in charge of my life, but now I have it and you'll never get it back." She headed toward the fireplace.

Story was tossing and turning, desperately trying to wake up. Somehow she began to know she was having a dream. Finally she opened her eyes in absolute relief that the dream was over. "Oh, God," she said, "oh, God, why that?" She turned over and looked at her watch. It was nine o'clock. Almost dark.

It was too hot in her room. The windows had not been opened for the evening. Story got up and went downstairs. She looked into the kitchen. Hermine had made herself some peanut butter sandwiches for supper. There were crusts of bread and an open jar on the table. Story opened Hermine's door. She was asleep with all her clothes on, a box of Kleenex by her pillow. Cecelia Too was on the bed under her arm.

Story closed the door and went into the kitchen. She must eat. She was so shaky and weak. She must keep going. It would not do for people to think she was destroyed by this. It would never do to let them know how upset she really was. She screwed the cap on the peanut butter jar and went looking for a can of soup. Spooning pea soup into herself as if feeding somebody else, she forced herself to think about how she was going to behave, and what she was going to do with her life.

The best thing to do probably was just to pick up and go on as if it had never happened. That's it. Just pretend that it had never happened. Like Mama pretended when her hair got cut off. Like Papa pretended when he beat her. She started unpacking the boxes. All night she unpacked, so that the next morning it barely looked like anyone had planned to leave.

In the morning she dressed carefully. She put on a sweater that would make her look alive, a bright red sweater with gold buttons. She worked carefully, curling her hair so that it didn't appear she had been up all night. Some stylish earrings in her ears and a black skirt completed the look. She looked in the mirror and noticed that her eyes were red and a little puffy, and she looked tired. That couldn't be helped. She'd say she had a cold. When Hermine got up, Story said, "Good morning, Hermine," like nothing had happened. She looked like herself again, only a little tired. They sat down to breakfast as usual, and as Story was pouring out Hermine's milk, she thought she might as well finish it all off.

"That Aleatha Joyce and her whole family is from common stock," she said. "She's the one who thought I should marry that Sam person and who influenced me. I don't want you around people like that, who are nothing and who never will be anything. She doesn't even know who her father is. And at least one of those children doesn't belong to that no-good husband of hers. It's people like that who traffic in drugs and bring down the race. I was stupid to listen to her, and I don't want you making the same mistake. When you take up with trash, you will eventually lie down with it. Eat your breakfast."

Hermine could hardly swallow her cereal. Story kept telling her not to waste food. She just ignored Hermine's tears. Hermine was getting too used to those people anyhow. There was no point in adding to the drama by discussing it.

"After breakfast, I want you to clean your room and unpack your things," Story said from the sink where she was washing up the dishes. "And don't ever mention Sam Tucker's or his daughter's name in this house. I hope he rots in jail." Her voice was as hard and as brittle as glass. She turned around to make sure she had made her point. Hermine looked as if she had been struck blind. Ignoring her, Story turned back to the dishes.

Something crashed to the floor. "You can't!" Hermine screamed. "You can't do that! You can't send them all away. Those are my friends! Faith is my blood sister! We were going to be real sisters! And Jamesina and all of them! And Aunt Aleatha! You can't! I'll run away. I will! I will! I hate you! I hate you!" She raised her small arms over her head and came after Story, beating her suddenly between the shoulder blades with her fists. Story whirled into her, knocking off Hermine's glasses, and slapped her twice. The ten-year-old collapsed in a pile of sobs on the floor.

Story was trembling with fury, her voice was loud and raspy. "Nobody hits me and gets away with it. I have had enough! Enough of your trashy friends! Enough of your unruly behavior! I'm trying to save you from making a stupid mistake, and this is how you repay me?" She jerked Hermine up by the arm. "Get up!" she yelled, shaking her. "Get up and get out of my sight! You can thank your Jesus I will not stoop to beating you, even though that's what you deserve. But if you so much as move from your room until I say so, I will put you out of my house! I can find someone to take you. Don't you think I can't."

Hermine stumbled through the kitchen door without her glasses, sobbing, half covering her eyes and holding her hand to her cheek.

"And don't you come back down here for these glasses either. I think I'll just keep them for a while, so you'll know how fortunate you really are!" Her heart was racing. She had to get her breath. Orange glass, pieces of broken cereal bowl, were under her feet. "Damn it! I hate a mess!" She kicked at them and swore to herself. How dare that child! How dare she lift a hand to strike her! After all she'd done and after all she'd given up for her. She had said "I hate you" again. Story was not even aware of her own tears for a few minutes. She was so angry! So angry at this whole mess! "I hate you"? She had never lifted a finger against her. Never even spanked her on the hands!

Then it all came down around her, Sam and all the rest of it. Her disgrace, and that awful dream about Bertie, almost like Bertie really was somewhere laughing at her. She put her head down on the table near Hermine's spilled Captain Whooies cereal. She was mad enough to kill Sam. That no-good lying dog of a bastard. She hoped they did ask her to testify against him. She would do her best to put him up under the jail. She wished Bertie was alive. They sure had something in common now. If you're out there, Bertie, she said to herself, let me tell you this. This is the last time I'll be a fool enough to believe in happiness. You can depend on it.

———

Sam had been arrested on several counts: possession of heroin, selling heroin, maintaining a dwelling to sell illegal drugs, operating a vehicle for the sale of drugs, and fraud. The evidence was so overwhelming, they didn't need Story's testimony. He was sentenced to jail for twenty-five years.

———

It was nine years later, when Hermine was in school in California and Story was being considered for vice-principal at her school, before Story heard from Sam. The letter was from New York City. Her first impulse was to throw it away unopened, but then she thought better of it. She was curious, after all. What did this man have to say to justify his behavior? She wanted to know how somebody who had done what he had done would have the nerve to approach his victim. So she opened the letter just to see how much gall he really had.

Dear Story,

I know you are shocked. I'm out on parole now, and I don't intend to go back in. I know you think I'm a monster. Perhaps you hate me and won't even read this letter, but I wanted to write you because there were lots of things on my mind after what happened. We had something together that was good, and I thought I'd write and say, if you're still available, if you still want me, I still want you. Before you laugh, hear me out.

What I'm thinking is that you're a real sophisticated woman, with real sophisticated taste. I can build things back up again. I know people. I know how fast people forget, when you have the ability to make money.

But that's not all I wanted to say to you. I also wanted to tell you something that has to do with who you are and who I am. See, we're more alike than you think we are. I know you like pretty things, I know you like a nice high-class life. I know you like what I can give you. There's no way a black man can get those things for a woman in this world except to do something like I did. I think those people that I sold to, well, they were going to buy it somewhere after all, and I just made it available to them, just made some money on it. But I don't think that's a real awful thing to do. I just got caught. That makes it real stupid, I guess. I made a couple of bad mistakes, but don't think you too good for a drug pusher, you know. 'Cause it ain't about being too good for anything. It's about who survives and who doesn't survive out there. It's about the big fish eating the little fish, it's about being a salesman, versus being a sucker. If you had grown up like me, you'd know what I mean. I'm a shark, and I know you're a shark too. You just a shark who's pretty. We could go somewhere together. We don't have to stay in North Carolina. We could go somewhere and have a good life. Ain't no need of you thinking that you better than all these other folks out here who are trying to make it.

And you know all those folks who are addicted to heroin? Those folks who are hooked on heroin that gave me their money? We ain't so much different from those folks, you know. We're hooked on something, we're hooked on lots of things. We're hooked on living well, and being first, on having what we want when we want it; that's what we're hooked on. So we don't have much business looking down our nose at *anybody, that's what I think. It's just that you have to have a different way of doin it if you're smart, that's all. It's just that you know how to look good doin it.*

You know how to look good, how to look smooth, and you try not to let folks know who you really are. You're a survivor just like me, Story, and I'm just saying what we need to do is hook up together and survive together. I just think that would be real smart of both of us, so I just wanted to tell you that I know who you really are, that we are birds of a feather so to speak. All your education and all those books you've read, and all your teachin, that's fine, but if I could "mix a metaphor" as you're always saying, this is coming from one big fish to another. And so, I'm sending you my love and saying there's a great big ocean out there and if you want to swim it with me, I'm yours.

Love you,
Sam

The letter left her with the most confused set of emotions she had felt in a long time. The nerve it took for a damn criminal to write to her like that! She had to sit down on this one. Her sofa was the nearest place; she perched on the edge of it. The nerve of him saying he knew who she was! Nobody knew who she was; nobody had ever known. Not Mama and Papa, not Herman, and certainly not Sam, not even in their wild lovemaking. Nobody knew how she had fought pain back and lived in that place behind her veil; nobody knew how she had pulled herself together and decided to live in spite of Papa's craziness and Mama's silence. Nobody knew how she had decided that they would have a family name in spite of it; in spite of whatever had made her father so desperate to break out of the prison he had been put in by life, by hatred, that he became twisted into that frightening shape. How did Sam dare to say he knew who she was!

There was something in him, though. Something entirely intriguing to her. Intriguing and even attractive. Of course she would never consider "going with" him again, or even seeing him. But there was something in his complete honesty, in his boldness and drive to be himself, that she had to respect and even like. It reminded her of herself. She laughed out loud. Only Sam would have enough unmitigated gall to pull off such a proposal.

Oh, well, she thought, that's one chapter of my life that will remain closed forever. She wished Sam all the best, and let the letter fall silently into the wastepaper basket.

CHAPTER VI

FREE AT LAST

SEPTEMBER 2012

Hermine slammed the screen door. A car rattled down Woodbark Lane. "You'd think they'd get that thing fixed," she grumbled, though she knew it was getting almost impossible to get anything fixed that had been made before 1990, and that you were supposed to dispose of cars over ten years old according to the new ordinance, because they didn't have the new ozone-saving device on them.

"Fixed," Story said. "What's that, your hair?" She liked pretending she couldn't hear. It forced people to shout, or to severely limit their conversation. Either choice gave her the upper hand.

"No," Hermine shouted, sitting in the plastic lounger, "the *cars*, the *cars*." She hated shouting, and so often she didn't talk to her aunt Story at all. "Want some lemonade?" She strained her voice and put her glass down.

"That would be nice, dear," Story said. She raised her voice. "And put it in the blue glass." Hermine got up out of the lounger and walked toward the kitchen.

The old house still didn't have central air. It was September, but still and hot. There was one unit in the living room. Some folks thought that was intolerable, but it suited Story, and it was her house. Hermine got out the ice and fixed some powdered lemonade, thinking she would put in a real lemon if she had one, just so she wouldn't have to hear Aunt Story's mouth. The old lady was a pain in the natural ass, she thought. Why do I do this? Why am I still here? Am I not already old? Haven't I paid my dues? The powdered stuff spilled a little on the floor—it always did—and she gritted her teeth thinking about her worsening arthritis and bending down to wipe up the sticky stuff. "Fuck it!" she swore aloud. She'd get it later. Everybody else in the world lived with central air. Story was an anachronism and a curio enough without adding to it by living like it was still 1950.

"Hermine?" She heard the old woman trying to get up.

"I'm coming! Just hold on."

"Hermine, dear, by the time you wait on somebody they could forget what they'd asked for." Story took the blue glass and carefully put it on the wicker table next to her. In the southern heat the ice began to melt quickly. "Couldn't you find any lemons?" she said, looking out of the sides of her weakened eyes. Hermine didn't answer. She was not going through that mess again about lemons only being available once a year now, and so on and so on. She drank her own glass of already lukewarm lemonade, hoping Story would drop the subject of fresh lemons.

Hermine was thinking about another night, another warm southern night, a night soon after she had lost Faith. That was the night Story had found her doing something "filthy." Hermine thought, Filthy is as filthy does, looking at the old woman in silence. She was just a little girl when it had happened, and she had never forgiven

Story for that night. She could feel her heart ice over when she thought about it.

Story wasn't so old that she couldn't still feel Hermine's energy change. They had been together for so long that they registered each other's shifts like barometers. "What's wrong now?" she said, looking directly at Hermine. "I know it's something. Something you're dragging up to throw at me." Suddenly there was bitterness hanging in the air.

"Why did you do it?" Hermine said. Then not knowing why she should bother, asking, "Why did you always cut me off from anybody who cared about me? Aunt Aleatha, Faith, anybody?" It was old, deep anger from a long time ago, still simmering.

"I was trying to raise you with some class, some standards to live by. But I failed. You insisted on taking up with trash anyhow. And worse, living like a common whore out there in Los Angeles. Like a common, filthy, whore—a freak!"

"Well, I guess I had to ask, didn't I?" Hermine put her glass down on the small table between them, her hand just a little unsteady, and looked out into the street, away from the old lady, away from the deep shadow that had fallen between them. But she couldn't free her mind from the memories, from the gnawing pain, from wondering what she had ever done that was really so wrong to deserve that awful summer that King Sam had left them.

———

The summer had stretched out before her like an endless, hot dusty road. She didn't know what she was going to do. Three days ago King Sam had been arrested, and Aunt Story went back inside herself, more distant and silent than ever.

Hermine could hardly eat. Nothing tasted right. Faith was gone. They had sent Faith away somewhere, Hermine thought, and she didn't belong to anybody anywhere in the whole world. She was an orphan. She had heard the kids talking about orphans in the Children's Home. That was what she was, even though she lived with her aunt. There was nobody left to talk to. Aunt Story had forbidden her to talk to the Joyces, and even though Aunt Aleatha had said Aunt Story would give in soon, Hermine didn't think so. It was hot. They were having a heat wave. There was nowhere to go to get away from home.

Hermine didn't think Aunt Aleatha knew Aunt Story very well. She didn't know how mean and stubborn she could be, and she didn't know that Aunt Story wouldn't care if she died of loneliness. She didn't know how much she missed Faith. Aunt Aleatha didn't know how hard Aunt Story could be.

Hermine had cried herself to sleep for three nights. And her *Heidi* book had disappeared. Now she was catching a cold. She sat under her tree for hours and hours, until Story told her to stop sulking and go find someone to play with, somebody nice. So she walked around the neighborhood, kicking stones that were sitting on the curb. She got out her favorite doll, Cecelia Too, and tried to sew, but she couldn't do it right. Nothing she did was right. She wasn't any good at sewing, she wasn't any good at anything. She tried reading *The Lion, The Witch and The Wardrobe*, but nothing worked. There wasn't anything she wanted to play with, and there was nothing to do except wonder and think and feel sad. She thought about the last three days and how horrible they felt. She wondered if life would always be this horrible.

The day finally got over. Hermine still didn't feel good. She was in her bed and in her warm place. She liked it there when she was sad and all by herself. She was by herself a lot because her real mama and daddy were killed in a car wreck when she was just a baby, and her aunt Story had to work to feed them. She knew that, because her aunt Story told her. And she was by herself more and more because Aunt Story was at work or doing something else a lot, and she told her to go to her room all the time, and she didn't have much to do. Now Faith was gone and there was nobody to touch her warm place and she knew Aunt Story was always mad.

Hermine began to suck her thumb and rub with her other hand, and she rocked herself some. Nobody would ever touch her there again. Story opened the door all at once and flicked on the light. She had come to look for dirty clothes, but instead she saw it. Hermine's warm place. Her voice was cold and straight. It had no curved edges in it.

"And what do you think you're doing?" Story demanded. Hermine jumped violently and hunched her shoulders together. She wanted to disappear. "Take your hands away from your body, and place them up over your head. If I ever so much as think that you are doing something that filthy again . . ." She was too angry to complete her threat. In her haste to obey, Hermine had left her nightgown up over her waist, and her little body was totally exposed. Story jerked the gown down in a violent motion. "If you want to grow up like some people I know," she warned, "you just keep that up. This is what I get for taking care of you. This is how you repay me. You have certainly failed *me*." She was to get up immediately and wash her hands, and put on her underclothes.

By this time Hermine was overcome with tears. She didn't know it was dirty. It was her warm place, that was all.

She was always to sleep with her hands outside the covers, Story told her, and she would be checked every night. Did she understand that? As if she didn't have enough to do without worrying about such filth . . . filth!

———

"Filth! I can't stand a fly!" Story slapped the green plastic fly swatter in a futile effort, and Hermine was jerked away from her memory. Just as Story pulled back to hit a fly on the blue glass, Hermine reached for it, but she was too late and the glass ended up on the floor, pieces of blue glass and a puddle of lemonade for Hermine to clean up.

The fly had settled on a shrub, just out of Story's reach. Hermine got up silently, staring at the street. It had been a long time since she'd thought of that night, and thinking about it didn't feel much better now than it had years ago.

"I see you are not in any hurry to get this sticky mess up," Story said. "And there will be more of those nasty flies any minute if you don't hurry." Her voice was getting more annoying and shrill.

"All right, all right!" Hermine said. "Don't *push* me." She looked her aunt in the eye. "Just don't push me!" She went through the house to get a bucket and a mop. Little else was said that day. The younger woman was wondering why she had ever come back, something she had wondered every day for the last twenty-five years.

1957

Hermine could hear the little kids in the next Sunday school room singing, "Jesus loves the little children. All the little children of the world." She was glad to be out of there. She was with the big kids now, thank goodness.

The only time she got to see the Joyce kids was in church. That's because Aunt Story didn't have the nerve to stop going to her own daddy's church because of King Sam. So they had to see Aunt Aleatha in church if nowhere else. Jamesina Joyce was eleven now. Hermine was twelve. They were still best buddies in spite of Aunt Story. They saw each other in the lunchroom, and in the halls, and after school whenever they could, and they were in the same Sunday school class. The big kids all hated going to Sunday school, but there was nothing they could do about it. All dressed up in those patent leather shoes and long socks. Jamesina never had patent leather, though, but she wore her school shoes to church, and a clean school dress. Today she had on red and yellow plaid.

Deacon Woods was boring to her. He was trying to explain to them something about Moses, who didn't get to the promised land. "It ain't everybody who get to cross over Jordan," he said. "Even Moses didn't get to go, 'cause the Lord had something in mind for him." Hermine stopped listening and opened her little purse. John Victor was throwing spitballs at Ruby Wright's back. He was a big bully. Always botherin' somebody. "Joshua was the one, he was the one chosen to go, to lead the children of Israel across the chilly waters of Jordan." Joshua Franklin from her sixth grade class was listening intently to Mr. Woods. "Will you be ready to lead your people like the man you're named after?" Hermine yawned and wrote Jamesina a note. "Joshua Franklin couldn't lead me to the A & P." Jamesina got the note and clapped her hand over her mouth to keep from laughing in Mr. Woods's face.

"Meet me behind the church after," Jamesina's note read. Jamesina was reaching around Ruby's back when the spitball hit her arm. "Ow, boy," she whispered fiercely to John Victor, who was looking at his Bible like an angel. He mouthed back silently some insult to her mama.

Mr. Woods had seen all this but he didn't quite know what was happening. "Jamesina," he said suddenly, "just how did they get that ark and all those people across that big river?"

"She don't know," yelled John Victor. "She don't know nothin'. She live in Downberry Street."

Jamesina stood up. She looked ready to kill John Victor. "Uh, well, Mr. Woods, I reckon they just rowed across." She made a face at John Victor.

Hermine said quickly, "God parted the waters, Deacon Woods." She knew Jamesina didn't know, and she knew Aunt Aleatha would give Jamesina all kinds of cleaning duty if she acted out in Sunday school. Jamesina had to keep her cool. She couldn't attack John Victor just yet. If they could just distract Mr. Woods from the spitballs and the notes and keep him from telling.

"Good girl! God sent a miracle and parted the waters, and that's what God will do for us if we're good Christian boys and girls. Time to stop now," he said, closing his Bible. "Go straight home. See you next Sunday."

They kept some order until they hit the door. And then Hermine and Jamesina headed for the church parking lot, their heads full of premeditated evil toward John Victor. "We don't have much time," Hermine said. "You know Aunt Story. 'Civilized people have dinner on time,' " she mocked her aunt.

"I'm gon' kill that boy for gettin' me in trouble with his ole spitballs. He wouldn'ta called on me if it hadn't been for John Victor! And talkin' 'bout my street and my mama!"

Hermine was hard at work, thinking. "A girl," she said. "A girl would be perfect." She knew about boy and girl stuff now. She was twelve. And she knew what would blow John Victor out of the water. "You're only eleven," she said. "You have to know about this stuff. You have to understand. All we have to do is find out who he likes."

Jamesina was rarin' to corner him behind the school and beat him up.

"Do you want your mama on your behind for the whole summer comin' up?" Hermine said. "We can't do nothin' like that. It has to be quiet!"

"I can't stand him," Jamesina snarled. "I can't stand his ole smelly ass. He stink! Talkin' 'bout where I live!"

"You know where they live?" Hermine asked. "Over behind the lumberyard in that trailer. They poor as dirt."

"Well I can't stand him anyway," Jamesina repeated.

"He got a nasty mouth," Hermine added.

"So anyway, what's the plan?" Jamesina was impatient.

"I think it's Ruby. He was tryin' to hit her with the spitball. But we can find out for sure. All we have to do is tell him she likes him too, and he will get himself in trouble."

"Do she?" Jamesina wasn't at all sure how these things worked.

"No, dummy! She can't stand him either. But he'll fall for it. You wait."

Monday brought clear cold weather, and clear cold malice on Hermine's part. She sought out John Victor at lunch and slipped a forged note in his lunch box when he went to get his milk. It read: "John Victor is a sweetheart, John Victor is a daisy. When John Victor kisses Ruby, he drive her all crazy. 2 sweet 2 be 4 gotten. Ruby."

He was ripe. Before the day was over, he had tried to get Ruby's pencil, sent her a note, and was waiting to walk her home. Hermine watched it all from a distance, waiting for Ruby to come out of the side door near the gym at three o'clock. John Victor paced up and down until Ruby's class emerged. Hermine and Jamesina edged forward so they could hear. Ruby wore a yellow wool sweater and yellow ribbons on her braids. John Victor sidled up to her and said, loud enough for all the hangers-on to hear, "Hey, babes, let's you and me walk together. I hear you really want to go with the meanest cat in the school. Let me drive you crazy, baby."

Ruby turned, her yellow ribbons bouncing at the ends of her long braids. "Boy, you better get away from me, 'fore I get my brother on you. Get outta here with yo' little nappy-headed skinny self." She flounced off the sidewalk and crossed the street, and half the sixth grade broke out in hoots. John Victor was left standing in the middle of a crowd of "oohs" and "she got yoou's." Hermine and Jamesina whooped and hollered all the way home. It was the best day of the school year. And the bully would never know who set him up.

That day bonded Jamesina and Hermine as fast friends. Jamesina never forgot that Hermine had gone to war for her, and Hermine never forgot that because of Jamesina, at least once in her life she had found a power place.

1961

When she was sixteen, Uncle Dee and Uncle Dum sent Hermine her first pair of blue jeans, and she was in love with jeans forever after that. Aunt Story thought the jeans were vulgar, and Hermine wore them as often as she could find an excuse to do so. "She lives in those filthy pants," Aunt Story said to a friend in disgust. But Hermine felt very powerful in her jeans, and they helped her when she was tempted to let people "push her around."

When the mail came that Saturday, Hermine was in her room. She heard the postman's step. There was almost never any mail for her, but she was supposed to bring in the mail every day anyway. It was one of her jobs. She had been doing her homework in American history. It was a welcome excuse to leave her books and dawdle downstairs for a while. The house was very quiet. She heard her own radio playing upstairs, "You Send Me." She loved Sam Cooke. She'd like to be one of those girls who could slow-dance to that with some boy plastered up against them. She looked at herself in the hall mirror and sighed. It would never happen.

It was an overcast day. She felt the cold breeze on her face when she opened the door to reach for the mail in the brass box by the left side of the door. 333 Mill Street. There were three big threes on the brass box. Lots of mail today, she thought, leafing through it, only half paying attention and sure that there would be nothing for her.

She was halfway up the stairs to her room before she saw it. She put the large stack of bills and other official-looking mail on Aunt Story's writing desk in her room next to the chocolate candy box without even realizing she was doing it. A letter for her! Postmarked Oklahoma! Wachomis, Oklahoma! She knew who it had to be from then. The radio announcer was screaming about some big sale at the hardware store, and she flipped it off. She turned the letter over once, twice, almost afraid to open it. But then she tore it open all at once. They were inviting her to visit them that summer. "God!" she said to herself. "God! I can't believe it. I can't believe it!"

On with the radio again, and she was dancing to "Lawdy Miss Claudie" when it hit her. Aunt Story might not let her go. Hermine sat down at the foot of her bed. Oh, there had to be a way, there just had to be a way; she was certain God couldn't be that cruel, but what about Aunt Story? She wandered about the house all day, American history forgotten. Finally, just before dark, she heard the key in the lock. Hermine picked up the letter, afraid to breathe. She was holding it next to her heart. One by one she went down the carpeted stairs, dreading the confrontation. She just stood there staring at her aunt, breathing very shallow breaths and holding the white envelope. It all took less than a minute.

"I got a letter today, Aunt Story," she almost whispered.

"Don't you know how to speak to people?" Story said. "I'm tired. It was a very long meeting and I would like a cup coffee." Story put her notebook and books down heavily and took off her tweed coat.

"Yes, ma'am. Hi, Aunt Story, how are you?" Hermine said all at once.

"Now what about a letter?" Story said, hanging her coat in the closet.

"Uncles Dee and Dum. I got a letter from them." She paused.

"What in the world could they be writing to you about?" Story said, moving toward the kitchen to put on her coffee.

Now she had to tell it. "They want me to come visit them this summer, and they're going to send me a ticket. Can I go?" She had followed Story into the kitchen.

Story turned around. "How ridiculous. Why would you want to go way out there to see those two old men? Put some rice on. We need to start dinner. I'll go change my clothes." She started out the kitchen door. "That's too much money to accept from them."

Hermine was still holding her letter. Her hands began to sweat. She was not giving this up without a fight. "Please, Aunt Story, listen for a minute! I can work. I can babysit in June and July and go in August. Please!" She saw only her aunt's very stiff back dressed in a gray and green dress.

She turned partially toward Hermine. "Hermine, what is it with you? All I want tonight is a little peace and quiet. There is always something with you, always something. I'm going to say it now once and for all. You are supposed to go to State in the fall. Your babysitting money will go to books and new clothes. Nowhere else. You don't need to go out there on some fool's errand. Please fix my coffee."

The gray and green dress made its way up the stairs. The dress was all Hermine saw, not a person with blood and bones, just a gray and green dress. It was so unfair and so senseless! Hermine dropped her letter on the floor. The coffeepot was boiling over. She didn't care. She'd like to throw all that hot coffee all over her damn dress, all over the kitchen! Cream, sugar, saucer, cup! She hated her! Now she knew why some of the white kids she knew were running away to join hippie farms. They were right. Old people were horrible and should all be exterminated, she thought. She'd like to put something awful in that cup. One day, she thought, one day I'll get even with her.

The next day she decided to try again, but it didn't do any good. She didn't pay the bills, and she didn't need to go way out there. That's what she was told. What's more, Story was determined not to owe those two old "crazy" men anything.

Maybe a strike, Hermine thought. Everybody else was sitting in and sitting down. Maybe she'd just stop doing the dishes and dusting. Let her see how she'd like that. For a week she didn't do the dishes. When Story's energy and her patience wore out, she lowered the boom. "I've had enough, young lady. I am not washing another dish. I hope you're prepared to miss all the social activities and all your movies until the fall," she said one morning as they were leaving the dirty breakfast dishes behind. "And you will be saving me a lot of money to put on your tuition because you won't be getting any allowance until you stop this stupid strike."

Being extra sweet didn't help. Tears didn't help. Wearing her jeans every day to annoy Story didn't help. Nothing moved Story to change what she said was a wise and sensible decision for her niece's own good. Short of running away, there was nothing Hermine could do. There was no way she could keep her promise to Uncle Dum. The last time she saw him, she had failed at dancing. She was not good enough to finish that waltz. Now he would think she had failed again, and maybe he'd be right. Maybe she was not good enough at anything, and she really didn't have a power place at all. Maybe Uncle Dum was just an old fool who didn't have any sense. She packed her jeans away with an aching heart. She couldn't quite bring herself to throw them out.

1961

The day she could run away or leave was the day she'd be free. Teachers noted her intelligence. She studied hard. Story had taught her one lesson she believed: that people of her race who were educated would have a chance to escape the gaping mouth of poverty, and those who didn't were doomed to stay behind in slavery. Slavery for Hermine meant life with Aunt Story.

She was in a hurry to grow up. She passed the test for an early admission to Hattenfield State, and found the work easy. Before the end of the first year, Hermine had given up on having a boyfriend. They were always saying stupid things to her like, "Hey, babe, what chu know good?" How could anybody with any intelligence answer that? Besides, she wore glasses and had a rather thick waist, and she knew they wouldn't really want her in the end, even if they pretended they did; she knew they thought she'd be easy sex, and they all did.

But all that didn't matter to her now; it didn't have to matter. It was the time of Freedom Now. Black Power and beautiful African queens. Hermine was in love with it all. She had never felt so alive. It was the time to stop apologizing for who you were, to claim your own people, to stamp out slavery forever. The gym was packed. She felt a little drunk. They were making history, not their parents. Not some old white men in Washington. They were the ones in the news. "Slavery was gone forever. Let no one and nothing have your soul," they said. "Be with us, brothers"—and somebody in the audience added "sisters," but nobody heard that but a few women. "The time is now," they shouted in a final climax. "The revolution is yours!" The rumble of stomping feet in the Hattenfield State gym got louder and louder. Hermine was in heaven. She had not known life could be like this; so full of energy, excitement, passion. She loved the wildness of it, the feeling of flying she got when five hundred students got carried away with the certainty that they had a right to live. All her life she had longed for someone to tell her those things. That she was a beautiful queen just because. That she had a place, something real to do, a reason to live. Something had always been missing for her.

She had believed in Faith. That Faith was going to be there for her always. But that had been a big joke. She had been a naive little girl. There were days when she wondered about the point of it all. She went to school, she went home. She worked and studied. Her friends always seemed to be freer than she was, happier, as if they had a secret. She reached up and felt her straightened hair. She would do it tonight.

Carol Jones was sitting on the bleachers directly across from Hermine. The beautiful Carol Jones, campus queen two years ago, was a senior with creamy skin and long brown hair. She reminded Hermine of Faith Tucker, only she didn't like Carol Jones. Hermine had never liked the parties and the flirting and the teasing that went on there, and she had never felt like she could compete with those fast girls who were already on birth control pills. Some of those girls had mothers who bought their pills for them. She wouldn't dare even mention them to Aunt Story.

There were strangers on the other side of her. She had been too late to hook up with her best friends for this rally. But this was something else. This didn't require you to be quick with jokes, or talk jive, or be flirty with boys or smooth and worldly. This was here for the taking, this power, this certainty that her life belonged to her and she deserved it. The crowd jostled her in their excitement. All around her she heard phrases being tried out—"sitting in," "passive resistance," snatches of political questions, "counterrevolutionary"—it was electric. Laughter mixed with excitement and the serious faces of young people ready to take on the world. They spilled out onto the campus. She loved it. It was a warm springlike evening. Stars were everywhere. The kind of evening in North Carolina that makes you think the warm weather has arrived, when really winter is just lurking in a corner like a hawk waiting to swoop down on you. But you don't care. For one day, anyway, it's spring.

"Hermine, wait up!" Someone was calling to her. "Hermine!" It was Judy, her roommate. "Girl! What a night! Black people are movin' out!" Judy was underweight and myopic, but she refused to wear glasses because "she could get more men without them." Hermine often teased Judy about the *more*. "More than what?" she would say. "More than none?" She liked Judy.

Hermine grinned widely. "Let's do it tonight!" she said, pulling on Judy's short straight hair.

"Let's do it?" Judy looked horrified. "Oh, God, I just got my knots busted—five dollars an hour. Oh God, you mean wear it *natural*?" Her voice had gone up to a squeal.

"We shall overcome the straightening comb!" Hermine shouted at the stars.

"We shall overcome the straightening comb!" Judy picked up the refrain.

They dashed into the dorm, sisters in their new liberation from the tyranny of feeling ugly. "Free at last!" Hermine shouted. "Free at last!" The world had suddenly lost its power to tell them that only women with yellow hair that didn't curl naturally would dare to call themselves beautiful. The shower had never known such power. In a ritual cleansing, they snipped, washed, and cut out of their heads three hundred years of ugliness, together in their mutual joy.

—

Spring vacation came. She was sitting on the porch reading the *Wretched of the Earth* when Story came home from work. Her aunt had not seen the new hairdo. She stared at Hermine silently and walked past her silently into the house. She had not said a word. Hermine got up to cook. It was hamburgers and fries. Story came to the table. "What's this junk food we've got tonight?" she said quietly. Hermine was about to take a bite. Here it was. She put her fork down. "Well, you can wear it that way if you wish," Story said, "but not in my house. You'll wear it in a respectable style, or you'll move out of here. You will not live with me and wear your hair in that ridiculous way."

Hermine's hamburger was getting colder. She didn't move. She was thinking of a way to get out of there. She'd never make good her threat over a hairdo. Hermine knew that. But maybe there was another way. The hair had given her an idea. And she was thinking of some magazines she had found hidden away in a closet. Story sat chewing quietly. Hermine was thinking. Thinking of the words "respectable style."

Her aunt had a birthday coming up. Her forty-fifth birthday. She had decided to have a small party; have a few friends over to help her celebrate. Aunt Story thought her friends were interesting. She was proud of her taste in people and said so. Hermine thought they were old as dirt and twice as dull. She already knew who would be there. The Twitchells, from church; Miriam and Norman, the Sandersons from school; Dr. and Mrs. Hinson; and a couple of old maids like Aunt Story, Dr. Elenora James from Hattenfield State, and Miss Lydia Turnbull. Hermine had never figured out what Miss Turnbull did for a living. She lived alone, and whenever she cornered you, you were trapped. Hermine called it the Turnbull trap. She droned on about whatever she was talking about until you started figuring out what you could do to get away. Mostly she talked about opportunity and being ready for its knock. There might be one or two white people too, from the school system, whose names she couldn't remember.

Hermine waited for the day of the party. I'll get her back for everything, she thought. For saying no to everything I ever wanted that would make me happy; especially for Faith, and for my trip to Oklahoma. She listed them in her mind, the worst times in her life. And she shopped carefully for her birthday surprise. She bought everything she was told to buy by Aunt Story, very carefully. The just-right napkins and tablecloth, just-right flowers and candles. She did everything she was told, and Aunt Story was pleased. She had fixed hot canapés and bought white wine and coffee and cream puffs. Aunt Story answered the door herself, dressed in a pastel-blue dress, with pastel-blue heels to match. She sparkled as each of her guests came through the door. "It's wonderful to see you!" she would say.

Hermine was supposed to bring in a platter of canapés and serve it at eight-thirty, shortly after everyone had arrived. She was wearing a yellow party dress that she hated. She had only worn it once, two years ago. Aunt Story had gone through Hermine's closet looking for "just the right thing," and was delighted to find that it still fit. Hermine sat at the kitchen table in the yellow dress, staring at the big canapé tray. It would have to be done at the right time or it wouldn't work. She had stashed everything she needed in the pantry in a brown paper grocery bag. As soon as she heard the doorbell ring a safe number of times, she darted into the pantry and squeezed between the sacks of potatoes and the cans of peaches. She stripped off her yellow dress, knocked off her pumps, and opened the paper bag. The chartreuse, neonlike sequins gleamed in the light coming from the kitchen in a crack through the door. It was perfect, tighter than a sausage skin, she thought, trying to wiggle her ample, seventeen-year-old figure into the size six dress. Good. It showed almost all of what she had in front, and she just knew her panty line would be seen.

Jamesina was right. It would make Aunt Story "drop her drawers." She stepped into a pair of three-inch heels borrowed from Justine, who had never liked Aunt Story since she had had her expelled from school. The dress reeked of My Sin. Whoever Jamesina had borrowed it from must have used a whole bottle. She had to hurry. It was almost time for the canapés. If she didn't get out there soon, Aunt Story would be coming through the kitchen door with her fake voice on. "Hermine, dear? Where are those canapés?" She fluffed out her thick Afro hairdo and quickly put on some huge rhinestone earrings. Slathered on some lipstick called Hot Cherry Pie without the help of a mirror, and put some on her cheeks for good measure. She grabbed the magazines out of the bag, darted out the door of the pantry and picked up the platter, magazines underneath as if they were shielding her hands from the heat.

Just as she heard Miss Lydia say "opportunity knocks," she got to the middle of the room and Aunt Story saw her. In a half second

Story had almost managed to find a voice to say something, but by then Hermine had put the tray on the coffee table and was waving the pornographic magazines in the air. Topless girls' breasts kept flopping slowly past Deacon Twitchell's nose. "I forgot," Hermine said loud enough for everybody in the room to hear. "I forgot just where you wanted me to put these magazines, Aunt Story. Just let me know, and then I'll serve the canapés. They're the ones King Sam left you, remember?" She spread them out on the coffee table. Three magazines entitled *Layin' and Playin'* stared up at Story, and all the rest of them. Hermine's right leg was slightly turned to the outside, one neon breast just barely grazing Miss Lydia Turnbull's arm.

Aunt Story was paralyzed. And then she startled everyone by laughing. She just threw back her head and laughed, and everyone else did too. "I have to give it to you, Hermine," she said, "this is quite a birthday surprise. How about fixing Dr. James a glass of white wine, would you?" And then she went on with the conversation she had been having with Deacon Twitchell as if nothing had happened.

Hermine saw in a flash Story had decided the best way to handle this was to pretend that nothing out of the ordinary had happened. But she also saw that cold as ice smile, and she heard the edge in the laugh. It wasn't Aunt Story's usual laugh. Hermine turned and walked out of the room. She wouldn't change. She wouldn't give her the satisfaction. So she wore the dress all evening, serving the food, changing the records, fixing the coffee, even though she began to feel awfully foolish. Her hair up in a bird's nest; her smeared lipstick; her chartreuse, sequined, too-tight dress. She smiled and she spoke, and when she saw her aunt's friends didn't know what to say to her, she smiled again. Aunt Story never said go change your clothes. She played out her hand till its end. But Hermine knew how angry and embarrassed and devastated her aunt was, because along with her cold as ice smile and her artificial laugh, she had noted the metallic brightness in her eyes, the quick swipe of the hand on the cheek when she thought no one was looking. She had brought Story Temple Greene to tears, in front of all these stuff-shirted bourgeois Negroes, and it made her feel powerful, at least for a little while. As the evening wore on, she thought about Uncle Dee and Uncle Dum, but somehow she knew they weren't talking about this when they talked about power.

By the time all the guests went home, Hermine was fast asleep. She never knew what happened to the magazines. They weren't there in the morning. Aunt Story was waiting for her when she appeared for breakfast, sitting on the sofa in her robe. "I think you'd better pack your things and leave, Hermine. Get one of those wild friends of yours to let you sleep at their house until spring break is over. Then go take a room on the campus. I'll pay for it. I don't care where you go. I don't want to see you until you can be a decent human being."

This was what she had been waiting for. Aunt Story had never wanted her anyway. She was glad to leave. Glad to be thrown out. She put some things into a bag, trying to convince herself that this was exactly what she wanted. Trying not to feel in the least bit guilty for what she had done last night. She stuck her snapshot of Uncle Dee and Uncle Dum in the side of her suitcase, hoping Aunt Story wouldn't tell them what had happened. And then she had to think about where she could go. There was no room in Aunt Aleatha's house. She always had relatives spilling out of the windows. Where did foreign students go during vacation? She called Jamesina, made a few more phone calls, and left while Story was at work. They never mentioned the party performance again.

———

Hermine let it grow. A big and wild Afro as close to the pictures of Angela Davis as she could get it. She had been born with big bones, a gift from her father, and she was rather startling, almost beautiful with her large brown face framed in the thick hair. Her looks had never been fashionable. Not too many men had seen her as pretty, but now there was a presence there they had to acknowledge, and some of them were truly attracted. Hermine found this interesting, but a little bothersome. She could never tell when to believe the jive talk and when to write it off as a game.

In her junior year she decided to take a chance. Stephen was nice. The kind you'd write home to your mother about if you had a mother who cared, she thought. She kicked a stone on the campus walk, frustrated, wondering who she could trust enough to talk to about this. For two months he'd been checking her out in the library, following her to the dining hall so he could get in line next to her, just by chance, showing up in the dorm living room. She'd known the signs even though she didn't usually play the games. So here she was with this decision to make. Three tests to take in the next two days, and Stephen wanting to push her into sex after a month or two of dating.

She had seen him with other girls, though. He was charming enough to be frightened of. Made her wonder if he was so used to having his pick of women that he would just use them up and drop them cold. She was a little scared of the whole idea of love anyway. Once in a while she thought about Faith and how she had wanted to live with her. She heard things about "queers" on campus, and blushed even when nobody on campus knew what she was thinking. She always felt ashamed to laugh when people talked behind their hands and giggled. If they knew about what she had done, she would be the one they were talking about. But then she laughed anyway. It was just the way it was, with everybody. She hadn't done it after Faith, but she felt funny about it, like she had. She'd almost decided to live alone forever, when Stephen showed up in her life.

Everybody liked him, even the guys, who seemed to sense he was a leader and looked to him for some kind of guidance. At the Black Student Union meetings, he was the one guy who was always clear-headed, the one who convinced everybody that his idea made sense. Last night they had almost split up into two organizations. He had brought them together again. She looked up when Bill Harper challenged the club's motives and the semester's project. "Y'all ain't really black!" Bill shouted, angry at the adoption of the activity which was to pressure the college for more help getting graduate schools. "What y'all doin', tryin' to go to these places? MIT, Yale, Harvard? Who the hell cares about their schools? We should be helping our brothers in the ghetto! Y'all a bunch of Toms!"

There was silence and then a general outcry. People were ready to fight over being called Toms. They were jammed into a little room in the student union, they were hot, and they were tired. Hermine looked at Stephen, who had lobbied hard for scholarship help. He wanted a law degree. She knew that. Stephen was mad. They had been at this debate for three months, and he didn't like being called a Tom, but he was always in control. Walking slowly and deliberately to the front of the room, Stephen raised his hand.

"Y'all cool out," he said. His low voice was commanding. Things quieted down a little bit. "My man," he said, smiling at Bill, "we all in this together, my man, we all soldiers on the front lines of bigotry and racism. I couldn't agree with you more, we need to go down on the block and help the brothers up. But you know if we don't have any black doctors or lawyers, who's gonna be there when you get hurt on the front lines or get put in jail on whitey's trumped-up charges? I for one don't want to have to give all my money to white doctors and lawyers! So point well taken, but we in this *together*." His deep voice soothed. He wasn't angry, he just made sense. She could feel the tension level out. People were beginning to see his point. The president called for tabling the decision and more discussion. There was no more talk about splitting into two groups. Yes, Stephen was definitely somebody she could like, a lot.

She adjusted her book bag and pushed her hands deeper into her pockets, needing some gloves. She was out of money until her next allowance, and never, never asked Aunt Story for it between times. Too much preaching to hear about budgeting and responsibility. Hermine kept walking toward the library, her favorite place on campus.

That's where she had met him, leaning over the *Who's Who in Black America*, trying to find Walter White's name. She asked him if he knew who Walter White was, and Stephen went on for ten minutes about the history of lynching in America and Walter White's work investigating the crimes. She liked him right away. He was majoring in pre-law, quiet and smart. He didn't scare her and he didn't boss her, so she thought she could risk a date or two, and then they just kept going out, and now he was really in love, he said.

She had reached the table she liked best, by the window, and pulled out the chair. She was still deep in thought when Judy said,

"Girl, you must be driftin' on some memory, 'cause I'm sittin' right here with a big stack of books, and you don't even see your own roommate!"

"Shhh," Hermine said, not wanting to draw attention to herself. "I got to talk to you, girl."

"Yeah, I figured. You were out there dreamin' about *the man*, no doubt. Gonna give it up or not?"

"Shhhh! Not now. After. I'm goin' to another table. Finish your term paper. See you at lunch. We'll go to Your Mama's."

Your Mama's was packed with State students because it was the only place black students could go for sandwiches. "If we had our rights," she heard someone say, "we wouldn't all be crammed in here like sardines in a can. We need to check out that sit-in business."

They found themselves a seat in a corner by the kitchen. Judy didn't even wait for her lunch. "So," she said, leaning on the red vinyl tabletop, her gloves still on her hands, "what chu gonna do, girl?"

"Oh God," Hermine said. "Oh God, I don't know. Sex is, you know, so complicated! There's periods and stuff to worry about, and then, you know, birth control!"

"What's to worry about? The man says he loves you. Do it! Ooh, makes me shiver just thinkin' about it."

Maybe she was right, Hermine thought, over her Coke and ham sandwich. He was nice and nice-lookin', and for once there would be somebody in her life who *said* he loved her, even if he didn't really. High school had not prepared her for this. There, she had simply acted as if the whole boy-girl thing had not existed. It was easier that way. Aunt Story had not helped, since none of Hermine's friends had ever come up to her standards. Still, she wasn't sure she wanted anybody that close to her. Finding out her secrets, seeing into her. Touching her, really touching her. It excited her, but it scared her too. This time is would be for real. Not two little girls practicing on each other.

He came to the dorm at seven, right on time. She wasn't ready. Judy said the red dress, Hermine said the African dashiki; they couldn't decide. Then finally she wore the purple tie-dye that looked kind of African but not too much, and the long silver earrings.

Stephen was not very tall, but he looked taller than he was because he was very sure of himself. Hermine thought of him as an older man, which he wasn't really. He was a senior, and she was a junior. Just serious, steady-eyed, not the silly jive talker that she'd come to have no respect for in high school. He had a small mustache, wore a beige sweater over his shirt, and mustard-colored trousers that showed off his strong physique.

They went to see *Pillow Talk*, but neither of them had their minds on the movie. He had a friend with a house. She never knew how college men did those things. Rented houses, apartments, so they had somewhere to take their girlfriends. It was near the campus movie. They walked slowly even though it was cold, both of them nervous once she had said, "Well, okay. I'll stop by for a few minutes for something to drink." He knew and she knew what that meant. They had red wine. They talked about the student movement and the civil rights movement and Martin Luther King, and then they were suddenly all out of talk and Stephen even blushed a little and moved very close to her.

"I love you, Hermine," he whispered. "I'll take care of you. Let's do it."

It was the "I'll take care of you" that got her. It sounded so warm and safe and homelike. Never to have to go back to Aunt Story's house. Never to feel the sting of her voice. She just slid into his arms, feeling red-wine warm, her insides and her body answering his, and even the pain she felt when he did it was not very intense.

"I didn't know you were a virgin," he said. His voice was very tender, very low. "I really didn't. But I'm glad."

She lay in his arms thinking about it all, for the first time finding her whole body was acceptable to someone. Feeling like she wasn't ugly and in the way and somebody's burden. She loved knowing that she could want to be with a man, like she had wanted to be with Faith. Only now she was grown-up. She was relieved. She was elated. She really wanted him. Maybe you didn't have to love either men or women, she thought. Maybe there were beautiful men *and* beautiful women, but she always kept her mouth shut when the girls started talking in the dorm. People would think she was a freak. Not only that, she knew they would trip out if she started saying what she thought. Then they'd label her "ac/dc." Well, maybe she was. She didn't know what she was. She was just who she was. But she kept quiet. She was not about to lose all her friends, much less Stephen. Living with Aunt Story had taught her when to be quiet, if nothing else.

———

It was nearing the middle of November. Thanksgiving soon. "What are you afraid of, Hermine?" Stephen asked. They were on their way to a dance. Social events always made her nervous. "You're always a little bit nervous with me. What are you afraid of, my Honey Bee? You look beautiful tonight." He loved her in turquoise, and it did show off her golden skin well.

Maybe she wasn't too bad-looking after all, she thought. Maybe the dance would be wonderful.

"I'm not afraid with you, Stephen," she lied. She was almost always thinking that she had fallen in love, and being in love scared her. It wasn't safe. It was like being in a boat if you couldn't swim. Suppose the bottom of the boat gave way and you were left out there drowning? Suppose he was only practicing on her like Faith?

But she loved him anyway. He was her first real love. She knew much of what she knew about her body because of him. He was her first real tenderness, and the first time she'd even been truly warm in her life was with him. It was just that she was always, always afraid of the bottom of that boat. Always testing it to see if it was still holding.

"Do you still love me?" she would say, cocking her head to the side. It was her routine question at the close of every phone conversation. And he would say in his deep southern voice, "What do you think, Honey Bee?" And he would say, "Is you lost yo' mind?" in mock dialect. "Yes, woman, yes, I love you!" and finally she would be satisfied for another day and she would hang up in a warm glow that lasted until the next time she felt the ocean under that boat.

That warm glow lasted all that year. He insisted on buying her some mittens for the winter. He worried about her health. He sent flowers at the right time for the right things. She was a little scared most of the time, worrying about her looks, her figure. Was the sex as good as he said? Would he really be there for her? Was he lying? Did he really love her? He said he called her his Honey Bee because she brought him sweetness.

Judy thought he was wonderful and thought Hermine was out of her mind for "throwing away her life," she said, when she found out what had happened.

"How can you just walk out of his life!" she cried. "A man like that who loves you! A *perfect man*. Do you know how many *perfect men* are out there?"

"He's not so perfect, if you ask me, Judy," Hermine answered, her head stuck in her political science textbook. She had cried her eyes out for two days. As far as she was concerned, it was a closed chapter. This was the last time she would ever let herself trust a man, she thought. They were all like King Sam, one thing on the outside, another on the inside.

"But Hermine," Judy protested, "if you'd just talk to him! He's devastated. He loves you. That girl was just someone he used to know. I think he wants to *marry* you!" Her voice went up to a squeak.

"He can take his tweed suits and his beautiful voice and his Pan-African talk and his long eyelashes and go to hell," Hermine said. "I got his letter. I know what it said. 'That was an old girlfriend who just wanted to say good-bye. She just got carried away and it only looked from a distance like they were deeply involved.' It looked to me like he enjoyed it all too much. I saw her damn miniskirt and her high heels and her . . . Oh shit! I don't want to talk about it, Judy. I'm not begging for anybody. I can do fine by myself. I've always been alone, and I can be alone again. What I saw from that balcony was enough to convince me; I was just his thing on the side." She wiped her eyes, mad at herself for starting to cry again. "I will never beg, and I will never be humiliated by a man."

"But he *talked* to me, Hermine. He loves *you*, he said, not that fly chick." Judy was about to give up. "You're makin' a terrible mistake." She gave it one last try. Stephen was waiting. He had confided in her, and he *was* devastated. "You'll be sorry all your life. I've got to tell him. I've got to give him your answer. He's waiting downstairs."

"Tell him to go ... Tell him to have a good life with what's-her-name." Hermine went behind her books and that was that for her. It took too much out of her. She felt drained, humiliated. Always, always, she had known that she was not attractive to men, and this certainly proved it to her. He had taken her for a ride, she decided, and it was too expensive to try again. She would never let a man use her again, she thought as Judy went slowly out the door, she would never give them the opportunity.

—

The days were full of meetings, political arguments, plans for protests and marches. She threw herself into the movement, partly to get over Stephen. The nights were for books and catching up on assignments and missed classes. Bleeding and war-damaged, they all somehow managed to graduate on time, Hermine with a degree in pre-law. She cut her Afro down to four inches in order to get the mortarboard on her head and painted "Off the Pigs" on the top of her cap.

"Your aunt is gonna have a hissy fit when she sees your cap," Judy said.

"Yeah," Hermine replied, "just the graduation present I'd like to give *her*." They were kind of numb. Happy that it was over, going their separate ways—Judy to Chicago, where her home was. Hermine to California and graduate school.

"I know you'll pick up that pen and write," Judy said, tears running down her face when it was all over. " 'Cause if you don't, I'm comin' after you to break both your hands."

Aunt Story was standing there, not too patiently waiting for this good-bye to be over. They exchanged summer addresses, and Judy was gone, into the arms of her large, emotional family.

"Well, Miss Hermine, you did it," Story said, smiling at her. That was as close as she got to congratulations. They walked in the sweltering heat, but Hermine noticed her aunt looked satisfied, even happy.

She really wished she had accepted the invitation to have dinner with Judy's family. Maybe they could go anyway. Why not? It was a special day; it was beautiful weather. "Aunt Story," she said impulsively, "let's go out to dinner. To the Eastern Gardens. Just you and me? Come on, after all, I graduated!"

Story smiled, looking satisfied. "You did indeed," she said. "All right! I'll take you out for a treat. I like the Eastern Gardens. It's just been integrated. We'll test them out."

Hermine couldn't believe she had agreed so easily. That was where Judy and her family were going! "I'll just turn in my cap," she said to her aunt, trying to cover the words she had painted on the mortarboard with the sleeve of her gown.

"Go on now," Story said, looking at the cap, "before I change my mind. Turn in your gown so we can go. And by the way," she called to Hermine, "tell the pigs hello if you see any."

Hermine ordered egg foo yung, and Story ordered something called Spring Rain with pork. Today there seemed to be a kind of truce between them. Maybe a moratorium, Hermine thought, remembering her political science teacher. They had been laughing about boring teachers, and he was one of them. And now all that was over, and she was happier than she'd ever been. Free, and going off to California. She was bouncy with excitement. Aunt Story looked pleased with her and with herself.

"A great meal," she said. "Pass the soy sauce, Hermine. And now you get out there, and I want you to learn as much as you can. You study hard and make something of yourself. You've got the mind, you know."

Hermine nodded between bites of the egg mixture. She was trying to use the chopsticks, because she was going out West where there were lots of Asian people. The food kept dropping onto the plate. Aunt Story seemed to think it was hilarious, and Hermine did too, clowning a little for her, because she was enjoying the novelty of laughing with her aunt.

"No," Aunt Story said, "let me show you. Here, I think it's done this way." She reached over the table and took Hermine's hand, trying to get the rice to stay on the stick, but it kept being a disaster in table manners. Her hand covered Hermine's as they both squeezed the long sticks, and for the first time Hermine noticed how similar their hands were. The same bone structure exactly, the same round, even nails. She was astonished. Except for the difference in the color of brown skin, they could have been the same person's hands.

"Aunt Story," she said impulsively, "thanks."

"Thanks?" Story said, her hand still clasped in Hermine's, still holding the chopsticks.

"Thanks for everything," Hermine said. "I mean, college and all." She shrugged her shoulders. "You know."

Story nodded, and just barely squeezed Hermine's hands. "You're quite welcome, Hermine, dear. You're quite welcome."

At that moment the restaurant door opened and Judy walked in with all her family. Hermine dropped her hands and the chopsticks, and in the excitement of introducing everybody, forgot entirely about the similarity of their hands.

—

On the way back to Hermine's apartment they were quiet, each lost in her own thoughts. "I expect you to do your best in California," Story finally said. Hermine nodded. She could go for her master's or law school with her UCLA Fellowship. The best of it for her was leaving 333 Mill Street forever. Forever, she thought, what a wonderful word. As they passed the library, she had a flash of Stephen's face, briefly, only briefly.

"Well, I must run, Hermine," Story said. They had reached the campus apartment. She pecked Hermine on the cheek. "Come by and see me before you take off for the City of Angels. 'Bye 'bye."

As she drove off into the late afternoon sunlight in her white Pontiac, Hermine thought, "relieved," that's the word. She's really very relieved that I'm going. Well, so am I.

CHAPTER VII

CALIFORNIA DREAMIN'

OCTOBER 2012

Today they could see the gold leaves of new trees the city had planted. Today it was clear that Indian summer had ended. They turned on the heat.

She knew she should get the blankets and quilts out. Except for Aunt Aleatha's quilt. Hermine kept it in its storage box where it had been ever since she got it, sealed and protected by professional cleaners. It was a long time ago now, soon after she came back from California, twenty-five years, it had been. She couldn't believe it had been that long. Aunt Aleatha had given clear instructions to Jamesina. "Send it to Hermine when I die. She might need it."

Jamesina shipped it to her all the way from Phoenix, where she had moved. It was worn and a little faded, but you could still see the material from Aleatha's dresses, and scraps from Jamesina's clothes. You could still see that tumbling blocks pattern, and Aunt Aleatha's clear and even stitching. Jamesina enclosed a little note: "Mama died last month. She wanted you to have this. Think of you often. Remember that girl I beat up for your glasses? (happy face) Love, Jamesina." Hermine remembered. Dear old Jamesina. She was gone now, too. "We're all connected," Aunt Aleatha had said.

Even to the dead, Hermine thought. She sighed. The furnace was making its noises.

"You ought to get that thing fixed, Hermine," Story said as the furnace started its knocking.

"Well hell, it's old," Hermine replied, "just like us. No wonder it knocks."

"Don't have to remind me, Hermine," Story said, leaning over her eggs, "my bones remind me enough. And you don't have to cuss." They were sitting at the kitchen table. In these houses built in the fifties, the kitchen often had a built-in breakfast nook. In their house, the table was not built-in, but it fit into a boxy area with windows all around. It was very pleasant most mornings.

"What's in these eggs? Pass me the salt."

"No salt. Doctor's orders," Hermine said. "And what's in there is good for you. Herbs and other things to season them. Here's the No-Salt." She was consummately ignored by Story, who stirred her eggs around, put her fork down, and then ate her toast.

Hermine opened the paper to the second section. There was a picture of a bunch of kids in dancing costumes. The lead story was about their group, Rainbow Dance Company. They were kids of all colors and backgrounds. "Good . . . nice," Hermine mumbled to herself.

"You might talk loud enough for me to hear you," Story said. "I do live here."

"I was just thinking," Hermine said aloud, "about when I took dancing as a kid. This is an article about kids."

"Um," Story replied. Hermine knew Story really didn't remember

her taking dance, but she wouldn't let on. As Hermine read the article, it all came back to her. The day she first went to dance. Story had
said yes, for once, to something she wanted to do. For some mysterious reason she had said yes. Hermine remembered how nervous she
got the day she asked. She was about seven or eight; she couldn't remember now. But she did remember her stomach had butterflies,
and she recalled her fear that she wouldn't get to do it.

She remembered the wonderful day the dancers came from the
colored high school, and their glamorous teacher, Mrs. Loy, and she
thought, She's got a movie star's name, Myrna Loy, and that's right
for a dancer. And the dancers from the colored high school per-
formed for them in the auditorium of Hampton Elementary. It was
ballet and tap, and she thought they danced like something from the
movies or a fairy tale in a book. Then Mrs. Loy made an announce-
ment that she was teaching dancing lessons, and if you wanted to
take them, you could tell your teacher, and so she did, and she had
to ask Aunt Story if she could sign up. It was in the kitchen on Mill
Street at the kitchen table where she asked, after she stood on one
foot and then the other, and started and stopped her sentences. After
she cleaned up as best she knew how and had taken out the trash. After she had said her prayers three times and washed her hands and
face. She asked. And Aunt Story looked up from her reading and
said, "For Heaven's sake, child, speak up!" And Hermine put every
kind of courage she had in her voice, and said, "Mrs. Loy said to ask
if we could take dance, and so I'm asking because I really want to, really I want to."

It looked like the usual discouraging words were going to come
out of Story's mouth, and then she said, "Dancing. Haven't thought
of that for years and years. Yes. Yes. You can do it. If you want, why
not? Just work hard and be a success at it. Do well. Don't fail me
now. I'll pay for the lessons."

It was the surprise of her lifetime, Hermine thought. One of the
few times she remembered spontaneously hugging Story and Story
patting her on the back. "Okay, enough of that," Story said. "Just do
good. Do good for me. I have my reasons for letting you do this, so
don't mess up."

"Be a success. Don't fail me."

Boy, that was sure a heavy one. How was she to know she wasn't cut out to be a star ballet dancer? She really tried, but she couldn't ever seem to get but so good. Mrs. Loy tried to explain that children were different, but Story kept asking, Why can't she get any better? Mrs. Loy couldn't soothe Story's disappointment a bit. She kept telling Story dance was good for Hermine even if she never made first row at the recitals. Just let her stay and keep trying, she said. "Please let her stay." Story said she'd pay for a few more lessons, and then they got home and Story had said she looked like a teddy bear in tulle and Hermine had quit. She just never went back. She never stayed after school for any more lessons, and nothing Mrs. Loy said could make her go back.

"You never could do eggs you know," Story said, interrupting Hermine's memory. "You never could make them taste like anything, even with salt."

"I never could do anything to suit you, could I?" Hermine scraped the eggs into the garbage, making more noise than necessary. "You just never got over the fact that I wasn't Mrs. Loy's top dancer. Remember?" There was no answer. "You never got over the fact that I didn't pass the bar. You never . . . Oh, just forget it. It's too late." The old lady's head was trembling slightly with age. She looked bewildered and a little lost. Hermine stared for a minute into those ancient eyes. She doesn't have a clue what I'm talking about, Hermine thought. I don't know why I bother.

"I want my medicine now," Story said. "I'm supposed to take it after I eat. And then I want to watch my show."

She doesn't remember my life, Hermine thought. She doesn't know how hard she was to grow up with, or what she did to me, or even why I get so mad at her. If I could just ask her somehow. Just ask her once why it was always always so frozen between us. She got Story settled in her chair and went to get the prescription and water.

If only there were somebody she could tell. A support group for survivors of mean old ladies, she thought. There must be other survivors out there, just dying to tell their stories. And she would say, "I was raised by my aunt, who should have put me in a Children's Home. And there was always a desolate space between us, like a

frozen waste, and I could never reach across it, and apparently neither could she."

Hermine ran the water into the glass. Story was calling. She
wanted the channel changed.

1965

California was wonderful, intoxicating after the hot, dense southern
mind-set in Hattenfield. She could at last breathe! There were people there who knew how to live, and women there who weren't enslaved, either by poverty or marriage or race. There was work with
the poor and the Black Panthers, and she found sisters everywhere,
Hispanic, Indians, blacks, whites. Hermine got an apartment with
another graduate student. She knew what Dr. King's "Free at last"
meant, at least for her, it meant free from limits, chains, don'ts,
can'ts, won'ts, and Aunt Story.

Story called every month on the first of the month. Hermine knew
Story was doing her duty. She wanted to see that she wasn't in trouble of any kind. She'd call and ask the same three questions: Are you
well? How are your grades? Don't fail me now. Are you paying your
bills? And she'd hang up. After she posed the questions, Story was
satisfied that she had fulfilled her role as a responsible parent figure.
Story said she didn't like California, but since she had never been
there, Hermine couldn't imagine what she based that on.

Anyway, it certainly did keep them out of each other's hair. After
the first few months, Hermine never called her back; there was nothing she could say that was safe. How do you say that you're breathing
for the first time in your life? That you're so glad to be away from
home that you thank the clouds, the sun, and the stars above for not
being "home"? No, there was nothing to say, so she wrote meaning-
less notes that spoke of weather, work routines, and asked no questions. Sometimes she was tempted to put a letter into the mailbox
that simply said: "Are you well? How are your grades? Are you paying
your bills? Don't fail me now."

She worked hard at law school and decided to put her energy into
being an advocate for the poor. Diana, her apartment mate, was a po-

litical science major, going for a Ph.D. She wanted to write books and teach and be influential with her scholarship. Her favorite saying was, "If you want to change the world, girl, you got to change the way people think!" Hermine would argue about direct action and laws, and they would go back to their black coffee. Long nights were spent poring over books with papers scattered everywhere. They never cleaned up, and they joked about not being able to find the bed some night. The bed was a mattress on the floor. Once, the phone rang, and they almost missed the call because the receiver was hidden under so much miscellaneous stuff on the bed. They slept together in the midst of the chaos, sometimes not bothering to undress; dirty coffee cups, pizza boxes, assorted clothing, and African objets d'art all mixed up together.

There were always parties to go to, always fascinating people to meet, never enough time to do all the work expected of them. One night after a party they sat on the side of their mattress finishing up beers, drawing on what was left of a joint and sleepily discussing a lesbian couple they had seen at a party. It was three A.M. "It makes sense, you know," Diana said. "After all, the population of the world is too great anyway. We've got to do something about the birth rate."

Hermine sipped some beer. She thought about the men she had dated. "Men suck for the most part anyway," she said quietly. She was angry at men. Angry at King Sam, angry at Stephen, angry even at her father for dying and leaving her with Aunt Story.

"Suck what?" Diana said, grinning. Hermine pushed her down and poured the rest of her beer between Diana's breasts, soaking her T-shirt. They were laughing and tussling on the bed.

"Shh, shh," Hermine said, "you'll get us evicted. J. Edgar Hoover is listening."

"J. Edgar Hoover is a fag pig," Diana shouted, "and I hope he hears me!" Hermine suddenly flashed on Story. God, she was glad to be away from there. God!

Diana was screaming about pigs and piglets in the FBI. She covered Diana's mouth with her hand and fell on top of her, suddenly wanting more than anything in the world to kiss her friend and bury her face in the hollow of her shoulder. Her heart was pounding. They were close. Diana would protect her. She knew Diana would understand because she had heard her talking about gay rights. Her mind was racing, but mostly she could hear her heart beating and nothing else, and mostly she knew she really wanted this. It was a chance she had to take. There was no struggle. It was where Hermine turned her pain into fire and touching.

Diana made it all right finally. It was a safe place for all her lost feeling. Diana welcomed her inside the soft places of her body and her heart, and all she had fantasized about having with Faith, she finally had. Hermine's tears were a dammed-up flood let loose, dammed up from the day long ago when King Sam had been arrested. Diana loved her. She would never go away. She would not do what Faith and Stephen had done.

They became addicted to each other very fast. It was new, wonderful, one more step into outer space. They knew what the brothers said: "Dykes are counterrevolutionary. It is a white woman's thing, decadent and corrupt." They'd sit in political meetings giving each other secret looks, smiling as if they agreed with every word, and then later fall into bed when they couldn't study one more minute.

All that political stuff didn't matter to Hermine. She didn't care what they said about what she was or wasn't. She didn't think she was any of those things. She was just herself. Like she'd always been. She didn't want to "come out." After all, it was nobody's business who she slept with. She tried to ignore the whole thing.

The one big argument they had going was whether to tell their families about their relationship. Diana wanted to be open about it. Hermine thought it was stupid. "Why ask for a problem you don't have?" she said. "That's what white women are always doing. They got to tell everybody what they're doing in the bedroom. Well, it's not for me. And if you knew my aunt Story, you'd know what I mean. 'Political integrity,' 'being real,' " she said scornfully. "Yes, I *am* sneaking. Yes, I *am* living a secret life, and it ain't nobody's business but my own. I don't see any reason to open *that* can of worms."

Diana was outraged. "You *know* why, Hermine," she said, pacing up and down in their two-room apartment. "It's like being a criminal or a fugitive or something. You can't even be a whole person when you're with her."

Hermine laughed out loud and strong. "That's how much you know!" she said, waving her arms. "That's how much you know about this woman! I've never been and never will be a whole person to her. She is a witch. The woman is a witch, and I will not have her dirtying our love, which is what she would do; oh, she would find a way to do that to me."

"But Hermine, your integrity comes from inside you, not from her. Can't you see that? It's just that you're pretending to her, pretending to be someone you're not."

"I am not pretending to be me. I am only what I am. Why can't I love both women and men? Lots of people do, you know. I *wanted* Stephen. I *loved* the man! I see no reason to tell her I'm gay when I'm not."

She was anxious to make it right between them. Her relationship with Diana was the most important thing in the world to her. She didn't care about this political stuff. And she was terrified that telling Aunt Story would create some kind of disaster that she wouldn't be able to handle. It was asking for trouble. She felt it in her bones. "She has never known me, never *seen* me anyhow, Diana. She doesn't *see* people. So if I told her about us, she wouldn't see us. Don't you understand? I might as well pretend. It makes no difference. She'd see some cartoon lesbian characters living in decadence and disgrace and bound for Hell."

Diana shook her head. "It's your wholeness I'm talking about. Yours and mine. I'm in this too, you know. My integrity is involved."

The argument stayed around for years, like dirt kicked into the corner but not thrown out. They walked through it, but they wouldn't get rid of it. The difference felt too much like an earthquake's rumble. Hermine carried a fault within her, a vulnerability that Diana gradually came to sense in later years, but she tolerated no shifting under her feet, no threat of pebbles breaking loose, and so she refused to pay heed to the echoes. Diana herself was solid ground, good soil; you could stomp your feet on her and she wouldn't break, and she wanted that for her partner.

1967

A rally and march were scheduled at the UCLA campus. It was a coalition of women's groups, blacks, antiwar people, and others. Diana wanted to go. She was pressuring Hermine to march with the women. Hermine was timid about revealing herself in public as a feminist, much less as a lesbian. She had friends who would be shocked, and might even reject both of them completely. Also there was her job, and her scholarship, and passing the bar. She was very nervous.

"Nothing's going to happen!" Diana insisted. She was chopping onions for their spaghetti dinner. "Nothing! Who will see you in all that crowd anyway? This is California, for God's sake."

"*Everybody* will see me. The television people will be there," Hermine protested, waving her arms wildly. "Everybody I care about will see me!"

"Well, you'll have to decide where you stand, then," Diana said, scraping all the onions off the chopping board with her big knife and into an iron skillet. "You'll just have to decide if you're black first or if you're a lesbian first, and that's a damn shame." She wiped her cheeks where the onions had brought tears. Hermine knew they weren't emotional tears. Diana was as unflappable as usual.

"Well, I'm *not* a lesbian," Hermine blurted out. "I never told you I was!" The old wound had surfaced again. There was a long silence.

"Oh, really," Diana finally said. She stopped chopping onions and put her knife down. "Then what are you, my dear? Have you been busy doing things I don't know about? You should make up your mind!"

Hermine stammered, "I never *told* you I was. I just love *you*, that's all. I just want to be free to love who I want to love. That's all! I don't mean to hurt you. Please, Diana, that's not how it is. I just don't *care* who people are. That's all. I just love you because of *you*."

"Well, I'll be damned. You could have fooled me," Diana said quietly.

The phone rang. It was Western Union with a telegram from North Carolina. They wanted to know if Hermine preferred to have it read over the phone or simply sent out. She said they should go ahead. What in the world would be announced to her in a telegram? The operator read: "Sorry to inform you. Stop. Uncle Dandridge McCloud and Uncle Dannell McCloud departed this life, March 28, 1967. Stop. Heart attacks. Stop. Call for details. Stop. Signed, Aunt Story."

Hermine put the phone down quietly, saying, "Thank you, operator," at the same time. Diana knew it was something upsetting. She was watching Hermine's face while she poured the tomato sauce into the onions. Hermine sat down heavily on a kitchen chair. "It was Uncle Dee and Uncle Dum," she said. "They're dead. And I never ever went to visit them. I don't do anything right." She started to cry then, remembering her childhood and the days of going to King Sam's.

"I'm so sorry, Hermine," Diana said softly. She turned off the burner and put her arms about Hermine. "Want to talk about it?"

"No, not right now, no." Hermine wandered off to her room, remembering the sunny spots they had brought to her, the fresh air, the honesty. And she hadn't even written them for years. She hadn't written a word or sent a birthday card since moving to California.

She went into her closet and rummaged around in the back of it, looking through boxes. They had to be there somewhere. She had never thrown them away. Oh, God, she hoped she hadn't thrown them away. She kept wiping away tears as she searched. Finally, at the bottom of the last box, she saw the faded blue denim of an old pair of jeans. The jeans her uncles had sent her years ago. She hugged them to her heart, remembering the evening at King Sam's when Uncle Dum had made her promise not to let anybody push her around and had told her about her power place.

Hermine knew she could no longer get into anything that had fit her at sixteen; even so, she tried, and then she began to rip the inner seams of the jeans. Once she had measured, she cut them off where a miniskirt would end and put the rest of the material aside for a halter top. So much time had gone by that Diana knocked softly on the door to see if she was all right. "The spaghetti's ready, Hermine. How about a little supper?"

Hermine opened the door. She hugged her partner. "Yeah," she said, "let's eat, and I'll tell you what I'm wearing when I march with the women's groups tomorrow."

———

Aretha Franklin belted out "Natural Woman" on the radio. Diana was pacing and flinging her hands up in the air. "No notice! No nothing. Tuesday. Tuesday!" The telegram had just come. It read: Coming to visit STOP Meet at Los Angeles Airport Tues. 3:30 P.M. STOP Flight 485 STOP Conference at UCLA STOP. Their house was in disarray. Neither one of them had much time these days to buy food, much less clean the house.

She was already in a panic about the bar exam coming up in a month. It would be her second try. The first time had been a washout. She'd studied herself into a tizzy, then during the test, she froze. It was as if her very brain was locked in ice and nothing would come out. She didn't like to think about it, much less anticipate explaining to Aunt Story why she hadn't passed. She couldn't explain it to herself even. She knew the stuff. But it was as if she'd never spent all those months studying all those cases. Nothing but a big zero, nothing there. All she could think about was the day she had danced for her uncles and made a fool of herself, and after the bar exam she felt the same way. So she just pretended to Aunt Story that the date for the exam hadn't come up yet, and tried to put it off as long as she could.

There were books and papers and dirty dishes everywhere. Hermine simply sat and stared, always her first reaction to extreme pain. This was like a soap opera; only it was worse. She'd get up, do a little paperwork, and return to the chair by the window. All day she sat fighting down panic.

She knew that love was not new for Diana. In college Diana had had one or two affairs with men and one with a woman. She had seen and heard almost everything that was considered daring. But Hermine felt like she would die without this love. She would do anything to keep it. And the prospect of her aunt coming was a threat she couldn't explain. After all, she was an adult, wasn't she? What kind of power did this woman have that she could make her feel just as she'd felt when she was going with Stephen? As if she were in that boat again, that boat that had a shaky bottom that would let you drown. What did Aunt Story have to do with Diana? She couldn't make Diana leave her; that didn't make any sense.

Still, she felt it. The sense that this was not safe, because even though she knew better, she still blamed Aunt Story for Faith. After fourteen years she still smarted when she thought about not even having a chance to say good-bye to Faith. Diana wanted her to be strong. She wanted her not to be jealous, and to be "mature" about everything Diana wanted to do. Diana said "let the past be the past." That was then; this was now. She wrapped her up in the only home she had ever known. The only problem was that Hermine wanted life to be solid for once. She wanted to depend on people. Things weren't as simple for her as they were for Diana.

And she didn't want to make another terrible mistake. What if she had been wrong about Stephen? What if he had really loved her, and she'd thrown all that away? Hermine slammed her book down on the desk. Damn it! He *had* left her. She was sure of it, no matter what Judy had said.

Diana didn't seem to have as much patience with her as she used to either. She still gave her lots of presents—flowers, treats, trips to concerts—but somehow she didn't seem quite the same these days. She was irritable more often, and she had started going to cocktail parties without her, even staying out all night if she was an hour away from home. Oh hell, Hermine thought, maybe she just needs something else right now. But the thought didn't help as much as she wanted it to. Aunt Story's coming was just a chink in the bottom of that boat. No matter what. There was no telling what kind of pressures it would put on Diana and on their life together.

It was Sunday. They had two days before certain calamity. She tried to calm herself down by eating sweets and junk food, even thought she knew she was eating too many snacks and colas, gaining weight and hating her reflection in the mirror. After all, what was the worst thing that could happen? she thought. Story might say horrible things to Diana, that's what, and Diana might lose what patience she had left and walk out of her life. Even worse, maybe Story would try to get Diana fired—or maybe she'd try to get *her* fired! And then she'd have to find another job or go back to North Carolina, 333 Mill Street. Never. She'd never go back there. Forever. She had said she was leaving forever.

Hermine's panic rose again like a familiar snake. She knew her aunt's meanness, her small, cramped places, places in her like a dank cellar where insects made nests, and an occasional rat made a resting place. She knew her well, and that's why she could taste the fear at the base of her tongue.

Diana found somewhere to go, anywhere to get out of the house. "She's your aunt," she said on her way out. "You figure something out. Didn't I say we should have told her!"

Hermine decided to do the laundry. It tended to clear the mind a little. The smell of the detergent, taking things from the dryer, folding the clothes—her hands needed something to do. They shook a little as she sorted the things in three piles—darks, lights, and not-so-brights. Sometimes she thought she belonged in the last category. There was no escaping this problem by going to work. Sunday. The office was closed. She turned on the small machine in their tiny laundry cubby, and heard the comforting sound of the water filling it up. She shook the detergent from her hands, and then slapped them together to get the grainy stuff off, flicked off the overhead light and went into the living room. It would be maybe a half hour before the clothes were done. Time enough for some coffee. The awful truth seemed to sit on her shoulders as she reached for the jar of decaf.

Hermine sighed a deep sigh and scratched her head, pulling her hair back from her face in a nervous gesture. She was still wearing her hair unstraightened, and she knew Story would still hate it. Beyond the all-present fact of Diana, she had told other lies, which Diana knew nothing about. Lies about her job, her house, the bar exam, and her car. She told Story what she thought she would want to hear. She told lies to keep her quiet and satisfied and out of her life.

Hermine looked around at the tiny house. Half of a duplex was not exactly what Story would call success. One bedroom, an "office," a living/dining area, a kitchen with laundry, and a bath and a half. And the neighborhood left something to be desired also. It just hadn't been important to either one of them. Leftover forties and fifties "ranch-style" homes, some bordering on poor and run-down. Her car was not the new Buick two-door sedan she had described in a letter to Story, but a 1958 Chevrolet in need of paint and some body work.

Anyhow, it wasn't fair. This whole thing wasn't fair. Coming like this with no notice, interrupting her peaceful life with Diana, causing conflict between them. It was like her, it was just like her! Hermine slammed her fist down onto the kitchen counter and burst into tears. Frantically looking for a Kleenex, and glad Diana wasn't home, she was disgusted with herself for lying, but she was determined to put up a good fight. She blew her nose brusquely and picked up her coffee; it was losing its heat.

There was no question about it. She would have to outthink her aunt, anticipate her moves, take her off guard. That wouldn't be easy to do. Story was an experienced old warrior. Hermine thought of the time she had been so terribly embarrassed by Story when she'd invited some high school "friends" over to the house, defying Story's orders. She had not told them to go, but she had certainly thrown them out of her house. They were not the right people, she'd said. "Loud and common, uncouth and dirty." Hermine had only brought them home out of pure rebellion; she really didn't like those kids and usually had nothing to do with them.

Hermine had counted on Story's sense of decorum, and the fact that Story knew their parents. They had been students of hers. She thought she'd won when John Henry Primes sat on the sofa and put his dirty sneakers on the coffee table alongside, and then on top of, Story's *Book of Renaissance Art*. She thought she had won when Shenetta put "Annie Had a Baby" on the record player and turned it up as far as it would go. Story had walked through the room as if they weren't there and gone upstairs without saying anything. Hermine thought, She can't bring herself to say anything. After all, she knows them.

Hermine was sure she had won until, during a lull in the rock and roll, she heard Story calling her, and she went to the bottom of the stairs. Story's voice came wafting down the stairs. "Hermine, darling, when your friends leave, be sure to spray that deodorant, won't you? You were quite right, you know, a certain class of people brings that smell in with them wherever they go. It must be in their clothes." Hermine almost died. It went all over the school that Hermine had insulted her classmates and that she had to spray after they left. It was the last time she'd risked so much with her aunt Story. She knew then that she was outclassed.

But this was her house, not Story's, and that ought to give her a little edge. The wash was done. Hermine transferred the whites to the dryer and put in another load. There was no way to avoid it. Aunt Story was too smart, and besides, Diana wouldn't pretend. Okay. She would learn the truth, but she didn't have to win the game, not this time.

Life had been good without having to spar with Story every step of the way. There had to be a way to wage this contest so she wouldn't come out the loser. She didn't want to go back into that crazy place. Maybe if she refused to play. Maybe they could just invite some friends over for dinner and wine and make polite conversation. Play it light, and not get into any sticky areas; she might squeeze through without any irreparable damage.

Nikki and Darby and Diana could do the cooking. She would pick Story up at the airport at three thirty. Diana might be political, but she wasn't a fool, and Nikki and Darby would know how to have fun sprinkled with a few serious things, so it would sound like they weren't complete idiots. No heavy "issues" for the evening.

Hermine picked up the phone and arranged the dinner for the evening, giving careful instructions to her friends, "No heavy issues; don't be political," she said. "Have a little fun." Hermine was holding on to a most desperate hope that everything was going to work. She had finished the darks and cleaned the house when Diana returned. "I have a plan," Hermine announced.

———

At three thirty Hermine was waiting at the gate for the 787 from North Carolina. She spotted her aunt right away. Story looked very professional and very jet-lagged. Hermine was dressed in a sundress, her earrings looked African, and her hair was still natural. She wasn't pleased. Story kissed the air beside Hermine's face, and Hermine did the same. "You've gained weight," she said. And then, "Is this your car?" She looked down at the old Chevrolet.

"Yes, I got rid of the other. It was always in the shop," Hermine said, trying not to sound nervous.

"Well, it makes no sense to change a new car for a ten-year-old wreck, I'd say. Did you think about what you were doing?" Hermine drove in silence, the stick shift grinding from one gear to another.

"One favor," Story said. "I'd like to stop somewhere and pick up a pair of stockings."

"No problem." Hermine smiled bravely. "We'll just run by the nearest shopping area; as you can see, they're everywhere." She waved her hand as if to show both sides of the street to a tourist. "On your left, a Boutique California, and on your right, an Elegant Wear shop. I just have to stop for Darby, if you don't mind. She's having dinner with us."

Darby was white, small, and dressed entirely in black leather— miniskirt, jacket, and jewelry. Her long brown hair reached her waist. She bounced out of the house and into the two-door Chevy. Story had to lean forward to make room for her to get in the backseat.

"Hello," Darby said cheerily. "So glad to meet you." She leaned across the seat partition to grip Story's hand. The L.A. traffic made for plenty of conversation time. Story thought, All I really want is a shower and a nap, not to make conversation with this overly exuberant young woman. Darby rattled on about all there was to see in Los Angeles. Out of her left ear Story heard words like Hollywood and Vine and the Mann Chinese Theater, and Venice Beach. Darby said something about "the famous Santa Monica Boulevard."

"Yes," she kept saying. "Oh? That's interesting. Yes."

Suddenly they were in a traffic jam. An antiwar demonstration had blocked the street. All kinds of people, mostly young, were sitting in the middle of the street. They had on clothes that were strange to Story, but she'd certainly seen their like on television. Some of them carried signs that read, HELL NO, WE WON'T GO, and OFF THE PIGS.

"Oh, cool man, far out," Darby said in Story's ear. "I bet you haven't seen this in the South yet!"

"We've had our share of demonstrations," Story said in a subdued voice. Could this young woman not know about what was going on in the South?

"Oh wow, yeah," Darby said. "Mississippi is an incredible place. Heavy. Yeah. Do you march, Mrs. Greene? Have you been to Mississippi?"

Hermine appeared to be nervous, as if she wanted to get by the demonstrations, find a dress shop, and get home. She rapped the steering wheel with her nails.

Los Angeles police waded into the crowd and diverted Darby's attention. As soon as a path was cleared, Hermine sped off down La Cienega Boulevard in the direction of a shopping area near her house.

"Aren't you going a little too fast?" Story said. Hermine didn't answer, but turned and pulled into a shopping plaza.

———

Diana was cooking, wearing a blue miniskirt and a tight sweater. "Come in," she said. She swallowed hard. "Come in. We're delighted to have you. I've heard so much about you, Aunt Story." She wiped her hand on a towel she had been carrying and extended it. Story shook it briefly. She was very suspicious of this young woman. When Hermine wrote she had a "housemate," as they called it these days, Story didn't like it. She didn't like it from the start. If a woman was not with a man or a relative, she should live alone. Hermine carried the large suitcase back to the bedroom. She had put Story in *their* room. There were photographs of them with other women on the dresser. She noticed there were no men in the pictures. "Your house is smaller than I'd expected, Hermine," Story said, "perhaps I—"

"No, no, there'll be plenty of room," Diana said quickly. "Hermine and I will take the sofa bed. You just come on back and freshen up." She shouted from the kitchen, "I hope you like Italian. Hermine and I love it. I do most of the cooking. She doesn't much like to do that, as you probably know." Diana continued her long-distance conversation. "The bed is very comfortable, and good for your back." Hermine wished she'd shut up about the bed.

Story saw only that it was a double. She sat down heavily at the foot of the bed. "I have a meeting tonight, Hermine. I'll be depending on you for a ride." She had no reservations at that hotel, but she was thinking she should have.

"No problem," Hermine said. Her voice seemed too loud, and it echoed in Story's head as if she were yelling from very far away. "I've nothing better to do tonight." Hermine disappeared into the kitchen.

Story was left in the little bedroom. She looked around, curious, uncomfortable, but unable to deny her obsession to know. She was poking at the truth while her whole instinct said to leave it alone. There were suspicious books on the shelves, books on women's rights, black power, and a magazine called *Gay Underground*. She leafed through it and tossed it on the chair in disgust. What could Hermine be doing with such trash?

The doorbell rang.

"Get the door please, Diana, I'm in the john!" Hermine called from the bathroom. Story cringed. Voices drifted into the bedroom. They were all female. She walked out into the living room. A woman she hadn't seen sat on the sofa that Hermine and Diana would sleep on that night. She was introduced as Nikki. Nikki was a large, black woman who wore long red pants and big earrings. Her hair was worn in a "bush," another variation of the Afro hairdo.

"We were having guests for dinner, Aunt Story," Hermine explained, "and when we got your telegram, we thought we'd just make it a party." Story managed a slight smile. She sat on the edge of the third cushion of the sofa, her back as straight as a telephone pole. The only other chair in the room was a bean bag. There were two large pillows on the floor.

"Let's have some music," Darby said, flouncing over to the stereo. She found a Jimi Hendrix album and put it on.

"So, Mrs. Greene," Nikki said, "how do you like California? Isn't it a gas?" Darby came back to the sofa, almost snuggling into her seat, and patted her foot to Hendrix.

"I just arrived," Story said tightly, "and I don't have any opinions yet." Diana announced dinner. They crowded into the dining area at the small table, two couples on either side, Story at the head.

Nikki was low-voiced, but gracious and attractive. "You know, Mrs. Greene," she said between bites of lasagna, "we'd be very interested in what you do for a living. Hermine hasn't told us what meeting you're attending." Story softened a little and gave a very careful explanation of her job as vice-principal of an elementary school and the conference she was attending.

The young women began to talk about the complications of school integration in the South; they were very interested in the black movement and the Vietnam War. Somebody said something about Watts and the problems in the northern cities and how much racial hatred there was in the North. They seemed to Story to be knowledgeable and sophisticated about politics. Story thought maybe they might be all right for Hermine as friends until Darby said, "And what do you think of gay rights and how that fits into the black movement?" Nikki and Diana glared at Darby as if she had stripped naked in the dining room.

Story's side of the table had suddenly become a frozen waste. She said, "I don't think about homosexuals at all. Do they have rights?"

Darby paled and coughed. Hermine excused herself from the table "for some water," and Diana put her fork down. "Until all lesbians and gay men are free, none of us is free," she said. There was a long, long silence. Hermine had to come back into the room. No glass of water could take that long. She heard her chair scrape the carpet, the sound magnified a thousand times. She sat down. The silent chewing overwhelmed her. Someone reached for the French bread. A knife scraped a plate. The heavy smell of oregano and cheeses seemed to fill the room. Hermine's face was shiny. Sweat was running down her back.

Finally, Story said, "Excuse me," and walked into the bathroom and shut the door. When she heard them starting to clean the kitchen, she picked up the bedroom phone and dialed a number. Nikki and Darby continued to play Joplin, Aretha, and Beatles albums. They all talked in low tones under the loud music.

Story appeared in her coat at the bedroom door in the midst of all this. Diana and the others were drying the dishes. Hermine was standing over to the side, looking as if she'd swallowed a brick, but it was her eyes Story noticed. Her eyes were frightened, like a trapped animal, but there was a deadness there too. She hadn't looked at her in so many years. Had her eyes always looked like this? Like she was hiding?

In the midst of the music a cab pulled up. Hermine waited for Story to speak. Nikki tried to smooth things out. "You aren't leaving us already?" She seemed genuinely sorry. "Mrs. Greene, we had dessert. You can't go already. We were just getting acquainted." Diana stood a little to the side. "Come on now," Nikki continued, "send the cab away. We'll have coffee."

"I hope your stay is pleasant here," Diana said, always the honest one, and not about to ask her to stay. She hadn't tried to hide anything, and Story knew then. Her suspicions were right. They heard a horn.

"I hope you and your friends are satisfied," she said, "now that you've ruined a perfectly good human being. Maybe you can find something better to do, like cruise down Santa Monica Boulevard." The silence was full of Story's and Hermine's unspoken rage.

Diana and the others retreated into the kitchen. It was the only thing to do under the circumstances. Hermine was left standing with the pieces of the evening.

"Hermine," Story said, her face expressionless. "if you would get my bag, I'll be going." Story felt old. Older than she had just two hours before. Tired. Very tired. Somehow she got down the steps and into the cab. Their good-byes were simple and quiet, as if they both wanted it to be over.

Story was weary. Weary of a world that had never been safe for her, of a world that was now telling her that her own flesh and blood was alien, one of *them* out there, and not to be trusted in ways she had never dreamed possible. She felt she had failed in some way. She had done her duty. The best she knew how. She was sure there was nothing wrong with the way she'd raised Hermine, but there must have been something she didn't know about. Something wrong somewhere. There was a right way to be, she was convinced of it. That night she knew she had failed in all those things she had fought so hard for. Papa had been right after all. There was a Hell. Hell was being in a world where you had no one you could depend on, and no one who understood what you stood for. She fought back her tears all the way to the hotel. There was such a shame in it. A shame that went deeper than she had ever felt.

Even poor Bertie tried. She tried to do something about her weakness. But this! This she wasn't prepared to accept. There was no excuse for this that she could understand. The girl wasn't stupid. Her success in school proved that. Maybe it was her father, in the genes or something. She went around and around with it, but got nowhere. It was like a fish in a pond. It kept swimming around and around to meet her. She couldn't say the word now, not ever. She hadn't said it for so many years that she'd almost forgotten the truth. The fish kept coming back to her. That word. It would make her sick to say it now. She closed her eyes in the Los Angeles traffic. The cab driver was saying something to pass the time on the long ride. The fish in the pond. Fish with dead eyes jumped into her mind. The fish in the pond opened his mouth and a baby tumbled out. She jerked her eyes open. The driver said, "This is it, lady. So, do you have any kids?" He was picking up from something he had said earlier. "Mine are all grown now, daughter too. Well, good luck." Daughter. The fish in the pond. They were her grandmother's eyes, she suddenly realized. Those same flat, unhappy eyes. She would not see those eyes for another twenty-two years.

1968

April. Diana was very busy, with the semester coming to an end. Hermine looked out of the kitchen window at their wild backyard. The house they were renting had belonged to a family in the fifties. They had a gas grill in the back. There was a rusty old swing set, and what must have been a sandbox, now just four rotted wooden planks in a vague square. There was no grass, only scrubby weeds and overgrown shrubs, choking what was left of the flowers. It was sunny. It was almost always sunny.

Chewing slowly, Hermine wondered about dinner. It was her

week to cook. Maybe she could light that thing and grill something. She hated her cooking weeks. It reminded her too much of North Carolina and Aunt Story's kitchen at 333 Mill Street. Maybe they would just have avocados and canned tuna. She hated to cook, period. Anyhow, her room was a mess. She should clean up instead of cooking. A bag of half-eaten nacho chips was in front of her on the counter. She reached for another one. Besides, she was always hungry during her week. Diana was a wonderful cook. She sighed and chewed. Gourmet cooking and Hawaiian dishes. She was a marvel in the kitchen. She was a marvel everywhere. Hermine sat down at the kitchen table. They had got it secondhand, an old wooden one they painted white. The walls were decorated with posters— freedom slogans, feminist images, African faces, Martin Luther King, Malcolm X. She switched on the TV. Marches; Walter Cronkite. Diana would be home soon. She'd want some dinner. A half hour later she heard the front door open. She was still sitting at the table.

"What's for dinner? I've a meeting tonight. I'll be very late. Did you cook?" Hermine was slowly chewing the last of the chips. Her eyes were red and swollen, and she looked straight at Diana like a child caught who had lost her favorite doll. Diana didn't know yet. She didn't look up at Hermine, but hurried into the bedroom, annoyed, very annoyed. She had been shepherding a visiting scholar around all day, and she was very tired. "Dammit, Hermine, I don't have time to eat out tonight! I *went* to the store, and we've got a house full of food!" She couldn't hear the news over her own chastising.

"Garbage workers strike . . . Memphis . . . King . . . no word on condition . . . King critical . . ."

Hermine heard drawers slamming. The toilet flushed. She still had not moved from the table and the TV.

"We cannot afford to eat out during your week all the time. What do you want, a mama? I can't feed you, I can't. Dammit, now I've got to speed or I'll never get anything to eat and make it on time." She ran through the living room and out the front door. The Volkswagen screeched out of the driveway and she was gone. She had not noticed the tears or even said hello, but she had twisted a knife in a very tender place that only she knew about, in a wound that only she knew was there. "What do you want anyway, a mama?" Diana's voice hung in the air between the torturous "special" bulletins and Hermine sitting at the table in front of the TV. She put her head down on the table and cried like a baby who had lost more than one fantasy in that half hour. Dr. King was gone. He couldn't save black people; the movement couldn't save them; but most of all, Diana had as much as said that Hermine was an immature burden, and that she couldn't or wouldn't save her.

———

The world didn't end when Dr. King died, even though it seemed to. And Hermine didn't die because Diana said she wanted a mama, even though she wanted to. Diana suggested a new job might help what she called Hermine's "black moods." There was an opening in a new black law firm for an office manager, but Hermine hadn't passed the bar. So, unless she took the exam again, this was as far as she could go in the profession. It was a dead-end job, but she liked the people, and it was decent money, so she took it. And she was good at what she did. Running the office for a bunch of young, energetic lawyers who wanted to help people. The job helped for a while, but mostly Hermine was so relieved that Diana didn't leave her that she was able to cope a little better.

Diana stayed on, and even if it was out of habit and convenience, Hermine was willing to take what she could get. Her loneliness drew her to groups of people. She didn't like to be alone. She heard someone mention a meditation group in the office, and it sounded like a place to meet people, so after work she found the bookshop where they were meeting. Someone was supposed to talk about mantras and explain how to put yourself in another state of consciousness. That's what she needed all right, escape from this state of consciousness. She didn't know what was wrong, but something sure was. She just never felt really happy. Days would turn gray and dull, and it would all seem worthless, everything, everything she'd ever done — college, graduate school, her affair with Stephen. All for what? Di-

ana had just been promoted, and they almost never spent time together; she was always too busy. There was no point in sharing this
meditation thing with her, Hermine thought. Diana wouldn't dream
of taking the time to sit and meditate. She was a young woman on
the way up.

Hermine found the shop with no trouble. The window was full of
the featured author's book, *Ten Minutes a Day Toward Enlightenment.* Then she saw other things, things like incense and candles.
She sat next to someone dressed in rainbow colors. A man with an
earring in each ear was on the other side of her. By the time the
teacher had demonstrated the technique for them, she was convinced that she had found an answer to her own aching heart. She
was sick of being lonely. Only for a few years, a few naive years with
Diana, had she felt that cold, frozen space inside her thaw out. She
was looking for warmth, how to find a cradle that would rock her.
She didn't much care where she got the answer because she had felt
Diana's warmth slipping away. She was desperate to find some way
to belong to someone.

After three or four times the meditation group was pleasant, but
she wasn't sure of herself. She always went late so she could walk into
a room already full of people and maybe not have to say hello to people already talking. The man with the silver hoops in each ear
walked over to where she was standing. "So, what's your name?" he
said, looking her over. "I noticed you last week, and I really like your
eyes, you know. What's your sign?"

She looked at his red watery eyes. "Hermine Greene and thanks."
His hair was long, stringy, and blond.

"So hey, what's your sign? Scorpio maybe? I'll bet it is."

"Yeah," she answered. He grinned, pleased that he had guessed
right.

She noticed that he smelled faintly of beer.

"How about after—a beer maybe?" It was time to start the
meditation.

"Why not?" Hermine answered, taking her sitting position. Nothing else was happening in her life. She didn't have anywhere else to
go on this Friday night. Diana was in Hawaii at a conference. He
didn't have to know she was in love with a woman.

They went to a little pub, and he had too many beers, and so did Hermine. His name was Alex, and he thought she was "really cool," and he said he always dated black women because they "had it together" and he liked that. She knew he wanted to get her in bed. He was obvious, and she was disgusted from the start. When they reached her front door, she had to push him off. She was dizzy and almost fell.

"Look, Alex, look, you're nice and all that. I'm glad you like me, but you don't know who I am. Look, Alex," she insisted, "I said *no*." His beer breath was on her neck. "You need me to call you a cab?"

"C'mon baby, you pretty thing, c'mon, please?" Hermine was getting really tired; it was late and he was getting to be a problem.

"Look, Alex. Like I told you, you don't know me at all." He had her pinned to the wall with his arms now. "Look," she said loud enough for the people walking down the street to hear, "I love women, okay? I'm not your type."

He stopped pushing on her and tried to stand up straight. "Well, you coulda fooled me," he said through his beer fuzz. "Nice knowin' ya, kid. Didn't mean to be a nuisance. Be cool." He staggered away, and she let herself in.

A deep sadness seemed to meet her as she closed her door. A big, empty, silent sadness. The same sadness she always felt at home. "The sad thing," she used to call it. She headed for the kitchen and remembered a big piece of chocolate cake was there. At three o'clock in the morning she was staring at the cake crumbs, wondering how she was going to get through Saturday with nothing to do and no one she wanted to be with.

———

Nikki was somebody who would understand. They were sitting on the L.A. beach. "Maybe it's California," Hermine said. "Maybe there's something about being out here that makes people treat other people like sea gulls—they just peck around them, like that bird after the McDonald's bag. Pick at them and leave when there's no more meat to eat."

Nikki said, "Yeah, maybe so." Hermine lit a cigarette and wished for a drink, at least a cup of coffee. She said she knew she was supposed to be working toward being above all those addictions, but she wasn't there yet; she didn't care what the books on enlightenment said. And that girl, who was she anyhow? A nobody; a straggly white bitch of no importance from nowhere. An uneducated fly-brain of a person. Diana was throwing herself away! She felt the tears come again. It was cold. Nikki just kept nodding her head in agreement. What did she know about it? She should go home. She should confront this. They agreed.

Diana was outraged. "I can't believe you," she said, her voice getting louder and louder. "You know you are first in my life. I've *told* you and *told* you. And now, over a phone call, and a stupid note. Anybody can *call* me. Or do you have a lock on the phone?"

Hermine sat staring at the ceiling and the floor alternately. She fiddled with her keys. "But you can't deny you broke our lunch date. You can't deny you didn't come home last night. You can't deny the letter."

"It wasn't a letter. It was a birthday note. That's all! I tell you, this is it. I can no longer be policed, taken for a liar, whined to, watched. I won't stand for it. I have told you and told you. And I said the last time something like this happened, either I am free or I split. And I am splitting. Now." She walked into the bedroom. Hermine had begun to cry. She was frantic, and Diana was also frantic, frightened that she would weaken. What Hermine had feared most in her life was happening. She was sliding downhill faster and faster. She could feel her whole world slipping out from under her. Everything was turning to Jell-O. She ran to the bedroom, but Diana slammed the door shut.

"Get out, then!" Hermine screamed. "Get out of here now, bitch! Go on to your white piece. Is she any good? Is she as good as me?" She began to throw record albums up against the bedroom door. They didn't break. The tough plastic was made to withstand punishment, and it seemed a mockery of her anger and frustration. "Take your damned classical music with you!" she screamed as Mozart, Beethoven, and Stravinsky bounced off the door and onto the carpeted floor. There was only silence on the other side of the door. Hermine ran to the study and locked herself in. The tears hadn't stopped. She fell on the sofa bed in an exhausted heap.

Diana had finished packing a bag. She was really sorry about it all. A great well of regret rose up inside her. They had loved so deeply and so well for such a long time, but there was no way to go on with this madness. She was not going to be controlled by anybody's fear. That was no life. She looked around the room, remembering, but she'd have more time for that. There was a lot of packing to do, and a place to find. Diana shrugged her shoulders, wondering if anybody ever "made it" these days. Same sex or not, what was the difference? Everybody seemed to break up sooner or later. She'd thrown things in the bag indiscriminately, just taking this and that. At the last minute she picked up a little African statue. It had elongated, pointed breasts and scarification marks visible on the face, and a huge pregnant belly. Hermine had given it to her years before. She stuffed it in with her stockings and sweaters.

On the way out she paused at the door of the study and knocked. "Hermine? Hermine, I'll call you?" she said kindly, her voice ending in a question mark. "You take care, and remember I love you." Her throat was full. She almost broke down on the word love.

Hermine heard the car start up. She held on to the railing of the sofa bed and moaned, rocking and rocking and rocking. "I want my mother," she began to say. "Oh God, I want my mother."

—

There were meditation groups, and cigarettes, and cats, and wine. She took the bar exam one more time, and froze up in panic, flunking it again. There was even an occasional man in her life.

The one man she really liked was Ben. He was massive and beautiful, a journalist from Atlanta. One night he took her to a bar to drink beer and watch the Los Angeles Rams. He told her he believed in reincarnation, karma, other dimensions, and football. She hadn't had so much fun in a long time.

"Why don't you come and go with me to South Africa," he said between swallows of beer. "Lot of stuff going on there."

"Yeah," she answered, "a lot of dangerous stuff. Why in the world are you going there?" She had only met him a few weeks ago, and she still wasn't sure what kind of journalism he wrote.

"I freelance, and right now I'm doing some articles for a liberal

Christian magazine. I'm really turned-on about going to the motherland, especially a place where I think I can do some good by telling the truth."

She could tell he really cared about what he was doing. He looked right into Hermine's eyes. His curly eyelashes and smooth brown skin made it hard for her to concentrate on South Africa. Instead she was thinking that she was glad she wore contacts, because he might not have asked her out if he had seen her in her glasses. Maybe so, but maybe not.

He ordered another beer. After the years with Diana, it felt sort of strange to be with a man, new and very exciting. She wondered what it would be like to go to bed with him, as he reviewed the current political situation for her and talked about apartheid. Here's hoping he doesn't read minds too, she thought, munching on her nachos. At that moment there was a touchdown or something, and Ben said to the man on his other side, "I'll drink to that," and raised his beer mug.

He was a very open person, she could tell. What if he could read her? What if he could sense what her life had been before she met him? Worse, what if they met someone on the street from her life with Diana? During halftime she impulsively asked him, "Ben, have you ever had a psychic experience?"

"Of course," he said. "Most of us do. Don't you? Once, I saw the person I think was my dead grandfather." Ben was looking at her intently. "I like you, pretty lady," he said softly. "I like you a lot. You are a very interesting lady, and it's a pleasure to be with you."

His apartment was full of ceiling-to-floor books, and magazines were all over the floor. They made love in the study on the pull-out sofa. "Where've you been all these years, Hermine?" he said, stretching his full length. His feet hung off the edge of the small mattress. "Sure you won't come and go with me to South Africa? You'll never regret it."

Hermine had visions of ending up in a South African prison. "But it's so dangerous, Ben. What are you going to do there?"

"Like I told you, write news stories from the point of view of the victims of apartheid. Somebody has to get the word out."

"I just can't. Dodging police and bullets, living with the underground. I don't have it in me, even though I care an awful lot about what happens to the people. I'd hold you back. I don't have that kind of courage." Her voice broke on the word "courage." She thought about Diana, and wondered why she was always falling in love with people who had no fear. She rubbed her hand across his chest. "How long will you be gone?"

"It depends. It's a series of articles I'm working on. I may make it into a book."

They had a three-week affair, and made love every other day. And then he left. It was as if he dropped off the earth. She missed him, she worried that he was dead, she worried that he was being tortured in some horrible place in South Africa. She even worried that somehow he had heard about Diana, even though it was much more probable that he had lost his freedom or his life. She never heard from him again, and gradually she had to let him go. But she never forgot Ben. His big, loving body, and his big, loving spirit. He was a wonderful and comforting memory.

There was never another woman.

She saw Diana once in a while, here and there with her new love, a dark, round-faced young woman with cornrow hair. There was never anything much to say to each other, so after a while they'd just wave across the room and try not to come too close. For Hermine it was a wound that wouldn't heal.

She had kept the house and shared it with three cats she called Dark, Light, and Not-So-Bright. Work as a paralegal went on. She became an office manager at a large firm and was good at her job. After Diana left, she had been sick for a while, some kind of bronchitis, and Darby and Nikki had taken turns caring for her. They seemed to be stuck in the sixties—they were still smoking pot—but they were good friends. That was when she developed the cough that wouldn't go away. But she kept at life. There was always another workshop to go to. One month there was one on deep breathing, and the next month she was going to auric visions or something.

Then the letters had started coming, first one every year, then more often. This one felt strange. Very close to the last one. But then

the whole idea of Story writing to her was strange. She put the envelope next to her on the blue and white bedspread. Hermine was
putting curlers in her hair. She had had a long day. Her chest hurt.
For a few minutes she stared at the dark blue carpet, deep in
thought. She put down her curlers and picked up a glass of bur-
gundy, thinking about Story's letter. She picked the letter up again
and ripped it open. "I know we haven't talked for quite a while," it
read.

I'll say, Hermine thought. Ten years qualifies as a long time not to
talk to your so-called surrogate mother! Dark jumped up on the bed.
She was blue-black, the most affectionate of the three cats.

"I do think," she continued, "that you might have thought once in
a while of me. I could use a word now and then. I just think we
should mend some fences and act like relatives are supposed to act."

Dark had turned over the shoe box that held her curlers. "Damn,"
Hermine swore at her cat, and at the letter. Would this woman ever
stop throwing her curves? Life would go along very peacefully, and
then suddenly there she'd be again, like the wicked witch in *Snow
White*, knocking at the door again with a poisoned apple. She never
gives up, Hermine thought, stuffing the letter back in the envelope.
Never mind that Story had been the one who refused phone calls. "I
don't want to mend fences; I don't care what her life is like. I just
fucking don't care!" she said aloud, picked up Dark and stroked her
back gently. It was time for sleep. She coughed, and lit one last cigarette before turning off the light. The moon was lighting up her
white curtains. Sleep did not come easy.

Story kept writing letters that suggested that she come back to Hattenfield to live. Even letters that asked, though she didn't yet plead.
The old lady's health was bad. She thought she might need surgery.
Someone to look after her. She suggested a law firm where Hermine
could get a good, well-paying job. Promised she'd let the past stay
past. Then she began to speak of her "duty" and the best years of her
life.

Hermine was tired of the letters, but she was also tired of California. It had begun to look cheap to her in the overly shiny sunlight,
facile and eternally vapid—all the worst characteristics of youth.

Fake Spanish architecture, tired stucco, taco restaurant after taco restaurant, water-bed stores, souvenir shops, one big ugly beach town. No one should stay young forever, and California felt like a fifty-year-old playing twenty.

Finally Story reminded Hermine that she had some investments to leave her, and a house. Hermine laughed at that one. When all else fails, she thought, try bribery. But her job was boring and there was no one special to take the chill off the evenings. Her life had become a dead end. Being single and middle-aged in Los Angeles didn't feel good. Still, the thought of living with Story brought ice water to her bones.

The morning she hit bottom, or thought she had, she was on her way to work in her old Buick, driving past truncated palm trees that had always looked out of place to her in that struggling city, not knowing what she was going to meet when she got to work, but feeling as out of place as the trees looked to her. Feeling somehow that things were not going to go well today. Just that sense of uneasiness.

The law firm was ominously quiet. Business had been slack for a while now. There were too many lawyers in this town, she had decided. When she got to her desk, she realized she was the last person to arrive, nobody called her in to take a letter, nobody asked her to look anything up. Joe Hamilton, the oldest lawyer, simply told her there was a staff meeting at ten. Hermine sensed something was wrong. She put the coffee out and lined up the cups for the microwave. She straightened her desk and dusted it twice. Finally they were ready.

As they settled in, Joe said, "This will only take a few minutes of your time. David and I have made a decision which will affect all of you." The two young lawyers and the secretaries were tense. "After a long, careful process, we've decided the partnership will be dissolved." Everyone's mouth was slightly ajar, though they struggled to keep their composure. They offered to help them find positions. They realized the recession had hit everybody hard. They offered severance pay. They gave them the day off. That was that.

They were all in a state of shock. It took Hermine a few minutes to grasp what had happened. She was let go. Just like that, it was over.

This job she had had for as long as she could remember. As she drove home she had to deliberately concentrate to avoid an accident on the freeway, mercifully not too crowded this time of day; but the smog was terrible; it was still too hot, and she had lost her damn job! At her exit she began to cry.

It was just too much. Now she'd have to look for work, she still hadn't paid off the house, there were her doctor bills, and she'd lent Nikki some money when her niece got into trouble. "Shit!" she said as she slammed her car door and wiped the tears off her face. "Shit! Damn! Shit! Why hasn't anything ever, *ever* worked out in my life?"

Los Angeles seemed to be full of office managers, especially those who worked in law firms. She couldn't understand it. What had she ever done to deserve such a life? All around her people who led depraved lives seemed to be happy. At least she thought they were depraved. They had jobs, though. Was she guilty of some awful sin she hadn't owned up to? Was her love for Diana really so terrible? Gay people had rights now. Where were hers? The bills were piling up. It had gotten to the point where she didn't want to open the mail. One afternoon she saw a letter hidden under a pile of bills that she had ignored for at least a week. The letter started, *"Dear Hermine."* She put it down, really afraid. It felt like every bill owed coming due all at once, or a letter from the devil, come to collect her soul. She knew if she read that note, her life would never be the same. Then she picked it up again, feeling silly, and read it all in a rush to get it over with.

I appeal to your sense of duty, right, and responsibility. You've worked with lawyers all your life. You must know about justice. I didn't tell you in my last letter. I don't like to complain, as you know. But my doctor has told me I have breast cancer, and I must have an operation. He thinks I will be able to go on living, that he can "get it all," as they say. Only God knows for sure. You must come home now. The operation will be next Thursday. I will probably lose both my breasts. There is no one to take care of me, and I won't have some complete stranger going through my things. By the way, I've bought a nice, new house. Of course you will get the house and whatever else I have. I've saved a

little money through the years. I have no one else. You see my position.
There's nothing else to do. I expect to hear from you soon.

Aunt Story

P.S. I've found a possible position here for you with a good law firm.
Come to 684 Woodbark.

Hermine said, "Shit!" stuffed the letter back in the envelope, and put her head down on her desk. Home, she thought bitterly. Home! That was never a word she associated with 333 Mill Street or Aunt Story. She used to have to go to church with her aunt and sing that song about "crossin' over home," and "being bound for the promised land." Well, if Hattenfield was home, she didn't ever want to get there, and she sure knew that wasn't the promised land, the home they were always singin' about in that dreary church. But yes, "she saw her position." There was nothing else to do. She was elected "it" by default, not out of affection or caring, but by default. Story had her. This time she had her. That would be it. Cancer. Cancer. Story would go so far as to give herself cancer to make her do what she wanted her to do! Hermine's second thought was that that was ridiculous, but then she threw back her head and laughed bitterly. Not with Story it wasn't ridiculous; nothing was ridiculous with Story.

Four days went by. Hermine didn't answer, she didn't call. She found excuse after excuse until Thursday went by. She called the hospital to make sure her aunt had survived the operation. Bills were coming every day now. Her chest had been hurting for a week, and she knew she was smoking more. She went to see her friend and psychic, Crystal Sherrill, who predicted the death of someone close. A past life with Story indicated there'd be some karma to work through. Then her last hope for an interview didn't work out. In despair she put her house up for sale and bought a ticket, vowing to return after Story's recuperation.

"C'mon, girl," Darby said. "It can't be as bad as all that. You can move in with us for a couple of months. You'll find something."

"Yeah," Hermine said. "Who's gonna hire me? A forty-one-year-old paralegal? They want the sweet young things for the front office, and besides, there aren't that many office jobs now. The economy is for shit, you know that. I'd end up in a dive restaurant serving those damn tacos."

"Well, we hate to see you go," Darby said. "It won't be the same around here without you. Promise you'll write and you'll fly out to see us? And Hermine," Darby said, making a point, "get your own apartment. Don't try to live with her." They were putting all three cats in a kitty carrier when Not-So-Bright got loose. She ran off the front stoop and into the street. Hermine was on the phone saying a brief good-bye to Diana when she heard the brakes screech. Diana was saying, "I wish you the best, dear. Let me hear from you, okay?"

As Hermine was saying "Gotta go. Gotta go," Nikki came in the front door. She knew it was only a cat, but her heart seemed to break right then. Crystal had said someone close, but she hadn't thought of her cats. They weren't people. She couldn't help crying. It all felt so wrong somehow. Not-So-Bright's little crushed body, the pain in her chest, the feeling she might never see her friends again, despite her vow to return. She broke down in Nikki's sympathetic embrace.

Hermine left for North Carolina in a kind of daze, trying to avoid the full realization that her worst nightmare had come true. She was eating too much again, she knew that, as she gobbled down the awful airplane meal. She thought about her therapist, who said overeating was self-abusive. Maybe she was right, but Hermine couldn't stop herself when she felt this way. Just like she couldn't stop herself from going to North Carolina. She felt as if she had set her own trap and stepped into it right on schedule. She didn't understand why, but she felt responsible for this disaster. She had always been horrified of this very thing, and now here she was returning to Aunt Story and North Carolina. It felt like a rerun of a bad TV show. It made her want to rewind the video of her life to see how she'd gone wrong.

She had this memory of Grandison Fox. Grandison Fox the sophomore class president, and the smartest boy in the school, or at least that's what everybody said. His father was a college teacher over at Hattenfield State. Everybody knew he would go on to college one day. He was just that kind. Yeah, Hermine thought, he was that kind.

The Great Pretender. That's what they kept playin' that night that Grandison walked out of her life before walking in. She was only in high school and so was he, but there was something old about him. There are some people who ripen before most of us, and he was one of those. A boy who looked like the man he would become before his time. A boy whose maleness made all the little girls scream their first scream before even he understood it, but who learned to enjoy it and even to count on it as his right and privilege. She guessed that's what happened that night. It was the beginning of a way of life for him. No wonder he forgot all about her and the note he had written, if he had really written it. That dance, that blue tulle dance. That dance with the punch bowl and the pubescent kids and the chaperones and Aunt Story's eagerness for her to know a "nice boy." It was a memory of confusion because it was a memory that told her that she didn't have what it took; that somehow she wasn't enough of anything.

He had danced the very first dance with some girl whose name she didn't even remember. What she remembered about her was that she had the biggest tits in the class. No wonder Grandison went right to her. She was a magnet with those knockers, a perfect chance for him to try out that new virility he had discovered. It wasn't about that girl or about Hermine. She laughed to herself. It was all about Grandison. She remembered Ruby was the one who started the whole thing. Ruby, object of John Victor's passion, Ruby, who was just learning how to wear lipstick and who had smeared it all over her top lip when she said, "Do I have something to tell you!" Ruby, who had chanted, "Hermine got a boyfriend, Hermine got a boyfriend." Ruby, who had gone on to marry the object of her contempt, John Victor, and had five kids with him, who started that strange alchemical change that occurs when someone thinks someone "likes" them. She was younger than most. Two years ahead of herself in school. Only fourteen.

It starts so young, Hermine thought, so young. Why do we let them carry our souls for us? Why do we care whether they like us or not? These people who seem to have the power of our heartbeats written in their little notes or in their slightest smile or in their touches? As if we've never been alive before we heard those words someone "likes" us. She remembered Ruby running down the street saying, "Wait up! I got to tell you somethin'," her lipstick smeared pink on the top lip. "Guess who likes you?"

"Search me," she had said. "Who?" They were turning the first corner toward Market Street. There were two blocks before they would split and go in different directions. "Ole beanhead John Victor?"

"No, stupid. Why would I even mention him?" Ruby skipped once and did a little dance step on the sidewalk.

"Willy Freeman, then?"

"No, he got a girlfriend. And anyway, he ain't tall as you and me yet. He's a runt."

"Well, all right, then. Who?"

"It's . . . get ready, it's Grandison Fox!"

"It ain't true. You lyin'." Hermine laughed. "Where'd you hear that?"

"Naw I ain't. Naw I ain't. Cross my heart and swear to God." Hermine remembered clearly. She had crossed her heart with two fingers twice just to prove it was true. She remembered it had mattered so much to her that she would have done anything, things unthinkable, anything, to be special to somebody.

Maybe he had never even said it. How did she know? He was only a sophomore, after all. Who could tell? Someone told someone else, someone said something, and all of a sudden Grandison Fox liked Hermine.

"You're lyin'," Hermine had said to her. "Where'd you hear that?"

" 'Cause he say so," Ruby had said. "He told Lewis Prenshaw. And he go with Louise, and she told me to tell you."

"I don't like that ole boy," Hermine had said, but she remembered her heart was pounding, and she had felt a little scared and a lot excited.

"Yes you do, yes you do," Ruby had chanted. "Hermine got a boyfriend, Hermine got a boyfriend."

"You go on, girl, and don't you tell nobody nothin'. Nothin'!"

"Hermine got a boyfriend, Hermine got a boyfriend." They had reached Ruby's street. Hermine started after Ruby to grab her, but she had taken off running down Market, running.

She knew now it wasn't that it was Grandison. It was just that it was somebody, anybody. Somebody to notice her. Somebody who would say that they liked her. By the time she reached her front door, the strange hypnosis had started, and she did "like" him, not ever having thought about it until ten minutes before then. And then there was that surprise when Aunt Story said that she could go, and she knew that it was only because he was the son of Dr. Fox who taught at Hattenfield State, but it didn't matter, none of it mattered. It was just that she had somebody who had said, or so somebody else had said, that he liked her. And maybe he was manipulated into writing that note. Ironic payback for John Victor, she thought. And maybe he really wanted to write it at the time because he too had been told "that somebody liked him." Maybe the girl with the big tits was just too much for his young maleness, but for whatever reason, she was no longer "2 sweet 2 be 4 gotten" when they got to that damn dance, and they were definitely not partners like his note had asked her to be. There was giggling around her and a pink punch bowl and a too-tight garter belt that kept cutting into her waist, and she remembered most the waiting, her shoes feeling tighter and tighter, waiting, and waiting, and waiting for the one who had said he "liked" her to ask her to dance, to ask her if she wanted some punch, to ask her anything at all. The Platters singing "The Great Pretender" over and over as Grandison danced by with first one girl and then another. And finally John Victor asked her to dance, and she struggled all the way through "Dedicated to the One I Love" because he was dancing too close for comfort, and she was not sophisticated enough to know how to handle it. And it was all too much. It was too much to think about having to talk about this in school; and not to understand how someone could say they liked you and then ignore you completely. Hermine shifted in her narrow airline seat. It was too much to feel so awful, she thought. It was too much, always searching your memory to analyze why you were never, ever enough.

Hermine read all the rest of the way to North Carolina to escape the pain and her own forebodings. She was reading *The Mayan Factor*, by José Arguelles, all about the lost Mayan civilization and the great healing of the planet earth that was supposed to start tomorrow.

It was August 16, 1987, and she stepped off the plane in North Carolina for the first time since she was twenty years old. The entire airport was new to her. She got a cab and gave the address, her mind still full of space visions. She was aware of how fast things seemed to be changing. Her own life seemed to slipping away from her without her permission; it was all sliding downhill like a great landslide. What did this mean anyway, this so-called transformation of the earth? She was exhausted. The driver said he didn't mind her smoking. This was North Carolina. Home of tobacco, after all. She let out a deep sigh with the first puff and looked out the cab windows at the streets of Hattenfield. Nothing was familiar, only a few abandoned buildings. She saw little except cheap bars, pawnshops, junk-food places, girlie shows, and massage parlors. Welcome home, she thought. Welcome home to the New Age.

How new would it be for her? she wondered. Would she see all those wonderful changes promised—a different way of life on earth? More love for people? More love for nature? Maybe all this metaphysical stuff was a big elaborate fantasy. If it wasn't a fantasy, they probably had it all wrong, and the transforming was going to be for the worst. What would Aunt Story be like after so many years? Same old Story, she thought, managing a chuckle. Same old Story. Hattenfield sure looked the worse for wear. It never had been much of a town.

She found Story at home. It wasn't 333. It was small and about ten years old now. Small but adequate, Cape Cod style in an integrated neighborhood. The surgery had revealed no cancer at all, only a few cysts that had to be removed. After she talked with the doctor, Hermine suspected that the whole sad story about cancer and breast removal was pure fabrication to get her back to North Carolina. She felt the old outrage rise into her throat, but she choked it back. What was the use? She didn't have the energy to confront Story with her deception. Now there was nothing in California for her to go back to. No job, no house, no love, no joy. But that was nothing new to her. Her joy in life had always been spirited away as if a thief in the night had stolen it, a thief who habitually left a message that said, "Never count on happiness, for it will always betray you." She settled in with resignation and despair, her ever-present, familiar sisters.

CHAPTER VIII

IF YOU KNEW ME

November 2012

This winter had come with a vengeance, as if to make up for the
warm winters of the past few years. Everyone complained about the
cold. All Story knew was that she was cold most of the time and that
her eyes always hurt. She was sitting in the living room under a reading light. Hermine had brought the album to her at her request. She
wanted to look at it even though she couldn't see very well. But she
remembered the photographs almost by heart. Her finger traced
the outline of FAMILY ALBUM. All remnants of what had been gold
leaf, or something like it, had long disappeared. Now there was only

the depression in the tattered cover where the letters had been. The cover was crumbling in places. You had to handle it very carefully.

Story ran her wrinkled forefinger around the grooves and remembered how much she had wanted to know. How she had stared at pictures of Grandma McCloud and Grandma and Grandpa Temple, at pictures of Mama and Papa. She opened the big book and leaned over so that her nose almost touched the photographs. That was the only way she could make out the faces. There she was with Bertie. They were dressed up for something, probably going to church. There used to be a picture of the church's choir here somewhere. They sure could sing. "Poor Wayfarin' Stranger" ran through her head. They sure could sing that one. "I'm just a-crossin' over Jordan . . . I'm just a-crossin' over home." Papa's church. Papa's choir. Wherever they were goin', it sure wasn't fun. They both looked miserable.

Well, havin' fun had nothing to do with real life anyway. She had always thought there were three things you had to do in life. Do your duty, pay your bills, and mind your own business. Having a good time had nothing to do with anything real. And if anybody ever got to the promised land, she didn't know anything about it. The problem with most people was that they didn't really know what the rules were, she thought, and they just went through life willy-nilly, acting like fools, doing what they wanted to do and behaving like the rules didn't really apply to them. Unlike most people, she knew life required that you go by certain rules, and she had always done it. That was why she had been able to go to college, get a good job, and always run a respectable home for Hermine. That was why nothing disastrous or disgraceful had ever happened in their family, because they had all played by the rules, except Bertie. Bertie had almost messed it up for all of them, but then *she* had fixed that.

Her old fingers and weak eyes went to the next photograph. There she was with Papa somewhere outside. She had on a dress, but she was helping him to do something. It looked like a rake in her hand. He used to say he'd like to have a man to talk to, and then he'd look at Mama and say, "You killed my only chance at that." Story shook her head and remembered how that convinced her that it wasn't good to be "womanish," so she tried to be strong "like a man," so Papa would be proud of her and stop beating her, and like her.

How hard I tried so he would like me, she thought, and maybe talk to me, and maybe stop thinking about his dead baby boys. But it never worked. It sure wasn't family life like they teach in the books. Used to say he was only trying to save our souls. She flinched, thinking of that one horrible night before he died. *That* sure could have been a disaster. And there was poor Mama, trying to look happy in her silk. Lord, the things she could tell if she coulda talked about it. Still, once or twice Mama did talk to her in little hints. And she found those notes when Mama died, on the backs of those old recipes. Oh well, let the dead rest, she thought. That's all water over the dam anyway.

When she left here, she would be at peace because she had kept Papa's church clean of riff-raff, and she had never brought shame to him and Mama's memories. She had never told anybody what happened that night, not even Bertie, who died confused about the whole thing and thinkin' Papa was just a violent mystery. Sweet, naive Bertie.

I was afraid of him too, she thought. Afraid of that belt. Guess he was afraid too, too afraid to love anybody. He sure loved that church of his, though. He didn't talk to us, but he sure did talk to that church. He put all his love into that church. He used to like that song about "crossin' over Jordan." Lord, couldn't he have preached up a sermon about drugs? They were putting addicted people in rehabilitation camps now. If you were found to be addicted, you had no choice but to go. In her opinion, the only problem with that was they'd waited too long to start doing it. She remembered when life was safe as long as you played by the rules, and respectable people didn't know what drugs were, had never heard of them. Only common folks, hoodlums, and wild musicians knew about drugs. Sam would have been all right too, if he hadn't been corrupted by those people he had grown up with. Lord, these pictures made your mind wander. Things she hadn't thought about for years.

She didn't understand how other folks thought. What went on in their heads? Except for a few people she knew, so many people seemed to be living some kind of wild, silly life that had no direction. Like that Penelope Somebody down the street. Running off like that to join a man she had only known six months in Europe. That was crazy! And Bertie . . . but then Bertie wasn't too bright, she guessed. Anyway, she thought, she could never figure out why Sam had let himself be sucked in like that, a smart, good-looking man like Sam who had everything going for him. She still remembered the humiliation. It was one of the worst times of her life. Aleatha had been the first person to mention Sam to her. Aleatha was dead now, like everybody else who had called her a friend.

There she was with somebody she didn't recognize anymore. She looked again and realized it was Sam, all dressed up in his fancy suit and tie. Imagine forgetting what Sam looked like. Old age is a trip, she thought. And there was one with her old friend. The name escaped her all of a sudden, and then she remembered again, it was Aleatha. And Hermine sitting in their yard on a fence. Lots of pictures that Herman had taken when Hermine was a year old.

She remembered she had wanted to know their secrets. She knew plenty of secrets now. Some she'd rather not know. There was Hermine with that girl she lived with.

And there she was with Hermine, a toddler, just starting to walk. They were in the park with Aleatha, all hugged up together.

Poor Hermine was looking a little worn these days. She should learn. It didn't pay to get so upset about things. Just didn't pay. Story pulled her sweater around her shoulders and tried to settle into the chair a little farther. One thing that she knew about all the people in these pictures. They had been uncomfortably cold too, all their lives, scratching and digging for some way to get warm, just like everybody else, or most everybody else, she thought. She knew their secrets, all right. She was not the only one who knew the pain of ice in the veins. She was not the only one who knew the desolation of unkept fires and a soul brought to a dead hearth. She had her own secrets, all right. She turned the page to a snapshot of Jim Black Wind in Egypt, his rough irregular features, his kind eyes.

1974

The waiter brought the Pink Lady and set it in front of her. She looked around. The only other nonwhite person on the trip wasn't in the bar. She was sure he had noticed her before she noticed him, because she made a great effort to be cool and unconnected to everybody, to all of them. It didn't do, she had reminded herself going through customs, to be too eager and to push yourself on others. Let them come to you, and that way they would be flattered if you received them well, and you would have no doubt that you were desired and valued. She didn't like to wonder about that. One wants to know, she thought, if one is an outsider with people. An outsider who knows she is an outsider can always put on a good appearance and be dignified and self-assured. But an outsider who thinks she has been accepted by people is open to making a fool of herself by assuming equality, even with this person, and she didn't know what he was, but he wasn't white. She always waited, and was never the one to make the first move. She considered that an unnecessary risk in a world full of unavoidable risks. Also, people were so available. Look at all these people on this ship, trying to introduce themselves to everybody on the first day. Missing one relationship because you avoid making the first move is not serious, she thought. People are very replaceable; pretty much the same wherever you are and whatever you do. Their games are rather predictable and boring, so why chance embarrassment?

She sipped a cocktail at the bar, glad to be away from North Carolina, which watched its schoolteachers like the Gestapo had watched German citizens. "Games People Play" was the song coming from some piped-in music system. Her mind wandered back to her career and the way it was ten years ago. Superintendent Link had requested that she come to the school board office.

I still hate him, she thought. I'll never forget his face that day. That phony-baloney smile, that smug sense of power. He knew how much I wanted that principalship, how I had worked for it since the first day I set foot in Hattenfield School. I had done everything right, everything. That was just their way of testing me, and they thought I would fail. Thought I would go with the tide, did they? They didn't know me at all. Story Temple Greene has never gone with anybody's tide. Folks were out marching. That Selma, Alabama, thing really had people fired up. Well, I couldn't blame people. If that's what they have to do, that's what they have to do. And what I had to do was what I had to do. I didn't see any point in giving up what I'd been working on all that time. That's progress too.

A black woman being a principal—all-black school or not—Link tried to maneuver me out of it. Telling me, "Of course you know how the school board expects its teachers to act, to use decorum, and not to condone violence." Saying that so I'd feel defiant and go out and march. I knew he was just waiting for me to show my face at the march, and zap! No principalship. And maybe no job at all. Well, they can wait all day for me to sacrifice myself, she thought, sipping her drink. I don't care what folks say about me being an Uncle Tom. When all that was over, Link was still Link, they were still niggers, and Story Temple Greene had a job.

She put her glass down and considered ordering another drink. She just might get drunk tonight. Something she had never done. She just might get drunk on Papa's birthday. After all, she could get a little high in the ship's lounge and then slip off quietly to her room and experience what so many people seemed to find excruciatingly wonderful— inebriation. Why not? The whole world was breaking the law, smoking weeds and doing unspeakable things with people of the same sex. She allowed the shadow of a memory too close to her to cross her face. Why shouldn't she try a little whiskey and see what it was like to be "smashed," as she had heard people say? She thought of her papa and laughed. And the more she thought, the funnier it was, because he couldn't get to her now. There was no beating her now. How she would love for him to see her sitting at a bar, "like a floozy," he would have said, "loose woman, trash," and his large underlip would have curled out as he spit out the word "trash." Story laughed out loud.

She knew he had noticed her yesterday when they got on the boat. She had been a little tense, clutching her smallish suitcase with determination, very alert, and she felt slightly out of place, like a woman wearing high heels in a Laundromat. He had noticed her, maybe because she was the only black woman, but she had worn her smartest suit, and she was trying very hard to be savvy about this overseas travel, very hard. As the customs officials waved her through, she was relieved that no one had stopped her for anything, and she bravely walked up the steps to the deck.

She took a sip from her glass, and there he was. He took his drink over to her at the bar. "Do you mind?" was in his eyes as he sat down. She said nothing, but bowed slightly in his direction, her heart beating slightly faster. Was she already noticeably high? What would this man think? She knew, of course, that he was one of the educators on the tour, but that made it all the more uncomfortable. She looked at him out of her peripheral vision. She'd forgotten his name. Distinguished, older, dark skin, the kind of face you call rugged, she thought, but not handsome. He must have been an Indian, because she remembered he had a funny name, like Red Foot or Black Sky. And then he said, "Jim Black Wind. Good to meet you."

"Story Temple Greene," she told him, reluctantly. She thought Story was a ridiculous name. People were always asking for an explanation of her name, and she didn't have an explanation. She liked it right away that he didn't ask her why her name was Story, and she made a note never to ask him if there was some meaning to Black Wind. She asked if he was going on tour to the Middle East for the first time. He said no, he'd been before, always flying, though; this was his first time on a liner. He'd been to Europe once and Egypt once. Story felt dumb. She hated to feel dumb. She hated to feel dumb more than anything she knew. She didn't say she'd never been out of the country before this trip. He didn't ask, having some sense of her experience from watching her. She kept ordering scotch and soda. Her head began to spin.

Jim was telling her about himself. He was fifty-eight. Same age I am, Story thought (but of course she didn't tell him), and a principal out in New Mexico. She looked younger. Let him think what he wanted to think. All the members of their tour were principals of schools. Jim ran a mostly Native American school, but not on a reservation. It was full of kids who didn't know what to do with themselves, poor Indian kids who were desperate to "make it big" and didn't have the first idea what they meant by that. He tried to keep them off drugs and out of fights. He was discouraged and looking forward to retirement. He had some land.

Her head was making a kind of spinning noise, and she immediately forgot the name of the town where he had land. Some Spanish word. She talked little. A few words about the Southeast, North Carolina, and what that meant for a school principal who was a black woman. Even though the South had changed, it hadn't changed that much, and things were still hard for blacks in the school system. She had taken a lot, being the first black woman principal in her town; a lot. What she noticed about him was that he listened to her. He wasn't looking past her eyes, but into them. He wasn't waiting for her to finish so he could get his next complaint in; he was really interested in her.

The alcohol seemed a little less influential. She straightened up a bit. Story had a gray streak in her black hair; she pushed on it gently, glad at the same time that age took away the pressure of both sexual need and sexual conquest. He seemed so relaxed, so calm. She wasn't used to such peace. It was like looking at a deep blue pool. It made her a little nervous.

She took another drink. Their work on the trip was to be done on the crossing—over and back. Committee meetings and proposals—and the tour would be mostly relaxation. Somewhere he slipped in being divorced and lonely for five years, and having a black grandmother from Kansas, but it was very subtle, so you could ignore it if you weren't interested. Jim asked her which committee she'd signed up for, and she said "Ethnic Concerns in Public Education," wondering if she'd be sorry she told him. Apparently he had not registered yet. Meetings began tomorrow morning.

She wondered what he wanted. Was he really just being friendly? Was there a hidden agenda? The music began again, and it was loud and heavy. She excused herself quickly, saying the usual "nice to have met you" speeches, and he asked if he could see her to her cabin. She thanked him politely and said something about how it wasn't likely she'd be mugged on a luxury liner, and carefully left the bar. *Carefully*, praying she wouldn't waver either to the left or right.

Once back in the cabin, the idea of getting really drunk was not nearly so attractive. Story stretched out in all her clothes on the narrow bed that was almost a cot. How interesting, she thought. She couldn't feel any motive on his part. It must have been the drinks. Dulls the perception, dims the brain. Herman's face came up from somewhere in the fuzzy past. Dims the brain, she repeated to herself and laughed quietly. She'd find out what he wanted tomorrow.

Story fell asleep suddenly, snoring slightly, her dress shoes making two little rounded shadows on the wall in the dim light of the cabin.

—

It was getting dark. The others were touring one of the many historical sights in that part of Jerusalem, and they had decided to steal a little time for themselves. After two weeks of working and relaxing, Jim had become a comfort, an adviser about travel, what to do about money, water to drink or not, things to buy. But he was mainly a safe harbor in the unruly sea of her consciousness. Things kept coming at her. Memories, fears, dreams. She had never talked to anyone this way in her life. She thought maybe this was a retarded mid-life crisis or something. She had always been too busy to stop and think about life this way, and it was good, but it was also scary. She trusted him the way she had never trusted anybody else. She trusted him in a way that was frightening to her. She had never had a real friend before in her life. She was fifty-eight years old, and she had never had a friend. There were people in her life who would call themselves her friends, but she knew better. She knew how much she had let them talk and never talked back.

The flowers in the garden brought a curiously bitter aroma along with their sweetness. They were near the Garden of Gethsemane. "It was Peter, wasn't it?" Story said quietly. Jim looked, rather than asked his question. "It was Peter who denied Jesus, wasn't it?"

"Well, yes," he said, "I think so. And then at the reservation school we were always told about Judas, you know, who turned him in."

"No, I mean Peter was the one who said he didn't know him when he really did."

"Yeah, I think so," Jim said quietly. They were silent for a few more minutes.

"Then I'll probably go to Hell," Story said, almost in a whisper.

Jim was silent, waiting for the story. She would tell him if she wanted to. Finally he said, "But it was Judas who hanged himself. And anyway, I don't believe in Hell."

"No," she said, as if she hadn't heard him, "it's too late. She's just like her father. I can't love her. She had the same openness. That fatuous acceptance, that lack of subtlety and need, and no sense of privacy. I can't love her; it's too late."

"Your daughter," was all he said. It was not a question. He knew the answer.

"I was afraid of losing myself, of being swallowed up in that thing they call motherhood, of not having any of myself left, like my mother. Besides, I couldn't take the risk of her really knowing me."

"You're pretty nice to know," Jim answered, lighting up his cigarette, carefully putting the match in his pocket, so as not to litter the grounds.

"You don't know me, Jim," she said. "You just think you do. Nobody really knows me." He knew there was great pain under the quiet eyes and voice. "If she had really known me, she wouldn't have liked me."

"Does she like what she knows?" he said, looking intently at her.

"No, I'm sure she doesn't," Story answered. She was very close to tears. She wasn't at all used to this. It felt like she was out of time and space, in another dimension almost, in a place where anything was possible and where the rules of real life didn't apply. As if she wouldn't have to pay for this feeling of closeness and love that she felt coming from this man. It was the most wonderful thing she had ever experienced, and she wished it wouldn't end like a good dream, but she knew it couldn't last. It wouldn't be like this at home.

"I like you," Jim said, his face very close to hers. He touched her once on the arm. Her dress was lightweight fabric for the summer weather and hot climate they were in.

"You don't understand," she said. "My mother was a slave. A slave to her husband and to her children. She did nothing but take care of all of us, morning to night, and when the day was over, sometimes he'd beat her, my papa, if he didn't beat me first. There was this hollow look in her eyes, like she had emptied out everything inside her and there was nothing but the skin left. She had no power. No self. At least I didn't know where it was. I couldn't stand to look at her. I couldn't stand it."

The sun was beginning to set. "It was Peter who denied Jesus," she said. "He said three times that he didn't know him."

"Yes," Jim answered. "Fear will make you do terrible things."

"Make you deny the right of someone to be themselves," she said, her voice breaking on the last word. "That's why I'm going to Hell. I don't see how that can be forgiven."

"But you can still fix it," he said. "Talk to her."

"Jim," Story protested, "you don't know what I did. I think she hates me, and I don't really like her very much. That's the truth. I never have. Some things you begin and put in motion, and there's no undoing them. They just have to run their course, like pregnancy or war. Stopping them costs lives. They become bigger than you, and more powerful, and they have a life of their own. Perhaps it's for that other one. I'm paying for that other one," she whispered, suddenly seeing Bertie's face. He didn't ask her who the other one was. "Stopping it costs lives." She was fumbling for a tissue. "My sister would have loved her the right way. I guess it's only fair to tell you; I've come this far." She wiped her eyes and nose.

"I wouldn't expect that," he said, putting out his cigarette.

"Jim, I never told her who she really is. She thinks she's my niece. All these years, I've let her think she's my niece."

He leaned his chin into his hand. "Well, that is a tough one," was all he said.

It was dark. There was some light from the city; the breeze was cooler. They could smell the flowers from the garden. They began to gather themselves to go. "I've never told a living soul," she said, looking anxious and drawn.

Jim took her by the shoulders. "Never forget," he said, "there was once someone who truly loved you." He took her in his arms in the dark night.

It was the first time Story had ever known the real safety of the love of another. Neither one of them remembered that Peter had gone on to become a tower of faith and a martyr in the name of the truth he had denied.

———

They loved well during that six weeks, and for most of the time, Story managed not to worry about what would happen when the trip was over. North Carolina seemed very unreal and far away. Feelings she had never experienced were alive in her. She knew why people seemed to lose their minds in the midst of this thing called "love." She lost all sense of what was appropriate, and she didn't care what the rest of the tour members thought. The tour went from Jerusalem to Cairo. The golden light of the city was magical to her. She was stunned by the Egyptian past, the way it imaged itself. The way it had owned itself, so obvious in the monumental pyramids and tombs and drawings. These artists had known who they were, had loved who they were. One day they visited a bazaar, a market in the city, and there were all kinds of trinkets, jewelry, and even carnival costumes. Story wanted to buy some golden glitter. It looked like something that might be used by Egyptian ladies of the evening, something like a glitter makeup. She bought a little bottle, not really knowing why she wanted it. Later, she would say, it was that glitter that made them lose all control, and that made her remember that she had to go back home.

They were in a small respectable hotel that catered to American tourists. The bus that would take them to Port Said was not due back for them for two more days. On the day of the last excursion, they stayed in, lost in their own hunger for sharing. It wasn't all physical at their age. It was the joy of unconditional acceptance, something they had both needed all their lives, and found in each other. As she laid her clothes out and got her bath ready that late afternoon, she thought about the evening ahead. Maybe they'd take a walk in the twilight. Maybe she'd tell him about that dream she had had last night. It was a dream that came and went often in her life. She didn't know how old she was in the dream, she only remembered the pain of being wrong.

It started behind the shed at the old home place. They had lived there when she was a very tiny child. She tried putting more of the pieces of the dream together as she showered. It always starts, she thought, with the sun coming up, or anyway it's early morning always. I am at peace playing in the dirt. There are glittery things under a pile of trash. I'm curious about what they are so I pull them out. The trash tumbles down in a heap, and somehow I reach the bottles. She reached for the shampoo bottle. Story thought, There are lots of flowers somewhere in this dream, and I begin to look into the bottles. I lift them up and look inside. The sun makes rainbows through the bottom of green bottles, and I think it's beautiful. There's some water or something on the bottles or inside the bottles, I can't tell which, but then just as I look at the rainbow, someone snatches me up from behind, yelling. I don't know what they are saying, I can't hear the words. I am so scared. As she dried her hair she remembered more and more. All I can feel in my dream is my fear, and then I know nothing except the searing pain across my buttocks and legs. It seems to go on for hours and hours, and in my dream I can see the blood running down my legs. I scream and scream.

Standing in the shower with her towel, damp from the shower, Story realized she had awakened herself with her own scream the night before. She was horrified that she had cried out in the night.

She and Jim had adjoining rooms. Maybe he had slept through her calling out. Otherwise he surely would have come in to check on her. It was a terrifying dream. She always tried to put it all the way out of her mind, but there was something in the dream that haunted her. She wished she knew more about dreams and what they meant.

Jim ordered a wonderful dinner of lamb with a very hot sauce and good wine. She knew that he wanted to make love, and there was something about the evening that felt very special, almost like a honeymoon to her. With Jim being so romantic, it didn't seem appropriate to talk about her silly dream. She let it go, maybe another time. She was undressing in the bathroom, still a little shy about him, when she did something she never expected to do. She took the gold glitter makeup and spread it between her thighs and onto her belly. Against the dark brown, almost black skin, it was magnificent, even on a woman her age. Story was still a beautiful woman. People often told her that. The skin between her legs was almost black, soft, like fine black wool with a downy fuzz on it.

In her closed parts this woman, who had never allowed herself to be loved, pressed gold light. This woman who had never loved herself, pressed the light of the sun, and her man, his tongue between the folds of purple plum skin, the Indian tongue, calling her home to sweat lodges, and spirits, and dark snakes. He loved it and she loved it, and she was in absolute terror. There it was, her self, her touching place, not hers now. Meeting, Indian and African, like two rivers under the world's surface, and making an unheard of color, so dark it sang, and gold gleaming, shining, like her forbidden and lost right to be who she was.

It was more than love for Story. It was the terror of the abyss, the loss of all the rules and the fences and the safe limits, and because of that, somewhere inside herself she decided it was doomed to failure, and she accepted the loss of her own abundance.

—

The closer she got to the States, the sicker she felt. On the last two days of the crossing, she did not emerge once from her cabin. Jim sent notes, flowers, messages by the steward, and there was no reply. He was not surprised. She had been pulling away gradually ever since they had boarded the ship. He was not devastated, simply saddened. It had been wonderful with her, and it could have gone on being rich, nurturing, something to make the harsh world a little less so. She would have to come out of her stateroom sooner or later, but he had neither the desire nor the need to push her into a place where there would be bad feelings and a destruction of what they had had.

When it was time to leave the ship, he saw to it that he was a discreet distance away from the customs line. He had sent her his last note with all the information she needed to find him, an invitation to come to New Mexico, and assurances of his love. She went through customs quickly, stepped into a cab, and only turned around when it had safely pulled out into the heavy traffic. He watched the cab until it disappeared into the crowd of vehicles near the waterfront, his right hand in the pocket of his trousers. He was fingering the amulet of the heart, a green marble scarab she had bought for him in Cairo, and the hieroglyphics cut in outline at the base read: "Thou are my double, the dweller in my body. May my heart be with me in the House of Hearts!"

She had never told him about the dream. She had never told him how much it hurt to give up the glitter of early morning sunlight making colors in the bottles.

—

Suppose she had been wrong. What if she had spent her whole life being wrong? Story began to laugh. It was just that she had never considered that fact before. Never. And it was entirely possible and entirely funny. She leaned back in the chair and laughed until the tears ran. Hermine was so unused to hearing laughter, she came running from the other part of the house. She thought the old lady was not in her right mind, and asked her if she needed a pill. Story just waved her away, shaking her head and wiping her eyes. This was her secret, this realization that she could have been wrong. Nobody would ever get this one out of her. "Here," she said, handing Hermine the family album. "Take this thing and put it up. It's a dangerous book."

CHAPTER IX

ICE STORM

DECEMBER 2012

The phone rang. Some woman calling for Hermine Greene. Hermine wasn't there. Story almost never answered the phone anymore. It was something Hermine had to take care of. Just too much trouble. Didn't they know she was too old? Too old to be bothered? Some woman from the Central Courthouse wanted Ms. Greene. She didn't know what that was anyhow. All she knew about was the County Courthouse and City Hall of Hattenfield. She didn't know what the Central Courthouse was. Everytime she turned around they were changing the name of things. She slammed the phone down and sucked on her hard candy, her favorite treat. "Planeteers" was the name of it. She hoped Hermine would bring her some more; she was almost out. She was always running out. It came in violet, green, and pink, and had chocolate insides. She like the pink best. Phone calls. She remembered some woman nosing around about Hermine once before. She couldn't remember when. Seemed a long time ago. Somebody called about the child's father or something. None of their damn business.

Nobody's business but hers. The child's father was who he was. For better or for worse, and nobody needed to know at this late date, least of all Hermine.

She wanted Hermine to come home. That woman, Mrs. King, was somewhere in the house. She thought she could hear the vacuum cleaner going. Fat lot of good she did, Story thought. I could die here and no one would know. She was in her television rocking chair. It had a little tray attached to the arm, where she could reach the medicine, water, and even her cordless phone, if she wanted to answer it. Mostly, she let it ring. Let that woman answer it, she thought. Hermine's spending my hard-earned retirement on her, when she should be here taking care of me. She was forever going out somewhere. She's no spring chicken anymore, Story thought. Hermine better be careful. It's too cold out for a woman her age. I could fall down. I could be sick or something.

One thing about Hermine, she was never sickly. She was enough trouble without being sick. Except for one time. She got real sick. I thought she was gone that time, Story thought. Scared me to death. Story flipped channels, impatient with commercials, loud music, and references to machines she didn't understand. She wanted another sweater. It was so chilly all the time now. She'd forgotten what month it was now, but it was cold. Where was that girl anyway? She should be here getting my sweater. I could get pneumonia, she thought. She ought to remember how it was for her. She got so sick, I thought she was leavin' here. Food poisoning, I think it was. Story remembered the afternoon the school had called her and the fourth grade teacher said Hermine was very ill. Running a high fever, and she had to go and get her.

Hermine was shivering and laid out on a cot in the school nurse's office. Temperature of 105. They rushed her to the doctor's office and on to Memorial Hospital. It was almost too late; it was almost fatal. "A deadly bacteria," they said. "We have to get her through this crisis. Only time will tell if she pulls through."

Story sat with her all through the night and the next day. The black hospital in Hattenfield, Williams Memorial. Story watched Hermine as she twisted and turned in her fever. Her golden skin turned sickly pale, her hair pasted to her damp forehead. Every so often she'd vomit, and Story would wipe her lips with ice and her forehead with a damp cloth. But the fever kept going up through the long night, and Story sat and thought about her life, her life as a wife, a mother, a teacher, a lover. She tried to read, but the words kept sticking in one place in her mind. The place that said she might die. She might die, and I'll be entirely alone then, because she's the last one, the last one of us. And she knew that it mattered. What happened to Hermine mattered a lot to her, more than she had ever been willing to admit. She sat there all night and held her hand and vowed to be nicer to her if she could just get well. If she could just live, she'd make it up to her somehow. And they'd be real family to each other. Story prayed whatever prayers she could muster there in the midnight, in the almost dark little room where they kept coming in to check the fever. She vowed to sue the school system which had given the children bad chicken for lunch, and made several children sick, but none so bad as Hermine.

Finally, in the gray hour of early morning, after insisting that she take a walk, the nurse running down the hall alarmed her so, she almost fainted, but it was only to tell her that the fever had broken and they thought she'd be all right. Story had been weak in the knees then, and had to sit down. The nurse helped her, brought her a drink and said, "I understand she's your only living relative," and Story said, "No, I have some uncles, but they're, well, not as close." Not as close was all she could get out. She wished, then, she could have said, But she's my *child*. Her tears were for relief that it was going to be all right, but not only; because she cried too for herself, and for what she had done, and what was. Because there was now no way she felt she could turn back the time and undo what she had done.

It was too late then, and it was too late now. Life was what it had been. She pulled her sweater tighter around her arms and thought she didn't really believe in reincarnation, but maybe it was true, maybe it was true that you got another chance, and next time maybe she could cross over this space between them, and she could be a real mother to Hermine.

———

Hermine didn't want to remember it, but there it was in her head word for word. It just reminded her of things best forgotten, like what she wanted from life and what she got instead. The day she went to the courthouse in Hattenfield she remembered it in spite of herself, and it had been twenty-six long years since she received that little package in Los Angeles. She had been to work, and she came home and found it in the mail. Inside the outer wrapping was a package addressed in a wavering hand. It said something that looked like "Sit Ever Vir," but the words were smudged out. Under that she saw "and for only her." Inside the package, wrapped in yellow newspaper, was another note, in a younger handwriting. It simply said, "I have reason to believe your aunt is not your aunt." And it was signed, "Sincerely, A Friend." There was no return address, nothing to indicate who it was from. Scratched in the same weak handwriting on what looked like a piece of paper bag was a message that read, "This pin should be give to my granddatta should she be foun." It was a man's gold stickpin, set with one small sapphire. Hermine had been undone by this thing all the next day. What the hell did it mean anyway? California was full of nuts. All kinds of nuts.

Anybody could have sent that stuff. It had frightened her, thinking of letter bombs and people who stalked other people, especially women. There were plenty of weird people who hated anybody whose sexual habits didn't fit theirs. She shuddered, but she put the pretty little stickpin away anyhow, feeling somehow drawn to it and a little superstitious about throwing it away. She must have had grandparents somewhere, and maybe . . . but what about that "your aunt is not your aunt" stuff? It was all too crazy. She told only one friend. The memory was very clear, all of it, as if her mind was trying to tell her something she needed to know. Darby had abandoned her black leather for more conventional "artsy" clothing, but she was still a good, loyal friend, Nikki's partner and Hermine's confidante. They were sitting in a vegetarian place on La Brea Avenue. It wasn't so full of kids talking valley talk or jumping around to boom box music as some places, and they could hear themselves think over the bean sprouts and tofu.

"You should take it to the police," Darby said. "No two ways about it. It's crazy."

"So, what will they do?" Hermine said, chewing furiously. This whole thing had her upset. "You know they never do anything until somebody turns up dead. I remember once a woman in Hattenfield died after this dude, her 'ex,' threatened to kill her every day, and they claimed since he hadn't done anything, they had no evidence. So the poor woman ends up dead in the front seat of her car with a bullet through her head." The waiter brought some herb tea just as she said "bullet through her head." He tried to keep a blank face but wasn't very good at it, clearly interested in their conversation.

"Well, yeah," Darby said, "you might be right. Still, maybe . . . I know, what about looking into it ourselves? Let's call Venetia."

"Why Venetia? Has she gone into being a private detective?" They had a good laugh, knowing Venetia was a tiny, little, soft-spoken woman who was afraid of her own shadow.

"She's a handwriting expert," Darby said between bites. She had to get back to work and was in a hurry. "The police might have hand-writing of suspects on file, but Venetia is like their source. She does the analysis for them."

"God, who would have suspected," Hermine said. "God! Venetia, an undercover for the police."

"Well, not exactly, but she does know a lot about it, and so we'll call her. Call me tonight, and I'll give you her number." She left Hermine sipping her tea and pondering the mysteries of people and their unknown identities. It was one of those memories that comes back with its trivialities that seem to mean nothing, the gleam of the chrome on the door, the green floor, the smell of bean soup.

Venetia picked up a somewhat ordinary personality, introverted, with a propensity toward the healing arts and music. An older per-son, probably a female. Nervous, withdrawn, and nonassertive. But Hermine never found out the identity of the "Concerned Friend."

That was a long time ago. Now she was at 684 Woodbark, which

might as well have been 333 Mill Street for all the difference it made
to Hermine. Still, she didn't know who had written that crazy note.
Things never changed, never seemed to get better. She had stopped
meditating and praying because it didn't make any difference. There
was never a day anymore when she woke up happy to be alive, and
she was tired of it all. She was shuffling through her closet floor trying to decide which shoes to wear. It was threatening rain and cold.
She decided on the leather sneakers and some sweat pants. Just
thinking of going to the governmental center made her tired. She
avoided it as often as possible.

She had decided to take the city tram. It was late as usual, and
crowded, but it was either that or walk. She had to go to the courthouse because Story had received a letter from the state tax service,
Property Tax Division. The letter told Story that the records on their
old house needed to be updated. Computer information was reviewed every twenty years. Story or someone representing her had to
go to the Central Courthouse and verify their records. She had not
responded to the phone call and would be penalized if she didn't re-
spond to the letter.

She stood in line for at least forty minutes to get a seat on the shuttle that would take her to the train and into the governmental center.
It was bone cold. Whatever happened to global warming? she
thought, stamping her feet. There was no heat in the waiting room.
You could only have a car now with special permission, and they
didn't qualify; even though Story was ninety-six years old, they didn't
have an "imminent emergency situation at all times" in their home.
Hermine's feet hurt. She hated going to town. It was dreary and full
of people wandering around looking for work. People on foot who
mirrored her own desperation.

The computer room was crowded. That meant another long wait
until her number was called. She went in and sat at one of the long
tables with seven other terminals, and punched in her aunt's name.
Routine information. Present address. Birth. Marriage. Children.
Children. There it was on the screen as plain as day. Hermine
Greene. *Born 1944 to Story Temple Greene and Herman T. Greene.
Rosefield, North Carolina. Washington Colored Hospital. 4:00 P.M.*

She punched it in again. Machines could make mistakes. There it was again. She sat there paralyzed, staring at the screen as if it had given her the date of her own death. Her mind was spinning. A carousel out of control; the voices of the people garbled in a crazy mix of noise in her head. The letters blurred and jumbled in front of her eyes, and she suddenly didn't know how to read. She couldn't make out the meaning. She knew these shapes somehow, but the letters didn't mean anything. Born1944tostory temple greene1944templegreeneborn storytempleborn1944greenetostoryhermineto1944hermine. She didn't know how to read? Why didn't she know how to read? Why couldn't she read? "Excuse me?" A voice miles away. "Excuse me, are you all right? Ma'am?" The carousel in her mind stopped. Her face, she knew all at once, was wet. Tears under the chin. She fumbled for a tissue, cursing herself, cursing some stranger because she couldn't find a tissue. The tissue appeared from an unknown hand. An arm steered her gently up from the table. Still, she wouldn't go. She couldn't move. Surely there was a mistake. A glitch in the computer. Something, she said. Anything.

Finally the attendant asked her to move on. Other people were waiting, she said. In a barely audible whisper Hermine said, "No," she wasn't finished, and asked if there could possibly be a way to see if a mistake had been made. Could the woman verify the information from the town of Rosefield for her? The woman looked annoyed. There were so many people in line. But she did ask the attendant to cross-reference her sources, and the sources were correct. There was nothing else she could do.

Hermine queried the computer for the names of Story's cousin Zach Greene and his wife, Grace Oglesby Greene, "her parents" killed in an automobile accident in Rosefield in 1945. No such people had ever existed.

In a daze, she completed her business, verified Story's ownership of the house, and walked back to the terminal to wait for the shuttle train. It was getting dark. She had forgotten her hat. Though it was beginning to sleet, she didn't feel the cold. She felt like a prisoner trapped in a crazy play, a captive held for an unidentified crime. But this wasn't a play or a TV show. This was her life! The anonymous note, the "Concerned Friend," they were real.

Your aunt is not your aunt? Your aunt is not your aunt? There was no sense to it! No sense! What was she to do now? Leave her? Her mother? Her mother! Leave her and go where? A sixty-eight-year-old woman leave a ninety-six-year-old woman? She could put her in a home, but she didn't have the money for that. Perhaps she could have her committed, but that would take a good lawyer, money again, and it was getting very hard to do these days. She could never prove incompetence on the grounds she had. All the hospitals were chronically overcrowded. They'd never believe her story anyway. Her mind was whirling with anger, helplessness, even laughter.

How she must have hated me! she thought. How she must have hated me to have carried this out. To deny me for my entire life. She began to cough, and had to get out of line. Someone got her a drink of water. People were very nice. They saw an elderly woman who must not be well, but they didn't see an enraged daughter who had discovered something ugly, something that made her sick at her stomach, that chewed at her insides, something that left her feeling so helpless, so infuriated, that it seemed to be stronger than she was, and alive.

The sleet was beginning to come down in earnest when she got off the shuttle. Good, she thought. Good. Let it freeze over everything. Let it come and imprison us in our darkness in our unclean wounds; then our little frozen souls will be fully at home in this world of ice-bound hearts and nasty little fires that burn only to tease us and go out. The magnitude of the lie lay on her like a cold, wet, winding sheet. She walked home, ice freezing in her hair, feeling nothing, and let herself in with her key.

Story was asleep. Hermine felt her chest tighten. She started coughing as soon as the heat hit her. The cough that never left her these days, and the ice began to melt into her gray hair. No! No! I refuse to let her kill me, she thought, hurrying up to dry her hair. She made herself a cup of whiskeyed tea. I've been a tough old bird all my life. I can outlast her even through this. She took four thousand milligrams of vitamin C and sat at the kitchen table wrapped up in a blanket, sweating out the chill and deciding to live. Hermine knew she could hold her tongue. She'd had long years of practice. There'd be a time. She would have her day.

All Hermine remembered when she woke up that night was that

she had dreamed of a knife in her hand. She was sitting bolt upright in her bed, sweat on her forehead and under her chin. It was only later that she knew the dream had told her something about her anger, about what she was capable of doing. It was only after the snow came, the snow that covered up the ice on the back steps, that she remembered the whole dream, the argument, the denial, the blood on the knife, and the cold fear that encircled her after plunging it in over and over. It was Story's denial that she feared. That ancient face would look up at her and say something like, "What do you mean 'deny you'? I don't know what you're talking about. Are you gettin' senile, Hermine? Your mind was never too strong, you know." Everytime she tried to imagine the scene, she found it impossible to get past that point. There was outrage in all her movements and in everything she did for the old lady, who was now only able to move from chair to chair with assistance.

There was breakfast, lunch, and dinner to fix. There was bathing and washing her hair and ironing her clothes. Their retirement gave them enough to pay for a cleaning lady, but just barely. There were still groceries to buy and put up and all the thousand little tasks that are part of living. Bills to pay, repair people to call—there was no one left but her. Story wanted poached eggs. She wanted cream of wheat. She needed trace minerals and vitamins. Story had even less patience with her than ever, it seemed, and Hermine could feel herself getting slower and slower, on purpose.

She was making some chicken soup with fresh vegetables the day that she almost lost control. Story insisted on sitting in the kitchen to watch. "I don't know why you want to sit on those hard chairs," Hermine said, chopping the broccoli up. "You'd be much more comfortable on the sofa."

"Nothing in there to watch," Story said. "I get tired of TV."

Hermine chuckled. Watching her make soup, she thought, was the show of the day. She threw the broccoli in the soup pot and took the carrots out of the refrigerator drawer.

"Don't put so many carrots in," Story ordered. "I hate carrots. We should have more meat."

Hermine tightened her mouth and kept cleaning carrots. "Well, I like carrots," she said. "You can't always have your way."

Story lifted her walker and set it down emphatically. "Just what are you implying? I never have my way," she said sharply. "You control everything around here. You never fix my meals on time or cook what I need to stay well."

Hermine was leaning on the counter, her hand over her face. It was too much. She was too old for this, and exhausted by her anger.

"Aunt Story, I like carrots, and *I* need to stay well. After all, somebody has to take care of you. Like I said, life doesn't always let you have your own way." She kept chopping the vegetables, one after the other.

Hermine knew it wasn't over. The old woman hated to lose a point. She resigned herself to a difficult evening. "You just don't care," Story said. "After all I've done for you. You're still self-centered. I don't think you care if I live or die!"

Hermine turned sharply. She controlled her voice, but she felt her throat close up, and she knew she was very close to confronting Story with her lie. "Oh, I care," she said. "I care, old lady, or you'd be dead now. Who the hell takes care of you? Who do you think takes care of all this?" She waved her hands in the air. She trembled slightly. "I don't have to stay here, you know, I could . . . I could . . ."

"You could what? At your age? Don't be ridiculous, Hermine. Help me into the living room. And have your own way with the carrots."

She just likes to beat me, Hermine thought. She likes to humiliate me or make me wrong. It just doesn't matter what the issue is. She waits for me to slip and then she lets me fall. Hermine knocked over a box of bouillon and the chopping knife fell between her feet. Suddenly her mind went back almost to the beginning of her life.

She was ten years old. She had let the milk bottle slip because she couldn't have a slumber party. She had let it happen just like that, so fast she didn't know it was happening. Her hands had stopped holding on because her heart was outraged. No slumber party, no girl-friends, no joy ever. She realized now that she had been trying to have that party all her life. She'd spent all her life missing that party. She remembered the imprisoning brown oxford shoes, and almost looked for them on the old lady's feet, expecting them still to be there.

What did I ever do except be born? Why does she hate me so much? She stood there staring at the old lady as if she couldn't believe any of it, their lives, their history. She couldn't understand how this could have happened. The kitchen, the white cupboards, the blue countertop, the windows and curtains, and orange and green vegetables, all seemed artificial for a minute, like a stage set that would be struck when this bad play was over. And she and Story, for just a split second that would be over when she blinked her eyes, were two actresses who had played out their roles almost to the end. At that moment none of it made any sense to her, except that they were caught there on the stage playing out a script that somehow had trapped them in its story.

"What are you waiting for?" Story asked, breaking the spell. "Are you going to finish that soup or not?"

—

Hermine had to hire someone to come in and help at night. She couldn't do it anymore because she didn't want to. The nurse talked of how Story had been her mother's teacher and how her mother had told her about Miss Story's classes. Hermine said nothing. A great acid wetness ate a hole inside her that got bigger and bigger, and she began to lose weight, despite her decision to live.

The days crept by. They were locked in by recurring ice storms. She was desperate. She had to get free. There had to be an answer to this. She knew enough to know that what she had found out could kill her if she let it. And how would they live together in the same house once she had spoken the truth—once she called a ninety-six-year-old woman a liar—a manipulator who made both of their lives a lie.

It had been a long while since Hermine had meditated on a regular basis. She'd decided that there was no point, that there was no help to be found through praying or anything else. Frantic to know what to do with herself, she decided to try her old habit anyway. Perhaps there would be some clues she hadn't thought about. It couldn't hurt to try. She got quiet and sat facing the window. At first, it was annoying. The old techniques she had known so well did not seem to be working. Like everything else in her life, she thought. It took about an hour of patience. She kept stopping and starting, but the old feeling came back to her finally, and soon she was inside her own head, descending into some deep, watery place. She went down deeper and deeper, until she found herself in a hypnotic state.

It was a capsule of gray light surrounded by water. The capsule opened onto land and Hermine stepped out. She looked down at her feet. White shoes, and the hem of a long white dress. She looked at her body, her arms, as much as she could see without a mirror. A gorgeous, rich dress full of beads and sequins, made with delicate lace. The kind of dress every teenage girl dreams of. She touched her ears. There were pearls in her ears. She couldn't see them, yet she knew they were pearls. She was full of anticipation. She felt high on something. A door appeared in front of her. A wooden door set in a wall. She opened it, feeling like Alice in the book she remembered from childhood, and stepped out onto a small dirt path.

Somehow she realized that the wedding was waiting at the end of that path. There was no questioning it. She started down the path, her bride's dress just barely skimming the ground. She held it up a little so it wouldn't get soiled. She walked slowly. The landscape was familiar, but also strange. There was an overlay to it, like looking at yourself in the mirror instead of directly. But it was unnaturally clear and all the colors were intense, as if the world had just been created. For a long while there were trees—palm trees, tropical lush trees—and then they stopped abruptly and the land was barren. The path led through it, through the desert sand. She saw only an occasional scrubby bush of some kind, not even any cactus. Something scurried off to the side under one of these bushes. In the split second before it was out of sight, she had seen it in the corner of her eye. Maybe. It was a scorpion, she thought with alarm. "What do you expect in the desert?" she said aloud to herself. "Don't be silly, and afraid. There's nothing to be afraid of. You're on the way to your wedding."

She had to keep going. She had to meet her bridegroom. He'd be looking for her. The dress was too hot for this place. The sound of rattlers caught her attention. Snakes. She stood absolutely still, afraid to turn around, afraid even to look from side to side. Finally she glanced to either side. A shadow startled her. It looked like a man, and then a light flashed quickly and she saw it was Stephen, Stephen from college, her first love, standing in the shadow.

"Stephen," she called, and started toward him. "Stephen, don't go, wait!" But just as quickly the light faded and he wasn't there anymore. There was only that slight sound every few seconds, and no one. Alone again. She was getting too hot, and she was very tired and confused. Maybe she had only imagined Stephen and the sounds and shadows.

Up ahead were some trees. Another rattler sounded, and she suddenly felt very thirsty, so thirsty she was in pain. There was nobody there, not even desert animals drinking at the river. She fell to her knees, heedless of the beautiful dress, and drank from the river as if she had spent her whole life in that desert without water. The dress was now spotted with soil and water, but the river led to a woods that seemed to have sprung up while she had her head down drinking. The cool of the woods was like paradise. It reminded her of her mission. She must keep on the path.

The woods smelled of mossy things, and something faintly rotten. She saw a rock formation up ahead that looked like a place where she could stop and catch her breath. As she got closer, she realized there was someone sitting near the rock on a tree stump. It was a woman, but she couldn't get to her. The river was between them. "Cross over," the woman called. "You've got to cross over." She was dressed in the oldest of clothes, an Aunt Jemima head rag, but something gold glittered on the side of the blue head wrap. Hermine was afraid she'd ruin her dress, she'd drown. She looked about for a boat, something to carry her across, but there was nothing and nobody else in sight.

"Cross over!" the woman called. She knew it was true. She had to go. Her feet felt the cold all at once; it was up to her waist. She struggled with the strong currents, but they seemed to carry her along by themselves, and then she was there, staring down at the woman's head wrap. A small pin set with a blue stone of some kind. The woman's face was turned toward the sheer gray rock that she had seen as she approached. The old woman spoke without turning around. "What can I help you with, dear?" she said. The voice had a curiously familiar timbre. Almost familiar, but not quite. It intrigued Hermine, but she was afraid to look. So she stood where she was, too frightened to walk around to the other side of the stump, enticed and repelled by the de-

sire to see the woman's face. The wedding dress was getting heavier and heavier. It lay on her shoulders as if it were made of lead. A dirty red rag hung from beneath the stranger's ancient skirts. What looked like bloodstains spotted the rag. She was filthy and all her clothes were filthy. There was a bundle of dark, curly hair on the ground by the woman. Her hands were naturally a dark brown, but they looked as if someone had spilled black ink all over them, and then they disappeared. There were only stumps where the woman's hands had been. When Hermine realized everything the woman had on was familiar, she was terrified. All the woman's clothes were made of material she had seen Aunt Story wear. The blue head rag was made of fabric from one of her aunt's dresses. She knew she had to get away from here.

The panic was beginning to rise into her throat. She could hardly speak, but the words came out of her mouth as if she had no control over them. "I was to meet the priestess here," she said, almost in a whisper. "To get married." She felt sweat in the center of her palms.

"That's what I am," said the voice, which was becoming more familiar to Hermine. "The bridegroom is not coming. You must marry yourself."

Hermine knew her aunt Story's voice. She swung around to the other side of the stump, grasping Story by the shoulder. What she saw was the face of a complete stranger, an old hag of a woman she had never seen before. In her shock, she stammered, "But . . . you . . ."

"He's not coming," she said. "You must marry yourself."

"But what about the pin? Where did you get that pin?" Hermine asked.

"Wait, they wanted you to have this," the old woman said. She held onto a porcelain slop jar with her disfigured arms and managed to hand it to Hermine. It was full of pieces of old food—rotting and moldy vegetable scraps and rancid meat—and there were also little fragments of paper in there with what looked like parts of recipes written on them. "Also, you must go to the river and drink it. Only then will you be married."

"But you can't mean that!" Hermine was near hysteria. "You don't understand. I've already been there. I swallowed half of it already! You told me to do that the last time!" Actually, she didn't remember a last time, but she knew she had to say that, and that somehow it was true. "Anyhow, you're the wrong person! You're supposed to be . . . and where did you get that pin?"

"Just who am I supposed to be?" The old woman leaned over toward Hermine, clutching the stinking slop jar. Hermine backed up. There was solid rock behind her. "There was no last time, dear. You must have the wrong person."

Hermine began to cry. She had the impulse to eat the garbage, without knowing why. Somebody seemed to be directing her actions, her feelings. She realized she was weak and hungry, and suddenly garbage didn't seem so revolting. She took the heavy slop jar full of pigs' food and reached in. Stir well, one strip of paper said. Mix in the secret ingredient and bake. But as her hand touched the disgusting stuff, her own strength seemed to return just a little.

The woman was silent. No one else was there. There would be no wedding, and no bridegroom. There was nowhere to go but back to the path. The forest looked impossibly thick and dangerous. She knew she'd get lost in there. She didn't know what the old woman meant by "marrying herself." She couldn't perform her own ceremony. That made no sense. She was weary and afraid of getting lost, and there was just this crazy old hag and this garbage to eat. The sheer wall of rock offered no opening. She turned again toward the woods and saw only darkness. When she turned around again, the woman dressed in Aunt Story's rags had disappeared. Only the bundle of hair was left.

What she felt mostly was rage. It was so unfair! So humiliating! There was nothing to do but cross the desert once more. This time she saw in the distance, here and there, bodies of people sprawled on the ground, dead and dying. The river she had crossed had disappeared. Vultures were circling above. She carried the pigs' food all the way back to the wooden door, and found herself coming to, gradually emerging from what seemed like a dream.

Maybe she had gone to sleep. She wanted answers, not puzzles, not cryptic mysteries, obscure symbols, and useless old recipes! She went out for a walk in the cold, just to be away from Story, just to have some thinking room. She felt like something or somebody, if there was a somebody out there, had played a great cosmic joke on her. A mystery inside a mystery, like that damn package—notes inside notes wrapped in layers of old withered paper, and one of the messages clear enough to be read.

She went over and over the meditation, turning it around in her mind, turning the symbols upside down, and she got confused at the same place every time, with the old lady who seemed to be Aunt Story. The stickpin had to have been her father's. The anonymous note must have been sent by somebody who had known her grandmother. Was the old woman in the vision really her grandmother? What did she mean "marry myself"? she pondered, and, Why do I have to drink the river? And why didn't she have any hands? Then there was the garbage, and that was where she really got stuck. Someone wanted her to carry it. But who? Who were "they"? Was it possible "they" were Story?

She got angry just thinking about that. How could you? How could you be expected to carry someone's garbage like that? And anyway, I ended up with that damn garbage in the end, Hermine thought desperately. *I* did! She broke down and cried on the street, walking furiously around the block. I carried the goddamn garbage my whole motherfuckin' life! she thought. I carried it all the way to California, and I lived with it in my living room, and I brought it back, and you never said a word, you never said a mumblin', fuckin' word!

Hermine was trembling. She walked up the porch steps, her body moving with the stiffness of an old lady, tears streaming down her face. I *have* drunk the river, she thought. I have. She was shaking and terrified, and not at all certain she would survive her own anger.

—

A soap opera that had no ending was on the television, she thought; just like their lives, it went on and on and on in misery, problem after problem, people piling one lie on top of the other. Well, this was going to be the end of this melodrama. She marched up to Story's chair and switched off the TV in mid-sentence. Story looked up, a little confused. The drone of the machine sometimes seemed to hypnotize her into a stupor.

"You want to tell me about Herman Greene?" Hermine shouted,

standing over Story and looking down at her. "Don't you lie, don't you even fix your mouth to lie, old lady."

Story blinked, her eyes adapting to real life versus the technicolored screen. "What you talkin' about?" she scowled. "Don't talk so loud, I'm not that deaf."

"You know, you know all right," Hermine answered, still talking very loud. "I should leave you here to die in your own poison. You are going to talk to me if I have to threaten it out of you! Tell me who Herman Greene was!"

"You threatenin' me, girl? How dare you." She ran her hand over her face, astounded. "I gave you everything I had. I deserve better. I'm old and sick; leave me alone." She waved her away as if she could make it end by this gesture.

Hermine pulled up a chair. Her legs seemed to be giving way beneath her, but she was not giving up. "Are you going to your grave with that lie? Only you would do that. I wouldn't put it past you." One hand gripped her chair, a spare dining room chair that was sitting next to Story's light green easy chair. One hand pulled a gold stickpin with a blue sapphire out of her pocket.

"Whose stickpin was this? Whose?" she shouted. Story peered at the object, and some dim memory came alive for her. "All right, talk to me. Now."

"I don't have to answer to you, Hermine," Story said. She had taken off her glasses and was rubbing her eyes. They had been bothering her lately. "But since you insist on dragging up old bones, I'll shut you up. Herman T. Greene was your father. That was his. I don't know where you got it, but it was his. Now leave me alone."

"Leave you alone! Just like that, leave you alone? Do you have any idea what you've done to me? Is that all you're going to say? Was I a piece of trash you could just throw away? A disposable module you could make into whatever you wanted? One of those robots they use to do housework for people?" The veins were pounding in her temples. She was coughing, spitting. She stood up again. She could hardly breathe, and she took desperate, wheezing breaths every two or three words. "I could have died, I could have died not knowing you were my mother, not knowing shit! And you would never have told me. That was the idea, wasn't it? That was the idea! Just make up a story, and everyone will believe you! You stole my life from me! And you had the nerve to say, *don't fail me!*"

Story stood up, leaning forward on the walker that was always in front of her and between them. She was close enough to kiss Hermine, who seemed to be rooted to the floor in her rage.

"You liar! You liar! Every step of your life has been a lie!" Hermine was shaking with fury, ugly in her rage, her old face gray with the strain, her heart pounding in her chest. "Who are you anyway? What kind of person are you?"

Story hesitated a long time. She looked off into the distance. "I am not the only liar," she said. "I seem to remember a certain lifestyle in California." After a long pause, she started again. It seemed to take a great deal of energy for her to talk. "Papa did it. Mama kept her mouth shut. He beat me so bad I threw up sometimes. They beat me till I was almost raw. And then Papa . . . your fine, upstanding grandfather, the great preacher, he decided he needed more than the pleasure of making me suffer. Mama saved me. She saved me from the touch of his hands and his need to have a willing sacrifice. All that talk about being pure and holy. She just couldn't stand it any longer. So don't you tell me about being done wrong and suffering. No, I never let myself be close to you. I never let myself be close to anybody. I'd had too much hurt to know love. I vowed to myself that I would survive, that was all. And I have done that. I have survived being beat on a regular basis by a father who had lost himself in rage, and desertion on a regular basis by a mother whose life was stolen by fear and white folks who took my father away and whose crazy eyesight blinded them to everything but themselves. I have survived my own stubbornness and pain and my own grief, and *you* turnin' on me, even though I did the best I knew how to teach you how to survive. But close? No. They taught me good and early in my life. As close as I ever got to my parents was a heart sliced in two. They took away my chance to be close. And somebody took it away from them, I reckon.

"It was all too much. Papa ragin' and grievin' over his lost chances and his lost mama and papa. Takin' out all that sorrow on Mama and me. I don't know all of it. They never talked about it. Never told me what the pain was between them.

"So don't tell me about what you missed. You had your chances like all the rest of us. Something's been taken away from you. I guess so. That's life. Take it back the best way you know how; that's what I did. Took back my life the only way I knew how by keeping what was left of myself for myself. When you been stole from, sometime all you can do is gather up the pieces and get through another day, till you forget the thief's broken into your private parts and everything *seems* normal. And that's the best you can do sometimes, make everything *seem* normal.

"Now get out of my way. I need to lie down and rest." She took a deep breath and struggled off with the walker, her slow, dragging step painfully familiar to Hermine.

Hermine suddenly sagged as if all her muscles had lost their power to hold her up, and she dropped into the old worn chair that was still warm with Story's body. Outside, freezing rain hit the windows. She felt as if she were choking to death, and she took deep, struggling breaths. It was too much to swallow. This story of rage and hidden passions, like the slimy bottom of a stagnant pool, like that garbage she had to eat in her dream. The cold January afternoon had gone completely dark. She was chilled, and she turned on the reading light next to her. Her hands were shaking, so the light wavered and then threw a circle of lonely light around her. The house was deeply silent, but the silence was full of questions.

—

But she would remember the eyes. Even when the ice that had locked them in together for two or three days went away, even then, the eyes. And she would walk, anywhere, it didn't matter where, just to get away from the eyes. To quiet her own fear of what she might do, to keep herself from spitting venom at the old lady who had become now, not a nuisance, but an obsession. To put some distance between them, for she was losing herself. When she gazed in the mirror now, she saw not herself, but Story. She walked only to pick up one foot after another, to lie to her body that she was going somewhere, she was getting away, but the walk always led back there. No matter how long she was out in the cold, she always had to go home. Every day for a week she walked her anger, braving the icy weather, unafraid of slipping, unafraid of her already thinning bones, only room in her heart for her rage.

In the house they were speaking in little frozen sentences. Daughter to mother—"dinner is ready." Mother to daughter—"I want some milk." Daughter to mother—"here's your medicine." Mother to daughter—"I want juice." Little sentences for little lives, confined to car, house, kitchen, bed. Little words. Time for your pill. Shut the door. Cold. Old fevers. Old eyes. They talked to Hermine. Held her even in the dark, so that she was never free of them. What had she done? What had they both done? And Lord have mercy, what would it be like to be free?

Her people had said it, asked it over and over, and what would it be like to be free? Hermine could not close the eyes that never slept, the eyes that stared back at her from her mirror. After she had decided she'd never call her mother, after she stopped looking into Story's face, her face, even after she put the sheet over her own mirror to hide from the face she saw there. The eyes told of the miles impossible to be crossed between them, of the abyss that had been dug too deep. The eyes spoke of guilty beginnings newly found, and the desperate need to catch some sunlight for once, before the cold settled in for good—the river Jordan, chilly and cold.

There was terror in the eyes, frightened of the words, frightened of the truth that had no mercy. Ice and cold reigned between them, never mind that Story had given her the pearls. "Grandma Sadie's pearls," she said, and pressed them into Hermine's hand. Grandma Sadie, a piece in the hurtful old mystery. Grandma Sadie, a picture in the album, a stranger to Hermine. And when she, Hermine, closed her eyes, she saw a headstone. She didn't know whose name was carved on it, but it was stone, cold. The river Jordan, chilly and cold.

She would remember fastening the coat against the weather. Pulling on the boots. A river of ice down the steps and out to the car. A river of ice chilly and cold. River Jordan, chilly and cold. And the eyes that she couldn't avoid as they made their way to the steps and then down, down that river of ice, and falling into the watery snow, that fall that said, over, it's over now and you are somehow free and somehow bound forever.

But it was more than somehow Hermine wanted. Free. To finally be there. What would it be like to finally get to the promised land? Free. And even then, as Story cried, "Bertie, where are you?" and in her old confusion mixed one with the other, even then the eyes held her. The hands were slipping, slipping, and she, the mother, lost her footing, and the hands of the younger one, the daughter, not able to reach quick enough, though the arms knew, they knew the fall meant it was over, that the ice had finally locked them in its cold. Those eyes that looked up at her in a final connection, in a final search for a way to be worthy, a way to be forgiven, to warm the soul, to be redeemed at last. Maybe Story could come home to someone who said, "Yes, you are my child, my mother, my kin, and you are home." Oh, Lord have mercy, what would it be like to be free?

She, the daughter, would always remember the back porch and the slippery wet under her feet, and her stiff bones, and that she needed to watch the old one, *her mother*, if only said with a tearing in her chest. It was so cold her coat seemed made of cotton, and she knew the old lady was cold under her gray and black fur. Story called her "Bertie." Bertie because her mind was finally going after ninety-six years. Maybe it was the shock of being called liar; liar. Even though Story had given her the pearl earrings that Jacob (now really her grandfather) had given Sadie (now really her grandmother) when they married; even if she did say, "Grandma Sadie's pearls," and had meant it. Had meant, "I want you to have this family re-membrance; you are my daughter."

Story called "Bertie" and then "Hermine" at the last because the two women were bound together like the pattern in the old slave quilt. They were bound together before the ships brought the flesh sellers; they were bound together, because they knew each other's songs by heart, because they knew each other's stories by heart; they were bound together by the sorrow chains. And how did you forgive such sorrow, and how did you forgive yourself?

She could smell the cold and snow. She could hear the ice dripping off the young trees. Why didn't she reach out fast enough? Was she so old herself that she had lost her quickness? Was she a liar? Did she forget that revenge was not enough, that revenge was not the name of the covenant that would get her across the river?

"We have to take you to the doctor," she had shouted in the old lady's ear. They had started down the slippery steps for the last time, for the last time. It was seeing everything all at once, seeing her for the first and what would be the last time. Because of the eyes, she saw her, because the eyes said, "I have been lost out here, Hermine. I am falling." And the old hands that shook with palsy and the many years of holding on simply let go, and she fell into forever. The daughter did not catch her in the space impossible to be crossed, did not catch her in time, and across the river of ice shouted, "*Mother, Mother*," and in that one word there was a thawing, a beginning at the end. Maybe there had been time, but just maybe; and she would never know if she could have caught her because it was all over in thirty seconds.

And the sorrow chains brought the daughter down like the tumbling blocks into the icy waters at the foot of the steps where the mother's eyes were already closed against the pain, against the confusion. The sorrow chains brought the daughter down in her desperation to catch the mother, after all. In her desperation she could not allow revenge to be the door to the final solution. Hermine caught the old head up out of the snow and water, but her mother's eyes were closed, finally.

———

It was a grief of not knowing; not knowing finally what might have been. It was a grief of silence. Now, there was no way to say, I want to know you, to know more about how you got this way, to know where the scars are. To know why you didn't call me your own. Now, there was no way to say, I want to know more about Aunt Bertie and what she thought and Grandma and Grandpa Temple and what the pain was between them and who stole what from whom.

The fall had given Hermine the gift of being seen for a few timeless seconds, and the gift of seeing in return, but the grief was in not knowing. So she sat for days in the house, now so deeply silent, wondering how it had been for her mother, not knowing the shape or feel of the life that had filled so much of her own life, and yet left it so very empty, how it had been for her father, who was only a name and a stickpin with a small blue stone. She sat and watched the ice thaw and drip from the trees for days. The furnace clicked off and on automatically, and the pale winter sun finally broke the freeze altogether. She heard the ice crack and still the silence was filled only with her questions, one upon the other.

———

One day when it seemed that winter would last forever and the questions would never stop, she found comfort in cleaning, in throwing away the past. First it was just an old box under the bed, an annoyance, another piece of trash, but on second thought it might have something in it; an old letter, car repair bills, "this is not an invoice"; *Hattenfield Times*, "Will Busing Ruin Our Schools?"; letters, cards, snapshots, Hermine with Uncles Dee and Dum; Story, young (twenty?), dressed for church; Story with Hermine, Christmas tree; Aleatha, Hermine, Jamesina, Christmas day.

Then another box and another. Boxes full of life, boxes full of Story. Birthday wrapping paper, fragile fragments, old grease-spattered pieces of paper from almost one hundred years ago. And so began a dialogue, a conversation missed by seven seconds. "I found you, Mother," Hermine would say. And in every corner of the house she searched and talked. And in every corner of the house she heard the answers. "I found you," she would say aloud to the photographs and the furniture and the walls in Story's house. Because I found the notes from you and from Grandmother, and from all of them speaking through you from so long ago, to me. She would say aloud what she thought, what she pieced together with the journals and the letters and the poor little recipes. She would say aloud because she had to, "Are you listening, Mother, are you there?" "I found the pieces of your life, Mother, of Grandmother's life, and my life. I found them where you had put them, knowing some part of you wanted to say to me, 'This is who you are, this is who you come from, Hermine.' You wanted to keep the promise of family, the covenant of kin." Hermine would say aloud that on the back of her meatloaf recipe Sadie Temple had written in shaky, fifth-grade hand, "J. beat me today," and on another one for white cream cake, "Story strapped again." And on another one just, "mercy, mercy." Old slips of paper stuffed in a box with a copy of a doctor bill and her aunt Bertie's death certificate and a thousand receipts for her grandfather's tools and supplies and

Bibles and God knows what else. In that same box a letter to Uncle
Dee and Uncle Dum, with a picture of her grandparents and Story
in fond embrace, never mailed. A pair of ancient glasses, old buttons, a small wooden box with carved figures on it, beautiful and elegant. More of Grandmother's recipes. Green snap beans with
bacon and "He done cut off my hair. There is a balm in Gilead."
And for Sadie's watermelon pickles, "my poor chile. God protect . . ."
Shrimp gumbo, bell peppers and onions, and on the other side, "J.
tell me they done cut off his daddy's hands."

And the unexpected journal of March 1955 written in her
mother's neat hand.

*March 1955—"Sam is after me, I'm sure of it. I really find him at-
tractive and exciting. Finally a man who can challenge me, a man
who has class! God, I hope it works out. I'm tired of being alone."*

*May, 1955—"I really like Sam. Love is a word I'm almost afraid to
use. It has too many sticky sides to it. Do I dare to marry again? Sam
is waiting for an answer. Going dancing tonight. Got to say yes or no."*

*June 1955—"I can hardly stand to look at myself in the mirror. I look
terrible. What a fool I've been. I should have known Sam wasn't real.
Love is a trap. Mama fell into it and I vow to stay out of it. I intend to
raise Hermine so she understands that. I thought about Herman for the
first time in years today. I'm sorry he had to die the way he did. Mama
used to say, 'you lucky if you chooses your own man.' Mama, if you only
knew. I didn't choose a man any better than you did."*

*August 1976—"Saw a man who reminded me of Jim Black Wind to-
day. Some days I long for him so. Why did I do that? Why did I throw
all that love away?"*

And the album, Hermine said. I see it now, Mother. Are you
there? I see the grief on your faces. Grandpapa Jacob twisted into
meanness, and Grandma Sadie's beauty frightened out of her. I
found the story of my daddy's accidental death in a newspaper article, carefully folded and stuck away in a journal for 1946. Now, I
know that revenge isn't enough, ever.

Hermine would never chop her own sweet green peppers without
remembering her mother was a captive in a house of fear and that

they might as well have lynched her grandfather along with his daddy because all of his love was squeezed into a place so tight and so fearful that it couldn't possibly breathe, and it twisted and twisted trying to get out until it finally killed him. "I'm beginning to understand, Mother," she shouted to the fireplace and the kitchen table . . . "to understand why your eyes were open, but dead and gone somewhere." The space seemed impossible to cross. The ice-covered bushes and the eyes that held her, eyes that finally saw clearly, for the first and last time. Hermine never had a chance to say, "I forgive you, Mother. I understand." She said it now. To the photographs and the letters and to Story's chair, to their places on the porch and to the window with the plants. To the dresses and the earrings and the shoes.

"You wanted to be free. Free of the sorrow chains they carried. You wanted me to get to the promised land, and so you tried to give it to me in rules, in education, in nice clothing. You wanted me to have a life without love because for you, in love, there was only pain. And so you tried never to touch me. But you touched me just the same, Mother, just like the colors in Aunt Aleatha's quilt touch each other, they can't help it and you couldn't help it. I've spent my whole life chained to Sadie and Jacob, their sorrow, your sorrow, my sorrow, just like the slavers wanted, oh, just like they wanted when they brought us to this place so long ago. But it's time to remember there was a life before slavery, a time when we weren't chained by sorrow."

———

Hermine wrapped Aleatha's quilt around her shoulders and put on her orange knit hat and dragged Story's rocking chair, now Hermine's, out into the winter sun and sat rocking and still talking to Story, if only in her head. Soon to be spring now, soon to be spring. The ice is all gone. And because the sun was out, there were children, too, who lived near, on their way home knowing what the sun meant, who saw her sitting on the porch at that strange time of year, talking to herself. They stared at her and then remembered some mother's words about politeness and looked away quickly, but Hermine had seen them and laughed, laughing at herself, an old lady wrapped up in a quilt in the middle of a winter's day in a rocking chair, talking to herself. Laughed and called to them, "Hello, nice day," and waved, and they waved in answer.

I must catch the living, Hermine thought, as the laughter of the children rang out from a distance. I must start today. Spring is coming. I must catch the sunlight. "I tried to catch you, Mama," she said, at last able to use that eternal word, and she knew the conversation was almost over now. She would no longer have to talk to the dead. She could talk to the living now. She could tell her story. She could talk it or tell it or write it, so it wouldn't have to be stuck away in boxes and on little pieces of paper. And even if I can't get there all the way, I can try, I can reach, and that's what makes us holy, Mama, that's all we have. That's what gives a bottom to the river and a refuge in the storm. That's what brings us to the journey's end, Mama, and that's what lets us cross over Jordan.

EPILOGUE

Bead by bead, thread by thread, stitch by stitch, one bit of lace at a time, the women dismantle their dresses. There will be no more bridegrooms, there will be no more virgins sitting at the loom. Not until each piece of cloth is stacked beside their chairs and the debt paid, the story theirs. It is long past bride time for them, long past the flush of the maiden and the lush fruit of the tree. But each bead and each scrap is carefully put in a box as if there will be some later need for it; carefully laid away. Not for the daughters, for the daughters have left this place. Not for the granddaughters, for they too are away harvesting their songs, and they will not be returning to this place. The grandmothers must begin to tell themselves the story that is owed them, that is long past due them.

They begin in their aloneness. They begin to listen to the story their hair is telling them. Their gray hair that is crinkled and alive, begins to speak of its pain and suffering. Its memories of the dead, for those who were enslaved and who enslaved, for those who were killed and who killed. The story in their hair is as thick as the tangles and as woven as the fibers in the matted gray mass of living vine that covers their heads. The hair teaches. Teaches of angers long past, of wounds not cleaned, of breaches not healed, of dried blood in the open cracks and crevices. The hair screams for justice first, mercy later.

Other fragments of the dresses are laid in boxes, and then the feet begin to move, and the feet take them to a cave. In front of the cave there is a hearth where the women made fires. And the feet say they must enter this place, for they will find there what they have lost and what they have forgotten. And the fingernails find in the darkness of the cave a wall of red stone to scratch on, to scratch out the names that were given. Men's names given to them in place of their own by traders of flesh. Names that were thrust upon them in place of their own by revilers. The torn, cracked nails will not stop writing. They must remember for the children and for the men and for themselves. They must remember every name that was ever given to a woman that did not belong to her. And every name that was given to their children that was a borrowed name, and every name that was given to a man that was not his own, every name that was pretend— Skundus, James, Toby, Sambo, Simuel, boy—for Kawaku, Akpan, Konyek, man. Sarah, Jemimah, Topsy, mammy, girl—for Enyonam, Umdhlubu, Anean, Manjanja, Nambi. And every name borrowed from a man's name—first Wo-man, daughter of man. Then borrowed names—Wilhemina, daughter of William; Arthura, daughter of Arthur; Hermine, daughter of Herman; Jamesina, daughter of James; Roberta, daughter of Robert. And the nails write on the wall until they have only a small place left, for they have written BETRAYED in large, uneven, tumbled-down letters all over the make-believe names that were not their own.

And the feet lead them out under the sky. Now they understand why the story is feared, for the story is truth. Now they understand why the silence was enforced, for the truth is the story. And more pieces of cloth are torn away and placed in the piles beside the Longmother at the foot of the baobab tree. The Longmother speaks and the skin whispers her message of truth, that when it is not allowed to breathe, it begins to lie. The skin tells the grandmothers all the lies it has ever been told. It whispers on the breeze, wisps of lies, like the lace the old women are piling up beside them, whispers of white gauzy lies that have allowed suffocations to feel natural and death to feel like life.

It takes a long time to tell these lies, so long that it seems the grandmothers are asleep. So long that the old ones begin to dream the lies in the life that feels like death; but the voice knows and the Longmother knows that all the pieces of gauze must be put in the box, or the magic of the story that belongs to them will never be heard. And the debt will never be paid, and the poem will never be whole again. And so the voice breaks through the whispers of the skin. Breaks through the dreamy half-awake place where the grandmothers sit forgetting their task, in love with the warm wind.

And the voice will not leave them alone. It must be finished. There are still threads to untangle, seams to unravel, and the debt to be paid. It must be finished. And it is the voice that comes that finally teaches them what they already know, the words they already have, the purifying fire that is in their bones. The voice comes on wings mysterium and on winds of fire. And only then the taking apart is done. Every bead, and every thread, and every bit of lace, and every stitch is undone, put down, and carefully collected, and there is great rejoicing. For they must make of these precious and terrible fragments a flying thing, a thing pieced together that spins and turns and dances, a thing that they can give to their daughters and to their daughters' daughters, a thing that rides on the heavenly waters and on the winds of fire, a thing of fierce work and holy delight; and there is great rejoicing, for in their work just begun they have found their story once more, and it does fly; it flies out over the great baobab tree and into the everywhere sky.

Georgia McCloud—died 1895—of cervical cancer.

Tom McCloud—cause of death unknown—disappeared.

Tobias McCloud, slave owner—died 1885—of liver cancer.

Prince William Rountree—died 1890—of typhoid fever.

Alexander McCloud (known by Rountree)—died 1915—in race riot, of gunshot wound.

Hezakiah McCloud—cause of death unknown—disappeared.

Leona June McCloud—cause of death unknown—disappeared.

Sadie Evelyn McCloud (known by Rountree) Temple—died 1932—crippled by arthritis; cause of death—congestive heart failure.

Jacob Abraham Temple—died 1932—of stroke.

Bertricia Mae Temple—died 1943—of illegal abortion.

Story Temple Greene—died 2013—of injuries sustained in a fall.

Hermine Rose Greene—died 2023—of emphysema.

ABOUT THE AUTHOR

LINDA BEATRICE BROWN is Distinguished Professor of Humanities and holds the Willa B. Player Chair in the Humanities at Bennett College in Greensboro, North Carolina. She is a poet and lecturer and has written for such publications as *The Black Scholar* and *Religion and Intellectual Life*. She is the author of the novel *Rainbow Roun' Mah Shoulder*, and a collection of poetry, *A Love Song to Black Men*.

Linda Brown lives in Greensboro, North Carolina.